BEAUTIFUL DECEIVER

Danae smiled up at him and whispered, "Kiss me, you conceited beast."

When his grin burst forth, it rivaled the warmth of the sun in her heart, and then he lowered his head, and his lips were devouring hers, the passion flaring high as they drank deeply of each other.

Frightened at the strength of the insidious urges raging through him again, Sion reached up and disentangled her grasping fingers from his hair. "I can't, Danae," he gasped as he tried to push her away. She fell back and blinked up at him, the hurt she was feeling all too obvious. The sight of her swollen lips, moist from his kisses, was driving him insane. Then he saw that damned impassive mask of hers slip back into place, concealing all her emotions from him again.

Could she be so naive that she didn't know what she was doing to him? he wondered in agony as he watched her turn her back on him. Then all his noble intentions disintegrated with the last of the morning mist . . .

BOOK YOUR PLACE ON OUR WEBSITE AND MAKE THE READING CONNECTION!

We've created a customized website just for our very special readers, where you can get the inside scoop on everything that's going on with Zebra, Pinnacle and Kensington books.

When you come online, you'll have the exciting opportunity to:

- View covers of upcoming books
- Read sample chapters
- Learn about our future publishing schedule (listed by publication month *and author*)
- Find out when your favorite authors will be visiting a city near you
- Search for and order backlist books from our online catalog
- Check out author bios and background information
- Send e-mail to your favorite authors
- Meet the Kensington staff online
- Join us in weekly chats with authors, readers and other guests
- Get writing guidelines
- AND MUCH MORE!

Visit our website at
http://www.kensingtonbooks.com

WHILE YOU SLEPT

Wendy Burge

ZEBRA BOOKS
Kensington Publishing Corp.
http://www.kensingtonbooks.com

This book is dedicated to the heroine in my son's life, his beautiful wife, Khara. In her gentle hands I entrust Matthew's happiness, and wish them a long and lovely life together.

ZEBRA BOOKS are published by

Kensington Publishing Corp.
850 Third Avenue
New York, NY 10022

All Kensington titles, imprints and distributed lines are available at special quantity discounts for bulk purchases for sales promotion, premiums, fund-raising, educational or institutional use.

Special book excerpts or customized printings can also be created to fit specific needs. For details, write or phone the office of the Kensington Special Sales Manager: Kensington Publishing Corp., 850 Third Avenue, New York, NY 10022. Attn. Special Sales Department. Phone: 1-800-221-2647.

Zebra and the Z logo Reg. U.S. Pat. & TM Off.

First Printing: February 2003
10 9 8 7 6 5 4 3 2 1

Printed in the United States of America

Prologue

Camden Abbey, March 1882
Oxfordshire

Mildly curious, Katherine reached out to part the velvet drape, flinching as a blinding arc of sunshine burst into the dimness of the room. It hit her with a ruthless brilliance that forced her to narrow her eyes as she watched the bustling melee in the courtyard below. Stoically she studied the laughing camaraderie of the young crowd she had not been invited to join, and she was equally indifferent to the fact that she would undoubtedly never be asked to participate—never mind that the young man being jostled about with good-nautured ribbing amidst the group was her own husband.

When the mindless clamor seemed only to increase in volume, with little accomplished to hurry them on their way, irritation began to knit her brow.

Why don't they just go? she wondered impatiently as she nudged her wire-rimmed spectacles lower on her nose so she could look over them.

Her mouth pursed in distaste, Katherine's gaze wandered over the crowd until her attention finally alighted on the dominant jewel of this little scene.

Her dispassion was almost cold-blooded as she observed the stunning picture Lady Alicia Barrows presented in her russet habit; the velvet clinging with immodest design to a figure that the gods themselves must have sculpted to match the equally dynamic lines of her current lover—Katherine's husband.

And both were quite aware of the startling picture they made together. They were two splendid predators feeding off of each other's vanity, and Katherine wished nothing more than to stay safely out of their malicious company. She first realized this need to shun her husband on the day of her wedding to this callous stranger. It was now a fundamental element to Katherine's peace of mind—if any such thing could exist in the hell that was her life.

With arrogant unconcern, the lovers stood indecently close amid the crush of preparation; so close, in fact, that the lady's breast brushed with a seeming casualness against the viscount's waistcoat. Well aware of her lover's wife watching from the study window, Lady Alicia reached up to tangle her fingers in Halsingham's golden mane. With a smile, she drew his head down, her taunting gaze deliberately meeting Katherine's over his shoulder. With a cruel little twist to her lips, the lady whispered something into his ear and immediately Halsingham's laughter floated up to his wife's ear. Katherine did not even flinch when he looked over his shoulder at her.

Ignoring him, Katherine returned Lady Alicia's smile coolly, knowing all the while that she had been the brunt of yet another cruel jest. It would not be the first time, nor would it be the last. And when Lady Alicia no longer amused her husband, there would be another to replace her, also whispering into her husband's ear some scathing little comment about the unfortunate wife he had been saddled with.

Finally, as if on cue, the milling mass of people began to mount horses and carriages for the long trek back to London. A sigh of contentment escaped Katherine's lips as her eyes rested one last time on her husband. Impatient for his absence, she watched as he brushed a last lingering kiss over lips still bruised from his arduous ministrations of last night. Katherine then wondered with cynical amusement if they treated each other so fondly when in the privacy of their lovers' bower, out of the presence of their fawning audience.

Satisfied that soon the courtyard would be emptied of the bothersome guests, Katherine let the curtain fall back into place, then moved across the room, the noise outside becoming a mere drone of annoyance.

One week had tried her patience sorely, but considering that it had been a year since the last invasion of so many interlopers, she could not complain too much. If she did not know her husband better, and was certain of his complete disregard of her existence, she could almost believe that he deliberately flaunted his mistresses before her out of a warped sense of humor. However, that would be flattering herself, she thought with a rueful smile as she entered the breakfast room. There, she paused abruptly when she noticed her father still seated at the table. Swallowing her disappointment, she slipped into the chair held out by the room's attendant footman.

With narrowed eyes, Lord Camden glanced up from his London newspaper and stared with undisguised loathing at his daughter. It still astonished him how he and the beautiful woman who had been his wife could have produced such an unappetizing lump of humanity.

At the age of twenty-one, Katherine Beatrice Camden-Carey. Viscountess Halsingham, had nothing to recommend her. Not only was she of an inferior height, but her lack of it was emphasized by the fact that she was fat. She was an unremarkable woman in every way, and he found it highly unpleasant to look at her. If someone were to ask him to describe the color of his only child's eyes, he doubted he would be able to do so, for not only were they nondescript behind those rose-tinted spectacles she always had perched on her nose, he did not give a damn what color they were. Just as he had no idea what color her hair was. All he knew was that she wore it pulled harshly back from her plump face and covered with the habitual white linen cap she always wore. At least seven stone of excess flesh padded her small frame, and the way she dressed, in gray drab, only added to the ungainly picture she presented. Her only assets, if one were of a mind to say she had any, was a velvety complexion and an innate grace of movement that was surprising considering the near obesity of her body. All in all, she looked much older than her youthful years and exceedingly forgettable.

Indeed, how he wished he could forget her existence altogether; however, he was not allowed that luxury as long as he needed that ungainly body of hers to breed his grandson and future heir of his ancient line that was on the threshold of extinction.

She was an insignificant person with an unfortunately quite significant part in the future of the

Camdens. Thank God he only had to deal with her during one brief visit each month. Even that was twelve times too many in a year and a constant waste of time since each month, as regular as clockwork, she had her cursed cycle. He refused to believe that she could be barren. If she were, he would disown her and take pleasure in the doing.

Glancing over her spectacles, Katherine noted the ever-present animosity in her sire's colorless eyes and unconsciously she nudged the frames higher so that he blurred into an undistinguishable mass. Nervous under his hostile regard, she reached for another pastry and retreated into herself, which was the only way she could deal with these onerous meals. Biting into the flaky pastry, it was not buttery enjoyment she tasted, but the metallic sourness of helpless hatred.

"I hope you had the courtesy to bid your husband and guests a safe journey?" Camden demanded, snapping his paper to another page.

Keeping her eyes lowered, she swallowed. She was always fearful of meeting his eyes, knowing he would see the hostility she felt for him. It would just give him another reason to punish her. Careful to keep her voice humble, she answered, "Of course, my lord."

Camden's lips thinned with disgust. He could almost sympathize with his son-in-law's avoidance of this cow's bed. Gad, who in his right mind would want to climb on top of her? But, Halsingham's desires had no bearing in their contract. The viscount had been offered the reprieve of debtor's prison in lieu of two things; to marry his daughter and get her with child. Camden didn't care where Halsingham spilled his seed as long as it was emptied with calculated regularity into his daughter. Whatever else the lackwit did with his life was of no concern to Camden.

However, Halsingham was presently treading on the dangerous edge of pushing Camden's patience to the breaking point. His absences would no longer be tolerated. The bastard was playing with fire, and the flames were beginning to run wild. Camden's jaw clenched as the pain began its insidious assault; his frustrated rage growing apace with the agony leeching into his arm and over into his chest. He was only too aware that the bastard had sneaked out of Katherine's room late last night. If Halsingham didn't quickly live up to his side of the contract, then he would soon start seeing his gambling chits and merchant debts unpaid and his credit insultingly denied. Obviously, the token one fuck a month was not accomplishing the job—and that was only when the man was able to drag himself from his debaucheries in London.

Well, all that was about to stop. He had been more than patient, and patience was a peculiarity he never tolerated.

"I would assume it is too much to hope for the possibility of a grandson in nine months?"

Katherine wanted to laugh in his face and goad him that he was too stupid to realize that the precious seed he had paid so dearly for had filled a more eager receptacle last night. Even knowing she took her life into her hands by deceiving Camden, the thought of being touched by a man who thought her hideous and repellent was unendurable. Just having him in the sanctity of her bedchamber for an hour as he snoozed in a chair by the fire was almost more than she could bear. After three years of marriage, she was still blessedly a virgin and she intended to stay that way. The thought of having her child taken from her and placed under the abusive control of this cold man was unthinkable. And if she was unfortunate enough to give birth to another worthless daughter such as herself . . . she shuddered at the thought.

Taking a deep breath, she lied with calm calculation. "Only time will tell, my lord."

Despite her outward coolness, she could feel perspiration beginning to shiver over her body. It was hard not to reach up and wipe away the telltale moisture of her nervousness from her upper lip. She knew she was losing her composure. Her secretive acts of rebellion never did seem to last very long when in his presence. Not knowing what else to do, her gaze darted to the plate of pastries set well within her reach.

Repelled, Camden watched as his daughter's plump hand reached for another cinnamon scone. His temples were beginning to pound with the blinding shards of pain slicing with insidious precision through his trembling body. He had to clench his jaw tight in order to bite off the howl of rage he so desperately wanted to let loose. Just being in the same room with this disgusting creature was enough to stretch his nerves to the frayed edge of sanity. It seemed the bitch deliberately set out to goad him.

Watching her dip her spoon into the jam pot suddenly shattered his strained demeanor into a million sparks of frenzied pain. Slamming his hand down on the table, he bellowed, "By God, madam, can't you do anything beside stuff your fat face all day long!"

Katherine's hand froze, then disappeared under the table to reappear with her napkin. With unnatural composure she touched her lips with the linen while surreptitiously dotting the moisture from her upper lip. Then placing the napkin with exaggerated neatness beside her plate, she rose to her feet and glanced down at her father's furious face, thankful of the distorted vision her mother's spectacles provided—it meant never having to meet his eye.

"Certainly, my lord. With your permission?" Before he gave it, she swept from the room, her head held proudly high.

Drawing a deep breath, Lord Camden again picked up his paper and continued to read in blessed solitude. Minutes later a hauntingly beautiful melody drifted through the corridors, the notes impeccably executed by fingers that had the genius of a true virtuoso. Camden's head jerked up from his paper, and once again he was enraged. With an obscene oath, he shot to his feet and, throwing the newsletter onto the floor, strode toward the offensive music.

When the doors crashed open behind her, Katherine jerked her fingers from the beloved keys and folded them in her lap. Staring straight ahead to the beautiful morning framed in the massive French doors, she refused to look into the cruelty she knew would be radiating from those soulless eyes.

As he came to stand over the gleaming piano, Camden resisted the urge to grab anything at hand and smash the magnificent instrument to bits. He satisfied himself by reaching over Katherine's shoulder and slamming down the keyboard cover. The reverberation of wood on wood and the discordant hum of vibration echoed in the tense silence that followed.

Katherine heard her father's steely voice behind

her as his heartless words struck her: "I can't stand the sight of you anymore!"

Camden stared down at her bowed head. His thoughts were a chaotic whirl as he fought the almost insane desire to put his hands about her neck and squeeze until he had wrung every drop of life from her ugly body. But, he couldn't. Not yet. His teeth clenched in a frenzy of frustration. He must remember the heir.

The pounding in his head increased till he could hear nothing else but the slamming pulse of his pain echoing in his ears. When he felt the insidious shiver of agony shoot up his left arm, he was almost grateful for the distraction. It brought back a sense of control.

Taking in a deep breath, he cradled his arm against his chest as he demanded, "You are to leave for Camden Square. Immediately. You will remain in London and in that stud's bed till you are stuffed with his seed, and I don't give a damn how you force him! He's nothing but a whore and he has his price just as they all do. I have already paid dearly enough and I will wait no longer for what I've paid good coin for! You will not come back until you are pregnant with my grandson! If you cannot seem to accomplish this most common of tasks, then mayhap Bridden will be more to your liking than this dismal residence you must suffer!" With that, he turned on his heel and strode from the room, his footsteps an angry echo in the tomblike room.

Katherine's eyes slid closed. Bridden, again. Camden Abbey or a lunatic asylum. Was there a difference anymore?

With quiet efficiency, a footman stepped to the double doors to give Lady Katherine privacy. His heart wrenched at the sight of the poor lady, head bent, sitting with the stillness of death at the instrument she could coax and command with such majesty.

Suddenly, she swung her head about and their gazes collided. A thrill of dread crept along his spine at the unholy light of hatred smoldering behind those rose-tinted lenses.

The smell of damp wool and mildew combined with the bone-jarring rocking of the carriage was steadily making her ill, and these were only minor irritants compared to all the other discomforts Katherine endured in the freezing carriage as it lurched down the rutted road to London. Having been literally tossed out into the sudden storm that had blown in, she had not been surprised when this dilapidated excuse of a traveling coach had rolled up to the front entrance with the Abbey's eldest retainer, Liam, perched precariously on top of the ancient structure.

Heaven knows, her father wouldn't put himself out to lend her one of his more comfortable conveyances, let alone spare the coin for a couple of train tickets so that she and her old governess, now companion, Jassy, could travel through this sudden tempest in relative safety and speed.

With gritted teeth, Katherine clung tenaciously to the hand strap as the coach jarred over yet another muddy pothole, barely saving herself from being flung to the wet floor. As she righted herself, she felt an icy wet sensation on her shoulder and turned to glare in disgust at the numerous rivulets of water trailing down the warped panels.

When the rocking torture chamber seemed to steady for the moment, she again sought what minuscule comfort she could by shifting about on the cold, cracked leather, trying to avoid the areas where the brittle hide was peeling off the wooden benches. Not an easy thing to do when every square inch was in danger of disintegrating.

Hearing a hacking cough, Katherine pulled off a glove, and leaning forward, she reached over and felt Jassy's face. She was shocked at how feverish her old governess had become in just the past half hour. In the next instant, a startling flash of lightning exposed the misery on Jassy's face as she sat huddled in her damp comer. The accompanying boom of thunder shuddered through the carriage, impressing upon Katherine the full extent of their helplessness against the raging elements beating against this ancient structure. Going more by touch than sight, she carefully tucked the blanket back up under her friend's chin. As with everything else, the interior lanterns had not been replenished with oil before setting off.

Feeling another shudder wrack the frail body beneath her hands, Katherine pulled her own lap robe from about her numb legs and wrapped it snugly around Jassy.

Biting her lip, Katherine worried about how Liam was coping on his own. His danger was much more immediate than just bearing up under the storm. The horses hitched to the carriage weren't the most predictable of the Abbey's stock and the likely chance that the thunder and lightning could spook them out of their traces was all too real. With desperate faith, she knew that no one knew horses and their quirks like Liam. Nervously she assured herself that if the old man felt he could not handle the situation he would pull up.

Katherine was startled as another blinding flash

of lightning baptized the interior with its eerie light. Before darkness had descended again an agonized scream was heard from above. Katherine froze in stunned disbelief; then, without a second thought she grabbed the latch on the door and flung it wide. It was ripped from her hand as she leaned out into the pelting rain and slammed against the side of the carriage, held there by the forceful gale. She cried out as the greedy wind wrenched her hat off, ripping at the roots of her hair. Her hands were clenched about the slippery sides of the door opening.

"Liam!" she screamed over the raging elements. Desperate for a sight of him, she strained to see atop the carriage seat. Another flash of lightning showed her the outline of a sprawled leg dangling over the side. There was an abrupt jolt; then the carriage veered off course, almost throwing her out the door. The door suddenly swung back at her, viciously striking her in the face. She screamed in pain as she flung herself back inside, just narrowly missing it as it swung back again, hard, and slammed shut. Hearing the shatter of glass, Katherine instinctively reached up to cover her face, just in time to protect herself from the shards of glass blown inward with the wind's fury.

Though sobbing in terror, she was up again and leaning out the door, this time using the door as a brace, her weight bearing down on the weakening hinges. Even as her grasping fingers reached up to grab Liam's leg, she watched, paralyzed, as his charred body tumbled over the side, brushing her arm before being swallowed by the merciless hunger of the storm. Though she knew he was lost to her, she still looked helplessly out into the blackness, the ground beneath her rushing past at an alarming speed.

Turning to look at the horses, she knew there was no hope for them. Terrified and maddened, they were running blind. She caught a glimpse of the reins slapping loose against their backs and within seconds the carriage was careering along at a deadly pace.

Panic-stricken, Katherine threw herself back into the relative safety of the carriage and dazedly wiped the rain from her face. Feeling pain, she blinked down at her hands. Her leather gloves were sliced to pieces, and beneath, so were her palms. She could feel bits of glass digging into her skin. Confused, she looked over at the door and, in a flash of light, saw blood smearing the jagged protrusions of glass still embedded in the window's casing.

On another plane of consciousness, she was aware of Jassy screaming, her cries barely heard above the pounding rain and thunder. When Katherine tried to make her way over to Jassy, she was thrown sideways and fell with a jarring thud against the sharp edge of her bench. Pain ripped through her chest, and for a few frightening minutes she could not catch her breath, no matter how hard she gasped. It seemed forever before she could draw breath again. Then, surprisingly, her panic seemed to subside, even as the agony piercing her side only grew more excruciating. Numbly she wondered if she had broken a rib.

Faint with pain, she lay there on the freezing floor, her saturated skirts weighing her down, and felt the vibration of the carriage beneath her. Even as inexperienced as she was, she knew that the groaning of stressed wood and iron did not sound encouraging; it was only a matter of minutes when the undercarriage would shatter under the unholy strain.

Slowly, painfully, she groped for Jassy's hand and held on tight. She was too numb to realize that Jassy's screams had ceased and her hand lay limp within hers, the frail fingers cold and still.

We are going to die, Katherine mused, not caring anymore what happened to them next. Then it struck her that her death would thwart her father's one obsessive desire: the vaunted Camden heir. It was with a sense of vindication that she realized all his years of neglect and abuse would not go unpunished. Grimly she smiled.

The heartening thought had barely passed when the carriage lurched violently out of control, throwing them about like fiddlesticks in a can. It was simple dogged determination that made her cling to Jassy's hand, needing to have her friend with her at the end, just as the gentle lady had been right by her side most of her life.

Chaos reigned as the coach tilted heavily onto its side, then began to slide sideways. She was conscious of the carriage breaking through a wooden barrier of some kind before toppling over. Then she felt herself falling, and with the piteous death screams of the maddened horses ringing in her ears, Katherine knew no more.

One

The two antagonists glared across the room at each other. Shattered glass and brown, wilted flowers littered the floor between them. Neither wanted to budge an inch, but the hefty housekeeper had the advantage of weight and soberness over the swaying red-eyed devil across from her.

"If ye think I'm meaning tae clean up this mess, ye've another think coming!" she blustered, her words almost swallowed in the strong Scottish brogue. As she noticed his dark eyebrows rising in derisive inquiry, she jerked her fist, perched on an ample hip, and indicated the vase he had just demolished in a childish fit of temper. Belligerently, she returned his glare.

Sion Sinclair, sixth Marquis of Dereham, turned slowly about, disdain curling his lips as he surveyed the disreputable room. Dust motes swirled through the dappled sunlight; cobwebs reflected like fragile lace high in the corners and dirty dishes were scattered over the desk, nearby chairs, and filthy floor. The sour smell of decaying food and spilled liquor permeated the stale air, a smell so pungent it had undoubtedly penetrated the dulled, dusty wainscoting. Finally, coming about full turn, his gaze flitted from the remains of the contested vase to settle with disdainful contemplation on the contentious servant.

Forcing himself upright, his muscles strained to their limit to prevent him from swaying, Sion murmured contemptuously, "Clean, Mrs. Turlow? Whatever does that mean? Obviously your interpretation of the word and mine differ. In fact, it differs so much that you are fired." As hard as he tried to speak clearly, his numb tongue stumbled over some words while slurring others. Yet he knew by her reaction that she had understood him well enough.

The housekeeper's eyes widened in shock, then narrowed spitefully as she sneered, "Is that so, yer lordship. And who, I'm thinking, are ye going tae get tae take me place? What other person in their right mind would work in this lunatic asylum? Ye, with yer drunken rages, pukin' up yer guts every other day, and tearing this beautiful manor apart. Clean, ye say? Tae what purpose? So ye've a clean slate tae demolish?" Then she continued, jabbing a shaking finger at the ceiling. "And her! That living corpse upstairs. Forcing food down her throat three times a day, cleaning foul-smelling sheets every day so's the poor thing dinna lie in them. And then, checking every minute o' the day just tae be certain she still lives! Ye're lucky tae have me!"

"You are fired," reiterated the steely-eyed lord. The fact that his eyes were also bloodshot to the point of looking painful appeared not to detract from the message he glared at her.

Breathing heavily, Mrs. Turlow stomped to the door, then spun to face her nemesis. "Verra well,

yer lordship, but when ye beg me tae return ye'll
pay dear for me forgiveness. Ye've steadily run off
every servant in three counties willin' tae try their
luck with the 'Hellhound o' Dereham,' and trust
me when I tell ye I was the last! God curse ye, and
good riddance!"

As her footsteps died down the corridor leading
to the kitchens, the already regretful lord gazed
helplessly about the shambles that had in better
days been an elegant, expensively paneled library.

"She's right," he muttered, almost losing his balance as he turned about to study the room with
blurry eyes. "I've turned two hundred years of
Dereham's pride into a hellhole." Staggering over
to his desk, his boots crunched loudly over broken
glass. He cursed as he bumped his hip against the
corner of the mammoth piece of furniture, then
reached with an unsteady hand to turn the battered
leather chair around. Another mumbled curse pre-
ceded the shattering of glass as he swept the seat
clear of several empty bottles.

With a sigh, he collapsed into the comfort of
torn leather and dropped his head back. Weary
and aching, his body melted into the chair, his
edgy nerves becoming a stagnant pool of apathy.
With bleary detachment he watched as a fly struggled to escape a web it had foolishly challenged.
A cynical smile twisted his lips for he could find
no sympathy to share with the hapless victim. They
both had nothing or no one to blame for their
pitiful state but themselves, both of them imprisoning themselves even more each time they
tried to struggle against their fate, the silken
threads winding tighter and tighter until there
was nowhere to turn. Tighter and tighter . . .
Reaching out, he grabbed a bottle and brought

it hurriedly to his lips. The sour liquor tasted like
bile, but it was numbing on nerves edgy with the
threat of sobriety. In one swallow he drained the
contents and tossed it negligently somewhere
around him.

Sion hated being drunk, hated not being in control of his life, but he hated the nightmares and the
memories even more. Paralyzing his mind with al-
cohol seemed the logical thing to do—either that
or putting a gun to his head. Yet for some depressing reason, one he still couldn't fathom, he
continued to hang on to his wreck of a life. Except
for nights, like last night, when the minutes seemed
to crawl by like the empty years stretching out before him, when the ticking of that damned clock
that Mrs. T. insisted on winding every day echoed
in his mind another wasted minute of his life. It was
at times like those that the thin shell of whatever
sanity he had left was stretched to the point of snapping. When the lure of eternal peace dangled so
enticingly close, reminding him of a dream that he
prayed would one day be his—a dream of forgiveness, of acceptance. The dream of lying down with
Tory in an undisturbed sleep that went on forever
into blessed infinity with their child safely slumbering between them.

And the answer to all his problems was only a
few insignificant inches away—just a matter of
stretching his fingers a bit until the gun was in his
hand. So why was he still here, struggling through
another meaningless day? Maybe this was God's
punishment for his crime, for his unforgivable
failure. Maybe this was hell. Alive or dead, this
was all that was left to him—this constant tormenting loneliness.

What was the saying? "Only the good die young?"

Squeezing his eyes shut, Sion ruthlessly thrust back the burning tears. *God, Tory, why? Why you?*

Instinctively he reached out, fumbling past the gun gleaming dully in the weak sunlight, to the bottle tilted precariously against a pile of books. Feeling its emptiness, Sion spit out a crude oath, then leaning forward he flung it into the cold fireplace—a graveyard of other such shattered yearnings.

The stomping of footsteps captured his ill-humored attention and slowly he turned to face the door, welcoming another confrontation with the aggressive widow.

Abruptly, the footsteps stopped. He flinched as the door was flung inward, swiping a clean swath of debris out of its way. A tray slid into view, clattering across the hardwood floor before it came to a halt a few feet from the door. Mystified, he studied the food sloshing about, even as it was congealing into an unrecognizable substance.

"'Tis for the girl. Ye do remember her, dinna ye?" Mrs. Turlow announced, barely stepping over the threshold as if leery of entering his den of iniquity. She didn't even give him the satisfaction of a flinch when he turned his baleful glare upon her. Instead, she calmly stared back at him while hitching her carpetbag higher and struggling with her coarsely woven cloak. It was pure torture not to close his eyes and relieve the pounding that seemed to center in each eyeball, but he would be damned if he would let her get the better of him. He was still a Dereham, blast her, and even drunk he was her superior. Unfortunately she knew him too well, and he realized he wasn't fooling her for a second when a smirk spread across her pursed lips.

"Ye be getting low on yer rotgut. What there be left is in the cellars." She paused for a second and looked at the carnage around her. For the barest instant he thought her frowning mien had softened with sympathy. God, how he hated that! He would not be pitied, and calling on what reserve he had left of his pride, he stiffened his back and glared down his nose at her. When a ring of keys was tossed down beside the battered tray, he immediately wondered which one opened the cellar, wherever the hell that was.

"The devil have mercy on yer soul, yer lordship, for surely God has forsaken ye long since." Then, with a shake of her head, his last servant was gone, the clamor of her boots reverberating back at him with devastating vindictiveness. Her final pound of flesh, he surmised as he rubbed his aching head. A rusty chuckle escaped him. God, indeed! God had forsaken him the day he had found his wife and child dead. And God had done nothing for him since but spit in his eye.

For some strange reason his bloodshot eyes slid curiously to the shimmering web above him. With morbid interest he watched the web's owner steadily advance upon the cursed fly, whose useless struggles only hastened its fate. As the spider began to cover its victim, Sion grimaced with distaste and grabbed for his pistol. Even drunk his aim was true. The explosive report split his head apart with a slice of agony that struck every nerve in his body before settling behind his eyes. The smell of the discharged powder burned his nose, causing a wave of nausea that instantly made him regret his noble deed. And now all he had to show for it was an ugly hole high in the uppermost corner of the intricately carved cornice; a work of art and history that until a moment ago had survived unscathed since the mid-sixteenth century. At least the fly was out of its misery. Lucky devil, Sion thought as he tossed the smoking pistol down. He only wished that he had someone as ruthless to release him from this endless trial called life.

Rising unsteadily to his feet, he approached the tray and again studied the unappetizing fare. So now he was suppose to feed this stranger upstairs? How in hell was he supposed to do that? By the constant grumbling of Mrs. T., the girl was in some kind of endless sleep. Anyway, if she wasn't already dead, this putrid mess would surely do the job. Reaching out a scuffed toe, he jostled the bowl of congealed broth, shuddering as a bit of it sloshed over onto his boot. If he was going to do this . . . this responsibility, he needed some fortification—now.

With a disgusted sigh, he spun on his heel, stumbled sideways, righted himself, then strode over to a map table cluttered with the usual assorted trash and bottles. With determination, he routed about, not even caring as a few of the empty bottles rolled over the edge. The sound of splintering glass was all too common in his self-imposed prison to elicit even a glance. At last, finding one not quite empty, he uncorked it and, with a shaking hand, hurriedly drained its meager contents. He closed his eyes in relief as the cheap gin snaked a path of fire down his throat.

Wiping his mouth with the back of his hand, Sion turned and weaved his way back to the door, then before he could talk himself out of it, he stooped down to pick up the tray. Immediately, the room tilted in crazed circles about him. His arm shot out with

clumsy speed to catch himself against the door, but
the damn thing slipped from his fingers and he
ended up tumbling onto his ass anyway—a not un-
common occurrence these days.

"Bloody hell!" he mumbled weakly. Crawling to
the wall, he leaned a shoulder against the door-
jamb and forced himself to breathe deeply. A fine
sheen of sweat coated his clammy skin and his
throat convulsed as he fought down the urge to
vomit. Hell and damnation, what was he doing?
Wallowing about on the filthy floor, all for some un-
guided sense of responsibility for a woman he
could hardly care less, for when all he truly wanted
was to escape into blessed oblivion.

Soon he was breathing easier, his body's inces-
sant craving silent for the moment. Irritation
spurred him on as he raised an arm and blotted his
clammy face against the soiled cambric of his shirt.
Then, gritting his teeth, he staggered to his feet,
the tray clenched in sweaty hands. His unsteady
footsteps resounded hollowly about him as he
walked into the foyer, then came to an abrupt halt
when he reached the foot of the stairs.

Sion's breathing accelerated to an alarming
speed as he looked up into the darkness looming
above him. It had been years since he had climbed
stairs. Any stairs. Glancing down at the noxious
brew, he silently battled with a rusty sense of obligation against the daily fear that ate at him every
waking and sleeping moment of his life. Again he
measured each tread of the stairway, and with each
beat of his heart, they became wider and higher.
Soon they were impassable in his feverish mind.

Even as he put the tray down, the dishes clattering at his feet, he felt like the basest of cowards.
Then resentment fueled his panic into anger. He

was not accountable to this girl. She was not *his* problem. She was Mrs. Turlow's, and that woman had brazenly walked out on her. Her death wouldn't be on his conscience, he tried to assure himself even as that deeply buried conscience of his stirred and nudged.

Rubbing his thighs, Sion backed up, the upper landing slowly receding from his sight with each step. His heart was pounding so hard he felt light-headed. Swaying, he sank down onto his haunches. She was not his responsibility, not like Tory had been—and, God help him, look what had happened to her. He had enough guilt weighing him down. After all, he had done his part in aiding the stranger upstairs, had he not? He had found her in that wrecked carriage, dragged her here, and given her into Mrs. Turlow's care. That was all that could be expected of him.

Why should the fate of this stranger matter to him, anyway? It wasn't any concern of his if she lived or died. Everyone lived and everyone died. Some sooner than others.

Besides, what could he do for her? He knew nothing of nursing. That was a woman's duty. What if he tried to care for her and she died?

All the eternal what-ifs continued to pound into his muddled mind until he thought he would go insane.

Closing his eyes, he saw red and his body began to tremble. *Not again. Not now.* A drop of sweat slithered down his temple as he realized he was becoming sober. His hands tingled, and slowly, as if in a trance, he looked down, already knowing what he would see.

Blood. Always there was her blood dripping from his fingers. He clenched his hands and felt the slickness and warmth of it. Her blood. Their child's blood. Always it was there, on his hands. Its metallic smell was an indelible, constant teasing of his senses, its unforgettable taste as cold in his memory as it had been on her lips. Always, always. His guilt wouldn't let him wash it away.

Tory! his mind screamed.

"Forgive me," he whispered in agony, his voice weighted with the tears that would never come. "Forgive me."

Forgetting about the girl upstairs, Sion spun around and blindly found his way back into his dark sanctuary. The slamming of the door echoed throughout the abandoned corridors of Dereham Hall.

In a dark room at the top of those impassable stairs lay a lone figure, forgotten and unwanted, as she had been all her life.

But now she slept peacefully in a cocoon of healing warmth, impervious to the world outside. With the instinct of any abused animal, she lay motionless, safely hidden away from all that would hurt her.

And as she slumbered on, patiently awaiting her time, she dreamed all the impossible dreams that had always passed her by. She now gloried in all the possibilities that were miraculously being offered to her.

Time, as the world knew it, had come to a standstill for her. As the minutes of her life slipped into days, and the days drifted into peaceful months, her body transformed itself, slowly, but steadily, shedding itself of all the shackles of her past life. Day by day, as the fleshy walls of her prison melted away, she grew stronger and more confident in herself, determined to live life to its fullest. Soon she would awaken to a new day—to the beginning of the rest of her life.

To a new life created especially for her.

Some time later, Sion stirred in the chair he was slumped into. He winced as he lifted heavy eyelids, the movements rasping like sandpaper against his dry eyes. Painfully he leaned forward and reached for the nearest bottle. He uttered a slurred curse as a single, sour drop teased his tongue. Feeling as though he had just been dragged through the sludge at the bottom of the Thames, Sion looked toward the dusty window, uncertain if the feeble light filtering through was the heralding of night or day, and not much caring in either case. Lurching to his feet, he made his unsteady way to the door. He fumbled with the latch before he was able to pull it open, then called out in a rusty croak, "Mrs. T.!"

Grabbing his head, he collapsed against the door frame and waited for her usual grumbling response. When none was forthcoming, Sion frowned and stepped reluctantly into the entry hall. He was about to yell again, when he paused in confusion.

The vast space crowding around him was as devoid of life as his heart. With each laborious step, Sion cursed as he supported his aching body down the long, narrow passageway that led to the kitchens.

The silence was just as heavy down there as he stepped into the dark cavern. The fire in the huge fireplace had long since burned into cold ash.

"What the hell?" he muttered as he turned about and retraced his steps. His head pounded with nauseating persistence as he contemplated the mystery confronting him. Back in the hall, he dragged leaded feet to the front door, and finding it unlocked, he inched it open. The sky was brighter now, telling of the day to come as the dawn breeze brushed softly against his face. He looked about, seeing nothing but the overgrown gardens and the sense of desolation that he had encouraged. Retreating back into the darkness of the manor, Sion slammed and locked the door against the world he no longer acknowledged.

Then he remembered. The bitch had deserted him. Angry, he made his way back to the door of his library and stared at the clock on the mantle as if it held all the answers. For the first time since he was a child and could remember such trivial details of life, the clock was silent. Now there was no one about to remember to wind the thing—not even Mrs. T., who had done so with mocking dispatch every morning while deriding him how the minutes of his life were ticking away into nothingness. Now it was as silent as death. Shrugging, he moved into the room.

He stopped midstride when his stomach growled with a painful insistence that caused him to wince.

With a weary sigh, he turned and again made his unsteady way to the kitchens. It took him several minutes of stumbling around before he was able to find a gas lamp and turn up the flame. A curse exploded from him as a startled rat scampered over his feet. Jumping back, he watched as the vermin scurried into a dark corner. His overly sensitized nerves were acutely aware of distant rustlings coming from every direction. Grimacing and careful of where he stepped, he walked over to the cavernous fireplace and saw neither wood nor coal about to restart the fire. His bleary gaze then swiveled toward the mammoth monstrosity sitting in all its blackened glory, intimidating him. The only thing he knew about the iron Goliath was how much it had cost him and that it was called a stove. Other than that, it was nothing more than a confusing array of doors, knobs, and grills.

Again he turned toward the centuries-old hearth. Rubbing his bristled jaw, he looked about helplessly, tempted to just walk out of this infernal pit, until the rumble in his belly demanded otherwise of him. However, no matter where he looked, he was certain of only one thing: there was no food—anywhere.

On the far wall he noticed several doors, two padlocked and one standing ajar. Hoping against hope, he raised the flame on another gaslight, and stepping before the door standing ajar, he pushed it in with a finger; the rusted hinges squealing. Peering inside, his lips turned up in disgust as the light reflected eerily off the beady eyes of at least a dozen rats helping themselves to sacks and barrels of foodstuffs now sadly depleted. He'd seen more food in soup kitchens in Spitalfields, for Christ's sake! What in hell had the Scottish harpy been doing down here? It wasn't as if he did not have the coin to buy enough foodstuffs to stock Buckingham Palace!

Cursing, he slammed the door shut and stepped back to glare at the other two portals securely locked against him and any other thief who was foolish enough to believe there could actually be anything of value down here. He began to doubt there was even any liquor behind one of those blasted doors.

Growing angrier by the minute, his gaze alighted on several trays hanging on the wall over a side table cluttered with various cooking paraphernalia.

He blinked as his groggy memory stirred—then he felt instantly sober. *The woman upstairs,* he thought with uneasiness.

Glancing up at the soot-stained ceiling, he felt a chill. With surprisingly steady steps, he hurried back into the hall. Sion paused for the briefest instant before with grim determination he started to climb the stairs. But even with this new fear driving him, his steps slowed with each upward tread. One hand clenched about the banister to pull himself forcefully upward, while the other reached up to wipe his brow. His fingers came away damp.

It felt as though hours had passed before he finally stood on the landing and looked about him. Wide, dim halls stretched out on either side of him, the ancient oaken doors standing as sentinels against his invasion. Hesitant, he looked at the rows of identical panels, wondering which one the woman lay behind.

Moving to the closest door on his right, he took a deep breath and reached for the tarnished latch. It swung silently inward. Standing on the threshold, Sion squinted through the shadowy light to the massive bed.

A body was stretched lifelessly upon the mattress, a thin covering delineating her slender outline. Cautiously, he moved farther into the room. The chills running up and down his body began to burn him. She looked . . . dead. Standing over her, he silently willed her to move, demanded that she give him some sign of life.

Suddenly, a bright ray of sunlight found its way through the loosely closed drapery and settled upon her stark profile, brutally defining her protruding bones beneath flesh that appeared bruised. His breath caught in his throat, choking him. She was dead, or so close it might as well be fact.

Closing his eyes, he prayed, *God, please, not again.*

Reaching out with shaking fingers, he felt her throat, searching for a pulse. He jerked his hand back at the feel of her cold flesh. Frightened, he glanced at his hand. No blood. He breathed again. Swallowing hard, he again touched the girl's throat, his temples throbbing as his finger roamed the cold skin, searching for a pulse. His breath expelled in a rush as he finally felt the slight evidence of the life-sustaining movement under his finger. Almost dizzy with relief, he continued to caress the feeble pulse with a gentle stroke as if trying to coax it to a stronger, steadier beat.

Not dead. At least not yet. He stared hard at the motionless girl. She was so thin. He winced as he gave a closer inspection of the protruding cheekbones and the stark delineation of the bone around her blue-tinged eyelids. Her hair was lusterless and tangled in thick snarls. She needed to be fed and cleaned. She needed to be taken care of.

And he had no idea how to go about it.

She may not be dead yet, but if he didn't do something soon, she certainly would be. He had to get food into her—but first he had to find the blasted stuff.

Stepping back, he thought of what lay before him and felt utter terror. This strange girl's life was now in his hands.

Taking a deep breath, he turned and left the room. Was this a test? he wondered. God's sense of humor, or a second chance? Hell and damnation, as if he did not have enough trials in his life—like getting through one day and into the next.

Where in the hell was he going to get food? Making his way back down the stairs, he found himself wishing that he hadn't fired that irascible old harpy. However, he would do well enough. After all, wasn't he a man of intelligence? He could do anything she could, and a damned sight better, he convinced himself. It would be a cold day in hell before he ever asked the sharp-tongued witch to step foot inside the walls of Dereham again.

Well, it must be snowing in hell today.

Sion Sinclair narrowed his eyes, infuriated as he watched the stubborn woman standing before him, her callused hands clasped firmly at her waist. Gritting his teeth, he reined in his temper and pride and bit out curtly, "I apologize!"

Mrs. Turlow watched him silently, her head cocked to the side.

Sion frowned as he waited for the presumed acceptance. She was looking at him as if she expected something else from him. His eyes narrowed as he glared at her. Not bloody likely!

So they both waited. In vain.

In the background the clock ticked monotonously on as both fought a silent battle. At last, with a disgusted snort, the former housekeeper raised her two chins and, with a final glare at the unrepentant man, spun around to leave.

Stunned, Sion watched this magnificent exit, not believing the woman's audacity. With an oath, he strode after her, bellowing, "Woman!" just as her hand reached for the latch on the door.

Mrs. Turlow hesitated; however, she did not deign to face him. "Yer lordship?" This query was followed by another lengthy pause. He glared at her proud back, clenching fists and teeth in frustration. "You obviously did not hear me," his voice was hoarse with anger. "I apologized."

"Aye, so I heard. The words, that is."

Struggling through his inebriated haze to understand the shrew, he glanced about the shabby entrance hall as if seeking assistance. "What more is there?"

She turned slowly and stared into his furious if confused eyes. "Words mean nothing, yer lordship. What I wish—nay, what I demand—is yer assurance that yer sorry for the abuse I've put up with all these years. Never once did I get an ounce o' kindness or consideration from ye. Despite the odds, meaning yer drunken fits and the poor lassie upstairs, I've done me best, I have. Granted, it wasna yer idea o' perfection, but ye, yer lordship, if ye dinna mind me saying, are a bit of a slummock, and dinna deserve the best from anyone. All I ever wanted was for ye tae meet me halfway, and ye dinna even do that!"

With a well-concealed shiver, Mrs. Turlow stood undaunted as the marquis's blood-shot eyes blazed into a stunned rage.

"Who the hell do you think you are? My equal?" Sion demanded, livid that this paid underling should even suppose to think he should meet her "halfway."

"Begging yer pardon, laddie, but in yer condition, I'd have tae lie flat on me arse tae be yer equal." She watched in satisfaction as his mouth dropped open in dumb shock. "A drunk be a drunk, if ye dinna mind me saying, be ye lord or sweep. Ye want me tae work for ye? Fine! But, ye will treat me like a loyal retainer and not yer whipping boy!"

Eyes blinking, Sion closed his mouth and felt shame. For the first time since the shock of his wife's violent death and the mockery of the investigation and trial that followed, he experienced an emotion other than depressed self-pity. With each year that had followed Tory's death, he'd had but one goal in life. And with a single-minded tenacity he had pursued this goal: a suicidal descent into the oblivion found at the bottom of any bottle he could get his hands on. Nothing else on this bloody earth had mattered, and anyone who had tried to convince him otherwise he had summarily tossed out.

Until today. Today he had a reason to think again before he did any tossing.

His head dropped forward as he closed tired eyes and actually saw himself through her eyes. Saw the shabby, filthy clothes that had undoubtedly cost the equivalent of months of this woman's hard-earned wages. Saw the lank, tangled hair. He couldn't even remember the last time he had taken the time to wash it—or bathe, for that matter. His nose twitched as he became aware of his body odor.

Lord, I'm disgusting! "Hellhound of Dereham Hall" was what the locals had dubbed him. An animal, indeed, and he had no one to blame but himself. Yet, was his shame strong enough to change him? he wondered despondently.

"I'm sorry. Forgive me." His whispered words echoed in the silence. He was so tired. So very, very tired. The smell of cloves tickled his nose as Mrs. Turlow came to stand beside him.

"I'll be seeing tae yer dinner, yer lordship," her no-nonsense voice told him.

Eyes still closed, he nodded. Then, as he heard her footsteps dying away, he turned abruptly. "Mrs. T."

She paused and looked back at him.

"I will be taking care of the girl from now on. I had no idea of the tremendous burden I had thrust upon you, and I do apologize for that. I . . ." He paused, running a shaking hand through his hair as he shamefully avoided the widow's direct stare. "I believe that the next few weeks may get a little . . . difficult. Last night I rid the manor of the last of the liquor. As I fight my dependence on the damn stuff I will need your help." Sion cast an uneasy look at her. "Do you have a problem with that?"

For once remaining silent, Mrs. Turlow shook her head. Sion offered her a lopsided smile. "I take it by the look in your eyes you know what to expect?"

"Aye, that I do, yer lordship. Me late husband, curse his sotted soul, had a love o' the bottle. Do I have yer permission tae summon the doctor if I have need tae?"

Sion winced. "If need be. I give you permission to do whatever you have to in order that we make it through the next month or so. I would have you bring back to the Hall as many retainers as you can persuade to return. However, I would ask that you protect my privacy as much as you are able." He knew he was dissembling in a very cowardly fashion, but the thought of strangers viewing him at times of great weakness made him blanch in horror and humiliation.

Mrs. Turlow watched the shifting emotion on his lordship's dissipated face. It was good to think that he could feel shame. Mayhap all could be well yet.

She knew well enough what was ahead of her. The thought of this large man going through the hell of passing on the bottle made her blood run cold. How could she possibly care for him and the lassie by herself? Be that as it may, she would do her best for his lordship. She did not know him well, but in the past few minutes he had earned a bit of her respect. 'Twasna easy for any man to admit to a weakness, especially a man of such pride as this one. To her way of thinking it showed a muckle bit o' courage. And that he had the strength to throw out the rotgut himself was proof enough to her that he was willing and ready for a helping hand. She had two strong hands and she was willing to give him both.

Sion caught her attention again as he looked around him. With a self-deprecating sense of humor, he said, "I would also appreciate it if you would concentrate on cleaning this pigsty I've created. I'll pay whatever is necessary to entice the villagers back into service. You can assure them the 'Hellhound' has been muzzled."

Mrs. Turlow smiled, wondering at his suddenly optimistic outlook. She knew it would be useless to try to rehire servants back into Dereham until his lordship had been purged of the evil humors he had been pouring down his throat all these years. The hellhound had been a mild puppy compared to what would come in a few days' time. Soon these halls would tremble with the fury of his howls.

She was skeptical of this pampered lord taking care of anything or anyone, but if shouldering the responsibilities of the girl pulled him from the lure of the bottle—even if it was only for a moment—it would be worth it. "We'll do what we must, yer lord-ship."

Sion smiled mirthlessly as he studied the in-domitable woman before him. "With your help, Mrs. Turlow, I doubt not we shall prevail."

He watched as she gathered up her battered car-petbag and cloak before heading toward the kitchens. Already he felt at ease knowing she was near.

Watching her retreating back, the marquis smiled, muttering, "How did I ever think to survive without you, you old witch? And blast if you didn't know it all the time!"

As he swung about to head toward the stairs the sight of himself in the large entry hall mirror caught his attention. Cobwebs and dust dulled the vision, but he saw all too clearly the picture he presented. He hardly recognized himself. Was this the same man who had once prided himself on his flawless appearance? As his gaze drifted over the shabby specter before him, his mind wandered back to another time and place—to an-other mirror reflecting back his pristine image and that of a pair of slender arms encircling his waist as he finished tying his ascot. Her laughter floated about the cheery room as he reached back and tickled her rib cage.

"Sion! Stop that," she gasped as she leaped back away from his teasing fingers. "I'm laced so tight as it is, I can hardly breathe." Again she danced away from his reaching fingers, him laughing as he pur-sued her. Then she stopped, her smile fading and she gazed at him with serious raptness. "You are so beautiful."

Her quiet words stopped him in midstride, and in wonder he drank in the love radiating from her eyes. "I pray he looks like you," she whispered. His smile froze, and cocking his head to the side, he paused, the question clear in his eyes.

Shyly she nodded, a hand covering her flat belly. "Tory," he breathed as he reached for her.

"Tory." His own moist eyes stared back at him through the dusty mirror. Biting down at the threatening tears, Sion turned away and headed for the stairs.

With a weary sigh, Mrs. Turlow pushed open the door and stepped into the room. Proudly she glanced about the now pristine decor as she breathed in the clean scent of beeswax and Castile soap. Moving to the bed, she stepped around a large armchair that hadn't been there earlier. She wasn't too surprised to see his lordship sleeping there; what she was surprised at was his appearance. She was shocked as she gazed down at the smooth shaven face and shining ebony hair lying upon relaxed shoulders. Her gaze shifted down, taking in the immaculate shirt and riding breeches, his boots recently oiled and buffed. Lord, was it just last week she had found him in a corner of the library, huddled in upon himself, ranting and raving with fever and pain? For weeks she had fallen into bed (when she could find the time to waste in the luxury of sleep), exhausted and afeared of waking in the morning to a house of death. If it wasn't for this forsaken lassie she shuddered to think what would have become of his lordship.

Smiling, she glanced at the still form on the bed and whispered fondly, "Just look what ye have done, hinny. Tae be sure, ye must be a gift from God."

Careful not to make a sound, she placed the tray on the bedside table, and reaching to the foot of the bed, she picked up the extra throw lying about the bedpost. As she placed it snugly over the deeply slumbering man, she realized that this was the first time she had ever seen him peacefully sleeping instead of passed out drunk. His breathing was slow and steady and finally silent of the inebriated whispers of a damned soul. With a gentle finger she soothed the deep grooves etched into his pale face—a face that still held too many remnants of the horror of the past years, but those too would ease with time.

Stepping back, she cast a final glance at the girl before slipping silently from the room. It was becoming stranger and stranger by the day, but life had purpose again, and even though weariness dragged at her stiff muscles as she thought of all the chores awaiting her on the morrow, she couldn't help but look forward to the coming day.

Leaving the room when she did, she never saw the girl's fingers twitch, nor her throat clench briefly. The highly anticipated event sadly went unnoticed by both her saviors.

Two

Setting down the basin on the bedside table, Sion stood over his patient and rolled up his sleeves. Close to eight weeks had passed since that fateful day when he had been thrust back into the reality of life, and he still wasn't sure how he felt about it. The withdrawal had been its own form of hell revisited, and the thought of going through that again kept his hand from the bottle just as much as did the enigma laid out before him.

The demons still nipped at his heels most nights, but they were tolerable, if waking in a cold sweat could be thought tolerable. Maybe the fact that this girl was still alive—in truth, thriving—under his care gave him the hope that he was not the failure that Tory's death had accused him of being.

Hands on hips, Sion studied his sleeping beauty, and his lips turned up in a smile. He was proud of his accomplishments. The motionless body stretched out before him could no longer be considered emaciated, although she was still far from the weight she should be. Her profile was now delicately defined, even though her cheekbones were still a bit too prominent. Her velvety skin now glowed with health instead of that sickly pallor which had bruised her skin before. It may not be the fashion to sport the kiss of the sun on a lady's countenance, but Sion rather preferred that to the paleness of the sickbed. Every morning, he carried her onto the balcony and sat with her as he pored over years of neglected estate accounts. Her hair, though now clean and shiny, still did not glow with the vitality of true health. That would come when she finally opened her eyes and partook of proper food. In the meantime, he fed her five times a day, painstakingly massaging her slender throat as he forced down as much of the nutritious broths Mrs. Turlow made for her as he was able.

The clock on the mantle softly chimed the hour, startling Sion out of his thoughts. With a sigh, he reached over and drew down the light coverlet. Picking up the washcloth, he soaped it liberally.

As he leaned over the girl, he lost all track of thought. Breathing deeply, he forced his mind to the chore at hand, and raising a fragile arm, he gently drew the warm cloth over her delicately tanned skin. He frowned, thinking how he needed to work these muscles a bit more. Wringing out the cloth again, Sion studied her profile. From time to time it was not unusual to catch a slight movement, whether it be the flutter of her lashes or the twitch of a finger. All his days were wrapped in these momentous events and he constantly feared that he would miss one.

"Well, what shall we talk about today, beauty?" he whispered as he dragged the cloth slowly across her collarbone. "Did you hear the swans calling this morning? How can a creature so beautiful have such an awful screech? It is a wonder that they mate for life considering they must listen to one another for the rest of their lives. Mrs. T. swears that if they don't shut up she's going to serve them up on silver platters." His eyes shifted reluctantly away from her pale breasts as he ever so slowly drew the cloth over one firm mound. Then he paused abruptly, for the strangest thing happened—the beat of her heart had accelerated under his ministrations. Putting the cloth aside, he gently cupped her left breast, feeling the frantic cadence. His eyes narrowed as he watched the fairness of her skin flush with color.

Sion's breath caught sharply as he watched her rosy nipples distend, budding into tantalizing fruit. Unconsciously, he licked his burning lips. His own heartbeat kicked up, and for the first time in years, he could feel the swelling of his desire. Ashamed and yet fascinated, his fingers tightened about her soft flesh. Yet, watching her face, there was still not a flicker of movement; the smoky fan of her eyelashes continued to lie still upon her flushed cheeks. Feeling the bud of her nipple press against his palm, he couldn't stop himself from bringing up his other hand to massage her other breast. Closing his eyes, he groaned low in his throat. She was so soft.

Suddenly, the picture of her in his arms, their limbs tangled in passionate disorder, flashed into his mind, and his hunger had him shaking as he began to reach for her. *He needed to be inside her.*

Sion lurched back from the bed, terrified as the disgusting thought swept through his mind. Even though it was a mere reflection of his fevered mind, it was still as close to rape as a man could get without committing the actual crime. Feeling a deep repugnance of himself, he drew a shaking hand over his face and thought of the comfort he could find downstairs in his library.

"No!" with clenched teeth he paced about the room. "Just take it easy," he admonished himself. "One step at a time." He inhaled deeply while keeping his back to the bed. "Get control of yourself."

Minute by minute he willed his trembling body to relax, and finally he found a semblance of control. Sion pulled his hand away from a face now damp with perspiration and turned cautiously toward the bed. His eyes snapped wide in shock.

Her beautiful eyes, whiskey gold and glistening with fear, were watching him from across the room.

"My God!" he whispered, taking a hesitant step forward.

The girl tried to speak, but finding she couldn't, she swallowed convulsively.

Jolted out of his shock, Sion strode to the bed and jerked up the glass that had always stood at the ready for this moment. With an unsteady hand he sloshed water into it, getting more on the floor than into the glass, then turned toward her. Seeing her flinch back from him, he came to a halt. Her hand shook as she tried to fend him off; however, it merely fell back to her side, limp.

Slowly, he raised the dripping glass. "Water," he offered in the calmest voice that he could manage as he moved toward her. "I just want to give you some water." He motioned toward his own throat. "You must be parched."

Her confused eyes focused on the glass. She swallowed again, then nodded. Sion watched her gaze dart about the room only to snap back to him as he sat beside her. They both eyed each other warily as he held the cool, wet rim to her lips.

It seemed her thirst was greater than her fear, for she allowed him to support her as she swallowed the water in greedy gulps. When most of it ran down her neck and onto her breasts, her gaze shifted down—and encountered her nakedness in his arms. With a cry, she fumbled with the blanket as she tried to cover herself.

Realizing her embarrassment, Sion pushed her hands aside and pulled the cover up all the way to her chin. He flinched at the fear widening her eyes. Forcing a smile, he sat back in his armchair, which was still positioned close to the bedside. For the first time since he could remember, he was at a loss for words. He bit down on his burning curiosity and gave her time to study her strange surroundings, noticing how she jumped at every little sound around her: the ticking of the clock, the warbling of the jay outside the window, his breathing.

Her attention finally settled on her hands, clenched white-knuckled about the covering. He could imagine the shock and dizzying sense of displacement she must be feeling at the sight of her unfamiliar limbs. Concerned, he watched her closely. When her body began to tremble, he reached out to hold her. No resistance met his effort as he drew her against his chest. "Shhh, it's going to be all right," he soothed as he gently stroked her hair back over her shoulders.

"What is happening to me? Where am I?" He barely heard the painful rasp of her whisper.

"You've been ill." During all the weeks he had taken care of her, never once had he thought about what he was going to say to her when she woke up. He had no idea how to even begin. How do you tell someone that she has lost months of her life? If there was ever a time he needed his no-nonsense, down-to-earth Mrs. T., it was now.

"Ill?" He felt her shudder and his arms tightened

about her. "I don't understand. Where's Jassy?" Her voice cracked, the last word forced out. It was obvious that this person was of great importance to her.

Dead and buried in an unmarked grave, he thought grimly, assuming she spoke of the old lady they had found in the ruins of the carriage. *Damn it! Where are you when I need you,* he silently cursed his unsuspecting housekeeper.

Pushing away from him, her manner becoming more hysterical by the second, she demanded again, "Where is Jassy?"

Sion opened his mouth, but still uncertain as to what he should say, he snapped it shut again. He paused a moment; then, glancing into her eyes he knew he had to say something—and quickly, for her agitation was growing by the second.

Suddenly the door crashed open, and in Mrs. Turlow's usual pandemonic way, she swept into the room while balancing a loaded lunch tray on her generous hip. As her eyes fell upon the couple on the bed, the tray crashed to the floor, scattering food and dishes in every direction.

Dropping to her knees, she raised clasped hands to heaven and cried, "Saints be praised, 'tis a miracle!"

The girl stared wide-eyed, open-mouthed at this spectacle before her.

Sion closed his eyes with a relieved sigh.

With much effort, Mrs. Turlow heaved herself to her feet and bustled over to the bed, pushing Sion out of the way in the process.

"Nay, none o' that, yer lordship," she scolded as she took the pale girl into her arms while ignoring her feeble struggles. "There, there, ye poor lambkin. Ye must be afeared out o' yer wee wittles."

Noticing the girl's lack of attire under the thin blanket, she shot Sion a censorious frown and again shooed him away.

Sion's eyes blankly followed the callused hand waving with brusque authority before his face. Confused, he remained where he was.

Mrs. Turlow swiveled about and glared at the dense man. "Out!" she barked.

"I beg your pardon?" Sion was starting to regret her presence.

"The poor lamb is hardly dressed tae receive ye, yer lordship."

"Receive me? Are you daft, woman?" Grinning, he motioned to the girl peeking around Mrs. T.'s protective shoulder. "I've been taking care of her every day for weeks. Believe me when I say I've seen everything there is to see beneath that blanket!" Seeing horror dawn in "Lambkin's" eyes, Sion bit his tongue.

Rubbing the back of his neck in irritation, he asked in a voice pitched to be heard above Mrs. T.'s blustering, "What is your name?"

At this question, even Mrs. Turlow quieted. Turning, she stared down into the girl's now emotionless face.

The silence that followed his lordship's question was uninterrupted as the girl stared back, her weary eyes blinking.

"Your name?" he asked again, more gently this time.

Again silence.

"I'm so tired," she finally whispered, slumping away from the woman's motherly embrace.

The marquis and housekeeper glanced at each other in frustration. After a few more minutes of

Mrs. Turlow's well-intentioned pampering, the patient was finally tucked in snugly.

Only Sion heard her sigh of relief as he shut the door behind him.

Katherine opened her eyes as the door clicked shut.

Am I going insane? she wondered through an exhausted haze? With much difficulty she finally managed to drag her arms from beneath the covers. Disoriented, she stared at the strange limbs. Her brain told the hand to move. After a long hesitation, it did, slowly. She stared at it with lethargic interest. It was hers—and yet it wasn't. It was not the color of her skin. The wrist bone protruded and the fingers were thin and bony. The entire arm was thin. It could not be hers.

She told the hand to clench. Inch by inch, the fingers curled into her palm, the nails digging into the tender flesh and she felt pain. Her nails were always bitten off and ragged, not long and buffed to a high shine.

She looked about her. Was this Bridden? Had she finally gone insane, just as her father had always said she would?

Her hand shaking with exhaustion, she touched her cheek and was amazed at the feel of the hollow beneath her protruding cheekbone. Her fingers wandered down, exploring skin now stretched tautly under her chin and along a slender neck. Again, her gaze wandered over the strange room. Where was Jassy? She couldn't remember. Had the strange man told her? A doctor. He must be a doctor. Remembering the man's words about what he had seen of her body, she weakly clutched the blanket to her breasts. This had to be some bizarre dream.

Succumbing to the lassitude pulling at her, Katherine closed her heavy lids.

Just imagine—she shook her head wryly just before drifting off to sleep—*me, thin!* What a wonderful dream.

It felt as if she had only closed her eyes for a second when she awoke again. Slowly she blinked several times as she looked about her. She frowned when she noticed that her surroundings were still unfamiliar.

Turning her head, she gasped as she looked straight into the black eyes of the same man from last night. Again he was sprawled comfortably in the oversized armchair beside the bed. His intent scrutiny alarmed her. Had she done something wrong? The sudden, heavy pounding of her heart quickly made her light-headed in her weakened condition.

Who was this man?

Where was her father?

Her husband?

Not knowing what else to do, she closed her eyes, blocking out all the strangeness about her. She was just too tired to deal with this stranger right now. All she wanted was to go back to sleep; that was blessedly familiar.

Sion frowned as his sleeping beauty closed her eyes as if to ignore him. He waited a few minutes, but after all this time, patience was not something he was willing to give her at this moment. Shifting in his chair, he cleared his throat.

At least he had the satisfaction of knowing she

was still awake behind those closed eyes, for he noticed a slight movement as she pressed herself back into the pillows, as if to burrow away from him.

"I know you are awake." His voice came out gruff, which was the last thing he intended. It was just so damn hard having to wait any longer for all the answers he had been burning for. Again he cleared his throat. It seemed strange to speak with her, knowing that she could actually hear him. "I would appreciate a few moments of your time, if you please. I promise not to keep you long."

After a long moment he watched her reluctantly open her eyes. She glared at him.

"Thank you," he acknowledged with a solemn nod.

Katherine stared at the man. Having lived with Camden all her life, being wary—being prepared for the worst—was second nature to her. He was very handsome, this stranger, she admitted with dispassion. Dark and brooding, just as she had always imagined Byron would have looked. She didn't like handsome men. But then, she didn't like men at all. There was a look of dissipation about his eyes and his wide mouth. She knew the signs of dissipation very well. And under that fine, dark skin of his, she could detect the unhealthy pallor of a drunkard. The stranger had a cruel look about him; possibly because of his dark coloring and the untidy length of his hair; however, the expression in those black eyes watching her appeared kindly enough. Were men capable of kindness? She scoffed at the silly thought as her gaze flicked along the long length of his sprawled form. For her it was not a matter of choice: he was a man, and men were her enemy, never to be trusted.

"Do you have any recollection of what has happened to you?" he asked gently.

That was easy enough to answer, she thought with relief. "No."

"What is your name?"

That gave her pause. *My name? He doesn't know my name?* She could feel her heart racing. So, she couldn't be at Bridden. If he did not know her, then that had to mean her father did not know she was here—wherever that might be. If she gave this stranger her name, would he summon her father? What a silly question! Of course he would. She felt cold all over at the thought of going back to the Abbey.

Her mind in a whirl, she dissembled: "I . . . I don't know." She realized with frustration that she was just too tired to deal with him right now. And this close examination of his unnerved her. Feeling as if he could read her thoughts, she lowered her eyes.

When the man started frowning, she tensed in alarm, noticing how even more threatening he appeared. Where were the servants? Was she alone here with him? Where was Jassy?

"You don't know your own name?" His voice was curt and she could sense how angered he was becoming. She knew the fear of living with anger all too well; however, she didn't know how this stranger dealt with his anger. And that frightened her even more.

"Please, could I see Jassy? My companion? Is she all right?" she asked in a hurry, needing the comfort of Jassy beside her. Jassy would know what to do.

She watched as all emotion was wiped from his face, and she started to tremble. Her breath became ragged. Something was wrong with Jassy. Her heart seemed to come to a standstill in her throat. "Jassy?" she whispered.

Sion looked away briefly from the stark fear in those golden, whiskey brown eyes. Taking a deep breath, he said slowly, "I'm so sorry, my dear, but the elderly lady with you was found dead."

"Found dead?" she parroted back blankly.

"There was a carriage accident," he prodded her slowly, afraid of shocking her again too soon.

Then it all came back to her in remembered flashes of horror: the storm, Liam, the carriage turning over. Tears sheened her vision. Jassy? Her own Jassy was gone? Choking, she managed to ask, "And Liam?"

He frowned. "Liam?"

"My coachman."

Sion shook his head. "I know of no one else. I'm sorry." He watched as she closed her eyes and turned her face away. Even as he sympathized with her loss, he wondered how she could remember her companions' names and yet could not recall her own. He bit down on his curiosity though; for it was obvious she was distraught and exhausted. Now was not the time to quiz her for answers. What she needed was the time and privacy to grieve.

He started to rise, but paused as her tearful gaze jerked up at him. As he continued to stand upright he watched her, his curiosity growing by the minute. She was acting like a cornered rabbit before the jaws of a badger. Even given the strangeness of her surroundings, the panic in her eyes was not normal.

"I'll leave you alone for now. My housekeeper,

Mrs. Turlow, will be bringing up your supper soon. Please let her know if there is anything you need." He waited a few more moments, hoping she would say something, but she just lay there staring up at him. There was no mistaking the look she was giving him—she just wanted him gone. His gut clenched tight, and suddenly he felt as alone as he had during all his past years of hell. He almost wished she was his sleeping beauty again, dependent on him for her every need. Awake, she obviously viewed him as a threat.

Nevertheless, awake or asleep, she was a mystery that he was going to unravel if it was the last thing he did. He just hoped he didn't lose her in the end, and then frowned at the absurdity of such a thought. Yet, the foolish fear persisted as he left her room.

Lord, am I getting fanciful, or what? he thought with disgust as he closed the door behind him, wishing he could drown these irrational feelings in a bottle of blue ruin. His hands shook with the need to wrap themselves around the smooth coolness of glass; his head pounded with the biting pain that only the smell of raw liquor could soothe, and the burning in his gut increased. Rubbing his damp face, he forced himself past his library and out into the bright sunshine, where he stood blinking as he glanced around him with renewed determination. Whether she admitted it or not, she still needed him, and by God, he would see this through sober if it killed him!

Three

Damn, but that woman is exasperating, Sion fumed as he paced to the French doors and again glared out upon the beautiful day.

Unaware of his furious regard bent upon her, the object of this ire was carefully making her way about the unkempt garden. Every now and then she would pause, leaning heavily on the ornate cane provided by his generosity, and turn her face to the healing warmth of the sun.

It had been a fortnight since that momentous day when she had finally broken free of her imprisoning slumber. And each of those days she had deftly eluded his numerous questions. He was certain that her claim of memory loss was nothing more than a convenient excuse. Those shadowed eyes revealed so much more than she could possibly know. Somewhere, somehow, someone had hurt her. It was obvious she was running from someone. But who?

He had to gain her trust somehow for they couldn't keep going on this way. Yet, despite his gentleness and patience with her, the ungrateful chit wouldn't even let him get close to her. She took her meals in her room, refusing to join him in the dining room, and every time he tried to accompany her on her daily rambles she would immediately return to her room, mouthing some inane excuse. Didn't she realize that if it had not been for his diligent care, his daily routine of massaging and manipulating her insensate limbs, she would not be enjoying the freedom of maneuvering on her own?

Then, as if he did not have enough problems, Mrs. Turlow was aiding and abetting the chit. It was a bloody conspiracy.

Well, enough was enough!

Setting his chin at a belligerent angle, Sion threw back the French doors and strode into the garden.

Katherine sighed as the heat of the sun seeped beneath her skin, healing her aching body and cleansing her troubled soul. She had never realized the beauty of the sun until she had been denied it for so long.

Opening her eyes, she actually savored the pain as she stared into the blinding brilliance. Now she could not allow a day to go by without spending time in its warmth. If she could, she would shed her clothes and immerse her naked body in the golden rays. She chuckled as she thought about her sun-kissed flesh. What a scandal! Actually, she didn't mind at all. She rather liked it. The delicate honey-golden hue actually made her look . . . different. Possibly even exotic?

Day by day, she could feel herself growing stronger, more confident. And like a butterfly emerging from its confining cocoon, she was eager to spread her wings.

A beautiful, wondrous creation. *I am becoming impossibly vain and I love it!* She smiled.

And what thrilled her the most was that everyone in her life had to believe her dead after all these months. Not that they seemed to care, made obvious by the absence of any search or even inquiries as to her whereabouts. This harsh realization of how unloved and unwanted she had been her whole life aroused no sadness or even anger in her; rather she felt relief that her long nightmare was finally over.

A strange sense of freedom dizzied her as the autumn breeze whispered over her slender body, still so unbelievably hers. Anxious, she drew a hand over her svelte curves. *I am still thin; it isn't a dream,* came the familiar litany, burned into her mind like a prayer by now.

Katherine tensed as she heard footsteps crunch along the graveled pathway behind her. Without turning, she knew who it was.

"Good afternoon." His deep voice, as always, sent shivers of apprehension down her spine.

With hard-won composure, Katherine turned slowly to confront him. She had too much at stake to ever be anything but cautious in his presence. She would never be able to forget that this man had saved her life, but she was also well aware of the fact that he had the power to take it away. Being returned to her father's oppressive charge would be unbearable. She would rather be dead.

Politely she nodded, "Lord Dereham." Heart beating a rapid tattoo, Katherine moved with feigned calmness down the path toward him, keeping a chary eye upon his formidable figure neatly blocking her escape. As she reached the last few feet before him, she paused.

"If you will excuse me, my lord, I'm not feeling too well. I believe I will retire to my room." She cocked her head and tried to stare him down. She could not do it, though. Quickly she looked over his shoulder, careful to avoid meeting his eyes.

Shifting further into the middle of the path, the marquis crossed his arms over his chest, feet planted firmly apart. His belligerent posture spoke eloquently of his frame of mind.

Pursing her lips, Katherine analyzed the situation and knew she was at a disadvantage. She could hardly push this imposing man aside, and if she headed off down another path he would simply intercept her before she got far.

The time of reckoning was upon her. Observing the militant light in his lordship's eyes, she knew she was cornered. *Like a rat in a trap*. Her mind quickly reviewed the numerous stories she had been playing with all week.

"I believe it is time we had a chat," he began, taking her elbow, and with gentle insistence he escorted her to a nearby bench. He lost no time once she was seated. "Now, first off, your name, please."

She hesitated, still frantically shifting possibilities about before committing herself. Finally, Katherine opened her mouth.

"And the truth, if you don't mind," his stern voice warned her.

She feigned affront as she jerked back. "I beg your pardon!"

Sion smiled grimly. Staring her in the eye, he assured her, "I am not as stupid as I apparently look to you, my dear. I know you never had a loss of memory, and right now I can see the wheels in that calculating mind of yours spinning some outrageous Banbury tale." Grabbing her chin none too gently, he forced her gaze up to clash with his.

"Know this, madam! *I* saved your ungrateful little hide and have cared for you for months. As I have already invested a considerable time with you, do you actually believe I would do anything to harm you?" He saw her eyes flicker with uncertainty. It was the mysterious shadows behind the uncertainty that would be the ruin of him yet. His voice deepened and grew husky as he continued, "I swear to you that never will I do, or say, anything to put you at risk. Moreover, never in this world would I return you to the persons who have harmed you. This I vow, upon my honor." Then, he added in a whisper, "Trust me."

The sun reappeared from behind a cloud, warming her face. On the breath of the afternoon breeze, the scent of roses enveloped her as the humming of bees echoed in the back of her mind. Still the intensity of his velvet black gaze compelled her.

Trust him, he says. How could she possibly trust any man?

Jerking her chin from his imprisoning fingers, Katherine charged impassively, "I grant you that you saved my life. However, after having done so you left me in an upstairs chamber and promptly forgot my existence. It was not until I was easier on the eyes that you deigned to offer any care to my person. Because I was able to ease your boredom, do you honestly think that gives you the right to my trust?" She forced a smile. "I give you my humble thanks, my lord, but that is all you are entitled to."

Katherine bravely ignored his clenched jaw and added quickly, "Of course, I will repay you for your time and any moneys spent on me. Somehow." She frowned as she remembered she did not have a farthing to her name. Out of habit, she started to adjust her spectacles, as she had always done when nervous, needing the comforting sense of anonymity they always afforded. But her pathetic little shield was long gone, so instead she nudged her chin a bit higher and tried to meet his intimidating perusal. Already she could feel the telltale dampness on her palms.

His eyes narrowed. "Your thanks! How magnanimous of you! And what the bloody hell are you talking about that I forgot about you?" he demanded, cursing Mrs. Turlow's wagging tongue.

Moving away from the marquis's overpowering heat, she answered with a detached smile, "I believe I have explained myself clearly enough, Lord Dereham."

The hurt she was trying so hard to hide was not lost on Sion; silent misery was etched on her beautiful profile. He knew in that moment that if he expected her trust he had to give a little of his own. Sion blanched at the thought of exposing himself so.

Taking a deep breath, he gazed out over the garden. "That had nothing to do with you. I was so drunk most of the time that I did not know day from night, let alone the fact that you were just upstairs from me." Standing up, he moved away from her. Now it was he who needed to put distance between them. He did not think he could bear to see the doubt and condemnation in her face when she heard the whole sordid story.

"Six years ago I met and fell in love with a girl by the name of Victoria Lansing." He paused for a long moment, and Katherine watched as his face eased its harsh lines, fond memories softening the dissipation marring the perfection of his features as he reminisced.

"She was everything to me. Tory had a whimsical sense of humor, where I had none. I was legend for the Dereham temper and bloody pride. Nevertheless, all she had to do was smile at me to make me realize what a pompous ass I could be. She made all my problems seem so damn trivial—and compared to what most people had to confront, they were."

His hands flexed before him as he stared down at them. Katherine could almost imagine a fragile white hand clasped gently in those strong fingers. Did he feel Tory's hand clinging to his? she wondered as she watched him studying his hands.

"We married not too soon after we met, despite all arguments against a hasty marriage and how it would appear. But we didn't care, so we turned a deaf ear to all their rantings and gave them an ultimatum: a quick marriage or elopement." He grinned at her. "You can imagine their unanimous decision."

The breeze soughed through the garden, ruffling his dark hair. Their eyes met briefly before he frowned and turned his back on her. Licking dry lips, she stared at his stiff back, his hands now clasped behind his waist. She noticed they were white-knuckled.

When he didn't continue, Katherine prodded gently. "What happened?"

Sion started at the sound of her voice, so lost had he been in his thoughts. This was so much harder than he had thought it would be. Clearing his throat, his voice was curt as he continued. "We had an argument that night. I didn't want her childhood friend in my home anymore and she was too tenderhearted to tell him. I was being unreasonable. I know that. I knew it then, it was just that I was so tired of him hanging on her skirts, whispering in her ear and openingly disparaging me. I had had enough and I told her so." He could still remember Tory's stricken face when he had stormed out of their bedroom that night. *God!* He squeezed his eyes closed as his head dropped back. That damned, ridiculous argument. She had asked such a little thing of him and he had been too much of a bastard to try to meet her halfway.

His jaw clenched as he remembered that last night. "She followed me out of our room, but I didn't stop. I was angry and she was trying to defend the rodent and I refused to listen. I had made it to the front entrance and had opened the door when . . ." The fog had been thicker than usual that evening. He could still feel it on his face, heavy and moist.

His voice sounded low and faraway to himself. "I heard Tory call out to me to come back, and then I heard her falling." He could still hear her cries, the sickening sound of her body striking each stair. The silence after. "Before I even reached her and took her into my arms I thought I had lost her." His breath became ragged as he remembered gathering her still form up in his arms. And the incredulous joy he had felt when she opened her eyes. Then the screaming started. The helpless screams as she doubled over in his confining embrace. She was alive, but in such complete and horrible pain. And the blood.

His eyes snapped open as the slashes of red washed over his memories. He turned toward

Katherine and bit out in a rush, "She was losing the child."

Even in the dimming of the late-afternoon light he could see the paling of Katherine's features. He felt a cool dampness shiver over his body. God, he needed a drink!

Rubbing his dry lips, he finished in a distracted manner. "She was seven months with child and I could do nothing to help them. I sent the servants for the doctor; I took her upstairs and put her into bed. I did everything I could think of, but nothing helped. She was bleeding so damned much and there was nothing I could do! She kept screaming and writhing on the bed. I could see her body trying to expel the child." Frantically he had tried to hold her close, hold the bloodied towel between her legs—but it hadn't helped. Nothing he had done had helped.

Katherine gaped up at him in wide-eyed shock, watching how caught up he was in the horror of the memory. After a long moment, helpless to help him, she just managed a strangled whisper, "I'm so sorry."

Sion dug his hands deep into his pockets. He could still remember the tacky feel of Tory's blood coating his hands, his arms, his chest. "Before the doctor even arrived she had died in my arms, screaming and begging my forgiveness for killing my child. She was begging me for my forgiveness." Sion looked up, blinking away the tears that scalded his eyes. "She died begging my forgiveness," he whispered into the cold sky. After a moment, he cleared his throat and continued, his voice husky with the strain of talking, "I hadn't even had a chance to bury her when her friend stepped in and accused me of killing her in a jealous rage. He lied to any who would listen how I had been abusing her and how she had confided to him repeatedly how she was in fear of her life. At first, I didn't refute his malicious charges because I felt I did kill her. Then, when I fought back it was too late; too many people were listening to him and charges were brought against me."

Agitated, he began to pace before her. He reminded her of a caged panther: restless, enraged, and helpless all at once. "The world said it was me. People I thought my friends, colleagues—even my family believed me guilty. Guilty of brutally murdering the woman who was bearing my child. And they tried me for her murder before my peers." His eyes were crystal hard when he stopped directly in front of her, his legs brushing her skirts. He stared down at her, his scorching gaze almost baiting her to make some comment of accord. It was quite evident to her that he did not expect her to believe him any more than the multitudes of London had.

Fighting against the instinct to run, she sat there and tried to meet his challenging scowl. Unconsciously she hid her shaking hands in her skirts and shrugged slightly. "But obviously they found you innocent, or else you would be . . ." She stumbled into silence.

"Executed?" Sion finished bluntly. He moved away again, to give her the distance she always seemed to need. "Oh, they tried, but I had an excellent barrister. The best money could buy." He could still bring to mind the pompous ass's smug face. "The bas—the man—had believed me guilty of beating a pregnant woman to death—quite viciously, I might add—but still he got me exonerated. To this day I don't know if he is a saint for saving my life, or the worst sort of scum for helping a man he believed committed such a heinous crime free to walk the streets."

Katherine shivered. Here she was, alone in an isolated garden with a man whose friends and family had believed him a murderer. Something was not right. There had to be something wrong with the marquis if all his family and acquaintances could turn so easily against him. There were so many questions she wanted to ask. Had there been a history of his beating her? Had his wife truly gone to her friend and confessed her fears. Why hadn't the marquis stayed to defend himself instead of fleeing to this isolated estate?

"The terrible thing is, though I am innocent of all their charges, I am guilty of her death," he said out into the void of the night.

Looking up from her hands, she watched as the breeze lifted his silken hair, inanely thinking that the disheveled mane needed to be trimmed. On the cool current, she discerned the faint scent of him. Not knowing what she was doing, she closed her eyes and breathed deeply, protecting herself from the chill of the approaching night.

For whatever foolish reason she couldn't even begin to fathom, she could not help but find herself believing in him. As she had been locked away from the outside world her entire life, she was certainly the last person qualified to judge people. However, she was very well acquainted with greed, vanity, selfishness, cruelty—and for some bizarre reason she could not decipher, she did not detect any of these traits in Lord Dereham. He had been nothing but kindness to her, an attribute she was not very well acquainted with, especially in a man.

As the silence stretched between them, she

shifted about, noticing that the evening mists were beginning to curl about their feet, lending a surrealistic aura to the small clearing. By his silence, it was obvious he was now expecting something from her. Her heart thumped painfully as she struggled with herself. How much should she give him? Could she give him anything? One part of her cried out for a sympathetic ear, but years of having her hopes dashed out from under her, and always by men, forced her to think twice. Camden's twisted hatred flashed before her panicked mind.

Trust. It was such a little word for such a seemingly impossible endeavor.

She looked over at Sion. His long body was no more than a silhouette in the dusky light. A premonition of just how little she knew him.

As if sensing her hesitation, Sion slowly moved toward her through the rising mist. Her gaze cautiously reached into the dark depths of a fellow tortured soul and suddenly she knew the truth. Dropping her gaze again, she fixated on her fingers, clenched painfully together. After a long moment she offered reluctantly, "My name is Katherine."

After a moment she felt him sit beside her, and glancing sideways at him she saw him staring at her. His face was oddly vulnerable as he met her gaze with a forthrightness that somewhat eased her lingering doubts. "I will do everything in my power to help you."

Katherine smiled. Not being able to help herself, she timidly touched the back of his hand that rested on his knee close to hers. "I believe you."

* * *

As the clock struck the ungodly hour of two, Sion cast a preoccupied glance in its direction. With an audible sigh, he stretched out his long legs and then recrossed them at the ankles. Frowning, his gaze returned to study Katherine, who had remained curled quietly in the opposite wing chair all evening.

Throughout the evening she had spoken little, revealing next to nothing about herself. Despite his baring his soul to her, she continued to deftly parry his questions. Disappointment, laced with a good dose of frustration, kept his large frame restless, his tired visage disgruntled. Had he revealed himself for naught?

Katherine peered over her bent knees and was unfortunate enough to meet Sion's irritated stare. *The man is certainly perverse,* Katherine thought ungraciously. He had hounded her for hours, gnawing and worrying her as though she were some meaty bone—and his last meal to boot.

Flicking her attention to the unfaded square of paneling above the mantel, she finally broke the silence, hoping to distract him. "Whose portrait used to hang there?"

Without taking his eyes from her face, he replied tersely, "My wife's."

Katherine's gaze snapped to his and narrowed. "You should not have done that." She felt anger and disappointment at this man of whom she had begun to think better.

He shifted irritably. "Done what?"

"Removed her portrait, of course."

"It is none of your bloody business!"

She remembered too well another portrait that had once hung in a place of honor. But that had all changed when one day her mother had died before giving Camden his heir. Her mother had not even been cold in her grave when Camden had raged through the hall and stripped her home of all reminders of her beloved mother. Katherine had been thankful that her mother's portrait had been merely relegated to the bowels of the attic, for everything else had been destroyed. And whenever her father had been away from the Abbey, she had hidden herself away in that dusty room and stared at her mother's beautiful face for hours on end. How those quiet times had soothed her. Even now she could recall how speaking to her mother's image had been like sharing all her grief with her personally. Those poignant eyes had gazed down on her with her own sorrow, apologizing for leaving her daughter alone to deal with the nightmare that was her father. If there was anything she missed from her past it was this portrait—the last remembrance of a woman who had dared to betray the earl by cursing him with a hated daughter.

Was this, ultimately, the fate of all wives and daughters who displeased their masters? To be exiled into ancestral obscurity?

Her voice hard, she accused, "I've heard you say how you loved your wife, yet you banish her likeness from the home you shared with her. Hiding her portrait is not going to make your pain go away. If she has earned a place in your heart, then she has earned the right to this place of honor in your home."

It was the look of reproach in her eyes more than her words, that angered Sion. "Look who's talking about banishing people from their lives," he scoffed, leaning forward abruptly.

Katherine's face stiffened, wiping any perceivable expression from her pale features. A blank canvas faced him. "That is different."

"Why?"

Katherine studied the empty space, wondering what the marchioness had looked like. There was no doubt that she had been beautiful. Sion's masculine beauty would demand no less than a mate to equal it. Years ago she had learned her lesson well, a lesson forced upon her by her father's callousness and reinforced by her husband's cruel disinterest: only the beautiful deserved to be loved. If love existed at all, that is.

Her lips remained stubbornly sealed. When his fingers touched her cheek, she flinched, pulling back as far as the chair would allow. In her distress she hadn't even seen him approach her. Now he was too close and she had nowhere to hide from him.

"Why?" his curt voice persisted. She almost flinched when his fingers touched her cheek. "Katherine . . ." His breath stirred the tendrils of hair at her temples as he knelt beside her, allowing her little respite from his body as he again crowded her. However, despite his gentleness there was a determination glimmering in his eyes that could not be mistaken. He was not going to give up until he started to get some answers.

"Some people don't deserve such an honor." Uneasy, she again shifted away from him. She hated it when he got too close. There was something in the heated scent of him surrounding her that unnerved her. It made her feel . . . anxious.

With a frown, Sion caught her chin firmly, compelling her reluctant eyes to meet his. "What the devil does that mean?"

The feel of his fingers on her skin began to

burn, sending tingling waves of awareness surging through her body. Her heart was soon pounding so hard that she was beginning to feel lightheaded. Narrowing her eyes, she glared at him and did the only thing she could think of doing in order to get rid of him—she attacked. "You might as well put her portrait back, for every time you look at that empty space you see her face anyway. Don't you understand what you are doing to yourself? Tell me, what do you see when you think of Tory?"

Sion leaned away from her, his face ashen.

"I'll tell you what you see. You see her body, bloodied and wracked with pain. That is what you remember when you look up there. For your own sanity, put it back. In time her portrait will eradicate that horrible vision."

Sion stared at her as if she was mad before he shot to his feet. For a long moment he looked about him as if lost; then, with a savage oath, he paced away from her toward the liquor cabinet. "What is wrong with you, woman?" he grated out as his hand instinctively reached for the brandy decanter. "It is none of your damn business what I do with my wife's portrait."

After filling the crystal tumbler, he turned toward the fireplace. His angry gaze darted from the bare wall in question down to the glass in his clenched hand. Drops of brandy glistened in the firelight where they had spilled onto his skin. Potent fumes floated up to tease his starved yearnings. His belly twisted painfully, and the little voices within began to howl and taunt him. Sion glanced at Katherine and flinched at the look of pity he saw on her face. With an even viler oath, he flung the tumbler into the fire, pleased at

Katherine's gasp as the sluggish flames exploded briefly.

Her shocked gaze clashed with his. He smiled grimly. "I took her portrait down because every time I looked into her face I felt guilt. Can you understand that emotion, Katherine?" He drilled her with sarcastic intent. "I loved her; she was blessing me with my child and I failed her. I should have been able to save her!"

"You cannot be held responsible for a horrible accident. However, you can be held accountable for what the world thinks of you. You knew what they would say when you ran. What they probably still believe. That, my lord, is your failure. That is why you will not let her rest in peace. Your last memory of her is your penance."

Sion swung away from her, sweat gleaming on his brow. She was so damn, bloody close! Damn her and her needle-sharp mind! "You speak as if she is some specter haunting me." He forced out a derisive laugh.

Katherine sighed sadly. Who wasn't haunted by his own ghosts? She certainly had her share. "If you are so bedeviled by the past, then you must go back. You must settle what has gone before in order to find contentment in what is to come. Go back. Clear your name and find your pride again. Give yourself the right to remember the good that your wife gave you. Maybe then you will even find a little peace." She wondered at her audacity. What gave her the right to fault this man's life and how he chose to live it? What had she ever done that gave her any pride in her existence?

Coming to her feet, she approached the marquis. When she stood before him she forced herself to brave the uneasiness she feared she would always feel in the presence of a man.

Her voice was muted, almost beseeching as she murmured, "I think it is time for a change, my lord. For both of us. We each, in our own way, need to face what life has tossed at us, and I believe we can help each other." She met his gaze and an immediate connection seemed to sizzle between them. Swallowing, she continued, "You need someone to believe in you again. And if I am going to survive in this new world I now find myself in, I know I am going to have to take a leap of faith. We are now both faced with a decision. Do we take a chance on each other? In my mind the giving and receiving of trust is a very fragile thing. It is so hard to build and so easily destroyed. So, where do we go from here? Do we continue as friends, or do we part as strangers?"

Pulling away from the lure of her eyes, Sion was bewildered and wary. The only thing he was sure of was that he wanted her trust with a yearning that was stronger than the lure of the bottle. And that scared the hell out of him. Finally, he shrugged, his lips twisting with wry amusement. "What have I got to lose? You already know everything about me and here you still are. I thank you for your belief in me, Katherine. I know you do not give it lightly. But, if you are seeking my help, I have a price: you have yet to answer any of my questions."

Katherine shook her head, muttering, "Just like a dog with a bone." Then, looking up at him sideways, she gifted him with one of her rare smiles. He felt a bubble of resentment that he should actually feel honored to be the recipient—it was so damn pathetic.

Turning toward the door, she said in a voice of

gentle rebuke, "I did say that I needed to take a leap of faith, and so I shall. However, you have exhausted me and I need a chance to gather my wits about me again."

Behind her back he quirked an amused brow and whispered, "Coward."

Glancing back over her shoulder, she gave him a grin. "You know what they say: 'He who fights and runs away lives to fight another day.' As you can see, I am taking that sage advice and running away."

He had to stifle a laugh. "Unrepentant coward," he teased again and watched as her silhouette melded into the black void beyond the study door.

"Good night, Lord Dereham," her voice floated back to him and soon a tomblike silence pressed in around him.

Lord, already he missed her.

Reluctantly Sion's gaze rested on that empty space where, once upon a happier time, Tory had smiled down at him. Katherine was right. He needed to find the strength to absolve himself of her death. How could Katherine know him such a short amount of time and yet read him so well? Each of her canny words struck him in the heart. She was so right: he needed to face his past and reclaim his pride, his confidence, and most important, his sanity.

And for the first time since crossing the threshold of Dereham Hall all those years ago, he now had the will to battle his inner demons, for he wasn't fighting them alone anymore. He now had someone who believed in him again, even if she was a reluctant ally.

Glancing down at the brandy, his gut clenched in anticipation but with a grim smile, he placed the stopper back onto the decanter and forced

himself to turn his back on the unholy temptation. His body was shuddering and he worried if
it would ever get easier. With resolute steps he
went upstairs to tackle another night of tortured
doubts, knowing that the only thing that made
him survive these dark, endless hours sober was
knowing that in the morning he would be with
Katherine again.

Four

The next morning, Mrs. Turlow threw open the door after peeking in discreetly. "I found it!" she announced, stepping aside to allow a young gardener to stagger in under the weight of a large trunk.

Used to Mrs. Turlow's unceremonious entrances by now, Katherine exclaimed with delight at the sight of her trunk and rose to her feet.

The poor lad looked imploringly from the housekeeper to the young lady, the weight bearing down on his undernourished shoulder. Taking pity on him, Katherine swiftly directed him to put it down where he stood. But even as he began to do so, Mrs. Turlow grabbed his ear and pulled him to the foot of the bed. "Here, laddie, here. 'Tis no good tae put it where the poor lamb will stumble over it."

With a sympathetic smile, Katherine followed the two, picking up a box of bonbons as she went. With a grunt the young man stowed the trunk against the bed and straightened his aching back. He quickly bobbed his head and backed to the door, just wanting to escape the inner sanctum of the beautiful lady he had admired from a distance for the past week. However, before he could duck out the door, he felt something pressed into his hands.

Stunned, he looked up into her sparkling eyes, then studied the treat she had given him. Chocolates! His mouth watered.

"Thank you, Ned." She paused. "It is Ned, isn't it?" Katherine asked hesitantly.

"Aye, m'lady." Shyly he ducked his head. "Thank ye." With the box clasped to his chest, he slipped away.

She turned to see Mrs. Turlow staring at her, hurt radiating from her. "I made those fer ye just last night," she groused.

"And they were delicious," Katherine soothed as she approached the trunk. "And much too tempting. I rather like my new figure, thank you very much. Next time some candied fruit would be splendid when you feel the urge to pamper me." She cast the disgruntled dame a winning smile.

"Ye could do with a wee bit o' meat on them bones."

Katherine felt her mouth purse with irritation. She had to force herself to keep her smile. "Please, Mrs. Turlow. Humor me in this."

The matron's mind flitted to the girl that Katherine had been once upon a time. With a new understanding of the tenacity of the mystery before her, she nodded. "Aye, lass. Candied fruit be a specialty o' me own."

Katherine reached out and squeezed one of the old dame's callused hands folded together at her starched shirtwaist. "Now, let's see what's in here. Was this the only one they found?" she asked as she leaned down to flick open the forced lock. Mrs. Turlow helped as she lifted the heavy lid, waterstained and splintered.

"Weel, 'tis the only one that wasna fully submerged, if I dinna be mistaken."

Katherine stared in dismay at the mildewed mess still folded neatly between tissues now rotted away. "Oh, dear," she sighed, and with a grimace of distaste she lifted the top garment. The stench rising from the ruined mess made her stomach turn over. With a jerk, she straightened and slammed down the lid. Her teeth sank into her bottom lip. She didn't know whether to be happy or sad that this last link with her past was gone.

With gentle insistence, Mrs. Turlow nudged Katherine aside, and falling to stiff knees, she again opened the trunk. "There must be something worth saving," she mumbled, her frugal nature coming to the forefront. As her fingers touched damp cloth, she clicked her tongue in disgust and plunged on. She quickly delved beneath the ruined dresses, coming up with a tarnished silver comb and brush set. With a satisfied nod, she set them aside and again attacked the contents. She routed about for a minute or so when, with an exclamation, she drew forth a large wooden case from the bottom.

Katherine's eyes widened in shock, and with a cry of joy, she grabbed the distorted case from the triumphant housekeeper. "My mother's jewels!" In wonder, she unlatched the lid and pried the top off as the case was warped from the damp.

As the jewels were exposed, the sunlight reflected off the stones, sending colorful prisms across the walls in kaleidoscopic splendor. Miraculously, the settings had escaped the tarnishing effects of the surrounding moisture.

"Blessed saints," Mrs. Turlow breathed in awe at the treasure displayed before her.

"However did you manage this, Jassy?" Katherine

wondered aloud, her stunned eyes taking in the
marvel resting in her hands.

"Now that be a sight, lass."

Katherine smiled into the matron's bemused
eyes. "Aye, that it be."

"Ah, weel, it dinna solve the problem of what yer
tae wear, now does it?"

Katherine almost laughed at the disgruntled statement. Here they were, gazing at a king's ransom in
jewels and Mrs. Turlow was worried about a few pal-
try dresses. As she held back her mirth, a faraway
look stole over the dame's face. "Mrs. Turlow?"

With a grunt, the housekeeper hoisted herself to
her feet, and without another word or look at the
temptation many would sell their souls for, she left
the room with its dancing prisms sprinkling the
walls.

Again Katherine contemplated the case in her
hands. Jassy had once shown her the jewels. These
were the bribes Camden had given to her mother
over the years of their marriage. Camden's way of
insuring himself his heir. No doubt, Camden was
still bitter about the waste of money. Katherine had
heard the story of how Camden had made her
mother suffer for her failures. His methods, even
back then, had been cruelly devious.

What kind of monster would force his dying wife
to listen to how he would make her three-year-old
daughter suffer the punishment that should have
been her own to endure? Had her mother cried as
she bled to death with the miscarriage of a second
daughter, while Camden watched with those pitiless
eyes of his? Or had she spit in his eye? She hoped
so, even though, ultimately, it had been her lot to
pay for her mother's last rebellious act. How her
mother must be smiling now, for the tables were fi-

nally being turned on Camden. Had Jassy always been expecting this chance? Was that why she had stolen the jewels?

She needed to speak with Jassy.

The grave was barren and unkempt, overgrown bracken almost concealing the lonely mound. Deep down, under that mass of dirt, was the only person she had ever loved and who had ever been kind to her.

Katherine smiled as she remembered the scatterbrained affection that the old governess had lavished on a confused and embittered girl. They had been on odd pair: she, sullen and overweight, always hiding her pain behind an impassive face; and Jassy, the complete opposite. Tiny and effervescent, she had always looked on the bright side of life, often with irritating enthusiasm. Nevertheless, each of them had filled a void in the other's life. What accomplishments she had managed in her secluded existence had been due to this indomitable woman. Jassy, knowing her father's animosity, had years ago learned to circumvent his edicts by playing up to this hatred. All the intrepid governess had to do was assure Lord Camden that whatever was planned for her was in the form of punishment for some nonexistent misdeed, and he complied easily enough. Never had he realized how his daughter had benefited from and enjoyed Jassy's "punishments." Not that Lord Camden had been around all that much, thank God. Nevertheless, he had made his rounds once a month, to assure himself that his daughter was suffering enough. And suffer she had. For her mother's failures, for Halsingham's failures, but most of all, for her own failure in not having been born his precious heir.

Katherine knelt down and slowly began to pull weeds from the unmarked grave. As a tear fell onto her hand and mixed with the dirt, leaving a muddy streak, she sat back on her heels. No longer could she hold back the pain constricting her heart, and soon her cheeks were damp and flushed with the first tears she had succumbed to in years.

"Oh, Jassy, how I miss you! I have found some new friends. Mrs. T. is wonderful. I think you would have liked her." She gave a wobbly smile, picturing Jassy and Mrs. Turlow in the same room, neither one allowing a word in edgewise. "And I believe Lord Dereham can be . . ." *Trusted?* ". . . understanding at times. Even so, they aren't you." With a sigh, she scrubbed a dirty hand over her eyes. "Oh, Jassy, what am I going to do?"

Just then a cool wind lifted and scattered the dead leaves about her skirts. As she looked up into the swaying boughs, it was almost as if gentle fingers brushed over her flushed cheeks and wiped away her tears.

Sniffing, Katherine heard Jassy's words whisper with the leaves dancing about her: *You don't need me now, my dear. Katherine Camden-Carey is no more. I have her safe, right here beside me. Don't you see what is before your very eyes, my dear? God has given you this chance, the chance to be whom you have always dreamed of—your own woman. You are finally free, my dear. Be strong and know I will always be watching over you. Just as God is. I love you.*

For endless moments, Katherine stared at the grave. Just as suddenly as it had come to life, the breeze died and the stillness pervading the air was deafening. Katherine leaned over and placed both hands, palms down, over the grave where she imagined Jassy's heart to be. Her fingers flexed, digging into the hard earth. Then she froze. Lifting her hands, she studied them as if seeing them for the first time. *Right before my eyes.* She turned over the slender, elegant hands. *Not Katherine anymore.*

Her heart thudding, she looked down on the grave again. "Jassy?" she whispered.

This time when the breeze kicked up, she closed her eyes and turned her face into the whispering current. She gasped, her hand leaping to her cheek in wonder. A kiss? Had Jassy just kissed her? Her brow furrowed in confusion, for somehow she just knew it had not been Jassy. Looking down on the grave, she felt an easing of the tension she had always carried with her. *Katherine?* Was Katherine bidding her farewell?

Squeezing her eyes shut, she bowed her head under the years and years of living under such a pathetic existence—and it had all been her own fault, a voice hidden deep in the recess of her accused. Long ago Camden had made her realize that freedom was something she could never aspire to; therefore, she had stopped waiting for it. And as she grew older, her youthful longings had withered within her heart, dulling her reason for living, for in truth, there had been more reasons to die. Then, when she had least expected it, her whole world had been tipped upside down. Her weary soul had been given a wonderful respite—sleep. Long, endless, rehabilitating sleep, and while she had dreamed all the forbidden dreams she had fantasized over the years, somehow they had passed from wishful yearning into reality. She had been set free!

She was now shocked to realize just how much she had resented the person she had been. Had resented her meek acceptance of what Camden had done to her, her cowardice not to stand up for herself, her inability to look him in the face and tell him to go to Hades and simply walk away. Camden had not killed her aspirations; Katherine had. She had let him intimidate her and then destroy any lingering pride or individuality that she still possessed. Now she did not know whether to feel sadness or relief that Katherine was no more than a bad dream that was gone with the morning.

She did not know how much time had passed when she lifted her head again. Her head felt fuzzy and pounded painfully behind her swollen eyes. She felt feverish, but she also felt purged of all her anger and frustration. Katherine had been a lost soul. Maybe now she would find peace.

Poor Katherine. Poor unwanted girl. *Forgive me.*

Standing, she stood by the grave and bowed her head in prayer. When she looked up again, she stared long into the beautiful blue sky.

"I love you, Jassy." Then she added slowly, "And you, Katherine. Thank you, and God keep you both. Please don't forget me."

Her steps were hesitant as she headed back to the Hall. Looking around her, she noticed that everything appeared sharper, more distinctive. Then she thought of all the possibilities that lay before her like a banquet of delectable choices. She was a creation of infinite hopes and desires. She could go anywhere and do anything. Her life now had no boundaries; no walls to hem her in, no scathing hatred to beat her down.

Her steps became lighter and more carefree the farther she distanced herself from the grave. Soon she was running toward her future. Before she reached the manor she knew who she was; what she wanted out of this new life she had been given. Bursting with hope of what lay ahead for her, she went in search of Sion.

If anyone could, Sion would understand her need for freedom from the demons of her past. It was as if she had been given into his care for this very reason. Two tortured souls in desperate need of each other, one helping the other.

Never would she forget this day. She laughed when she thought that she was probably the only person who could ever honestly say that she remembered the day she was born.

This day of September 30, 1882—the first day of the rest of her life.

"You want *what?*" Dumbfounded, Sion took in the bedraggled appearance of the woman who had walked in unannounced. As she repeated herself, he paid much closer attention.

"I would like a headstone carved with the inscription 'Katherine Beatrice Camden-Carey, Viscountess Halsingham, 1860–1882'."

Sion stared at her impassive face as his mind flashed briefly on the name Camden. "Why would you put your headstone on Jassy's grave?" he inquired gently.

Her startled eyes leaped to his. He was certainly going to get his answers now.

"I did not quite know what I wanted to do until about an hour ago." As she spoke, she slipped into the chair before his desk. "Actually, Jassy told me what I must do." With apparent nonchalance, she pleated the folds of the over-abundant material at her waist.

Sion leaned back in his chair. "Jassy?"

With a polite smile, she nodded. Her gaze darted to his, then dropped back to her busy fingers.

"Care to elaborate on that?"

Her fingers paused for a second. "Must I?"

"Oh, definitely, you must," he assured her dryly.

With a sigh, she leaned forward. "Do you remember what Katherine looked like when you first brought her here?"

Sion thought for a moment, his brow frowning in concentration; then, shrugging, he admitted ruefully, "Not really; I'm sorry, but I wasn't in a state to remember much of anything, if you will recall Mrs. Turlow's account of the situation."

"Come now, stop being diplomatic."

His lips twitched. *So much for chivalrous evasion.* "Very well. I don't recollect much other than the fact that you were . . ." He fished about for the least offensive word.

"Fat," she supplied brutally.

His eyes narrowed. "I don't appreciate words being put into my mouth. But if you insist."

Acknowledging his rebuttal with a nod, she spread her hands, "Who do you see before you now?"

Arms propped on the armrests, he steepled his fingers, and hiding smiling lips, he answered slowly, "I see a very beautiful if somewhat bedraggled woman speaking a bit of gibberish."

The girl sniffed impatiently. "I'm not angling for compliments, my lord. Nor insults. What I'm trying to point out is that the woman you rescued all those months ago is no more."

Sion continued to stare at her. "Forgive me; I must be extremely slow-witted today, but here I sit and, unless I'm mistaken, so do you."

Warming to her topic, she scooted her slim posterior to the edge of the seat. "Would you recognize me for that woman?"

"No, but I didn't know you then."

"Trust me when I say you would have paid Katherine no notice; therefore, you would have had no concept of what she looked like."

Finally comprehending her train of thought, he answered thoughtfully, "No, but anyone close to you would probably have no problem."

"I beg to differ with you. Every time I look in the mirror I see no resemblance to Katherine whatsoever."

"You won't get away with it," he warned her softly.

She paused, wary. "Get away with what?" *Yes, I will. It had all been arranged long before I knew anything about it.*

He jerked upright in his chair. "You know what. Stop treating me like some sotted fool. There has to be someone in your life close enough to call your bluff."

No, at Camden Abbey Katherine had been a nonentity. After all, who remembered what a whipping post looked liked? For the first time in her life, she was thankful for that very obscurity, for it would now be her ticket to freedom.

With a sense of pity, she answered slowly, "Believe me, no one would be able to recognize Katherine Camden-Carey in the woman you see before you now."

"Why all this deception?"

A small smile curled her normally somber lips. "Freedom, Lord Dereham."

He pounced on this. "You are married?"

She admitted, with a nod, "Katherine was married three years."

Sion frowned. He suddenly realized she was responding to him as if she were speaking of another person. "And you are saying your own husband would not recognize you?"

"Absolutely."

"Amazing." Confused, as if he had just walked into the middle of this conversation, Sion studied her more closely. Her expression was quite calm, and for the first time she seemed to exude a sense of confidence he had found lacking before. He shook his head in bewilderment. "I find this hard to believe, to say the least."

Her face was impassive again as she assured him, "Trust me."

After a tense moment, he asked, "What of your parents?"

"Katherine's mother died when she was a child of three. And as far as her father is concerned, she was dead to him on the day of her birth."

"Names, please," he persisted.

With an inward sigh, she steeled herself. *Trust him,* her heart urged. However, years of past experience made her balk. Her heart speeded up to an alarming rate as she finally supplied him with the means to betray her. "The Earl of Camden, Arthur Phillip Marlowe. Her husband is the Viscount Halsingham, Reidlen Carey."

"Camden," he murmured, his thoughts turning inward, spinning back to years before. So this was the daughter of "Crazy" Camden, a neighboring peer whom his family had always avoided. "And it is your intent to . . ." he paused, wanting to be sure he understood her thoughts completely.

"To inform them of Katherine's demise," she finished in a voice so low he had to lean forward to catch her words.

He frowned, then leaned back again. "Aha." *Does*

this tendency toward madness run in the family? he wondered cryptically? "And who sits before me now, pray tell?"

Rising, she dipped into a graceful curtsy. When she rose, a delicious smile played havoc on his already dazed senses. "Danae Suriano, *la Contessa di Sala.*" The heavy Italian accent she inflected into her words and voice was impeccable.

He blinked. He could not decide if she was mad or merely delusional. "Aha. Danae is an unusual name." He didn't know what else to say.

That infernal cool mask she was always hiding behind was once again intact as she resumed her seat. Disappointed to see the mischievous sparkle quenched, he realized he had just been given a rare glimpse of such frivolity. He found himself wanting more. One thing he remembered about Camden was his utter lack of humor. How dismal it must have been, growing up under the earl's harsh regard all these years.

"Danae is a heroine of Greek mythology. Her father, in a fit of rage, locked her in a coffin and cast her to sea. To die." Somber, she returned his intent scrutiny.

"And did she?" he inquired gently.

She shook her head, not breaking eye contact with him. "No. She drifted for days until she finally washed up onto a distant shore where a king rescued her."

The ensuing silence crackled with a strained undercurrent as they continued to study each other. Finally, clearing his throat, he looked away. Those cat eyes of hers were all too compelling. "And so who is this Danae Suriano to be?"

She noticed his sudden preoccupation with a

paper on his desk before she answered tentatively, "Your lover."

He bolted upright. "I beg your pardon?"

"Or mistress, or whatever the title." She shrugged, striving for a nonchalance that was rapidly fading under his shocked gaze. She added quickly, "Not in reality, of course. It would just be a charade, you understand. You could establish my identity as the widow of an Italian nobleman, whom you have taken as your lover. Who would know you were not in Italy? You have secluded yourself out here for years, and what better way to prove my identity. Who would doubt such a brazen relationship—or the woman embroiled in it?" she ended lamely, now embarrassed at her forwardness.

He again scrutinized her, this time in much the same way one would inspect some unknown species of insect under a magnifying lens. Finally, he asked, still perplexed, "Why?" When her eyes questioned him, he reiterated, "Why this elaborate scheme?"

"I have the chance for the first time in my life to experience life, to meet people, to find something to make me laugh." She paused in stunned surprise, her brow furrowed in deep thought. She did not realize she spoke aloud when she admitted in amazement, "I don't think I know how to laugh. Isn't that funny?"

Sion felt himself tense as he watched her confusion, then her struggle to hold back the tears that trembled on her lowered lashes. When she finally raised her gaze, he was shocked at the austerity lurking in the amber depths. It was true that he had never heard her laugh, but not know how to laugh? *How bloody sad.* Within the next second he made his decision. And his reason was too simplistic. He wanted to hear her laugh. Just for him.

Sitting forward, his voice was stern as he told her, "If you go forward with this foolhardy plan, *Katherine*"—he emphasized the name—"you will be in violation of every parliamentary and canon law that is written. If you are found out, the life you are deriding so blithely will be stripped from you so fast you will be praying for what you are now tossing aside. Even Camden would be preferable to the inside of a prison."

Danae's head jerked up, her eyes flashing. "Never! You hear me? Never! *Anything* would be preferable to that hell!" Swallowing her panic, she wondered if she had been so very wrong about this man. Bravely she faced him, trying one more time to make him understand. "I am twenty-two years old. Until the day of my marriage I had not seen the outside of the Abbey. Literally. On the day of my marriage to a man I had never even heard of, I was told, in the privacy of the bridal chamber, that he couldn't stand the sight of me. He slept on the floor that night, and in the morning he was gone, much to Camden's displeasure. The reluctant groom had been ordered back. Again he slept on the floor, but this time in my dressing chamber for he could not stomach even being in the same room with me.

"As we each had our self-interests to serve, we came to an understanding: he would leave me untouched and I would not tell Camden that his precious stud was unable to perform the one thing that he was purchased for. In fact, I rather liked the idea of spoiling Camden's obsessive plans. However, the next month, when I began my mon . . ." She stumbled to a halt, her face burning with embarrassment at what she had almost said. "Well, when Camden found out that I could not be carrying his grandson, he beat me for my failure, then sent for Halsingham. Every month I did not conceive, I was beaten. But it was worth it," she cried out with rebellious anger. "Can you imagine what the fate of my son or daughter, God help her, would have been had I been unfortunate enough to give that man another child to dominate? I swore I would die first."

Shocked at how she had just lost control of her emotions, Katherine's age-old habit of retreating within herself surfaced in Danae. She hated feeling the same instinctive need to escape. Breathing deeply, she fought for control. She was *not* that unfortunate girl.

After a few moments, she continued, pleased at how collected she sounded. "The humiliation Katherine suffered at being abandoned by a man paid to marry her was nothing compared to the fear she lived with every day of her life, wondering when Camden would become wise to the fact that she was still a virgin." Refusing to be embarrassed, she forced herself to return his piercing scrutiny. Her hands shook, hidden away in the folds of her skirt. When she held his gaze without backing down, she felt a shiver of satisfaction. Katherine would never have stared someone down.

"Well?" she prompted, her voice deliberately loud.

What choice did he have? He felt a jolt about his heart. *No choice in hell.* "I will help you in any way I can . . . Danae." He tried to inject a light note into the somber conversation but failed miserably. He was too damn angry. He had always guessed that Camden was a bastard, but . . .

And this Halsingham . . . He felt a muscle spasm in his cheek as he unclenched his jaw. Unfortunately, there was nothing he could do about them—yet. Not wanting to frighten her, Sion tried to mask his anger and murmured, "Well, why not? It has possibilities."

Danae studied the angry man sitting across from her. He suddenly seemed so overpowering, so . . . dominating. With a frisson of fear, she had a moment of doubt, worrying that maybe this wasn't such a good idea. What did she really know about him except that he was a drunkard and had been tried for murdering his wife? Hardly a good recommendation. With haste, she explained again, "It would just be a charade, you understand, till I'm established."

A mocking smile stretched his tensed lips. "I regret to inform you that I'm abominable at charades. I will certainly need to get to know you better if I'm going to be convincing as your . . . lover." He still sounded so angry. Was he angry with her for daring to embroil him in a scheme he obviously had no faith in?

Danae simply stared back at him, biting her lip.

Clasping his hands atop the desk, Sion leaned forward, and Danae breathed a sigh of relief when she notice the sparkle of humor back in his black eyes. "Now you are teasing me," she smiled. Then her eyes narrowed as she watched Sion settle back in his chair, propping newly shined boots atop his desk.

"Not a bit of it. I assure you, you will need as much practice as I can give you. I am well known for my discerning taste in lovers. I realize you have no experience in this sort of thing, and I promise you I shall be the soul of patience. We will practice for as long as it takes you to feel comfortable in your role." He cocked a menacing brow at her. "The role you choose for yourself, let us not forget. Merely consider me your humble tutor."

Danae's mouth dropped open at the cheek of the man. Then, before she even had a second thought, she bolted out of her chair and was gone. She was further mortified when she heard his chuckle as she fled to the sanctuary of her room.

Sion's feet fell to the floor with a thud, all humor wiped from his face. Damn and bloody hell! This was all he needed. Why on earth was he taunting her like this, almost daring her to run? Yet how could he possibly survive this foolish charade? He knew that the moment he held her in his arms, he would have a bloody hard time letting her go again. Then what was he going to do? If he wasn't damn careful, she could bolt on him. She was such an innocent.

At that moment, he selfishly wished she *were* the bold and worldly *Contessa di* Sala.

Swiveling his chair around, he looked sullenly out the window, thinking how much easier life had been when he had been drunk.

Five

Camden Abbey
December 1882

After taking a sip of his brandy, Camden again read the neatly scripted letter, this time more slowly. A log in the fire popped, then fell into glowing red embers, drawing his attention. It was a good thing that the pain had been unbearable this morning, for the only thing keeping him sane at this moment was the opium haze that still held him. The letter dangled from his relaxed fingers with a negligence the complete opposite of the fury that the narcotic held at bay. His eyes narrowed as he watched the mesmerizing flames writhe and flicker, just as his gut was twisting and burning. Slowly he lifted the glass to his lips and swallowed back the last bit, reveling in the streak of fire shooting down his throat.

So Katherine was dead. And with her the continuation of his line.

Flicking the page up again, Camden's eyes searched for the signature and seal. It had been years since he had even heard the name mentioned. Sion Sinclair. This time he let the missive slip from his nerveless fingers onto the plush Aubusson.

Damn her! Since the moment of her birth, she had been a thorn in his side, a constant reminder of his failure to the earldom. Now this final defiance of hers—and with Dereham, no less! He could almost believe that she had planned this, her death, just to spite him. Now what was he to do? He didn't even have the good fortune of claiming a bastard son to fulfill his dream. Always he had been careful not to waste his precious seed, saving it for the legitimacy of marriage. He had always feared that one day a bastard might step forward to cause his legal heir problems. And for his judiciousness, what does fate dole out to him? One wife dead at the birth of a bloody girl, and the second wife cursing him with the greatest evil of all. Now there was no possible chance of ever siring a healthy heir. To hell with that! There was no chance of any heir anymore, healthy or otherwise.

And Katherine, his last hope, had to go and get herself killed. It was just like the ungrateful bitch. He should have drowned her at birth, as he had wanted to.

His lips twisted, thoughts turning beyond bitter to ugly as he continued to watch the dying embers.

Well, just to be sure, he would go and find out for himself. He had to find out what part Dereham had played in this debacle. What did he know? Camden frowned as he felt a quiver of apprehension. Absently he rubbed his arm as the shivers of pain became harder to ignore. Then, with deliberate care he turned his thoughts to the sour contemplation of Halsingham. Doubtless, that scum would soon be wallowing in his good fortune. The dashing, rich widower, sod him.

But, you will pay, the earl assured the unsuspecting viscount brutally. *Oh, yes, you worthless prick! Before I'm through with you, you will be on your knees, groveling for my forgiveness.*

Damn, but it made him want to howl with rage when he thought of the bloody fortune he had paid for Halsingham's seed. And what had it gotten him but to look like a frigging fool!

At that moment he wanted nothing more than to castrate the bastard.

Camden smiled coldly as he poured himself another brandy. That was not such a bad idea, considering he owned the cock. His restless gaze shifted to the animal heads mounted on the walls of the library. Mayhap he would even have the useless thing mounted in a place of honor.

Camden's eyes glinted with a feral intensity when, instead of drinking the brandy, he hurled the glass into the dying embers. The embers exploded outward in a flash of flames, sealing his pledge in fire.

"Your father will be here at the end of the week. With your husband, I might add," Sion announced as he strode into the dining room.

Already seated and nibbling on a breakfast of assorted fruits, Danae glanced up, her expressionless eyes finding the correspondence he held out to her. After she had dabbed her lips, she accepted the extended letter with an air of distaste. She didn't even give it a glance as she set it aside. "He is not my husband, remember?" She took a sip of tea. "Nor do I have a father."

Sion's attention was riveted on her as he seated himself. Silence extended between them while the

newly acquired footman poured his coffee and set
a steaming plate of sirloin before him. With a slight
smile, Danae glanced at the generous portion and
wondered with envy how he stayed so fit. With an
inward sigh, she turned back to her own sparse
repast.

"Are you not the least bit curious?" Sion finally
asked after the door had closed behind the footman. When Danae glanced at him, he nodded
toward the missive.

No, she wasn't the least bit interested in what
Camden had to say. Instead, she watched as he sys-
tematically cut and devoured his plentiful
breakfast. Her nose twitched, and she had to bite
her tongue to hold back a plea to have a taste of the
juicy meat. Instead, she looked down at her plate.
The slices of peaches and pears arranged artfully
on her plate were already turning brown and
looked as unappetizing as they tasted. They weren't
even fresh. She hated canned fruit. The pomegranate was fresh though, right from the scrawny
tree that was Mrs. T.'s pride and joy.

With a sigh, she picked up her fork again.

"Danae?" Sion's voice jerked her back.

"No," she finally acknowledged, her voice slightly
curt. "I don't care what he has to say." Her stomach
grumbled.

"I still say you won't get away with it." Leaning
over, he helped himself to an indecent amount of
potatoes and kippers.

Her lips thinned as she studied the mounded
plate. Tamping down her resentment, she retorted,
"That is not what you said last week." Her fork was
poised over the slice of pomegranate. She blinked
down at all the little, bloodshot eyes staring up at
her. With relish she began to poke each one out.

The smell of the onion and potatoes was making her more and more ravenous with each breath she drew. Her gaze snapped up to follow Sion's hand as he reached out for a pastry. Closing her eyes didn't help, for she could hear the flaky crescent crumble in his hands as he tore it apart. Her brow felt cool with perspiration, and valiantly she fought the terrible compulsion to snatch it out of his hand and stuff it into her mouth.

"Would you please pass the jam?" Sion asked politely.

Her eyes snapped open and she glared at him angrily. She was so tempted to smash her tasteless peach into his busy mouth. Didn't he know what he was doing to her? Tilting her head she contemplated the silver dish set much too close to her.

I can do this, she assured herself. She was relieved to see that her hand was steady as she reached out and clenched her fingers about the cool metal. With unconscious deliberation, she brought the dish close to her nose and breathed deeply of the sweet aroma before passing it on to Sion. It *would* have to be gooseberry, her absolute favorite. Danae's mouth watered as she remembered how the tart-sweet flavor wrapped around her tongue. She shivered in ecstasy, her tastebuds tingling, so real did the image feel. Memories could be a deuced nuisance, she was beginning to realize.

With a smile Sion thanked her, then cast her a quizzical look when she didn't let go of the jam, her hold unbreakable. Confused, he pulled his hand back, then almost dropped the bowl when she suddenly thrust it at him.

Danae found it impossible to ignore him as he dipped a spoon into the server and withdrew the luscious jam. Hypnotized, she watched the way he lavishly spread it over the flaky roll. Her gaze became fixated on a gelatinous glob as it quivered on the edge of the pastry, teasing her. As it slipped over the edge and began to fall, she held her breath and watched as it fell . . . and fell, as if in slow motion, before it landed with a plop on the pristine table linen. To her over-sensitized nerves, it landed with the force of a cannonball. She almost groaned as the little drop of berry sweetness shimmered in the morning sunlight that streamed in through the windows behind her.

Sion paused when he noticed Danae's preoccupation with the glaring evidence of his clumsiness. Was she appalled at his table manners? he mused with a smile. Then his smile died when the sun's rays shot a brutal light onto her strained profile. He suddenly couldn't remember the last time he saw a morsel of food pass her lips. "You're not hungry, my dear?" he quizzed her gently while he critically examined her neck and shoulders.

Danae's gaze snapped up, and she glared across the table at him. She tensed when she saw that Sion's narrowed eyes were far too perceptive . . . and far too pitying. Shoving back her chair, Danae rose to her feet and tossed her napkin down. Then, without a word of excuse, she marched from the room. It took all her concentration not to lift her skirts and bolt from the lingering aromas tormenting her—and from Sion's too perceptive regard.

Worried, Sion watched her abrupt departure, then looked around him as if something in the room would help him understand what was bedeviling Danae. She was becoming increasingly moody and short-tempered by the day. It was possible that she was much more intimidated by the thought of facing Camden and Halsingham than she was willing to admit. She could be so proud, hoarding her feelings close. Sadly, he wondered if she would ever truly trust him.

As he turned back to his now-cold breakfast, Sion again wondered about this sudden aversion to food that Danae had acquired. Was it from an unconscious sense of determination to see that Katherine remained dead and buried? It was steadily becoming an obsession, and he knew the horror of an obsession feeding off one's insecurities. Moreover, he was getting damned tired of feeling guilty every time he sat down to a meal with her. He compared their two plates, measuring his own liberal serving against the monastic austerity of hers. The luscious curves that she had acquired in the weeks after rising from her bed were slowly melting away again, and even then she hadn't had any weight to spare. In his estimation, she needed a good stone or more on her small frame.

If he didn't stop this foolishness now, she would soon be right back where they started when she had awakened from her deep sleep: pale, gaunt, and weak as a baby, with her grand plans naught but tattered dreams stuffing the mattress beneath her. Somehow he was going to have to get her to eat more, even if he had to tie her down in order to accomplish it. Now that brought some interesting possibilities to mind.

Shaking his head clear, he called for fresh servings from the kitchen. He wasn't about to let her insecurities ruin his appetite, by God! Now that he was sober, his appetite had grown prodigiously— and he was damn proud of it!

Out in the hall, Danae was brought up short by Mrs. Turlow's strident voice calling out, "Katherine!"

With an almost painful hunger twisting her in-

sides, Danae swung about and let all her frustrations boil over onto the hapless housekeeper. "Mrs.
Turlow, how many times do we have to go over this?
My name is now Danae. A slip of the tongue such as
this could ruin everything for me." Realizing that
she was almost shouting, Danae snapped her
mouth shut. She winced with self-reproach when
she saw the stricken look on Mrs. T.'s face. Closing
her eyes, she shook her head, "I am so sorry, Mrs.
T." Her stomach growled its agreement.

The housekeeper frowned at her, noticing the
girl's paleness.

"It's not your fault I'm so irritable. It's Sion! He
can be so . . . irritating at times." Then she added reluctantly, "Not that he really did anything to deserve
it, but . . . oh, drat! I vow, he can goad me without
even trying. Why is that? When I set out to provoke
him, he simply gives me that patronizing"—*beautiful,
enticing*—"smile of his as if I was some wayward puppy
who had just mangled an old pair of slippers he was
getting ready to throw out anyway. Has he always
been so pompous?" *Does he always eat so much?* That
could certainly make living in the same residence
with him hazardous to her new life.

When the muted rumble of Danae's stomach further spoke of her stubborn self-deprivation, Mrs.
Turlow bent a stern eye on her. "Aye, pompous, but
I canna say he was ever as mulish as ye." The honest old dame winced at that outright lie and
mentally crossed herself.

Knowing where this was going, Danae turned
away and stared with longing at the closed dining
room door, where his lordship was, no doubt, still
satisfying his gluttonous nature. *It just isn't fair!*
Danae lamented. *I starve myself, and I can still feel the
weight of every meager morsel of food I put into my mouth*

sticking to my body. And there sits that dratted man, stuffing himself till he is cross-eyed, and he remains gorgeous! It's just not fair!

When she heard the muted scraping of silverware from beyond the closed panel, she was close to pulling her hair out by the roots. Crispy, tender potatoes with sautéed onions; tender, juicy, thick slices of beefsteak; and kippers, salty and . . . Forget the kippers; she never liked them anyway. But oh, the hot, flaky pastries as light as air and last, but best, gooseberry jam—and that was only breakfast! She was tempted to set fire to the kitchen before Mrs. Turlow could start on the dinner meal.

Her nerves stretched to the point of pain, Danae turned back to Mrs. Turlow. Heavens, how her stomach hurt! For a bewildered minute, she blinked at Mrs. Turlow, forgetting what she was about to say. It was then that her restless gaze alighted on the crumbs on the housekeeper's apron. She could feel her blood heat feverishly. Sniffing, she could smell freshly baked buns. Closing her eyes, she inhaled again, deeper. *Hot sticky buns!*

Mrs. Turlow's hand shot out to steady Danae as she began to sway weakly.

"Do you smell sticky buns?" Danae asked faintly, hoping she was hallucinating.

"Aye," the housekeeper nodded, then glanced slyly at the wistful look on Danae's face. Soon the heavenly aroma filled the hall. Lowering her gruff voice to a comforting, hypnotic lull, Mrs. Turlow deviously taunted the weakening girl. "Come with me, hinny, and help me take the bunnies out o' the oven. Din ye smell 'em? The wonderful steam arisin', jus' begging tae be lathered with butter. Hot n' moist, they be. The butter be fresh n' sweet. They be awaiting ye, lassie."

The soothing hum called to her. The aroma compelled her. *Hot buns and sweet butter.* Danae closed her eyes and stepped forward. "And gooseberry jam?" Her plea whispered about her. Then she heard Katherine whisper in her ear and her eyes blinked open.

A single tear slipped down Danae's pale cheek as she stared reproachfully at her well-meaning friend. "Oh, Mrs. T., how could you?"

Mrs. Turlow assumed a meek, guilt-ridden attitude as she looked down at her sturdy shoes, when what she actually felt was the need to grab the wee witling by the ear, drag her into the kitchen and set her bum down at the table.

Lord, what was happening to her? Danae wondered in despair. She was becoming as unbalanced as Camden. She froze, panic choking her. *Where in the world did that thought come from?* Most likely from hell.

At that unfortunate moment, Sion threw wide the doors and stepped into the hall, smelling like the decadent breakfast he had just consumed. With a replete smile, he patted his lean stomach as he glanced at both women with a feeling of goodwill. "So, what goes on?"

He instinctively ducked as a missile flew past his face. Shocked, he whipped around to see Danae's slipper at the base of the wall behind him, and now a black streak of boot-lacquer smudged the freshly stained paneling at a height with his head. Hearing a rapid, uneven tread, he turned again and watched as Danae limped up the stairs.

Thoroughly confused, he sought out Mrs. T. "What is wrong with her?"

With a sniff, the housekeeper spun about on her heel and stomped off, muttering to herself.

In the distance, the slamming of two doors echoed out to him.

Retracing the past few minutes in his mind, Sion frowned as he contemplated the stairs. Just a few weeks ago Danae had gazed at him as if he was her knight in shining armor. Now, she was treating him like the village idiot who had stood out in the rain till he was a rusted pile of scrap metal.

If it was the last thing he did he was going to get food down that stubborn throat. He didn't know how much more of this he could take.

He could almost hear his knees squeak as he strode toward his study. Even though he was tempted, he decided that he would not go up and coddle Danae. This had to be another of her hair-brained schemes: starving herself to prove something to herself. If that wasn't just like a female, fighting common sense with no sense at all. He slammed the study door behind him with just as much force as the ladies had.

It didn't help.

Immediately, Sion yanked open the door again, and muttering to himself, he stalked back into the hall and over to the foot of the stairs. There he stood, glaring up the curving length stretched out before him. He just knew she was daring him to come up and confront her. That was rich! What did she expect? For him to go up there and stand at attention while she threw her other slipper at his head?

Frustrated with indecision, he dragged his fingers through hair already too disheveled for so early in the day. Hell and damnation, she had to be starving by now! Rubbing his eyes, he again tried to remember when he had last seen her eat.

"Bloody hell," he cursed low. Damn, how could

the chit vex him so easily? Why should he care? Forcing himself to turn away, he strode back into the study, shoving the door behind him. But his hand darted out just in time to catch it in midswing. Gingerly he eased it shut, pleased that the latching was soundless. He could just picture Danae with her ear to her door, listening for what he would do next. Well, he refused to play along with her puerile games today. Let her suffer one more day with an empty belly cramping on her; let her get a little weaker and faint—hopefully it would scare some sense into her.

On that thought came a flash of ingenuity. Sion snapped his fingers, grinning as he thought of the slipper still in the hall. He would make her come to him. If she wanted it back, that was—and she would. It was the only pair that they could find to fit her until he had some made for her.

Cracking the door open, he peered out. Good, the hall was still empty. Holding his breath, he practically tiptoed across the hall to where she had pitched the damn thing at him.

His grin died.

The slipper was gone, with only the glaring smudge on his wall as testament to the incident.

Eyes narrowed, ears alert, he listened to the hollow silence around him. Then he heard it—a faint scraping sound. He smiled as he tipped his head back and stared up at the second-floor landing. It was just his luck that the grating hinges on her door hadn't been oiled yet, otherwise he wouldn't have heard her sneaking back into her room.

Sion shook his head with amused indulgence as he headed for the last time to his study. For such a self-possessed woman she could be so childish at times. Sion was fast realizing that the last thing

Danae needed from him was pity or condescension. What she really needed was to be upended over his knee. And she also needed a few rules explained to her—for instance, that his head was not a target for her tantrums. God knew what she would lob at him next. The possibilities made him blanch.

She may not have much sense, but she abounded in creativity.

Sion stood beside the elegantly set table, again checking to see that all he had ordered had been seen to. The morning sun shone with a muted iridescence over the fine china, and a lovely breeze fluttered the lace table cover. Impatiently he glanced toward the French doors that opened out onto the main terrace. He shouldn't be surprised she was late. Giving an irritated sigh, he leaned over and fingered a silver fork. A rustling sound brought him around again, and a welcoming smile curved his lips.

Danae was standing in the archway of the doors, looking distinctly unhappy about being here. Sion sauntered over to her, and taking hold of her hand, he brought it to his lips. Just as he expected, it was ice-cold. "Good morning, my dear. I missed you at dinner last night."

He almost laughed aloud at the disgruntled glare she turned on him. "Why was I ordered down here? I'm not feeling too well and would rather have stayed abed." She looked past him to the gleaming table. She was surprised to see a bouquet of hot-house flowers gracing the center and she felt a sense of gratitude at his thoughtfulness. However, she had no intention of giving in to him.

Pulling her hand with a firm insistence about his

arm, Sion literally pulled her forward. "Not pulling that old line on me again, Danae, are you? I had thought we had long ago agreed to forget that prevarication. Besides, I know very well that you are not feeling well. That is why I *requested*"—he slanted a look of gentle rebuke down on her—"that you honor me with your company this morning." They stopped beside the table.

Danae was staring off into the distance, her nose struck in the air.

"It won't work, my dear. Not this time." He pulled out her chair.

"What won't work?"

"Ignoring me. I'm in the best of moods today and I shall not let you provoke me. Look around you, Danae. The sky is unusually brilliant, no heavy mist to dampen our spirits. The air is humming with the sounds of birds and bees. You have my charming company, and the food is still warm." He leaned over and plucked out a delicate rosebud from the arrangement. Moving to stand behind her, he gently brushed the velvet petals against her cheek. "What more could you possibly ask for?"

Danae slowly reached up and took the blush-pink bud. Raising it to her nose, she sniffed the sweet scent, then peeked over her shoulder and gave Sion a curious glance. "Do I truly provoke you?"

He blinked at her. For a moment he was confused about what she was asking. She sounded so hopeful, her whiskey-brown eyes gazing up at him. What was she asking? If she had the power to torment him? *God, yes!* Did she deserve to know how she could turn him inside out?

Sion turned away from her anxious scrutiny, an ironic smile twisting his lips. This morning as he had dressed he had vowed to himself that he would not let her goad him into one of their typical squabbles that day. He had had every intention of being the soul of tolerance. However, it appeared that that was not what she wanted at all. Needing to know exactly what she was alluding to with this perplexing turn, he asked slowly, "And if I said yes, would that please you?"

Throwing him a hesitant peek, she gave a little shrug.

Well, I'll be damned, he mused, truly understanding her for the first time. All the uncharacteristic remarks and tantrums all made sense now. "Would it please you if I told you I found gray hairs this morning? You are making me old before my time, Danae. My teeth are wearing down to nubs. I apparently grind them in my sleep, you confound me so much." He watched her closely.

She gave him a shy, tentative smile.

Sighing, he stepped to her side and again raised her hand to his lips. This time he allowed his kiss to linger. Looking deep into her eyes, he smiled ruefully. "Yes, my dear, you provoke me endlessly. You give me no respect, but I find I can't just chuck you out the door. I am afraid to say it, but I believe we are stuck with each other. For better or worse."

Danae's smile then turned brilliant. As she moved past him she gave him a pat on the cheek with her rose before she slipped into her chair.

Stunned, Sion just stood behind her, staring down at the cascade of dark tresses. Was that what all this has been about? He took his chair across from her as he puzzled over this peculiar lady. Snapping his napkin open, he asked in a nonchalant drawl, "I take it you like contention in your life?"

Danae was studying the repast set before them. "I don't believe anyone would want contention in their life. However, I do find it stimulating at times. I'm not used to being able to express myself when I am angered. It's rather . . ." She cocked her head to the side, searching for the right word.

"Liberating," he supplied gently. "A feeling that your opinions matter?"

She turned glowing eyes on him. "Exactly so! I have always had to hold my feelings so close that now when I let them loose it is like . . ." Her voice trailed off as a soaring jay caught her eye. A secretive little smile tugged at her lips. "It is like flying," she whispered, her gaze still following the jay. Snapping out of her trance, she again dazzled him with her smile.

Suddenly, the light reflecting off his shining armor blinded him. His knighthood had been restored to him. Day by day, he was chipping away at her shell, amazed at all the facets he was exposing. He wondered if he would ever learn them all. "Well, then, feel free to express yourself at any time. Though," he turned a stern eye upon her, "my person is inviolate. You shall not punch it, kick it, nor loft things at it. In return, you may verbally abuse me without mercy. Pact?" He held out his hand.

She paused, again looking down at the table. "I have no problem with those conditions; after all, my aim has never been a threat to you, but . . ." She paused and then finished hurriedly, "I will not be dictated to." Lifting her chin to a belligerent angle, she stared him down. "For example, I will not be bullied into eating if I am not hungry."

Sion withdrew his hand, his face hardening. "I'm sorry, Danae, but I cannot just sit back and watch while you slowly kill yourself."

She jerked back in shock. "I have no intention of killing myself!"

Leaning back in his chair, Sion crossed his arms

over his chest and studied her for a long moment. How was he to be diplomatic while trying to make her understand the brutal facts? He decided to skip the diplomacy. "There were weeks during your recovery that I thought you the most beautiful woman I had ever seen." He saw Danae's face blush an unbecoming shade against her sallow skin. "However, I'm truly sorry that I can't say the same anymore."

A charged silence fell over the table. The expression in her eyes was stark as she returned his steady stare. Licking her lips, she shrugged. "But at least I'm not—"

"Fat?" He cut her off brutally, his brows rising in derision.

Danae dropped her gaze, her face paling. Her voice was thin as she grated out, "God, you can be cruel!"

If anything Sion's manner became more brittle. "I am not being cruel. I'm being honest. Going from one extreme to the other is no answer to your problems. In the end, all you will accomplish is to ruin your health. You've already destroyed your beauty—the same beauty, I doubt not, that you have dreamed all your life of having. My God, woman, look at yourself! You look pathetic. You are horribly pallid; your bones are stark against skin that looks much too fragile. Good lord, every time I look at you I fear your skin is going to tear if your cheekbones become any sharper. You look no better than those pathetic creatures locked in gaol for years. Your lovely complexion is gone. You look no more exotic than Mrs. Turlow does. No, I take that back. She puts you into the shade!"

He couldn't see the expression in her eyes, as they were still lowered, but he saw her mouth working slightly. When she did raise her gaze, he felt as if he had taken a fist to his gut. Tears shimmered in the amber depths. She looked at him like a little girl who has just lost her only puppy. This time he lowered his eyes, his jaw clenching.

"What am I going to do, Sion?" her voice whispered across to him.

His head jerked up. "I'll support you in anything you want to do, Danae, but not this."

Her fear was palpable as she leaned toward him. "But, I was putting so much weight on—"

He cut her off sharply, "No, you were not! You were becoming lovelier by the day! Your health was improving and you had almost gained back all your strength. Damnation, girl, you were senseless for over four months; your body had gone through months of trauma. At times, you were burning with a fever so high, you almost died from dehydration! In order to survive, your body depleted you of every ounce of sustenance it could draw on. Lord knows, we couldn't get much nourishment down you. You were practically a corpse by the time you woke up. Not too far off from what you look like right now, I might add. Over the following weeks your body was simply replenishing itself, settling into its natural, healthy weight."

When she blanched at those words, he could have bitten his tongue. How in hell was he going to reach her? He cursed Camden to the foulest pits of hell. For all her cool demeanor and her displays of independence, Danae had little, if any, self-esteem. Underneath, no matter how much she denied it, she was still Katherine. He felt his only course was to give her the inducement to start taking pride in herself. Being a typical man, he could think of but one way: to play up to any minute sense of vanity she possessed.

Taking a chance again, but with a bit more hesitance, he confessed to her, "You are a desirable woman, Danae. I sensed the passion in you during those weeks you blossomed. You made my mind spin with thoughts of you, and every night my body yearned for yours." His gaze was direct as he stared at her. "You were gaining pride and confidence. You were *Danae,* but now I see Katherine, frightened and letting those fears control her again. Which are you? The flamboyant, desirable *contessa* or the lonely woman too ashamed to reach out for what she wants?"

Danae twisted the napkin in her lap, the tips of her fingers white. "But what if my body doesn't stop?"

"Let nature take care of itself, Danae. I have never seen you overindulge yourself during a meal. You have always been cautious and aware of what you were doing. Katherine had no such luxury. Her anger and despair could only be soothed by her compulsion to compensate herself in some abstract way. She didn't have someone like me to spill her rage and frustrations onto. See how lucky you are?" He gave her a winsome smile.

She nodded, returning his smile, though it didn't quite reach her eyes. "Yes, I have been very lucky since I came here. You and Mrs. Turlow have been heaven-sent." She stared out into the garden, the bees busy at their work, the droning hum of their toil soothing her.

Finally, with a sigh, she turned back to face him. "Very well, Sion. Since I have your permission to abuse you—verbally, that is—then I feel it should only be fair that I give you some compensation. But as you said, the body is inviolate. You can drool all you like, but you can't touch." She twisted a curl about her finger. "That is, unless I give you leave to do so."

Sion frowned at her. "Well, I don't know about this. How about a little compromise? If I let you . . ." His eyes narrowed in thought. "Let us say, kick me—without slippers, mind you—then I should be able to get a kiss in return." He looked at her expectantly.

Danae scoffed at that. "You would like that, wouldn't you? I get bruised toes and you get kisses. How about this?" She studied him for a moment. "If I let you kiss me, I am allowed the opportunity to 'lob' something at you when I feel the urge—my choice of projectiles, of course." She smiled, satisfied, then added quickly, "And you can't touch me. Lips only."

Sion gave an emphatic shake of his head. "Absolutely not! Where is the fun in that, I ask you? A simple kiss for a possible concussion? It has to be hands, too, or nothing. After all, I have to place some value on my head." He enjoyed the sight of her scowl.

"Well, I would rather not stir up that hornet's nest, for it is obvious the values we would each place on your head differ widely. But, let us not forget my abysmal aim. Lord knows, you could get all the 'fun' and I nothing more satisfying than the chance to dent your walls," she told him with a reasonable shrug.

Sion wasn't about to tell her that with practice her aim could improve, for he did rather like the shape of his noggin just the way it was. He studied her sphinx-like demeanor, only her eyes giving away her impish delight in their absurd game. But frivolity aside, he found himself dealing with a true diplomat here. Therefore, he had better stop beating about the bush and close these negotiations before he came out with nothing more than a bruised ego, for hadn't she already stomped on it, telling him that only he would find any "fun" in their kisses?

This game now took an abrupt turn for him and was no longer a matter of light banter. He now urgently wanted those kisses they were bandying around. And as many as he could get!

Clearing his throat, he leaned forward and proposed in a very businesslike manner, "Very well. Let us skip all this shilly-shallying and get down to business. Now, I'm being very generous here, for you've proved yourself to be one formidable negotiator." Her gimlet-eyed scrutiny didn't alter in the least at his compliment. She was going to be exacting to the very end. "I have ordered a few nags from a stud farm I trust implicitly. If all goes well, they should be delivered no later than next week. One little mare is destined to be yours, with my compliments, under two conditions. First, you must regain your strength, and that means sitting down to meals and eating them. Second, you must prove to me that you can keep your seat on the mare before she is yours."

"But I can't ride—"

He cut off her indignant cry. "I know you can't ride. So, this is my last offer. For every riding lesson I give you—and there will be many, as there is much to learn if you are to be able to conduct yourself with some grace on a hunt—I get . . ." He paused for a long second, watching as she struggled to hide her excitement from him. "I get a kiss from

you of my choosing, the use of hands included."
His breath hitched at the tantalizing thought.

"In addition, I promise that you'll have no wor-
ries about certain portions of your anatomy
spreading. I'll find the hardest saddle made, guar-
anteed to pound the flesh right from your
charming derriere. Now, how is that for a compromise?" He sat back, satisfaction gleaming in his
eyes. He knew he had her now.

Danae studied him, careful not to jump to any
hasty decisions. However, the thought of her own
horse, and the freedom to ride it wherever she
wanted, was worth anything to her at that moment. In fact, it sounded too good. A kiss for every
lesson. And he had just warned her that there
would be many. And in any way he chose. Now,
that gave her pause. On one hand, she was terribly insulted; did he believe her to be some doxy
he could buy? On the other hand, the thought of
having the moral issue of whether she should or
shouldn't allow him to kiss her would be taken
out of her hands. An honorable person always
paid her obligations. This whole game suddenly
made her ashamed of herself—ashamed that she
was even considering the ludicrous suggestion.
And yet she was terribly tempted by the sheer audacity of it. A horse, riding lessons, and Sion's
kisses—how could she lose? Still, the negotiator
in her weighed every angle again, not wanting to
give in too fast. And being a typical woman, she
had to have the last word. "Very well, but during
the kissing, we remain standing at all times." She
cocked an uncompromising eye at him.

Sion fought hard to hide his triumph. *Oh, the glo-
ries of dealing with an innocent!* Trying to look a little
downcast, he heaved a heavy sigh and extended his

hand. "Very well. You drive a hard bargain, my dear. Pact?"

Smiling, she placed her hand into his. "Pact." He was so easy, she gloated as she looked down at her plate. Suddenly, everything looked beautiful: her future, the stunning morning, and the food Sion was placing on her plate.

However, Sion's thoughts were far away, his only concern now a matter of when the damned horses would arrive. Sitting back down in his chair, he smiled as he watched Danae raise a sticky bun to her lips and take a dainty bite. His indulgent smile died a slow death as he watched her tongue dart out to catch a bit of sweetness on the corner of her lips. He swallowed a groan as he realized that all of a sudden the thought of a mere week's time seemed to stretch before him like a hellish eternity.

Maybe it would be a good idea to send a missive to Rotherham and hurry along the date of delivery of his new stable. It would be such a shame to make Danae wait all that time, Sion selflessly assured himself as he shifted about in his chair, trying to ignore the way the sunlight glistened on her ruby lips.

Hell and damnation! A whole week! He would soon be inviting her to lob things at his head just for a simple kiss.

The absurdity of it all!

Six

Danae watched as another hank of hair tumbled over her shoulder to land in her lap. She picked up the long tress and again was amazed at the new color and shine. Gone was the lusterless light-brown hue that had been as nondescript as poor Katherine herself. She smiled as she pulled the silken curl in and about her fingers, holding it up to the sunlight. Twisting it this way and that, she was able to catch the teasing glimpse of henna that Mrs. Turlow had rinsed into her newly dyed hair, now a deep auburn. With this change, matched along with the richer, dusky hue of her skin, she was confident that she would have no problems passing for an Italian *contessa*. It was amazing what a few herbs thrown together could accomplish. Just one more reason to bless Mrs. Turlow and her endless abilities. The woman was a veritable wellspring of knowledge.

Then her smile froze as she felt and heard the shears sever another hank of hair. The shorn section above her brow flopped forward, causing her to blink rapidly. Raising her hand, she brushed the hair from her eyes, then grimaced as she felt the blunt-cut fringe. What was the sense of going through that laborious and messy, not to mention smelly, process of changing the color of her hair if now Mrs. T. was going to hack it all off?

"Oh, dearie me," she heard Mrs. Turlow mutter behind her.

Peeking over her shoulder, Danae saw the woman frowning at the top of her head. It was with amazing willpower that she did not raise her hand to investigate the cause of such concern. Instead, she turned her attention back to the growing pile of hair in her lap. There was so much of it. Never had her hair been cut. Not that it had been of any importance to her. But, now . . . Again she fingered the silken coil about her fingers. It was such a pretty color, she lamented to herself as a wave of doubt washed over her. Behind her, Mrs. Turlow clucked out her frustration as the rhythm of the shears picked up speed once more. Bravely, Danae held back the tears threatening to burst forth and watched the pile of shorn tresses in her lap grow.

It is going to be just fine, she assured herself with a deep inhalation of courage. Wanting again to study the style her friend was trying to emulate, Danae turned her head slightly, then gasped when Mrs. Turlow jerked it forward again. This time, making sure she held her head steady, she peeked sideways at the opened page of an outdated fashion magazine. The beautiful coiffure was so lovely, and it had been with an excited thrill of optimism that she had chosen this particular style for herself. Now, however, she cocked a dubious eye upon the fringe of tight curls framing the sketched face. She had not realized how much of her hair would have to be sacrificed when she had pointed to it. And it now appeared too impossibly intricate for anyone, let alone an elderly Scottish housekeeper, to fashion.

How in heaven had she thought she could even carry off such an extravagant style?

"There we be. Now fer the irons."

Danae's attention whipped over to the fire, where five thin curling irons were smoking in the embers. She watched in trepidation as Mrs. Turlow wrapped her apron about the handle of one and withdrew it. Then the widow approached her with an almost militant glint in her eyes.

Dropping the curl still wrapped about her fingers, Danae grabbed hold of the armrests and leaned as far sideways as she could from the lethal-looking weapon.

"Now, none o' that, hinny," the old lady admonished as she grabbed Danae's shoulder and pulled her upright.

"Mrs. T., I don't know about this! Mind you, its not that I don't trust you—yeowww!" she screeched as the woman grabbed a hank of hair and tugged hard. Immediately, Danae could hear a slight hissing sound.

Was that *smoke* she smelled? Panic then set in.

"Oh, please, Mrs. T., I really do not—" Her words were cut short as her head was jerked to the other side and another section caught up. Well, at least the hair wasn't hanging in her eyes anymore. Doubtless, it had been singed to the roots. Danae tried to convince herself she was being silly. After all, Mrs. T. knew what she was doing.

She cringed as her right ear was blasted with a string of Gaelic obscenities.

Swallowing, she asked timidly, "Is there a problem, Mrs. T.?"

She was quickly answered with another string of obscenities. At least they sounded like obscenities; she was just thankful she could not understand them. However, whatever the context of the widow's ire, it did not bode well for her hair; of that Danae was sure. Not wanting to upset the lady any further, she kept her fears to herself and bit down on her tongue. When she saw Mrs. T. stomp back to the fireplace for a fresh iron, she seriously considered making a run for the door. But where would she go with a head full of half-crimped, smoking curls? Sion would likely laugh himself ill.

With a sigh, she looked down at the long, silken ribbons of hair on the floor around her skirts. Should she save them? Perhaps a hairpiece could be fashioned from them.

When Mrs. T. finally grunted her satisfaction and stepped back, Danae glanced up startled, so lost had she been wallowing in her self-pity.

"Ah, weel, a masterpiece, if I do say so meself." A broad smile stretching her weathered face, Mrs. T. came about the chair to face Danae's skeptical gaze. The housekeeper's hands were clasped at her waist, her head cocked to the side—a master studying her creation. "Aye, *loesome* ye be!"

Danae's eyes snapped wide. In the next instant she was out of the chair, crying, "Loathsome! You made me loathsome?" She came to an inelegant stumble in front of the floor-length mirror. Her mouth dropped open as she stared at her reflection. "Oh, my heavens!" she managed to gasp out.

Mrs. Turlow chuckled as she came to stand beside her. "Nae, hinny. *Loesome* in me tongue means"—and with motherly pride she cupped Danae's face in her hands—"*lovely*. Yer a beautiful woman, hinny."

Danae was speechless. She turned back to the mirror, and blinking back the sudden tears that stung her eyes, she took in Mrs. Turlow's artistry. She was afraid to touch the confection of tiny curls

framing her face. The sunlight filtering into the
room behind her seemed to cast a glow of reddish highlights in the dark auburn of the elegant
coiffure that in turn gave her honey-hued skin an
exotic cast. And her eyes! They now appeared
huge, almost catlike, and the whiskey-gold coloring was quite startling against her dusky
complexion. Never had she realized what a pretty
color they were. Before, she had always worn her
mother's delicate wire-rimmed spectacles, the
rose tinting of the glass obscuring their true color.
The senseless bit of artifice had been more trouble than help, of course, since she had no problem
with her eyesight; but they had been a precious
crutch to hide behind. Now they were gone, lost
somewhere in the swirling waters that had claimed
Katherine. Although she sorely missed that last
link with her mother, she had to admit it was only
right, for they had belonged to Katherine. Danae
did not need them.

Blinking, Danae again focused on the miraculous transformation. Even the shape of her face
appeared altered. The cluster of curls seemed to
emphasize her high cheekbones and the slender
oval of her face. Her neck now appeared longer
and so graceful as it blended into the delicate
sloop of her shoulders, giving her upper torso the
elegance of balance that she had always admired
on the aristocratic ladies of her limited acquaintance. She was a lady now. A true lady. Not some
lump of humanity hidden away in shame on some
remote country estate. *I am a lady,* Danae thought
defiantly. For the first time in her life, she looked
back at her image in a mirror and smiled. *Camden, you can go to hell! You may have broken Katherine,
but you'll not touch me!*

Not being able to help herself, Danae gently patted the soft curls arranged with such painstaking accuracy that they gave the illusion of a naturalness that was astounding. Turning her head right, then left, she admired the remaining waist-length hair flowing smoothly down her back, just a hint of curling teasing the silken ends. She had never had the nerve to wear her hair loose. It felt so . . . decadent!

"Oh, my," she breathed in wonder. "You truly are a master, Mrs. T. You are wasted here, you realize. You should be tending the great ladies of London." Her eyes met those of Mrs. Turlow in the mirror. Danae spun around to impulsively grab her friend's hand and brought it up to her cheek. "Thank you so very much," she whispered.

Ducking her head, Mrs. T. flapped her hands about as if she were trying to shoo away her embarrassment. "Nae, none o' that, hinny. Why din I waste meself on them hoity-toity crows when I 'ave me own angel tae care fer?"

Blinking, Danae turned back to the mirror. With a more critical eye, she looked herself over. Ignoring the sack of a dress hanging around her body, she could honestly say she looked sophisticated enough to pass for the brazen Italian widow who would not think twice about flaunting herself with her lover before the cold censure of London society. Unfortunately, just *thinking* of Sion in the role of her lover made her blush furiously.

Wonderful! She may as well have a town crier go before her, proclaiming her the ignorant virgin that she was! A sophisticated lady of the world, indeed!

Suddenly, she felt intimidated by the task she had set for herself. Could she do it? There was still so much to learn and so little time in which to achieve perfection, and she had to be perfect in order for this crazy scheme to work. She had to be perfect, for not only would she fall, but also Sion and Mrs. T. She grew faint at the thought.

"Weel, we dinna be finished yet," she heard Mrs. Turlow announce as she bustled about behind her. After a minute, she stepped up to Danae's side, a basket brimming with small boxes, vials, and tins in her hand. Her callused fingers tilted Danae's face at various angles while she plotted her next miracle.

"Close yer eyes, hinny."

Obediently they snapped shut. Danae heard a crackle and caught a whiff of some strange smell she could not identify. When she felt something smooth and ticklish brushed over her eyelids, she jumped in alarm. Mrs. Turlow *tsk*ed, muttering that she was to stay as still as possible. She then felt a slight pressure against her eyelashes as something was dragged upward against them. Hearing Mrs. Turlow rummaging through the basket, she opened her right eye a slit and watched as the artist, muttering to herself, pulled various things out from the jumbled contents of the basket. When the old dame turned back to her, Danae snapped her eye closed and patiently waited for whatever came next. Then she smelled something suspicious. Taking another sniff, she detected the acrid scent of something charred. Her eyes flew open just in time to see Mrs. T. pinch out a curl of smoke rising from the end of what looked like a pencil.

"Close yer eyes, hinny."

Danae hesitated, before complying. It was difficult not to flinch away when she felt the tip of the object pulling across the base of her eyelashes.

Then the callused tip of Mrs. T.'s fingertip brushed back and forth.

"Ye can open yer eyes now, hinny."

Blinking, Danae turned and looked at herself closely in the mirror. She smiled as she shook her head. Again, Mrs. T.'s nimble fingers had created an illusion of magic, for it surely was not her eyes staring back at her. She turned again obediently when Mrs. T. reached for her chin, and watched as a little sack, tinged red, was pounced along the high point of her cheek.

"Now, give me a pucker, hinny" Mrs. T. directed, pulling a tiny pot out of her basket of miracles.

Danae frowned. "What?"

"Yer lips." Mrs. T. looked up from the pot with a distracted smile. "Pucker."

Pucker? Danae thought about that for a second before she cautiously stretched them taunt against her teeth, her cheeks straining to hold the uncomfortable grimace.

A crack of laughter exploded from her friend.

With a sigh, Danae waited until Mrs. T.'s mirth subsided into a chuckle. She could not help but smile at the old woman's high spirits. "What in heaven's name is 'pucker'? It sounds positively lewd!"

"Must I teach you everything? Even the most basics?" A masculine voice startled them from across the room. Both women spun about and stared open-mouthed at his lordship, who was leaning casually against the door frame watching them.

Pushing away from the frame, Sion strolled forward, his lazy gaze capturing and holding Danae's. "And, yes, it can be very lewd if done with a certain—" He cut himself short after taking in the wide eyes of innocence gazing up at him. With a sigh, he murmured low, "However, that particular lesson shall have to keep till another time." A wicked smile teasing his lips, he reached out and grasped Danae's chin. With a mysterious glint in his eyes, he slowly studied each of her newly defined features.

Danae, for once at a loss for words, simply looked up into Sion's mesmerizing gaze.

"This is the value of puckering, my dear," he whispered as he leaned down and, with the barest pressure, laid warm lips over her open mouth. Danae jerked back, but he only moved in closer, crowding her against the mirror. "Gently, my dear. Now, once more. You still do not have it right. No one would believe that my 'lover' does not even know how to 'pucker'," he softly teased. "Just relax and let your lips do what comes naturally."

Nothing, however, seemed to come naturally when she was in the clutches of Sion Sinclair, Danae thought frantically as his lips again closed over hers. One part of her wanted to slap him silly, while the other wanted to cling to him in the most forward manner. Too unsure of what she should do, her widened eyes sought out Mrs. Turlow over Sion's shoulder. Silently, she implored the frowning woman to do something. Yet, even though her displeasure was quite evident, Mrs. Turlow just shrugged back.

"Pay attention to me," Sion growled warmly into her mouth before he sank into his kiss again. Then Danae was aware of nothing else but him.

Closing her eyes, she was lost in an avalanche of sensations as Sion's tongue slid a delicate path along the seam of her burning lips. She shivered in places she never knew she had. The blood in her veins rushed dizzily along until she felt drunk on the taste of Sion Sinclair. She had read about such lewd urges besetting one's body when engaged in sinful exercises. But her virgin's body and her equally virginal mind had been too broken to think she could ever feel such things. The evocative awakening he was stirring deep inside her was as thrilling as it was terrifying. She felt a jolt of fire as Sion's tongue slipped passed her lips to gently stroke the tender flesh within. Her world as she had known it was forever shattered as his tongue touched and mated with hers. Her heart stood still, and suddenly she felt the floor rushing up to meet her.

"Steady," he murmured as he stepped slightly back from her, his strong hands grasping her upper arms, holding her upright.

When she felt him slowly pull away from her, she almost cried out. Her lips felt scalded as the cool air struck them. Oblivious to what she was doing, Danae leaned toward him, only knowing she wanted to feel his lips again. Instead, she felt his hands turning her around. Blinking her eyes open, at first she felt confused as if awakening from a long sleep. Then she focused on his face in the mirror, and what she saw there confused her even more. It wasn't fair that he should appear so cool when in the mere span of a moment, he had tipped her whole world off its axis.

She felt his fingers again take possession of her chin. Still lost somewhere back in the kiss that he had cut too short, she was aware of his warm breath feathering over her feverish cheek. Her own breath shivered in and held when she felt the hardness of his chest pressing indecently close against her back.

"There, my love," he whispered hotly into her ear. "That is a most impressive pucker."

She suddenly realized she was facing the mirror

again. At first, all she could see were Sion's eyes
staring at her from over her shoulder. Then she
looked at herself. As he said, her moist lips were
pursed in a most obvious manner. Then, as if coming out of a trance, the cad's words finally sank in
and then plummeted like a rock to the bottom of
her heart.

A lesson! It had been nothing but a dratted lesson!
Heat seared her cheeks as she pushed away from
his imprisoning arms. For a moment she turned
her back to him while she literally pulled herself
together. Had he been merely mocking her the entire time? Swallowing the sob that almost escaped
her, she took a deep, deep breath. Then, tipping up
her chin, she turned back toward him, pulling her
lacy kerchief from her sleeve as she did so. Never
again would she allow anyone to use her as the
brunt of their tasteless jokes! *Men!* It appeared they
were all the same! Well, this was one woman who
would no longer just turn the other cheek.

Staring him straight in the eye, she painstakingly
wiped her lips dry. She smiled thinly as she watched
a flicker of anger come and go in Sion's eyes.
"Thank you, my lord. I vow, you lend a certain . . .
flair to your lessons. How ingenious of you, to be
sure." Then she grimaced. "However, though you
may have enjoyed the taste of your cigars, I can't say
the same."

Sion felt a flash of anger and embarrassment at
her words. Then he paused before lashing back
with some scathing rejoinder. His lips twitched after
a moment's reflection. The lady was good; he had
to give her that—cool and disdainful, she was learning to play her part to perfection. Nevertheless, he
knew the truth of their kiss.

Stepping back, he sketched her a low, teasing

bow, his gaze unerringly landing on those lush lips of hers. The moist, plump flesh spoke a much different tale from the words that had just fallen from them. "I am your humble servant, my dear. I shall always strive to *satisfy* your every whim."

Danae's eyes narrowed. She did not like the sound of that at all! Watching the smug beast, she was tempted to kick him where he would suffer it the longest. And she was not thinking of his arse! Instead, she returned his bow with a disdainful curtsy.

"Mrs. Turlow, an excellent job, if I may say so and still retain my head." Though his words were directed elsewhere, his heavy-lidded gaze never left Danae.

He chuckled when those wicked eyes of hers flashed an equally wicked promise toward him. He felt his pulse quicken. *Egad! One look from those feline orbs and she can send me tumbling into thoughts of silken skin and satin sheets!* His smile froze as his attention again traveled down to her kiss-stung lips. Licking his own lips, he could still taste her on his tongue, and insidiously his loins began to ache even more. He had to hold himself rigid, so tempted was he to yank her back into his arms, to force her up against the mirror and reclaim that sleek tongue of hers. He blinked when something moved behind him in the mirror, catching his muddled attention. Mrs. Turlow's reflection was glaring at him with the promise of an avenging Fury. For some unknown reason she had allowed him that one indiscretion, but it was obvious she wasn't going to be so blind a second time.

Sion cleared his throat and looked over into Danae's wary eyes. All of a sudden he felt hot and stifled and wanted nothing more than to be quit of the room. Stretching his neck against the collar that seemed to be strangling him, he forced out as smoothly as he was able, "By the way, I would appreciate a few moments of your time in my study. At your own convenience, of course, my dear." He hoped his smile didn't look as strained as it felt, for he was amazed that he could even manage one at all.

Danae, just wanting him gone, nodded wordlessly to his request. She felt the strain of resisting him when she watched those black velvet eyes of his falling to her lips again. She just knew that if she closed her eyes, she would recall every shattering sensation as those firm lips moved over hers. It was already a memory indelibly etched onto her heart. *Please, just go away!*

For one unguarded moment, Sion spied a flash of vulnerability cross Danae's cool features. Not wanting to think he had distressed her, he shifted his gaze away and found himself staring at her bed. It was still unmade, the sheets rumpled and appearing to him as if they were still warm from her body. It was inevitable that the thought of her lying nude upon those tousled sheets, her limbs and hair wrapped about him, would hit him in the gut with the power to double him over. *Damn*, Sion cursed.

Abruptly he swung about and strode for the door. However, before leaving, he paused and looked over his shoulder. Unerringly, his intense gaze found hers. "Her lips look perfect just the way they are, Mrs. T. Do not rouge them."

Danae's eyes narrowing, she turned slowly around. He had just reached the door as her hand swept over the cluttered surface beside her.

"My lord?" She called out to him.

He spun around. "Yes, my dear?"

"Whether you consider it a lesson or not, I choose to think of your kiss as a breach of our pact. As my riding lessons have not yet commenced, I am entitled to compensation. I choose this!" And before he could blink twice, she lobbed her weapon at his head. As expected, it only bounced harmlessly off the wall behind him. However, the powder in the projectile did what could only be expected.

A long moment of silence fell upon the threesome as the cloud of talcum settled gently over Sion's motionless figure. When Danae and Mrs. Turlow exploded into gut-wrenching laughter, Sion just looked down at himself. Knowing himself to be a fool for having goaded Danae too far with that last little jab, he shook his head in disgust at his own stupidity. He sneezed in a puff of white powder, sending both women off into fresh bouts of giggles. Then he froze in stunned amazement.

Danae was laughing!

He looked over at her and thought he had never seen anything more beautiful. Her cheeks were flushed and vibrant with color. Her beautiful eyes were shimmering with her mirthful tears. She looked positively gorgeous!

Noticing Sion's strange scrutiny, Danae's giggles slipped away and she slowly became self-conscious under his steady stare. Shooting Mrs. T. a perplexed glance, she asked with hesitance, "Is something wrong? I only did what we agreed upon. I guess I should not have grabbed the powder jar, but it was the closest."

Sion shook his head, sending more talcum sprinkling down about his shoulders. "No, don't apologize, Danae. As you say, it was only what we agreed on. I'm just thankful you didn't lob more than one item at me. After all, I took more than one kiss."

Biting her lip, Danae reached out her hand again.

Sion raised his arms in defense and stepped back, striking the wall. He nimbly caught what she tossed to him. A clothes brush. Puzzled, he looked up.

"Mrs. Turlow borrowed that from your room. I believe you have more need of it than I. Are we now even? Two kisses. Two lobs."

Sion's smile flashed with its own wicked charm, and she felt her heart lurch and flip. *He is such a rogue,* she thought fondly.

With a tumble of powder, he gave her a dashing bow.

She swept him an elegant curtsy.

Then he was gone. Only the shape of his boots remained on the carpet, outlined with talcum.

"An' who's tae clean up that mess, I'd like tae be knowin?"

Danae's smile dropped away as she took in the white disaster. *Dratted man!*

Seven

For the fourth time, Danae pounded on the door, this time with quite a bit of impatience. When she again received no answer, she stepped back, and with hands on her hips she glared at the barrier. It never occurred to her to simply walk in, even though she was expected. "Well, for goodness' sake, where is the dratted man?"

"Well, come in, for dratted sake." Sion's voice drifted through the door.

Danae pursed her lips in irritation. Obviously, he was playing another game with her. Retaliation for the talcum incident, no doubt. With a deep breath and a sharp tug on Mrs. T.'s oversized bodice, she pushed the door open, and strode in, her head set at an impudent tilt.

Sion cocked an amused eye her way. "Danae, when I request your presence in my *dratted* study, I don't expect you to stand out there in the *dratted* hall, banging on the *dratted* door."

She could not help but smile as she sat down. "I believe I see your dratted point." With interest she inspected the stacks of old newsletters spread across his desk. "What are you up to? Mrs. T. said you had buried yourself in here with years' worth of entrail wrappings."

Sion's feet, perched on the corner of the desk, slipped over the edge and landed with a thud on the floor. He then leaned forward and, squinting, looked closer at Danae, his gaze irresistibly drawn to her reddened lips. He opened his mouth to say something, but when she narrowed those cat eyes at him, he thought better of it. While he may admit to being flippant at times, dull-witted he certainly wasn't. Wisely he refrained from saying a word. Instead, he picked up a London newsletter, yellowed and torn, from his desk.

"Yes, Jonas will be pleased to know that the subscriptions he continued to pay all these years have been put to some worthwhile use. I dug these out of a moldy corner in the pantry."

"Who is Jonas?"

Absentmindedly he waved her question aside. "Not now. Listen to this. It is dated March 18, 1882:

> *Parliament has redressed the subject of Women's Rights and has debated changes to the existing laws already in force—particularly the rights of married women. This new act further establishes their rights to a greater and indisputable degree than the provisions already set forth through prior bills. The Married Women's Property Act of 1882 will emphasize that women, married, separated, or deserted, can retain full ownership and manage their own property acquired before marriage. They have the right to manage their own businesses, to assume and be responsible for their own debt. Their signatures, on all contracts that have to do with said properties and moneys, will be honored without the need and/or consent of spouses. Upon their death, they have the right to bequeath these same properties and moneys,*

or any moneys acquired on said property through investments, any way they deem, even in perpetuity."

Sion glanced up, a twinkle in his eye.

Danae shrugged, then paused. Looking up, she gazed at Sion with an arrested expression.

Cocking an eyebrow, he grinned. "You are going to be a very rich young widow, *Contessa.*"

"Do you think it is possible?" she asked, her voice a breathy whisper. Her heart was pumping erratically.

Sion handed her the paper. "Parliament says it is. What we will have to do now is draw up a will. I remember you telling me that your mother had bequeathed all her dower estates to you upon her death. These properties were acquired before your . . ." He faltered as he noticed Danae's frown. With a sigh, he cast his eyes heavenward. "Forgive me, *Katherine's* marriage to Halsingham; therefore, by law, they are not entailed to the properties or moneys acquired during the marriage. To be more succinct, Halsingham has no legal claim to Katherine's property. So Katherine has the right to settle these properties where she wishes, and it will be her dying wish to bequeath her estate to Danae Suriano, *la Contessa di Sala*, in gratitude for all her selfless support and attention during the long and painful months of her illness. It was very wise of you to have refused to sign over these properties at the marriage."

Danae had listened to him with openmouthed amazement. When he finished, she said lamely, "Jassy refused to let me."

Sion smiled, "Then she was indeed a true friend looking out for you."

Danae simply nodded as she quickly scanned the

article he had handed her. *If only it were possible.* Not only would she be financially independent for the rest of her life, but Halsingham would not benefit one shilling from Katherine's death. He would continue to be beholden to Camden for his livelihood.

She smiled at that revelation. Such poetic justice it would be! It would almost be worth the years of abuse Katherine had suffered at Camden's hands. Now Camden's wrath would be directed on Halsingham, and there would be no escape for him unless he was willing to give up the lifestyle Camden provided him. A pity his reputation was so damaged that his beauty could not land himself a wealthy heiress. Halsingham, though, was barely tolerated in Society. Even his coronet was not enticing enough to the rich papas searching for a titled spouse for their daughters. It was a good thing Camden had come along when he had to bail the profligate rake out of his troubles, and now Halsingham was caught like the rat he was.

"Well?"

After a moment of contemplation, Danae looked up, shaking her head. "You don't know Halsingham's greed like I do. He will contest this, and he will not care a fig what scandal ensues because of it. Freedom from Camden is going to be his first priority." *Just like mine.*

"The last thing I will want is too much notoriety. We will have enough of it when we live together in London establishing my new persona. He'll fight it, and the last thing I believe either of us wants is to be tied up in litigation in the courts." Just the thought of it made her queasy. What if they investigated her? Adamantly she shook her head, tossing the paper back on Sion's desk. "I can't risk it, Sion.

The jewels are more than enough. Becoming greedy could mean my downfall."

Sion leaned back in his chair again, shaking his head. "This is only an amendment to an existing law that has been around since the late sixties. It did have its loopholes, but generally it was effective. However, even if he does insist on causing trouble, we will simply present our trump card." A smug grin teased his lips, and Danae found herself distracted for a moment as she watched them, remembering what those lips had done to her earlier.

Giving herself a mental shake, she asked, "What is a trump card?"

Sion chuckled. "My poor innocent, I am going to have to do something about your abysmal lack of education in the finer aspects of decadence. However"—he shot upright again, holding out a finger—"it is this very innocence that will get you your money. Uncontested."

Danae frowned at him; then, with a shrug she apologized. "I'm so sorry, but my innocent mind has lost you. What are you talking about?"

Again he pointed his finger at her. "You are a virgin."

A blush stung her cheeks as her eyes narrowed. "How kind of you to remind me. Do you realize I had almost forgotten this fact? But what possible interest it could hold for you, trump or otherwise, is beyond my feeble mind."

Sion slumped back with a sigh of disgust. "Think for a moment, Danae."

At the moment she was becoming too angered to think, but she refused to let the cad get the best of her. Concentrating on the dearth of facts—and silly ones at that!—given to her, she warily glanced at Sion and noticed his black gaze locked on her. She hated it when he studied her in that assiduous way of his; it always made her feel like a butterfly with its wings pinned to a board.

Shifting a bit in her chair, she tried to ignore him as she pondered this puzzle he had thrown at her. *You can do this, my girl. It cannot be all that difficult if he thought of it.*

Fact one: I am a virgin.

She shot him a disgusted look.

Fact two: Because of fact one, I am also a trump card.

Fact three: Why in heaven's name am I even trying to make sense of this nonsense?

Because deep down, every insecurity Katherine had ever known came up to sting Danae's cheeks in shame. She could picture Camden standing over the cowering girl, deriding her for her lack of intelligence or beauty or any redeeming quality at all.

And now, here was another man mocking her. *Oh, what I would give not to be a virgin! That would show him, the arrogant goat!*

She jumped when Sion smacked his hand on the desk. "Lord, Danae, I thought you had more intelligence than this!"

Shooting to her feet, she leaned over the desk and shouted, "Don't you sit there and insult me, you dratted man!"

Sion also jumped to his feet and easily came nose to nose with her across the desk. "Then use your mind and think!"

"I am using my mind! It just doesn't dare to go where yours has been! It happens to have more rationality than that!"

That caught Sion up short. He frowned as he mentally repeated her slur, then threw his head back in booming laughter. Collapsing back into his chair, he laughed with a belly-deep joviality that took a while before it slowly eased into soft chuckles. Finally, wiping his eyes, he admired her over the desk. God, it felt *so good* to laugh again! However, Danae was staring at him as if he were a snake that had just slithered out from under the desk. Shaking his head, he murmured with admiration, "I have to concede that you pole-axed me with no mercy with that one. My compliments, madam. Your wit is truly a force to be reckoned with."

Danae grinned back at him, preening a bit. "It was fairly well done of me, wasn't it?"

"Oh, yes. I give you no arguments there." Tamping down his humor, he cleared his throat, meaning to get back to the point.

But she broached it first. "Now, would you mind telling me what that was all about?"

"To the victor go the spoils, as they say. What I was alluding to, in my usual clumsy fashion—"

"No arguments there," she interjected dryly.

Sion bit down on his lip, stifling the urge to laugh again. "As I was saying, technically, you are not married."

Danae shrugged. "I *know I'm* not married." Defiantly she stressed both words as she frowned at him.

Sion rubbed his face, growling with frustration.

Danae held up her hand in surrender. "All right. I am sorry. I shall not say another word. Until I hear something that demands a rebuttal, that is." *Which is everything,* she thought peevishly.

Lowering his hands, Sion just sat there and stared stubbornly at her. After a few moments of silence, Danae folded her hands in her lap and snapped, "Very well, I'll not say another word." His brows rose in dubious reflection as he continued to stare at her. "I promise!" she shouted at him.

"If the fact comes to light that Katherine's marriage had never been consummated, it would be devastating to Halsingham. Camden would doubtless cut him off without a farthing and probably sue him in court for breach of contract. The last thing Halsingham can chance is this information getting to Camden."

"You are speaking of blackmail, I presume?"

Sion cocked a brow at her. "You have some problem with this?"

"Heaven's no!" Danae quickly assured him. Halsingham's welfare was of no interest whatsoever to her, and she certainly could not disagree with Sion's logic. He had the situation exactly correct. Halsingham feared Camden much more than Katherine ever had. In fact, his utter disgust of Katherine was only reinforced by the foolhardy chance he had been willing to take by repudiating her. Though intelligence was not one of Halsingham's long suits, he was not exactly ignorant of the enormous risk he had been taking in thwarting Camden. And he probably had not been ignorant of the abuse his wife had suffered because of their pact. It had been Katherine's choice to protect their secret for her own reasons and certainly not because of any concern for his vainglorious hide.

However, she was still a bit confused. "So you are saying that because I'm . . . I mean, Katherine was a virgin at her death that her marriage to Halsingham is not legal?"

Sion nodded. "Actually, was never legal. A marriage never consummated is not binding." He studied her for a long moment. "As Katherine, you could just go to London and petition for an annulment," Sion said softly.

She cocked a doubtful brow at him. "Then what? Sit back meekly while Camden unearths some other miscreant to force upon me? No, Halsingham has never been my problem. It is Camden I need to get away from. But if what you say is true, with Katherine dead, how could you prove her virginity?"

Sion studied his nails. "I can get a doctor's signed affidavit attesting to Katherine's virginity."

"You know of a doctor who will do this?"

Sion's gaze slid to hers. "Yes."

She cocked her head and stared at him in wonderment. "Have you always been this devious, or am I just a bad influence on you?"

Sion smiled at her. "Oh, you definitely have some influence on me." His penetrating gaze dropped down to her lips. "Whether it is bad or not has yet to be determined," he murmured as he absently rubbed his lower lip.

Blushing, Danae looked down at the newsletter on the desk. At a loss for a pert comeback, she instead picked the paper up and scanned the article again. "You realize that if you are a party to this fraud, you could be held just as liable as I will be if it fails?"

"Yes, of course." Sion opened a drawer and took out a vellum and pen. "Oh, and another thing: since you are going to claim being from Italy, it would not hurt to have someone in Italy corroborate your story if either Camden or Halsingham actually has the sense to look into your background. I happen to have a cousin in the consulate in Naples, who I am sure would not mind giving you credentials should they receive a letter inquiring into a certain *Contessa di* Sala. I shall write to him today." Sion looked up at her. "Any problem with that?"

Danae just stared at him. Dumbly she shook her head, overwhelmed with his generosity and deviousness.

"Well, then, back to the dispensation of Katherine's estate." Dipping the pen into the inkwell, he began, "I, Katherine Beatrice Camden-Carey, Viscountess Halsingham, on this day . . ."

Danae blinked furiously as tears stung her eyes. With an almost reverent appreciation of his selflessness, she watched his hand dance across the page, his deep voice a mere hum at the back of her mind. No one had ever risked anything, let alone his life, in an attempt to help her. The concept was humbling, to say the very least. But, even more, it was downright frightening. What if she couldn't live up to the faith he was entrusting in her? As his bold script filled the blankness of the page, she worried and fretted. Not about herself. She had nothing to lose. But Sion . . .

"Well . . ." Sion put the pen down, his eyes skimming what he had just written. "How does it sound to you?" He glanced up, seeking her approval, but instead his breath caught at the look in her eyes.

"It sounds wonderful," she whispered.

Sion shook his head ruefully, still blinded by the appreciation shining in her eyes. He didn't dare imagine it could be something more. "You didn't listen to a word of what I just wrote, did you?"

"No."

He picked up the sheet and handed it across the desk to her. "You had better read it carefully, then sign at the bottom. Be sure the signature is a bit shaky. Don't forget, you are signing this on your

deathbed." Frowning, he sat back in his chair.
"Next I'll have to get the magistrate to witness it."

Danae was pushing a few things out of her way.
At his words, she looked up. "Will that be a problem?"

There was a dangerous glint to Sion's eyes when
he looked at her. "Oh, no, he'll give me no problems. He owes me too much to deny me anything."
His lips twisted in disgust. Not eager to get into that
kettle of fish, Danae dipped the pen in the ink.

"You had better read that first," he warned softly
when she bent her head over the last will and testament of the Viscountess Halsingham.

"Why?" she asked absently, glancing up. "I trust
you in this. It's not as if I have much choice in any
case, now do I?" Then she paused and teased him
with a slight smile. "Do you trust me?" She didn't
even wait for his answer before she returned her attention to the vellum. The sound of the pen
scratching against the paper was the only sound in
the study.

Sion watched as the sun glinted in her newly
dyed hair. Her transformation was amazing. Every
day she changed something: the way she walked,
the tone of her voice, a new mannerism. He
frowned at the black frock hanging on her slender
frame. It looked to be one of Mrs. Turlow's. All that
was needed now was new plumage and their creation would be perfect. He almost regretted that
soon the old Katherine would be completely laid to
rest. She had been a soul in pain, but her bravery
had been rather inspiring. Look what she had done
for him. He glanced about the pristine study.
Across the room, he caught his reflection in a mirror. If he had not actually lived through these last

hellish years, he would almost swear it had been nothing but a horrible nightmare.

Aware of the silence in the room, he looked over at Danae and caught her staring at him.

"Are you all right?" she asked with a worried frown.

"Just reminiscing," he shrugged.

Danae's eyes sympathized with him. "Tory?"

He shook his head. "Katherine. She was quite a lady. I shall never forget her."

Tears welled in Danae's eyes. "Neither shall I," she whispered. No matter how she might wish to deny it, she knew that Katherine would always remain a part of her.

Sion leaned forward and held out his hand.

Danae leaned forward and placed hers within his. She felt his warmth and strength enfold her.

With a wistful smile, he said, "Now it's just the two of us."

"And Mrs. T.," she reminded him with a grin, her fingers clinging to his.

His lips quirked wryly as he murmured, "How could I forget."

"Where are you taking me, Mrs. T.?" Danae panted, amazed at how weak she could still be at times. After a short pause, she hurried on, trying to catch up with the vigorous woman's pace.

"Tae the attic."

Danae came to an abrupt halt on the stairs. The last thing she wanted to do was spend time in the murky maze of some dusty attic. She had better things to do with her days now, thank heavens.

Mrs. Turlow also paused and looked down at her.

"Is there some reason why you are taking me up there?"

"Aye, I found the trunk." Mrs. Turlow waved her on as she continued up the stairs.

"But I thought you told me all the other trunks had been lost or past saving."

"Nay, lassie. 'Tis her ladyship's." Stopping before a worn door, Mrs. Turlow lifted the chatelaine hanging from her waist, selected a key, then bent over to slip it into the lock.

Danae frowned, then she felt a surge of curiosity. "Oh, you mean the marchioness's?"

"Aye." Mrs. Turlow disappeared into the darkness beyond the open door. Soon a dim light seeped down the stairs, and Danae, holding her skirts high, stepped into the musty air.

It was a montage of sights and smells not too different from the ones she had spent most of her life in. The lanterns cast an eerie glow over the vast cavernous rooms. Hundreds of years of heirlooms and casual clutter were weighed down with faded cloths and smothering dust—dour sentinels to generations of Derehams. Cobwebs fluttered in a helter-skelter pattern from floor to ceiling, and everywhere she looked were the tiny paw prints of the attic's occupants.

Hearing the bumps and mutterings of Mrs. Turlow, Danae turned toward the noise. Even before she saw her friend she could see that the air was laden with a film of disturbed dust.

Coughing and batting at the cloying stuff swirling around her, Danae came upon the energetic lady, bumside up, kneeling upon a huge wardrobe trunk. She could see by the drag marks on the dusty floor that it had just recently been manhandled out of some hidey-hole and brushed clean. Mrs. Turlow's broad bottom twitched back and forth as she struggled to pull something out from behind the trunk she was unsteadily perched on.

"Let me help you with that," Danae said as she stepped gingerly over indefinable objects strewn about the floor.

"Nay," the now filthy woman grunted, "Nae sense we both be tousy. I dinna have the chance tae look in this one afore." She groaned as she strained against the stubborn object.

Ignoring Mrs. T.'s grumbles not to get dirty, Danae pushed her way over to her side. Steadying the old lady with one hand, she helped yank at what appeared to be a large millinery storage chest that was definitely stuck beneath an untidy stack of small tables. After several minutes of an unyielding tug-of-war, they straightened, Mrs. Turlow pressing a callused hand to her back.

"Perhaps I should go down and get Ned?" Danae offered, but the stubborn dame just shook her head. Deferring to her elder, Danae followed the instructions given, and on the count of three, they both applied all their combined muscle in one mighty tug. Danae yelped when the chest popped free with a suddenness that sent both women tumbling backward onto the floor in a puff of dust. Unfortunately, on their way down, they tipped over an unsteady object, its holland-cloth dumping an accumulation of years of dust and debris over them.

Coughing and sputtering, they sat up and blinked at each other, the loose dust on their eyelashes sprinkling down over their gray-laden cheeks. Each woman looked like a ghost to the other: dust now coated their frocks, turning the unrelieved black into a chimney-sweep's rags. Their hair was matted with clinging cobwebs sporting all sorts of gruesome adornments. Only their dust-fringed eyes were a startling shock of brilliance in the colorless masks as they blinked at each other.

Bursting into laughter, they each raised a hand and pointed at the other's absurd appearance. Soon tears were streaking muddy paths down their faces, which, unfortunately, make them laugh even more. It took a bit of mirthful stumbling, but somehow they finally managed to help each other to their feet. Still chuckling, they tried to slap away the worst of the damage while giving their heads a vigorous shake. It took a good quarter hour before their good-natured efforts bore some remedy.

Satisfied they had done the best they could, they turned to raise the heavy lid of the wardrobe trunk. It was packed to the rim, tissue covering the top frocks, their vibrant colors barely discernible through the thin paper. Mrs. Turlow swept the packing paper off and placed it over her dirty shoulder while Danae's eyes widened in wonder as she took in the sight of a sapphire blue riding habit, carefully folded. She reached out a tentative finger and brushed the plush nape.

"Weel, what do ye ken?"

Danae was almost mesmerized by the rich material. Never had she seen the like. She jumped when Mrs. Turlow's arm reached past her and whisked the habit aside, careful as she placed it over the tissue on her broad shoulder. The shimmering silk exposed beneath made Danae gasp. She didn't know if it was a pale lilac-gray or a fragile turquoise, the two hints of colors shifting and melding with such delicacy in the muted light. This time she did not dare touch the exquisite fabric.

"Oh, Mrs. T., they are so beautiful." Then her brows knitted in doubt. Slowly, she backed away from the temptation. "I don't think this is a good idea, though. After all, these are the marchioness's and shouldn't be touched. His lordship, I'm sure, would not approve."

Mrs. Turlow shrugged. "I dinna think he even knows they're here."

Danae watched as Mrs. Turlow next pulled out a couple of ballgowns until she revealed a lovely plaid, all soft purples, grays, and pinks. It looked to be a daydress. Not being able to help herself, she gently drew it out and held it up, careful not to brush it against her dusty skirts. The bodice was soft gray velvet with a cascade of the palest pink lace at the high collar. The sleeves were tight-fitted with a fall of the same lace gracing the cuffs. The skirt flared out in a slimmer cut, designed to hug the hips. The bustle was light and unobtrusive. The delicate wool appeared to be as luxuriant to the touch as the velvet bodice. The gown was perfectly enchanting and looked to be close to her size. Sighing, she carefully refolded and placed it back into the trunk.

Mrs. Turlow bumped her shoulder as she came to stand beside her, also looking down into the trunk. "Ye dinna like it, lassie?"

"Oh, no, it is perfect." She turned away to step from the trunk when her shoulder was grabbed from behind and pulled with an abruptness that sent her staggering in a circle. She found herself facing Mrs. Turlow, who was trying to hold the dress up against her. Her heart thumping, Danae stood still as the soft folds fell about her dusty skirts, the lace tickling her chin. "Careful, Mrs. T., of the dust," she worried aloud.

"Dinna fash yerself. 'Twill brush off."

Danae squinted down and bit off a groan. It was so lovely. Never had she been this close to such beauty. Hopeful, she peeked up at Mrs. Turlow and felt an odd sense of relief when she saw the satisfied nod. Did that mean she did the dress justice?

"Aye, 'twill fit."

Then the lovely frock was thrown over her own shoulder. Quickly, she snatched it off her dusty arm, despite Mrs. Turlow's reassurances. Danae could smell the faint scent of rose sachet and wondered if it had been Tory's favorite scent. She had such an urge to take the dress and run. It was almost too tempting to just follow Mrs. Turlow's lead.

However, she knew she could not. "No," she told Mrs. Turlow, adamant in her decision. Swallowing her disappointment, she began to replace it in the trunk, pushing aside Mrs. Turlow's hands when she tried to stop her. "I cannot intrude on the marchioness's things, Mrs. T. It is disrespectful."

Mrs. Turlow shot her a fierce scowl. "So ye would rather deprive me o' me few frocks?"

Danae blushed, not realizing that she had been causing the old lady such an inconvenience. "Mrs. T., why didn't you tell me sooner? Now I feel just awful." Biting her lip, Danae again looked down at the dress. It was so pretty, so feminine. Already she could feel the lush velvet and wool encase her body. "I suppose just taking one couldn't hurt." Then she added in a rush, "But, it would only be until I can get into town and exchange a few of my jewels. Then I can get my own frocks made." The thought of her new independence made her glow inside.

Then a sudden thought struck Danae. Looking around, she asked, "Where are the portraits kept, Mrs. Turlow?"

The woman shrugged, all her attention devoted to repacking the gowns still thrown over her shoulder. After a moment, she paused and straightened up, looking toward her left. "I ken I saw them o'er there."

Taking one of the lanterns, Danae moved through the eerie clutter while searching about her. A good distance away from the circle of light surrounding Mrs. Turlow, she spied rows of holland-covered frames leaning against a wall. Careful to hold her lamp high, she weaved her way around shrouded shapes, her flickering light causing weird shadows to dance about her. When she reached the wall, she set the lantern upon a tilted tabletop and cautiously lifted the filthy cloths.

Tory wasn't hard to find; her huge portrait was leaning on the top of the fourth row to Danae's right. For a long time Danae stared down at it, trying to swallow past a sudden lump in her throat.

Seated on a garden bench, Tory's saffron skirts spread out about her in a gay splash of color amid the muted background of Dereham's gardens. Standing behind her, Sion smiled down on his wife, his hand reaching down over her right shoulder. Tory was reaching up with her left hand, her fingers clasped firmly in his and her cheek rested against their entwined fingers. Against the flesh tones of their skin, Danae could see the gold of their wedding bands.

Tory's green eyes peeked sideways at Danae, a slight smile gracing her softly tinted lips. Danae unconsciously bit her own lip, her smudged fingertips pressing tight against her mouth.

So this was the tragic Marchioness of Dereham, Sion's beloved wife.

Hello, Tory.

Of course, only silence was Tory's response to her greeting.

Having learned something of the powerful man

who had been this girl's husband, Danae had to admit that Tory wasn't anything like what she had imagined—other than her youth. Her smile was endearing and shy, and her deepset eyes were wide with girlish innocence and a fragile vulnerability. Otherwise, Sion's wife was almost plain, possessed of nothing remarkable that one would take note of. Her fey features, even in full maturity, would never have laid any claim to beauty. Yet there was something about her that drew you to her—an aura of gentleness that seemed to warm you as you looked into her eyes. Tory had been one of those rare people who instinctively inspired trust—a trust so deep that there would have been no hesitation in sharing one's innermost secrets. This had been a truly gentle lady.

Even so, if her beauty was to be judged by the look in Sion's gaze as he smiled down on her, Tory was, without a doubt, the most beautiful woman who had ever graced this earth. Danae gained a new prospective of Sion that day. It was now easy to see why he was still in such pain over the loss of his young marchioness. Heavens, it made her melancholy just standing there and gazing up into Tory's face, for Danae knew that, had fate taken another turn, she might have been able to call Tory her friend.

Danae didn't know how long she stood there before she felt Mrs. Turlow behind her.

"They must have loved each other very much," she whispered, trying to hide her twinge of envy.

"Aye, she was a bonny one. And his lordship doted on her something fierce."

The attic was quiet as they stood there shoulder to shoulder studying the painting.

I promise I will watch over him for you, Tory. Leaning

down, Danae wiped away a tiny snarl of old cobweb from the inner corner of the frame. *And you will find peace,* she vowed, taking one last look into Tory's wistful eyes.

Making a hasty decision, perhaps without giving it the proper reflection, Danae turned toward Mrs. Turlow. "Please have this brought down and hung in the study where it belongs."

The old lady stared at her, openmouthed. "Well, now, I dinna ken—"

Danae cut her off as she picked up the lamp and headed back toward the trunk, still standing open in the middle of the circle of light. "I will take full responsibility, Mrs. T."

Frowning, Mrs. Turlow hurried after her. "'Tis nae me I'm aworrin' about. . . ."

Danae threw a smile over her shoulder, again interrupting her. "Well, there you are. Nothing to worry about."

Mrs. Turlow's mouth screwed up. The girl dinna know what she was going up against. As always, she wanted to protect her lamb, but mayhap it was best to just stand back this time and let them tussle it out. Danae was becoming overly confident if she thought she could manipulate his lordship. In too many ways, Danae was like a toddler learning to find its unsteady way in the world. And just like that innocent explorer, the lassie would have to learn from her fair share of bumps and scrapes. It was sad but true that life couldn't be all hugs and kisses.

However, she wasn't too sure that his lordship wouldn't come out with a few bruises himself afore the dust all settled.

Eight

Sion raised his head as he heard a bump, crash, curse, and admonishment, all in that order. With a frown, he wiped the lather from his face and hastily buttoned his shirt as he stepped out onto the landing. Leaning over the balustrade, he peered into the hall below. After a minute, he again heard a gruff scolding followed by an ominous thump.

"Mrs. T.?" he called down.

Almost instantly, she appeared below, glancing around. "Aye?"

"Up here." Sion leaned over farther. "What is all the racket down there? Did I hear something break?"

"Aye." She waved, disgruntled, into the study. "The beetlehead bumped intae the drum an' knocked it o'er. Now, dinna fash yerself. 'Twas but a cup what broke."

Before she had even finished, a surly voice lambasted her from the room's interior, "An' watch wha' ye say aboot me, woman, or I'm thinkin' I'll jus' be a-droppin' the bleedin' thing right 'ere an' let ye 'ang it yerself!" The invective trailed off to muffled curses as Sion stepped down the stairs.

"What are you doing?" His curiosity overrode his irritation.

It was obvious by the militant light in Mrs. Turlow's

eyes as she glared into the study that she wanted to take care of the knave forthwith instead of replying to her employer. Distracted, she explained, "We're hanging the marchioness's portrait."

Sion froze on his descent, surprise widening his eyes. Then, as rage suffused his features, his eyes narrowed and lips thinned as he bounded down the rest of the stairs and strode past the startled housekeeper into the study. There he stopped in disbelief and took in the sight before him. A complete stranger was balancing on an old chair while he tried, with valiant effort, to set the huge oil of himself and Tory over the mantel in its prior place. Sion felt his blood surging to his head, and within seconds he could swear he saw red as he glared up at the portrait.

"What is the meaning of this?" His voice was so controlled, so softly spoken, that Mrs. Turlow swallowed anxiously. He swung about, impaling her with piercing black eyes. "Who authorized this?" As if he didn't know!

She swore she could see red glints sparking in his lordship's eyes, and cautiously she stepped back. It was almost like seeing the Hellhound of Dereham unleashed again and taking a vindictive piss on the new carpet. She opened her mouth to speak, then promptly shut it. The last thing she wanted to do was sic him on her little lamb.

Sion's eyes narrowed as he watched her stalwart effort to protect the culprit. Grim lips twisted into an unpleasant grimace. He did not like the thought that his servant was more loyal to that ungrateful chit than to him.

"Where is she?" he demanded softly.

Even as she was casting about for a way to divert

him, her eyes involuntarily flicked to the open French doors leading out to the gardens.

"Thank you," he spoke with heavy sarcasm.

Sion flung one more glare at the stranger who was now staring curiously over his straining shoulder at him. His stance wide, Sion pointed at the poor man with a threatening scowl. The man jumped and almost tottered off his unsteady perch when Sion's voice thundered at him, "Remove it! Now! And if that stubborn hellion is so taken with it, you may hang it in her rooms!" With this, he stormed through the doors and out into the gardens.

Mrs. Turlow bit her lip and glanced at the portrait, shrugging as she met her brother's bulging eyes. Biting out a curse, he hurriedly began to struggle with the frame, crumbling under its weight as he pulled it from the mantle. He had just managed to set the frame onto the floor with a thump before he fell over backward with an obscenity.

"Shut yer disgustin' mouth, Jamie! 'Tis a noble manor ye are in, nae some boozy-house." Mrs. Turlow stood over her bruised brother, scowling down on him.

Shooting her a glare, he rubbed his sore bum and mumbled sullenly, "'Tis nae what I be hearin'."

The ominous silence that followed had Jamie tensing. In a flash his arms came up over his head, seeking to protect himself from the usual boxing his elder sister dealt out. Instead, Mrs. Turlow chose to kick the exposed crack of his arse—hard.

Never had the clumsy witling ever found a pair of trousers that didn't sag low over his scrawny hips, exposing half his bum to the world. She was beginning to know that odious sight as well as the back of her hand. Mrs. Turlow sighed in disgust, already regretting her soft heart in giving the bobble a job, blood or nae.

As Sion strode down the path, he found himself so angry that he could hardly keep his thoughts straight.

How dare she? Couldn't she understand that this was not helping him to put his past firmly behind him? He had a new life and he liked it. As much as he had loved Tory, he had to leave her out; otherwise, he was afraid that she might drag him down again to where he had just fought like hell to escape. He shuddered when he remembered the bottomless abyss he had inhabited for so long. He loved the feel of the sunshine and fresh air, the laughter and the cleanliness. But, most of all, he loved the pride he was taking in himself again. And he was *damned* if he would let "Danae" pull him back into that morass of self-pity and guilt by having to stare into Tory's innocent face every day. After all, he had admitted that he needed to go back and finish the mystery once and for all. What more did the woman want of him?

Spotting a flash of color among the shrubbery, the marquis veered in that direction, and around the next hedge he came upon her engaged in an animated conversation with the new gardener. As he took in her appearance, he stopped cold in his tracks. He couldn't believe it! There she stood, her waist-length hair cascading down her slender back in rich auburn waves, the sun dancing about its red highlights. Her face, for the first time that he could remember, was truly carefree and joyous. And forming to her newly found svelte curves like a glove was one of Tory's dresses.

Sion closed his eyes as the world swayed about him. He remembered that dress; it had been delivered to the town house just days after Tory's death. Breathing deeply, he opened his eyes and charged ahead, glaring into Danae's surprised amber eyes as she looked up.

"My lord," she greeted hesitantly, watching as he bore down on her with death radiating from ruthless eyes.

"What the hell do you think you are doing, my girl?"

She blinked, wordless at the sight of his rage. With a perplexed look at Ned, who had stepped closer behind her, she waved the timid boy back. "Have I done something?" she asked in bewilderment, then she could feel the color bleed from her face. She swallowed, her hands clenching the folds of her skirt. It was just as she had predicted in the attic, only she hadn't expected quite this reaction.

His harsh laugh grated painfully on her ears. "Done something? What haven't you done? would be more to the point." He stepped nose to nose with her. When he spoke, a shiver of unease crept along her spine. "It was bad enough dredging up Tory's face and putting it up in my study without even consulting me, but this . . ." He flicked the lace at her throat with fingers that trembled with the urge to throttle her. "Now you even have the audacity to traipse about in her clothes. Who gave you permission?" He did not even know why he said the last. It wasn't that she was wearing one of his wife's frocks; it was this one that brought the bile of self-condemnation surging up his throat.

With an effort, Danae bit back her own anger, guilt, and hurt. He was making it all too obvious that the sight of her in his precious wife's dress was intolerable. The pain that ripped through her left her breathless. All the old insecurities were starting to nip at her again.

Through stiff lips she apologized, almost stumbling over the first words. "Forgive me. I thought you wouldn't mind if I borrowed just one," she lied. Of course she had suspected that he would not be pleased, but this rage had her stunned. "I had been taking advantage of Mrs. T.'s thoughtfulness much too long. Obviously, I misjudged your friendship. I will retire to my room and remove it immediately." Her cheeks burning and tears threatening, Danae tried to step around him. However, he blocked her path, his belligerent frown a warning that this was not over yet.

"Don't be ridiculous! Of course we are friends!" he grated out, glaring down at her now impassive face. He paused and counted to ten, forcing his rage down. He knew that dictating to Danae would get him nowhere—fast. Taking a deep breath, he tried to address her in a reasonable tone, though his voice came across harsh and embittered even to his ears. "There is no need for you to wear Tory's dresses. If you had only asked me you would have known that I had already sent for the damned seamstress."

Now it was her turn to become livid. Such generosity! As if she hadn't been walking about all these months in Mrs. Turlow's belted-in smocks. Then he called the seamstress and did not even afford her the courtesy to inform her. The arrogant fool! As if she would come begging to him to clothe her! Never again would she be at the mercy of a man to clothe her, feed her, or dictate to her. In addition, *never* again would she cower before some bully!

"Forgive me," she bit out. Reaching behind her,

Danae began tugging at the row of buttons with furious haste, her trembling fingers making a botch of it. "I did not mean to desecrate your wife's memory, and never again will I defile her precious relics." Almost screaming in frustration, she yanked the front apart, scattering pearl buttons at their feet.

Sion was stupefied as he watched her jerk at the beautiful gown in an attempt to strip it off. After wrestling it over her petticoated hips, she stepped angrily out of the circle of pastel plaid. His eyes almost popped as he watched her full breasts straining against a corset cut to the thinner, less breathtaking dimensions of Tory's figure. A vision of another time, when Danae had lain insensate beneath his touch, his fingers barely skimming flesh glistening in candlelight, made his blood rush in dizzying waves to his head. It was with a deep-rooted sense of self-preservation that he refused to take notice of where else his hot blood was racing. He forgot to breathe when he caught a fleeting glimpse of a pink nipple through sheer cambric.

However, before he could do more than blink, it was hidden behind frilly folds as she gathered the contested dress into her arms. A movement behind Danae distracted him for a second. His glare flicked up and fixed on Ned. A possessive fury blinded him when he noticed the youth's slack mouth and dazed, worshipping eyes gaping at Danae's scantily clad curves. He was about to let loose a scathing diatribe down on the innocent boy, when all of a sudden his head was swathed in the soft, feminine depths of a heady scent and warm cloth. He cursed when something sharp scratched his cheek.

"There!" he heard her yell. "And with my com-

pliments! Be sure you put it into a shrine, then
we mere mortals will know better in the future!"
And as he struggled to free himself of the suffocating material, he heard her footsteps retreat
down the path.

He swore loudly and fluently as he batted at the
smothering folds, finally managing to fling the co-
pious yards of material from him—right into the
unsuspecting arms of Ned—before he took out
after her. His frown faded when he focused on her
swinging hips as she strode with unrestrained violence ahead of him. Lengthening his stride and
pace, he came up behind her, the graveled path
crunching under his shoes. Sion reached out to
grab her arm, but unfortunately, she just happened
to look over her shoulder at that moment.

With a shriek, Danae gave up whatever dignity she
had left and bolted for the safety of the study doors.

"Oh, no, you don't," he swore as he reached out
grasping fingers and latched onto the cambric
petticoat, dragging behind her. He wasn't displeased at all when the thin material gave way with
a rending tear.

Stunned, Danae came to a slipping halt, staring down at her legs now displayed to whoever
cared to look with only the transparent pantalettes
to preserve any modesty. Enraged, hands fisted
at her side, Danae's glare inched up his long legs,
now partially hidden by her ruined petticoat. His
hand was still extended, the damaging evidence
dangling from his fist. Her eyes narrowed when
they reached the wide grin spread across his face
as he casually took in her dishabille, those lazy
black eyes roaming over her body. Her eyes then
popped wide when she happened to glance over
his shoulder and saw Ned standing halfway down

the path, the dress cradled lovingly in his arms, his whole attention riveted on her as he strained to see around the marquis's broad back. Absolute humiliation coursed through her veins as she turned back to the marquis. Pulling her hand back, she dealt the arrogant bastard a wicked slap. Her hand hurt, but it felt *so* good to see that she had literally slapped the smug grin from his conceited face.

Almost, that is, until his reaction erupted.

"That does it!" he spat out, balling up the petticoat in his hands before flinging it down onto the path between them as if he were tossing down the proverbial gauntlet.

Realizing her mistake too late, Danae fruitlessly tried to hold him off as she backed up, but nothing was about to deter him this time as he reached out and, bending slightly, tossed her over his shoulder. All her screams and flailing limbs failed to slow him in the least as he stepped through the study, into the hall, then up the stairs, ignoring a stunned Mrs. Turlow on the way. He did, however, find the time to deliver a retaliating slap to her upended fanny as he came into her room. There he tossed her, none too gently, upon the bed. Hearing Mrs. Turlow charging up the stairs, he calmly stepped to the door and slammed it in her sputtering face, turning the lock and a deaf ear to her fervid pounding.

"I wouldn't do that if I were you," he warned her in a low drawl as he turned about, catching Danae in a headlong rush for his back.

Noticing the hard glint in his eyes, she took his advice to heart and halted midway. She stuck her nose in the air and struggled for some semblance of calm. "You proved your point, my lord. Now would you please get out!"

Sion feigned a sorrowful sigh. "Danae, Danae, what am I going to do with you? Have you learned nothing yet? Well, I suppose now would be a good time to teach you the art of reconciliation after a lovers' spat." His blood was running hot, and he found himself with the compelling urge to dominate her, to claim her as his. Nothing seemed to make sense to him anymore. Even as he started to stalk her, forcing her back step by step, he damned his heartless soul, confused by this insane compulsion. It was not his intent to humiliate or frighten her, their argument in the garden already long forgotten. He could hardly remember what had even started the altercation in the first place.

He felt it when she bumped up against a bedpost, halting her retreat. Danae's cool facade didn't fool him for a moment, for her eyes spoke clearly of other emotions that he doubted she was even aware of. The little bit of remaining space between them sparked and surged with the power of an undertow, pulling their most primal instincts together. He could almost feel the rushing of her blood thrumming with his. His heavy-lidded eyes shifted down, and he found himself spellbound by the sight of her breasts, heaving in rhythm with his own heartbeat.

Sion reached out with gentle fingers and began to toy with the silk drawstring holding in her curves. He yearned, with a biting hunger, for another glimpse of her teasing pink nipples. Again the blood pounded in his head, but this time anger had nothing to do with the turmoil rushing through his veins.

Danae's breath caught as his fingers tugged lightly on the ribbon holding her chemise together. She gasped as his eyes lifted to impale her with the scorching fervor of his frown. Needing to hold on to something, her hands reached behind her and grabbed on to the post digging into her back. Even as she was telling herself to run, her breasts tightened with yearning for the touch of those long, elegant fingers.

Then he did touch her.

She bit back the cry that leaped to her throat as she felt a single fingertip drag along her flesh, just above the edge of her chemise. If his finger had been a brand, she was sure the scalding heat it left behind could not have been any more painful.

Watching him with a helpless fascination, Danae wet her lips. His eyes were instantly on her mouth, his own opening slightly in response.

"Please," she breathed.

The burning possessiveness of his gaze bore into hers as he demanded with a gentle ruthlessness, "Please what, Danae?"

She swallowed. "I don't know. I can't seem to think straight."

Sion's mouth inched closer till he was a mere breath away. His tongue flicked out, moistening his own lips. Her eyes closed when the wet heat of the stroke just barely brushed her own.

"Then I must assume you mean this?" She heard his husky murmur, then he was devouring her lips, his tongue slipping deep into her mouth. She felt his body crowding her, and the weight of him pressing against her breasts and belly was mind-shattering. Her mouth widened as she deliriously drank of him, her tongue dueling with his.

He groaned as she came alive against him, and,

not really meaning to do so or to go so far, his fingers clenched about the drawstring and he tugged it. The delicate material fell away, revealing the erotic sight of her breasts thrusting high in her corset, both nipples straining against their cruel confinement. He pulled away from her insatiable mouth, panting while he marveled at the sight of her berry-tinted buds, hardened with her desire for him, almost startling against the glowing hue of her moist skin. His nostrils flared as he caught the scent of an aroused woman, the essence of her perspiring flesh blinding him to all morality. Instinctively he widened his stance, the surge of his manhood painful as his testes drew up tight and he ground himself into her belly. The single most primal urge of man was suffocating him, making him numb to all but his need to mate with her.

Groaning, he rubbed his erection against the moist juncture of her thighs. His hands reached down to grasp her satin-clad hips, helping her as she strove to arch up closer to him. When her leg came up to embrace his buttocks, he could swear his heart stopped beating. Then more dizzying impressions crowded upon others as he felt Danae's mouth tantalize his neck, the velvet roughness of her tongue stroking along his jaw, sending shivers down his spine to further inflame his cock.

He became aware of the warm, sensuous weight of her breasts now cupped in his hands. The sensation of Danae was all around him: her moist heat cradling his loins, her satin flesh tantalizing the sensitive tips of his fingers, her silken tresses imprisoning his senses with their lush scent. When the pebbled hardness of her nipples rubbed against his palms, his hold on her breasts tightened possessively. The room spun around him as he forced her back onto the bed. His mouth came down hungrily on one of her sweet buds, suckling with the greediness of a babe at its mother's teat. After coming onto the bed next to her body, Sion immediately forced her legs apart with his knees, then pushed them wider still before he laid himself full-length upon her. He rested his damp brow against hers for a suspended moment as he gloried in the heat of her loins welcoming his, only the wool of his trousers impeding his chance to bury himself deep within her. Then his fingers sought the slit in her pantalets, already damp with her desire, and again his lips sought her sweet breast. Sion felt a deep sense of satisfaction when Danae moaned deliriously, her body bucking under his as he stroked through the tender, damp curls into the luscious center of her.

Numb to anything around him but his pounding need, Sion didn't feel Danae suddenly tense beneath him. His fingers only plundered deeper, the intoxicating scent of their passion surrounding him.

"No!" Danae panicked as his demanding fingers claimed more of her, his hot mouth pulling on her nipple, his tongue thrilling her unmercifully as he suckled her. With each gentle tug of his teeth on the sensitized tip of her breast, shards of delicious pain throbbed through her belly to mingle with the unrelenting pleasure his fingers were giving her. Fire was consuming her body; the earthy pleasure-pain was driving her sanity to the edge of a chasm that was widening with every stroke of his tongue and fingers. Sion was too easily claiming her as his, in the most elemental way known to woman, and she did not want him to stop—not ever! He was helping her to realize her wildest fantasies—and a few she had never known existed.

However, on the edge of this maelstrom of sensations was a confused fear at her unbridled response to what Sion was doing to her. She could feel Jassy's condemnation of her, even as she tried to push the elusive threat away. Was she becoming no better then the fallen women Jassy had always warned her about? She stiffened as Sion's fingers shifted; then she cried out, like an animal in pain, as his thumb stroked an unknown point of pleasure. In the next instant her erotic haze exploded around her, and her body shattered as she gave up to Sion the violent release of her repressed desires. Her scream echoed about them, and his ravaged breathing played counterpoint with her cries.

But before she even gave herself a chance to recover from the cataclysmic miracle, she sat up with a frightened cry and gave Sion's hot body a mighty shove, unbalancing him. Free of his weight, she stumbled to her feet, and dazed, she stared down on him. His long body was trembling, the width of his chest heaving with the effort to control his erratic breathing. He was magnificent to behold, and too overpowering.

Seeing the befuddled confusion on Sion's face, she felt lower than the most immoral slut. She had led him on, let him touch her in the most forbidden of places, her body urging him on to even more indecent acts. With a cry of humiliation, she buried her face in her hands. Hearing Sion shift about on the bed, she glanced up and, through a mist of tears, saw a look of rage suffuse the already hectic color staining his face. Instinctively she shrank away from him as he surged up onto his knees in the middle of the bed, his fists clenched at his sides. Still, she stood her ground, for if ever she had deserved a beating, it was now.

Still trying to understand what had just happened, Sion remained on his knees, glaring at Danae, his whole body thrumming with the pain of his interrupted orgasm. He felt like howling with the frustrated desires that were twisting his insides into knots of agony. The sensitized nerves under his skin felt on fire. He had to hold his trembling body motionless or he was afraid that the tenuous grip he had on his emotions would shatter into a million pieces.

God, he had to get out and rid his body of these dangerous urges. What he needed was a woman to relieve his body of four hellish years of celibacy. Then he cursed vilely as he moved from the bed, each movement an agony to his unsated loins. His helplessness made him even angrier because he knew he did not want just any woman; he wanted Danae and only her.

As he towered over her, his anger turned to confusion when he saw her flinch back from him, her eyes wide with a strange combination of fright, embarrassment, and resignation. Slowly he stepped back a good arm's length from her. He could not believe it. She was expecting him to beat her! He didn't know whether to laugh, bang his head against the wall, or find Camden and strangle the bastard with his bare hands! Frowning, he looked away from her stark eyes. Unfortunately, his gaze rested on the lovely nakedness of her breasts, and his gut tightened again.

Danae blinked at Sion as he stepped away from her. She saw his eyes flicker down to her breasts before his gaze shifted away. Embarrassed, she fumbled with the tangled ribbon to draw her chemise closed. She was almost in tears before she finally just yanked at the edges and held them together in her trembling fingers.

A muscle jumped in his clenched jaw when he murmured, "I'm so sorry, Danae. I didn't mean it to go this far." He felt such remorse, even as another part of him wanted to pick her up and bear them both down onto the bed again.

Danae turned away, hiding her tears. What was he trying to tell her? That he was sorry to have let his desire for her get so out of control, or that he was sorry his intention to humiliate her had gone too far. Did she really want to know? Her trembling hands, clenched about the fragile chemise, were pressed against the feverish skin of her chest as if she could contain the wild beating of her heart. "Please go," she whispered, yet her heart cried, *Please stay!*

With a sigh, he turned away after having spent a long minute studying her defenseless back. He longed to hold her and soothe away her fears, to entreat her to trust him again. However, he was worried how she would react if he were to touch her at this moment.

Danae watched his reflection in the wardrobe mirror as he crossed the room. She opened her mouth to call him back, but immediately lost her courage. Instead, she closed her eyes. But she needed to know! Would he look back at her or simply walk away without another thought? Hesitant, she peeked over her shoulder.

Sion stood before the door, still undecided what to do. It did not seem right that he should just walk away after giving her such an insult, treating her like some two-penny whore. He stared at the door as if it would solve his dilemma. He started to turn toward her, then lost the courage. She probably hated him again, not to mention fearing him now. Damn, he had acted like some crazed animal!

Angered and disgusted with his own indecision, Sion unlocked the door. Before he could even turn the handle, the door was thrown inward, forcing him to jump aside. Then, before he could say a word, he was literally yanked, by his lapels, out of Danae's room and into the hall by a ranting and disheveled Mrs. Turlow. He turned quickly to look back into the room and barely caught sight of Danae. For a suspended moment, their gazes locked before the door was slammed in his face. Rubbing pounding temples, Sion headed for the stairs. Then he caught the scent of Danae's essence on his fingers and he groaned.

God, he had such a headache! He did not even want to think about the other parts of him that still ached. Retribution was supposed to cleanse the soul, was it not? Or was that forgiveness? Well, he had already been given Danae's retribution; his frustrated body was a walking testimony to that. However, would he be given her forgiveness?

That evening, Danae slipped into her chair at the dining table before Sion even had a chance to rise. She acknowledged his greeting with the barest nod of her head, while avoiding any eye contact with him.

It soon became evident to him that there would be no forgiveness offered him during this meal, and he sighed as he glanced at the suddenly unappetizing fare before him. Believing his wisest course was to respect her desire to torture him a while longer, Sion followed her lead, and a heavy silence hovered over the dining room as the first course was served. When the silence continued with nerve-shattering persistence into the second course, Sion found, despite his best intentions, that his patient consideration was crumbling with the passing of each tedious minute. Every time he tried to offer a topic for conversation, she pointedly ignored him: glancing over his head to peruse the room, smiling at the footman as he poured her wine, pushing her food around her plate, yet taking small bites of the delicious meal with reassuring regularity. At least she was past trying to starve herself, he thought with pride. It was encouraging to know that he had succeeded in helping her with this problem, at least.

After a while, he stopped trying to gain her attention and simply stared at her, his fork suspended in midair. Was he being childish in wanting some kind of acknowledgment from her that he was even in the same blasted room with her? With a savage curse, Sion let his fork clatter to his plate. His voice was curt as he dismissed the new butler, Mr. Simmons, and the footman.

"I see that you are in one of those contentious moods of yours. Bloody hell, Danae, how many times must I apologize? I went too far; I'm sorry! So what do you want this time? Blood?"

"Now, that's an interesting thought," she mused softly. With care she tilted her head aside so he could not see her smile.

With ill-concealed impatience, Sion extended both muscled forearms after having bared them to his elbows. "So pick a vein, Danae. Any vein. Just be sure the blood spills onto your plate. I wouldn't want to lose my appetite any more than I already have."

Her eyes slid sideways to study the bronzed flesh. Then, without batting an eye, she swooped down, sinking white teeth deeply into the wrist closest to her.

With a surprised yelp, Sion shook her free and leaped to his feet. Astonished, he watched as she daintily touched the corner of her napkin to smiling lips. Mischievous eyes met his as she purred, "Delicious."

With a grin, he glanced down at the perfect indentation of her teeth on his wrist. Though the mark was red and hurting, she had not broken skin. He chuckled, "You blood-thirsty little witch." As he spoke, he had moved behind her chair. Leaning over her now still figure, he promised with a sensuous dark whisper, "But as the Bible preaches . . ."

And before she could blink, his lips latched onto her vulnerable throat, teeth nipping gently, his tongue soothing her racing pulse with long, hot strokes. He suckled deep on her tender flesh, wanting to mark her as she had done him. When he heard her gasp, he opened his eyes and again saw fear on her unguarded profile. Immediately, he stepped back. If it had been physically possible, Sion would have kicked himself in the ass.

"I'm sorry, Danae. God, that is starting to sound so redundant! I'm sorry that this morning things got so . . ." *Hot, wild, unbelievably erotic?* He continued, his voice strained, "I should have exercised more control. I am appalled at my behavior; yet, despite all that, you have to know that I would never deliberately hurt you."

Her continued coolness had him bewildered. He

knew they were attracted to each other. And even though she was still a virgin, he had tasted of that leashed passion she kept suppressed beneath her cool demeanor. All he had to do was convince her that she had the right to experience all or none of her fantasies, but not hide from her natural passions simply because she had doubts about her worthiness to share them.

Danae had slipped from her seat and put her chair between them. His nearness unsettled her. "How can you say you haven't hurt me?"

An exasperated curse exploded from him as he paced restlessly away from her. Taking a turn about the room to steady himself, he stopped in front of her and studied her face intently. With a sigh, he admitted softly, "I didn't mean to hit you this morning, nor was it my intention to offer you insult by . . ." Uncomfortable, Sion felt his cheeks flush hot. God! Now she even had him blushing, for chrissakes! Fumbling for the right words, he continued, "I didn't mean to . . . to subject you to such unbridled . . . that is . . . well, what I mean is, it was not my intention to treat you with such . . . disrespect." Damn it, he wasn't sorry! Moreover, he certainly had not been disrespectful to her this morning—he had been loving her, wanting to share what he was feeling with her. "I promise it will never happen again." He looked quickly away, worried that she might read that lie in his eyes.

Sion, tongue-tied? It boggles the mind, Danae thought as she shook her head, wondering at his obtuseness. As if, with all the abuse she had suffered, he could possibly be so dim-witted as to think his pat on her derriere had hurt her. It was ridiculous! As for what had followed . . . well, she simply refused to dwell on that. "You have nothing to apologize for."

"What is that suppose to mean?" he asked, irritated by the withdrawn coolness of her expression and her avoidance of his gaze.

"It doesn't matter," Danae assured him in a distant voice.

Stepping closer, he grabbed her by the shoulders and gave her a little shake. "Damnation, of course it matters! Everything about you matters to me. Now tell me what I did to deserve this coldness again. I feel I'm right back where I started."

Imprisoned in his strong hands, Danae felt crowded, breathless. "Please, my lord, let me go."

His jaw clenched. "Not until you tell me."

It was getting more and more difficult to hide herself behind an impassive mask. He brought out the worst and the best in her when he persisted to delve into her most vulnerable secrets like this. Wasn't she to be allowed any privacy?

Watching her, Sion frowned, and dropping his hands, he stepped away. "You are likening me to Camden, aren't you?" He could not disguise the hurt he felt. It was close to a sense of betrayal.

Danae cast a sideways glance at him. Yes, the rage and derision she had heard in his voice this morning when he had confronted her in the garden had brought back hated memories. Not wanting to express her thoughts, she shrugged.

Sion just stared at her for a long while, not able to believe what she was telling him. After several tense moments, he turned away and returned to his seat. He sat down to carefully contemplate his cold plate and felt nausea.

Well, he thought, not knowing what he should do next. *That settles that.*

Without thinking, he searched the table and sideboards for a bottle of wine or something to appease the sudden craving tearing into his vitals.

Danae bit her lip. She had never seen those proud shoulders anything but squared. Yet now an air of defeat hung about Sion. How could she be so senselessly cruel? *Because he was cruel to me this morning,* she ruthlessly reminded herself.

The thought that he felt her so far beneath his beloved wife that the sight of her in Tory's dress had enraged him to such an extent had hurt her as Camden's scathing diatribes had never been able to do. Camden had never cared for her, but she had begun to believe that Sion did. And for all her burgeoning faith in Sion's acceptance of her, it had been made abundantly clear this morning that his so-called friendship only went so far. How could anyone offer friendship and then place such restrictions on it? To her, friendship was akin to love; an all-or-nothing situation. If Sion had merely wanted her acquaintance, he should have made it clearer.

Clamping down on her impulse to go to him, she stiffened her spine and her resolve. It was best she had learned this now, before it was too late. It appeared she would have to change her plans.

Swallowing the lump in her throat, she told him stiffly, "I have replaced the marchioness's dress from where I had borrowed it."

He did not move or acknowledge her in any way. Danae looked down at her clenched hands. She was surprised to see them trembling. She wanted to say something else, but everything she thought of would only make her look more of a fool. She was too used to being ignored to expect any further response from him. She knew when she was no longer wanted.

"Good night, my lord."

Silence followed her steps to the door. Just as she reached for the latch, she heard his low voice behind her.

"I received word from the seamstress this afternoon. She is expected back into town tomorrow and will be able to attend you Thursday."

Danae paused, praying he would say something else. *Anything. Yell at me. Laugh at me. Just do not ignore me.* But he said nothing more. Not able to speak without the fear of her voice breaking, she simply nodded, and needing to get away, she pulled open the door.

And as she made her escape, she felt Katherine treading on her heels.

Nine

Early the next morning, the dawn barely discernible on the horizon, Danae let herself out the front door into the brisk fall air. The dew cracked under her feet as she walked the distance to Jassy's grave. Shivering, with her breath misting before her, she wrapped Mrs. Turlow's thick shawl securely about herself. She felt terrible, her depression feeling more like an illness than a state of mind. Her steps felt leaden, her eyes swollen, and her head pounded with a lack of sleep.

As she crested the hill, she stopped short, squinting in the lightening gloom. Sion's tall silhouette was unmistakable in the distance. Her initial urge was to retreat, but after a moment of studying him and gnawing on her lip, she trudged on. She had this compelling need to talk with him—strange for a girl who had always run from confrontations.

Keeping a curious eye on his still figure, she came up behind him. His head was bowed as if in prayer. What was he doing here? Looking past him, she was surprised to see the grave well tended, all weeds gone, the gentle mound smoothed out and delicate moss covering the cold dirt. Over Jassy's grave was a gleaming marble headstone:

IN HONOR OF OUR DEAR FRIEND,
KATHERINE
MAY SHE REST IN PEACE
1860–1882
MAY ALL HER DREAMS
FINALLY COME TRUE

Tears fell onto cold cheeks as she stared down in wonder. Not even realizing she was moving, Danae stepped to Sion's side. She felt him jerk, but she kept her gaze trained on Jassy and Katherine's grave. "When was this done?" she asked, a hoarse whisper all she could manage.

Sion stiffened and moved slightly away from her. She felt cold again. "The stone was set just yesterday," he told her, his voice oddly flat.

"Thank you." She glanced sideways at him, then quickly averted her eyes.

He nodded. After a minute, he turned away. "I'll leave you alone."

She heard his steps descend the shallow knoll. Danae bit into her lower lip until the metallic taste of blood blossomed in her mouth. Then she spun around, crying out, "Sion!"

He stopped and turned slightly back toward her. His eyes were wary and distant as his gaze met hers. It was obvious that this time he had no intention of meeting her halfway. Her breathing ragged, Danae stepped toward him. Sion didn't move or blink an eye; his mouth set into a grim line. Licking at the blood, she tentatively offered. "I'm sorry. About last night."

He just continued to stare at her.

She was sweating under Mrs. Turlow's woolen shawl. "I don't think you are like Camden, you know."

He shrugged. "You believe all men to be Camden. Why should you think any differently of me." He then continued on his way, his long legs taking him farther from her.

Panicked, Danae ran after him, her hand outstretched to grab him, but she didn't. "No! You are wrong. I could never think that of you! Even when I thought I did, I could not. Don't you see?"

Sion stopped again, sighing. He looked up at the pinkening sky. "You don't have to do this, Danae."

Confused, she stared at his back. "Do what?"

"Lie, just so you can be certain of my help. You have it. I gave my word and I intend to keep it."

Rage burned her cheeks. "Why, you . . . you conceited baboon! As if I would crawl to you! I don't need your help! I was just trying to . . ." *What am I trying to do?*

He spun around, glaring at her through narrowed eyes, his anger wiping away any pretense of impassivity. "Just trying to what, Danae?"

Her mouth snapped shut. She forgot what she was going to say. With a sigh, she stretched out her hands. "I was just trying to . . . I don't know what I was trying to say. You hurt me yesterday, Sion."

The look in her beseeching eyes made him pause. He was tired, and irritable and numb. He didn't know if he could deal with this right now. He did not want to be manipulated by her again. Rubbing his burning eyes, he snapped at her, "I don't know anymore what you want, Danae. If I hurt you yesterday, it was not deliberate. You should know that by now."

"Even when you look at me in your wife's dress with murder in your eyes?"

Sion paused, then dropped his hand. He

frowned at her, confusion in his voice. "What in Hell are you talking about?"

Now she frowned at him, wondering if they were speaking of the same thing. "You know very well. Yesterday. In the garden. You yelled at me about disgracing Tory."

Sion snapped upright. "I did not!" he shouted out.

"You did so!" she shouted right back at him.

Just then the glory of the sun burst upon them in warming, golden rays. Yet the beauty of this daily miracle was lost on both of them as Sion stepped closer, emphasizing in a lethal voice, "I don't know what you read into that little confrontation, but it had nothing to do with you wearing Tory's dress." He felt a stab of guilt as he vaguely remembered some of their words yesterday.

Danae stared at him, open-mouthed. "Well, if that is going to be your attitude, then I retract my apology." She began to turn away.

"Oh, no, you don't! We will have this out." He followed her back to the grave. "I can see where you might have misinterpreted my words yesterday, but I assure you it had nothing to do with you wearing her dress. God, how can you think me so petty?"

She spun around and jabbed him in the chest with a stiff finger. "Easily. You made yourself very clear. Why don't you be a man and admit it!"

Sion had to clasp his hands behind his back, or else he was afraid of what he might do. He looked down into her flushed face, pleased to see that she looked just as tired as he felt. Clenching his teeth, he said, "All right, I admit that what I said yesterday could have been taken in that context. But it wasn't meant so."

Danae frowned up at him. "Well, then what did it mean?"

He drew a deep breath. "It was the fact that you had gone against my wishes and tried again to force me to face Tory. I just cannot do it right now, Danae. I wish you would, just this once, try to understand that. As for the dress, it was just unfortunate that you chose the one that had brought forward some particularly bad memories."

Danae felt devastated about the dress. She had an insane urge to confront Mrs. Turlow and shout, "I told you so!"

"I'm sorry," she murmured, not knowing what else to say. However, she was confused by his first words. Wanting there to be no more misunderstandings, she asked, bewildered, "So, you claim I went up against your wishes? Maybe I did—unintentionally, mind you. But, what of your intrusion into my wishes? You always seem to think you have the right to bully me. No more will I cower before a man, Sion, and be denied the right to speak my mind."

His lips quirked down on her. "When have I ever gone against your wishes?"

When haven't you? she thought, angry at his convenient loss of memory. But it would do her no good to beat that subject to death. Trying to settle on something he could not possibly protest, she charged, "Well, you have been kissing me quite often, and I have yet to receive one riding lesson."

"I though we were speaking of going against your wishes. If I recall aright, you were claiming your share of those kisses yesterday," he snapped back, incensed at the injustice of it all.

Her cheeks bloomed with color. "Oh! You conceited beast! I didn't toss you over my shoulder and

carry you kicking and screaming to your room!"
She took a deep breath and calmed her galloping
heart. "And that is not the point. We had an agreement, if you will recall."

Sion closed his eyes and counted to ten. He
hated it when she was right! "All right. I concede
that. What else have I done against your wishes?"

She in turn counted to ten. "We could be here all
day if I begin to recite my list of complaints against
you, Sion. But I shan't, for I will not let you change
the subject that we began. If it was not the dress
that you were angered about, then how was I going
against your wishes yesterday?"

Sion shook his head and sighed. "I've already
told you time and again, Danae. I cannot deal with
facing Tory right now. Give me some time.
Please?"

She glanced up hesitantly at him and felt chas-
tised by the haunted look in his ebony eyes. "I'm
sorry, Sion. It's just that she looked so lost up
there. Camden had done that to my mother, you
know. Exiled her to the attic because she had displeased him. I liked Tory as soon as I saw her and
I just couldn't leave her up there forgotten."

Sion dropped his head back and closed his eyes.
Hell and damnation, what an ass he was. He remembered all too starkly their conversation about
her mother. And here he thought she had done it
simply to goad him. His beautiful, enigmatic Danae
was going to be the death of him yet, if he wasn't
more careful.

Reaching out, he pulled her into his arms, ready
to push her protests aside. However, her head fell
wearily onto his shoulder and lay there, trusting,
and for the first time she seemed content to let him
hold her. He smiled against her hair, feeling that a

milestone had just been reached in their rocky relationship.

"I'm sorry, my dear," he murmured gently, his lips warm against her temple. "Tory is never forgotten; you above all should know this. And I thank you for taking her into your heart. She has a true champion in you. The two of you would have liked each other very much." He looked over Danae's head and sadly pondered the past. Danae was right: Tory did not deserve to be locked away simply because he was still too much of a coward to face her.

"Very well." He felt the usual sense of helplessness grip him as he continued, "If it is so important to you, then put her portrait where you will." *Only please, not in my study. Maybe later, but not right now.*

Danae felt his tenseness. "Thank you, Sion. I will put her somewhere you can slowly come to terms with her being with us. I won't put her into any of the rooms you occupy. Is that all right?" She felt the stiffness melt from his body.

Sion tipped up her face and smiled tenderly down on her. "Thank you." Then his cool lips met hers. She stiffened slightly and he began to pull away. With a murmured protest, her hand came up to wrap around his neck, and she tugged him back down to her. He resisted for a moment as he searched her face for any sign of discomfort.

She smiled up at him and whispered, "Kiss me, you conceited beast."

When his grin burst forth, it rivaled the warmth of the sun in her heart, and then he lowered his head, and his lips were devouring hers, the passion flaring high as they drank deeply of each other.

Frightened at the strength of the insidious urges raging through him again, Sion reached up and disentangled her grasping fingers from his hair. "I can't, Danae," he gasped as he tried to push her away. She fell back and blinked up at him, the hurt she was feeling all too obvious. The sight of her swollen lips, moist from his kisses, was driving him insane. Then he saw that damned impassive mask of hers slip back into place, concealing all her emotions from him again.

Could she be so naive that she didn't know what she was doing to him? he wondered in agony as he watched her turn her back on him. Then all his noble intentions disintegrated with the last of the morning mist as hunger and anger surged forth.

"All right, damn you," he hissed as he almost brutally yanked her back into his arms. Her low moan was captured in his mouth as he covered hers, his tongue plunging deep. The pain of her fingernails digging into his nape was a delicious price to pay for his fleeting moment of guilt in taking advantage of her innocence again. His arms crushed her closer as she grabbed hanks of his hair and held on for dear life. Their groans mingled as their tongues sparred with each other. For the first time, neither drew back but instead gloried in this newfound passion—each needing the other with an intensity that bound them all the closer together, indelibly sealing their fate.

Suddenly, a turbulent flurry of choking dust and brittle leaves kicked up and spun madly about them. Sputtering and coughing, they broke apart, then blinked about them in confusion, for as soon as they had separated the flurry was just as abruptly and mysteriously gone. Disconcerted, they looked down and saw not one speck of dust on themselves, nor one clinging leaf. Sion jerked around and studied the pastoral panorama surrounding the little hill. The sky was clear, the air still, any hint of a breeze nonexistent, and all around could be heard the harmony of birds busy at their foraging.

Turning back to Danae, Sion was surprised to see a sheepish smile on her lips. Mystified, he asked, "What was that?"

Danae shrugged as she avoided meeting his eyes. Then she reluctantly admitted, trying hard to keep the laughter from her voice, "I believe Jassy was just trying to do her job."

Sion stared at her and then broke out into laughter. His chuckling died slowly when he noticed that Danae was studying him with dignified impatience. Smiling, he shook his head. "Come now, Danae. Enough is enough. I didn't say a word when you gave me that ridiculous story of Jassy talking with you, but this is taking the farce a bit far."

"Believe what you will, Sion. Nevertheless, just because you may not believe in events that are not quite explainable, it does not mean that they did not happen. I am not mad, or delusional, but I do know that Jassy communicated with me. And you cannot deny this strange little episode just now." Her stubborn chin angled a little higher as she eyed him coolly.

Sighing, Sion turned to look down on Jassy. Danae was right. Just because he gave no credence to the eccentric experiences that many had acknowledged, it did not mean they did not happen. Lord knew he had his own ghost bedeviling his life, so if anyone should believe in the supernatural, it should be him. He started when he felt Danae at his shoulder. Together they stood there looking down on the grave.

It appeared to be such a common-looking grave. Squinting, he searched for a red, or blue—or whatever the hell color it was supposed to be—aura that should be floating over the grave. All ghostly phenomena were supposed to be accompanied by an aura or some putrid smell, or so Sion had been told. He gave a tentative sniff. Nothing unusual that he could detect.

Hesitant, he turned to Danae. "Is this how it happened before?"

Biting her lip, she shook her head.

Scratching his ear, Sion frowned. "So, she actually did talk with you?"

Danae nodded.

"Do you think she whipped up that little melodrama because she doesn't approve of me?" He could not believe he had just asked such an idiotic question.

God, he was getting such a headache! And he was staying sober for this!

Danae grinned up at him, watching as he rubbed his forehead. Stepping closer, she hugged his arm to her breasts. "Oh, I shouldn't worry about her not liking you. If she did not approve of you, she would have struck you down with a bolt of lightning, or something just as effective. Jassy had never been shy about expressing her opinions or getting her point across, so there could be no room for doubt. I think she likes you."

Sion turned a look of complete disgust upon her.

Laughing, she turned to head back toward the manor and tugged him along with her. As they strolled along, they spoke of the scheduled meeting with Camden and Halsingham, each sharing their thoughts on how the crucial interview should be handled.

Again a sharp breeze ruffled Sion's hair, causing it to stick out every which way, and a strange shiver skittered up the back of his neck. Dropping Danae's hand, he stopped and looked about him, his fingers instinctively combing his hair back into place. The grove they were walking through appeared no different from before. He rubbed the back of his neck. It still felt like the hair there was standing on end.

When he saw Danae watching him with a quizzical frown, he noticed that the breeze hadn't disturbed a hair on her head. His imagination? He certainly hoped so. Uncertain, he glanced over his shoulder and studied the path they had been walking down. Scoffing at himself for his witless imaginings, he turned to reach out for Danae—and stumbled.

Cursing, he glared down at her. "She did that, didn't she!" he charged irritably.

Danae laughed as she pointed down at an exposed root, barely visible through the thick moss covering the ground. "This time I think it only fair to blame your own clumsiness, as you can see.

Secretly he doubted that. Never in his life had he stumbled over his own feet—well, at least not when he was sober. Thank God, drunkenness was not an issue in his life anymore.

An ethereal breeze, barely felt, tickled along his ear. *No, and it had better never be again, young man!*

Stunned, he stopped dead still.

"Hell and damnation!" he swore as he spun around, looking everywhere. "Did you hear that?"

Danae cocked her head, dutifully listening. "Hear what?"

"Never mind," he growled, feeling like an idiot. "Let's get back to the manor; I'm starved," he lied as he grabbed her hand and pulled her into a trot beside his ground-eating strides.

He could hardly wait to see her. A sense of urgency drove him as the carriage came to a lurching halt before the town house. Flinging open the door, he sprang onto the dangerously slick pavement. A dense mist seemed to enshroud him as he turned to the ornate front entrance that now seemed miles away. The same sense of dread made his heart hammer as he ran up the steps and reached for the latch. However, before he could touch it, the oaken door swung silently in and the entrance yawned before him like a great, threatening chasm.

In a flash, the world turned a brilliant red, blinding him.

Tory! *His mind screamed as he ran into the foyer. Again his mind flashed with the frightening streaks of red, now splattered and dripping down silk-covered walls. The constantly shifting juxtaposition of reds, in garish spatters and bold streaks, continued to blind him as he fumbled his way to the stairs, careening into walls and furniture as he went.*

What seemed like an eternity later, he reached the stairs. As he ran up them, they swayed and buckled beneath him, tossing him about. But he held firmly to the banister, managing to pull himself up to the landing. Blood saturated the wool runners, and as he started to run down the hall, his boots became sodden with blood, slowing him down. He was choking on the heavy miasma misting the air, but still he ran . . . and ran . . . trying desperately to reach her door—but the hall seemed to go on forever.

At last, with a gasping cry, he flung open her door and

staggered in, brought up short at the carnage of the once
beautiful room. His eyes sought and found her body. With
leaden feet, he walked across the room and fell to his knees,
slipping in her blood. Tears blinded him as he gathered her
limp body into trembling arms. Crying, he turned her over.
A silent scream tore through his mind, rending his heart.
There, covered in blood, almost unrecognizable was . . .
Danae.

With a cry, Sion threw himself forward. Heart
pounding, his head felt as if it was about to burst.
His perspiring body shivered as he convulsively
gripped the sheets tangled tightly about his naked
hips and thighs.

His gaze shot about the room and, disoriented,
he scanned the freshly oiled paneling of the walls.

A harsh laugh caught his throat.

God, not again!

His hands gripped his face, scrubbing furiously,
as if by doing so he could erase the terrifying memory from his mind. Never had Danae been in his
dream. But then again, he hadn't had the dream
for more months than he could remember—certainly not since Danae had awakened. Why now?

Without thinking, he threw off the sheets, and
grabbing a pair of breeches, he jerked them up his
unsteady legs, not bothering to fasten them completely. In the next instant he was headed for the
library.

Guilt nipped at him as he stared with burning urgency at the liquor caddy. The candlelight reflected
with delicate prisms off the cut crystal, beckoning
him closer.

One drink wouldn't hurt. It will help me sleep, he rea-
soned. Licking his lips, he stepped forward. *Just one.*

Losing the battle with his conscience, he tossed off the crystal stopper and sloshed a generous helping of brandy into the matching tumbler.

"Do you really want to do that?" the soft query jolted him as he began to raise the glass to parched lips.

His nerveless fingers dropped the tumbler, and as it bounced on the thick carpet, he spun about, guilty, to face Danae. She stood framed in the open doorway, the candle in her hand limning her silhouette with a gentle luminosity. Wordlessly, he stared at her as she stepped into the room and came to stand before him. Her eyes flickered briefly over his nearly naked body before she turned to replace the stopper on the crystal decanter.

Her finger lingered on the stopper, and his eyes were riveted on that finger as it caressed the carved design. His breath caught as his eyes shifted up to her face. For the first time in their odd relationship, they stared deeply and honestly into each other's eyes, neither timid in showing their true feelings. Intense, smoldering black probed the sensuous amber, and the tension in the room sizzled, searing his breath.

With deliberate slowness, Danae moved her hand to his throat, and softly her finger teased a drop of perspiration, which clung like a jewel in its hollow. His bronzed chest swelled with the gasp that shuddered through his hard frame. Watching her finger, Danae carefully traced the droplet down, over his collarbone, through the black hair curling over his wide chest. A fine sheen glistened on his body as the finger continued its trek down over his ridged abdomen and followed the tormenting drop into his navel. Sion's eyes slid closed;

his head dropped back as he bit back a tortured moan.

A moment later, though, his groan ripped through the silence as her finger explored even lower, barely teasing the wiry hairs sprinkled lightly above the haphazardly buttoned breeches that clung low on his hips.

"You see, it's not liquor you need," came her sultry whisper.

His manhood strained painfully against the wool, and his mind cried out to her to touch him.

"You are so beautiful. Never have I seen such beauty."

His mind reeled with her barely heard words. However, nothing could have prepared him for the bolt of desire that ripped through his body as he felt her tongue dip into his navel, drinking of the salty drop.

As a cooling wisp of air washed over his heated body, his eyes jerked open and he faced an empty room. Confused, his head snapped about, seeing nothing, hearing nothing. His fists clenched as his eyes fell on the liquor caddy. There in its place, as if it had never been disturbed, was the sparkling decanter and its matching tumbler.

Sion's narrowed eyes drifted to the door, searching the darkness beyond. If he did not know better, he could almost believe that he was losing his mind. Nevertheless, as his flaring nostrils drank in her elusive scent and his taunted loins throbbed, he knew differently.

Teasing little witch. He smiled grimly. So, she thought to teach him a lesson of her own, did she? Test her new wings a bit. She had innocently awakened the sleeping beast within him, and now she thought to play with him.

Well, as far as he was concerned, as of this night, all negotiations were null and void. From now on, they would confront each other on equal ground, as two adults quite aware of the consequences of their little games. And with his experience, Danae did not stand a chance.

As he glanced down at the decanter, Sion's smile turned ruthless. She was so right; it wasn't liquor he needed. He was starved for something much more intoxicating—and possibly just as damning to his soul.

Ten

When the carriage rounded a bend in the road, Lord Camden's eyes widened fractionally as he took in the breathtaking view of Dereham Hall. Nestled in a tight circle of wooded hills, the three-hundred-year-old manor was almost lost in its lush setting, but for the rich glow of the mottled raspberry bricks against the surrounding lush green. A meandering moat angled lazily around the Elizabethan structure to disappear through the only gap in the surrounding hills; in the distance a quaint windmill could be seen silhouetted on the horizon of the moat before its sparkling waters vanished from view beyond the vale. The slopes of the valley were terraced into yew-filled gardens and grass walkways, bursting with a symphony of color that almost hurt the eye. The picture was magnificent, dazzling—and exceedingly irritating.

So, this was the country seat of Sion Sinclair, the sixth Marquis of Dereham. Camden remembered the arrogant bastard very well. On first acquaintance, some ten years earlier, there had been a mutual dislike, and neither had ever tried to hide it. He smiled when he remembered the cub's arrogance shot down as Dereham stood tall and aloof before the House of Lords answering to the accu-

sation of murder. When the horrific news of Lady
Dereham's murder had hit the weeklies, Camden
had felt nothing but elation. And the fact that Dereham had also lost his heir made the tragedy all the
sweeter. Of course, Dereham had been innocent,
but Camden would not have minded seeing that
proud neck snapped at the end of a rope. It had
been a big disappointment the day Dereham had
walked away a free man, though not a forgiven man
in the eyes of Society.

Again his curious gaze scanned the hall as the
carriage jolted to a halt before the modest entrance. Dewdrops glistened upon the meticulous
lawn and a pink haze seemed to shimmer over the
courtyard, reflecting off the diamond-paned oriel
windows.

Everywhere Camden looked—the gardens, the
manor, the village and tenant dwellings, not to
mention the well-fed livestock—all appeared
meticulously tended, lovingly pruned, and pros-
perous. Unfortunately, nowhere did he see any
signs of the dereliction of an uncaring lord. For
years rumors had circulated about Dereham and
his suicidal attachment to the bottle. His lips
twisted with disgust as he realized that the rumors
were no more than the bored fabrication of addled
minds. Such a pity. The image of the arrogant
Dereham passed out in his own vomit had always
held a special appeal.

Biting back a gasp of pain, Camden moved to
exit the carriage. Irritably he waved his footman's
aid away and carefully put his foot on the step just
unfolded—he hated to be touched, and the idiot
should know that by now. With one hand clasped
firmly about the side of the opening, Camden
began to climb down, already expecting the pain

that would flash up his right leg, then down through his right arm and hand as his foot hit the pavement. No one observing the cold reserve he held about his person like a shield would have known of the pain surging through his body; nor the agony pounding, with the impact of a hammer upon an anvil, behind his eyes. Without a quiver to give his weakness away, the earl made a credible descent, leaning only slightly on his gold-headed cane as he stepped away from the carriage. Camden turned slightly as Halsingham came to stand beside him.

As usual, his son-in-law appeared bored; doubtless wondering what frivolous pastime he was missing in London. Every time he looked upon that handsome face, Camden felt a surge of rage that almost choked him. The useless cock could prove his potency all over the kingdom without a thought, but not one seed had taken root in his worthless daughter. He knew for a fact that Halsingham's bastards littered the cities and the countryside of England from one end to the other; but not one was his grandson.

He glared at his son-in-law's unsuspecting back as Halsingham strode to the front entrance just now being opened. Maliciously he watched as the vain man adjusted the cuffs of his immaculate coat. The worthless prick.

You are too stupid by half to realize how fucked you are. By the time I finish with you, you will pray for hell to give you sanctuary.

Slowly he followed his son-in-law into the manor, not allowing himself even a hint of a limp to help ease his pain.

* * *

Before he even heard the masculine voices in the entrance hall, Sion knew by Danae's tensed posture at the window that they had arrived. Closing the ledger he had been studying, he moved to stand behind her. Danae's eyes were riveted on the impressive coach blocking the drive, and when he placed his hands upon her shoulders she hardly moved.

"Are you sure you are up to this?" he asked softly.

After a moment, she nodded. "Too many years were wasted in fear of this man. I mean to continue this life as I start—in control." With a stiff smile pasted on her pale face, Danae faced the door as it opened; her fingers clenched almost painfully about his supporting arm.

"You look beautiful," Sion whispered into her ear as his eyes swept her figure. A rich pearl gray faille hugged her lush breasts and tiny waist to perfection. The bustle and train, trimmed with bands of burgundy and pearl gray velvet, ingeniously twisted with burgundy cords and tassels, lent an air of sophisticated elegance to her proud carriage. She appeared to be exactly what she was claiming to be: a worldly, independent Italian *contessa*. His lover.

Curiously his eyes appraised the two men being escorted into the library. It was with a distinct sense of jealousy that Sion focused on the striking young man elegantly poised in a muted shaft of sunlight. He scowled as he took in Halsingham's classic good looks, the shining blond hair, and the athletically fit body encased snugly in the expensive togs of a true dandy. He shot a quick glance at Danae, relieved to see her beautiful, wide eyes watching himself instead of the posturing peacock.

Forcing a smile, Sion nodded coolly to Katherine's father and husband, in that order. In a rush of bitter memories, he stared into the chilling eyes of Arthur Marlowe, the Earl of Camden. The earl's soulless gaze touched briefly yet quite thoroughly upon his person, leaving Sion with the uneasy sensation of having just been tainted by a touch of evil. Unconsciously his fingers tightened about Danae's cold hand, still clenched about his forearm.

Again he shifted his attention to Katherine's husband, irritated to see the fop gaping at Danae. Sion could see the scoundrel's glittering gaze slithering over her body, no doubt stripping her nude in his filthy mind. Clenching his teeth, he swallowed the urge to step over to the bastard and snap his neck, all quick and bloodless. His body would be gone and dumped into his carriage before Danae even realized what had happened and could yell at him about his abysmal lack of subtlety.

It was time to get this farce going. The sooner both of these men were out of Dereham, the better. Sion sketched a curt bow as he gathered his wits about him. "Gentlemen, welcome to Dereham. I'm sorry that this meeting had to take place under such sad circumstances." His dry voice belied the polite words, for he had just noticed the absence of mourning bands on the men's sleeves.

"You claim my daughter is dead." The words were cruelly abrupt as Camden ignored Sion's greeting and stepped past his motionless son-in-law into the room.

A slight tremor passed through Danae's hand, and reassuringly Sion stroked her fingers. He wasn't sure if the tremor came from fear or anger. In return, Sion ignored the earl's rude question.

"Won't you have a seat and I'll ring for refreshments. Would you mind, my dear?"

Snapped out of her trance at his words, Danae cast a brief smile his way before she moved gracefully to the bellpull. Sion noticed Halsingham's attention fixed on her gently swaying hips as she moved across the room. Never would Sion have believed that one day he would be thankful for fashion's absurd styles as he smiled approvingly at the cumbersome bustle obliterating Danae's rounded hips and beautiful bottom.

With a casualness that was becoming more and more forced by the minute, Sion stepped toward the peacock and held out his hand. "I don't believe we've ever met. Let me introduce myself." After cutting off Halsingham's view of Danae, Sion was finally able to pull the younger man's focus onto him. *The pompous lout.* Not only had he never spared a moment of his narcissistic life to offer a kind word to his abused wife, but now he had the crassness to show no pang of remorse for his deceased wife as he immediately attached his roving eye on the very lady who was the last to see her alive.

With a start, Sion felt Danae at his side, and in a manner that indicated years of intimate ease, he cupped the small of her back with a proprietary hand. He almost laughed out loud as Halsingham's eyes narrowed in irritation. *Think again, boyo. This is one lady who will never fall at your feet—or into your bed.*

"My dear, this is the Viscount Halsingham." When he looked down on her, their gazes locked for a brief moment, and almost immediately he felt her relaxing under his hand. For a precious moment, his fingers caressed her side, then he forced his expression into indifference as he turned back toward the peacock. "May I present *la Contessa di Sala.*"

The hand Danae extended to the viscount was offered with a cool smile. Sion was impressed that she was able to mask her emotions so effectively. She came across exactly as she wished to appear: a bored lady politely suffering the forward attentions of a man she found bothersome. Halsingham gallantly kissed her hand, and as his lips lingered on her skin, his enamored regard demanded her attention. When she realized her fingers were being held hostage in his, Danae's smile became strained.

Giving a rude tug, she finally freed herself from his clutching fingers and quickly stepped away from his offensive presence. Sion noticed how her hand dropped to her side to be hidden in the folds of her skirt. Knowing Danae well enough to deduce her next action, Sion stepped slightly in front of her, shielding her from Halsingham's scrutiny. Out of the corner of his eye, he saw her wiping her fingers with covert thoroughness on the expensive fabric of her skirt.

Camden's impatient voice broke into the subtle tension, as he demanded, "I find it hard to believe that my daughter was here all the months that you claim without anyone knowing who she was." Turning around, Sion saw Camden seated, the earl's shrewd eyes piercing the dimness of the room as he studied the little scene before him as if critiquing a vignette.

With seeming casualness, Danae turned away and stepped to a table farther away as she idly pretended to rearrange the flowers in a crystal vase. With her head tipped at a slight angle, all Camden could see of her was a portion of her profile and the elegantly coiffed auburn tresses.

"A sad circumstance, to be sure," Sion murmured as he sat opposite Katherine's father. Though he realized that Halsingham posed no serious threat to them, he was equally aware of what a danger this cold-blooded monster could be. "The *contessa* and I were coming back from a short jaunt to Paris when we came upon an over turned carriage. The freak storm had caused untold damage to the roads, and apparently her driver, the unfortunate soul, had been struck by lightning. The poor lady hadn't a chance. She was barely alive when we found her, partially submerged in a flooded tributary. Her companion we pulled from under the wreckage dead. Your daughter had already been deathly ill when we found her; there is no telling how long she had lain unconscious in that freezing water." Sion paused, waiting for some questions or comments—anything that would indicate even the faintest glimmer of remorse on their part.

The look of irritation and anger on Camden's face was unmistakable; his pale claw of a hand gripping his gold-headed cane as if it were a weapon. Halsingham simply looked bored as he sprawled gracefully in a chair not too far from Camden, his unwavering attention studying Danae's every movement. If Sion had had any doubts about Danae's claims about her past life, they were as dust now.

Sion continued, his voice now cold steel as his pretense of sorrow fell away. He just wanted them gone. "For weeks she was in and out of dangerously high fevers, apparently causing her a loss of memory, or so the doctor told us."

"How convenient," Camden murmured, his voice dry. Looking at the earl's twisted lips, Sion assumed the old man was mocking him with a semblance of a smile. However, on Camden's cadaverous face it took on the repugnant appearance of a death mask's grimace.

Deciding to ignore the feeble old bastard, Sion continued, "As ill as she was, it was not a surprise when infection set into her lungs."

"But of course." The viperous stare remained fixed on him. Sion found himself curious as to when those crepe-thin eyelids would finally descend over Camden's eerie, translucent orbs. How long was it possible for the eye to go without moisture, he wondered inanely?

Never known for his patience, Sion decided it was time to go on the attack. Subtlety was lost on a mind as warped as the earl's. "We thought it extremely strange that no one had been around to inquire of her. Of course, we had no idea she was of the peerage, having based our conclusions on the decrepit carriage that she had been traveling in and the worn rags upon her person. I had not been aware you had fallen on such hard times, Camden, that your family must appear in public so shabbily outfitted. How distressing for you, to be sure." Bored, he inspected the earl's impeccable and expensive suit. Behind him, he heard a choked sound, and hoped that Danae would behave herself. When his gaze finally ended its inspection on the earl's face, Sion was pleased to see the cad's typically expressionless features suffused with a lethal rage.

Camden looked out the window as he tried to rein in his wayward emotions. After a long moment, he replied woodenly, "I only arrived in London a month ago. It was then I was told by her husband that she had never arrived." He cast a withering glare at Halsingham even as he secretly realized his own fatal error in believing that either of those bumbling idiots could ever do anything as they were told.

Halsingham gave a shrug, his expression sullen, as he mumbled, "How was I supposed to know you were sending her to London? Not my fault she never arrived." Sion's brows rose in amazement. "You are telling me that after almost ten months since her accident you have only within the last month apprised yourselves of her disappearance?" Sion stared at the two silent men as they stared unrepentantly back at him. "I find this almost . . . criminal, gentlemen." And Sion was indeed flummoxed. How was that possible? Of course, he had believed some of Katherine's tales of abuse and neglect, but, still . . .

Halsingham gave an insouciant shrug as he straightened a cuff.

Sion saw Camden's hand shake, then clench before he shoved it into his coat pocket. All the while, those chilling, colorless eyes contemplated his son-in-law. Halsingham was a fool to bait this devil, Sion thought curiously as he watched the two's obvious dislike of each other. However, Camden didn't need a son-in-law anymore, and Halsingham was just too stupid to realize it. What kind of fool would not even know when his life was suddenly worthless and a bloody irritation, to boot? He could almost feel sorry for the bastard—almost, until he remembered the abuse Katherine had suffered for this man's selfishness.

With a start, Sion perceived that Camden was speaking again, "Be that as it may, I just assumed that my daughter had run off. That is why I did not contact the Yard. I wasn't too concerned, for I knew that soon enough she would discover she couldn't possibly survive on her own—after all, how would she be able to afford the amount of food she shoveled into her mouth every day? As grossly fat as she was, she wouldn't even have been able to peddle herself in the gutters of Spitalfields. It was just a matter of waiting her out. She always had been ungrateful and difficult to deal with."

The vase rattled slightly behind Sion, drawing the men's attention. Unhurried, Danae put the finishing touches on her arrangement, then moved to sit in the chair beside Sion. He noticed a distinct glint in her eyes as she stared directly at Camden.

Her Italian accent tripped convincingly over her tongue as she joined the battle. "But *signore,* see 'ow wrong you are? So, *tragico* what 'appen to poor *Katerina.* She become my dear *amica* when I take care of her. We do all we can for her, but . . ." Delicate shoulders lifted sadly; then she continued as she glanced sideways out of dark, lush eyelashes into Halsingham's riveted gaze. Danae's soft lips curled with seductive design. The peacock did not even know she was playing with him, Sion thought with little remorse. "You must be so . . . 'ow you say, heartbroke?" Her question had dropped to an intimate whisper as she easily twisted him around her little finger.

Sion hid his smile as he leaned into his hand, elbow propped on the armrest next to her. What power the little imp must be feeling, Sion wondered in amusement as he silently applauded her.

Mesmerized, Halsingham stared at her lush lips. "Disconsolate. Katherine was the most faithful of wives." His gaze lifted to be caught in the lure of her almond-shaped eyes, their enticing amber robbing him of all other speech.

Camden snorted rudely as he shifted in his seat. His reptilian regard was unblinking as he examined Danae's every move and expression. Sion knew the old man was trying to place where he had seen her before. Almost defiantly she leaned slightly toward Camden, her bold scrutiny blatantly challenging him.

Sion extended his hand and clasped her forearm, giving it a slight warning squeeze. He relaxed as she immediately settled back in her chair. Then he addressed Camden. "The *contessa* had faithfully tended to Katherine all those harrowing months. In truth, they had become quite close. It was not surprising to me when Katherine had asked for the services of a solicitor. She knew she hadn't long to live." He smiled affectionately at his supposed lover. "In gratitude for all her loving care and attention, Katherine had decided to leave her estate to the *contessa.* "

The silence that followed these words was absolute . . . and spoke a thousand words. Both men turned incredulous eyes upon their daughter and wife.

Danae's calm voice sliced the silence. *"Certemente,* I try to speak her out of this *decisione,* but . . ."* An insouciant shrug indicated she obviously hadn't tried very hard. Sion bit his lip. "She was so *insistente. Katerina* say this inheritance from her *madre* is only thing she call her own and she want it to go to someone *meritévole.* " Seeing Camden's expression harden, she added, *"Scusami,* 'ow you say . . ." She squinted as she thought; then, smiling brightly, she finished, "deserving. Yes, that is what she say to me." Her pseudo-innocent gaze flicked to Halsingham's stunned face before it returned to Camden's. Her smile then hardened, the playfulness twinkling in her eyes quickly fading as another indefinable emotion took its place. Immediately, she dropped her gaze to her hand, clasped warmly in Sion's.

Finally, minutes later, Camden stirred. "I will, of course, wish my solicitors to inspect this . . . document." His eyes flicked to Sion's. "And you will not mind if I send a constable to verify this story? After all, it is what . . . now *two* young women dead while under your care?" The softly voiced threat was not missed by anyone is the silent room.

Danae jerked her hand out of Sion's tightened grasp, then shot to her feet. Her voice was chillingly distinct as she glared at the monster; her flashing eyes narrowed with revulsion as she struggled to maintain her role. *"Signore,* if you say this to the *marchese* that he play foul, then you give to me these *assurdo* words! It is me who take care of *Katerina,* as I tell you. My *amante* do nothing! You insult the *vedova,* me! The widow of the *Conte di Sala!* Me!" She dramatically struck her heart with her fist. "From the most powerful *famiglia* of *Napoli,* you insult!" From there, she erupted into a tirade of the most wild, Latin proportions. Sion was amazed with the speed of the words tumbling from her mouth, her voice low and outraged. Even knowing no Italian, he recognized a few of the more international insults known in any port in any country, and he winced. Where on earth had she learned such gutter filth? Surely not from prim Jassy. He wondered if she even knew what some of the words tripping so easily off her tongue meant. Obviously not. Danae's only foray into the art of vulgarity was limited to "drat," a far cry from what was now tripping off her tongue.

Camden sat frozen as he watched her, his expression blank, while Halsingham watched the tirade open-mouthed, admiration gleaming from his greedy blue eyes.

Trying desperately not to laugh, Sion grabbed hold of her madly gesticulating hands and tried to calm her. After having finally subdued her and making sure she remained seated, Sion turned a mocking smile upon the earl. If Danae could be so dazzlingly creative at the drop of a hat, so could he; after all, they were partners and he could not let her down.

"As you can see, the *contessa* detests any insults to her person. It is a Latin trait, I believe. An insult to her is as much a slap in the face to her family and that of her late husband's, both powerful forces in Italy. The *contessa* is most passionate about her honor, and you have grievously overstepped the bounds of what is tolerated. Men have been found floating in a river for much less." He gave Danae's cold hand a soothing pat. It trembled with her rage, and he felt drunk with the joy of her defense of him.

"Are you actually threatening my life, Dereham?" Camden asked in amused curiosity.

"Not at all, Camden. However, I would advise against traveling in Italy any time soon. Assassinations are as prevalent there as a pocket picked here. We are still so much more civilized, even in these advanced times, wouldn't you agree?" Unconcerned with Camden's cold scrutiny, he forced a patronizing smile and assured the earl, "But, getting back to *your* original threat, of course you must speak with the constables if you feel so strong

in your convictions. I would never think of inter-
fering when you are about to make a fool of
yourself." His bored gaze flicked up and met Camden's. "Please, don't think I shall intrude upon
your fun."

Despite his nonchalant manner, Sion was very
close to throttling the bastard. An accusation of
Katherine's murder had not been figured in his
plans. Katherine's estate was sizable and would no
doubt be challenged. They were expecting that, but
not an accusation of murder.

Camden was wily, no denying that, and there certainly was no love lost between them. Right from
their first introduction there had been enmity between them, and Sion couldn't even remember
why. It would be just like Camden to play on Sion's
questionable past.

"You say my daughter died from consumption. It
is hard to believe, since the girl had the constitu-
tion of an ox." Camden's statement was spoken
with his usual cruelty as his restless gaze shifted
about the room; it was as if he was trying to avoid
Danae's still smoldering presence. Both Danae and
Sion were aware of the fact that Camden had offered her no apology.

No longer able to hide his animosity behind
flippant baiting, and no longer caring to try, Sion
leaned back in his chair, his heavy-lidded eyes staring at Camden as if he were contemplating a pile
of cow manure. "I can now see why Katherine detested you and your"—he briefly cast Halsingham
a disgusted look—"purchased stud." Sion's smile
was a slice of hell as he watched the slight stiffening in Camden's relaxed posture. "Do not think
you can come into my home and insult my lady,
threaten me, and mock Katherine. You see, I know

what you are, both of you. Just because I am a gentleman, do not delude yourselves that I won't act
just as dishonorably as you have done in the past.
If you wish to interest yourself in my affairs, so be
it. But I warn you, I'm not the same man I was four
years ago."

The gauntlet had been thrown down and
acknowledged. Into the extended void of sound-
lessness, the two adversaries continued to stare
each other down, the monotonous ticking of the
mantel clock echoing in the tense atmosphere,
neither intending to give ground. The lengthening shadows cast a very unkind light on the earl's
hollow-eyed, hollow-cheeked visage. For the flash
of a moment, Sion thought he was staring into
the empty sockets of a skull. Grimly, he concentrated on this confrontation, for the outcome of
today's dealings would follow them into their future dealings, and Sion wanted to make sure that
there would be no doubt as to where he stood.
Trying to measure the extent of Camden's ire was
almost impossible, as the man was a cold, motionless statue, which worried Sion much more
than if he had been venting his wrath at them.

Just as Sion thought he had no choice but to
kill the monster, Camden's eyes blinked before
he looked away. There could be little doubt now:
Sion had just earned himself a powerful enemy.
So be it. He actually relished the thought of future
skirmishes with this devil, especially if it deterred
Camden's spite from ever centering on Danae.

Danae and Halsingham had literally sat frozen as
the tense scene before them had been played out.
Not being able to help herself, Danae darted a
quick peek at the viscount and found him as as-
tounded as she that Camden had actually backed

down from Sion. It was the first time either of them
had ever seen Camden back down from anyone or
anything.

Halsingham then produced a thin smile, and
as he tried to ignore the combustible tension
around them, he turned to Danae. Sion did not
doubt for a moment what Halsingham's main concern was: his multiplying debts and how he was
going to pay them off before the bailiffs started
stalking him. Sion had sent out some inquiries
and was disgusted at the amount of gambling and
trade debts he had racked up since learning of
his wife's demise. It was obvious the peacock was
sweating now.

Speaking directly to Danae, Halsingham explained slowly, as though to a child, "Of course, you
realize that Katherine had no right to dispose of
her estate in such a manner. As her husband . . ."

Camden's disgusted snort underlined Sion's
words as he rudely interrupted the viscount, his
fuse burning very near the explosive edge thrumming just under his skin, "Obviously, you do not
keep abreast of the laws passed by Parliament.
The Married Woman's Property Act, a revision of
the same act passed years ago, now gives a married woman the right to dispose of her property,
which had been acquired outside of her marriage,
in any way she so desires. As Katherine inherited
her estate some fifteen years before her marriage,
I would think that grants her the right, under Parliamentary law, to do anything she wanted with
it. As you and her father"—his eyes drifted to Camden, then snapped back—"never afforded her an
ounce of kindness, and her dear nurse had tragically died in the accident, she wished to leave all
she owned to the *contessa* in gratitude for her gen-

erous care. It is my belief, however, that she would have left it to a beggar in the street before she let you profit from her demise—she hated the two of you that much."

Camden's eyes had narrowed. Through stiff lips, he murmured, "You go too far, sir."

Sion's smile was pure dislike. "On Katherine's behalf, I could never go too far." Danae's fingers tightened slightly about his hand.

Again Camden's gaze shifted to Danae. For a long moment he studied her. She, in return, studied him. Her contempt was as clear as Sion's.

Camden rose slowly to his feet, the white-knuckled grip on his cane the only indication that he used it for more than mere affectation. "Of course, you know that this is not finished. We will see you in the courts."

Sion nodded coldly. "Of course." Deliberately he and Danae remained seated. The insult was not missed by either man.

"I would have thought you had seen enough of the inside of our courts, Dereham."

Sion returned Camden's sneer, unconcerned. "Not at all. In fact, I am looking forward to it. You see, Katherine was not as alone in this world as you would have preferred."

Camden's tensing was barely discernible before he continued to the door. He even had to open it himself, Sion noted with a grim smile. He must remember to commend Simmons on his lack of punctuality.

One down, and one to go.

As one, Sion and Danae turned cool eyes on Halsingham. He paused before the opened door as if waiting for a word or something from Danae. When she simply continued to stare at him, he

sketched a slight bow in her direction, then strode
hurriedly after Camden, like a dog called to heel.
Sion covertly watched Danae's reaction to the peacock's departure. He was pleased to see nothing
but relief in her suddenly weary face that they
were gone.

When the door had clicked shut, Danae
slumped back into her chair. She glanced at Sion,
noting his thoughtful contemplation of the closed
door. "Thank heavens that is over. How do you
think it went?"

Choosing not to answer, Sion brought her hand
to his lips. "You were magnificent! Camden could
not quite place where he had seen you before.
I'm sure he will be racking that devious mind of
his for months."

Danae thought of Camden's cold eyes assessing her. Nervously she licked dry lips. "Whatever
happened to Mrs. T.?" She desperately needed a
cup of tea.

"As if we don't know. It's no wonder Simmons
was not at his post; Mrs. T. obviously had to get rid
of him if she was going to listen at the keyhole. Did
you even ring for refreshments?"

Rising to her feet, she shrugged. "No. It would
have been an excuse for them to linger, and I
wanted them out of here." She drifted over to the
windows just in time to see the carriage rolling out
of sight. "I wonder if this was such a good idea."

Sion laughed as he strode over to the bellpull
and rang for tea. "I think it is a little late to get an
attack of remorse."

She spun about. "Remorse! What do I have to
feel guilty about?"

Sion stood before her, hands behind his back,
rocking back and forth on the balls of his feet. "Oh,

nothing much, I suppose; other than lying, cheating, and breaking the law."

Angry and unrepentant, Danae glared at him. "I am cheating no one! The money is mine! And talking about being cheated, my whole life that man cheated me! If Camden had once, just once, mind you, shown me the slightest degree of caring, no matter how insignificant, I would never, *never* have even conceived of such a plan. As for Halsingham, I have no feelings about him, whatsoever. I just want to be free of him, and a divorce would solve nothing. After all, he was just being another unfaithful husband to another unwanted wife."

"Now I resent that!" Sion snapped back as he crossed his arms. Being likened to Halsingham was like pouring salt on his lacerated nerves. "Not all men are like your cad of a husband."

"Were you faithful to your wife?" she taunted.

An emotion she swore was pain flashed through his eyes before they became shuttered to her. Silently he turned away.

Reaching out, she grabbed his sleeve. "Sion, I'm sorry. You know I am still not used to fighting back. Sometimes my tongue runs away from me. I'm sorry."

Restlessly he strode over to the oriel window she had stood before only minutes before.

Danae drew back, unsure of herself. She couldn't tell if he was seriously upset with her or not. As she contemplated this, Mrs. Turlow bustled into the room, dispelling the tension.

"So, how did it go?"

"As if you didn't know," Sion murmured dryly, his back to the room as he stared out into the late-afternoon shadows.

Mrs. Turlow huffed, indignant. "I resent that, yer

lordship." Placing the tray on the silver caddy, she moved about the room, turning up the gaslight.

"Don't we all." Danae walked over to the tray and poured a cup of tea. She glanced at Sion and saw him smiling wryly over his shoulder at her. Raising the cup of tea, she enticed him over. He sprawled into the roomy chair before the fire and thanked her as he took the cup of soothing elixir.

Danae poured another, then also seated herself. "It went as expected, Mrs. T." When Sion snorted rudely, she sighed, putting down her cup and saucer. "All right, so it didn't go quite as planned, but overall, I believe it went very well."

"Yes, yes. Quite."

Danae chewed on her lip at his derision. Had they made everything worse? she wondered despondently. It had been so exhilarating, though, to see Camden taken down a peg for a change. Her smile died when she thought of Camden's cruel words today.

As the two sat lost in their own depressing retrospection, Mrs. Turlow busied herself with serving a generous portion of gingerbread to each. Danae's vulnerable eyes touched upon her friend's, only briefly, when she looked up and accepted the proffered dish. "He did not even ask where I . . . I mean, where Katherine was buried," she whispered.

Sion and Mrs. Turlow exchanged a glance over Danae's head as she bent over her cake. Clearing his throat, Sion said lightly, "Well, then. No sense worrying over the repercussions of this afternoon. Monday we will be in London and then the real fun will begin." And raising his cup in salute, he winked at them.

Danae smiled superficially as she took a bit of cake and almost choked.

Fun? No, indeed. This was war, and they had launched the first salvo, with much more bravado than they had intended. One thing they had been adamant about during their preparations for today: that they not earn the enmity of Camden. Then, instead of following their own wisdom, they had let their emotions get the better of them and had gone out of their way to poke at a slumbering snake.

The result was that they had foolishly roused an enemy who would strike when least expected.

Eleven

London! Danae couldn't believe she was finally here. With a smile, she closed her eyes and inhaled, long and deep—and took in a healthy lungful of the city's sooty, noxious mist.

Her eyes flew open wide, her throat convulsed, and she fell helpless to a fit of coughing. Across from her, she heard Sion chuckle and was grateful for the handkerchief that was thrust under her nose. She snatched it up and buried her face in it, thankful that the scent of starched linen and sandalwood eased her throat, and slowly she was able to breath again. Never in her life had she associated the sense of smell to any particular person, but she did now. For the rest of her life would she think of Sion whenever a trace of sandalwood drifted past her?

"London is renowned for many things, but the air isn't one of them," Sion murmured as he leaned forward and, with the tip of a gloved finger, lifted her face out of his kerchief. His thumb brushed gently over a reddened eye. "I should have warned you that the air will take some getting used to."

Not being able to help herself, Danae looked out the window again. There was so much to see, but the thing that struck her the most was the congestion of people and the noise. It was absolutely fascinating. "I've never seen anything like it."

"Don't worry, I'll make sure you see it all. Twice, if you like."

She glanced over at him, and as always his smile warmed her. She was just about to say something when a shrill whistle blasted close by, startling her.

Her eyes wide, her excitement evident, she demanded, "Is that a train?"

Sion frowned at her. "Haven't you ever seen a train?"

Shaking her head, she scooted over to the window and leaned out.

Amazed that she had never even seen a train, considering England was crisscrossed with rail, he tried to push her back so he could close the window.

"No." She pushed him away, "I want to see."

"I recommend that you close the window. We are right next to the tracks, Paddington Station is just ahead of us, and the soot is unbearable."

"Please, Sion." She cast a pleading glance over her shoulder at him, and bravely Sion resigned himself to the inevitable.

"Very well, but don't blame me. . . ."

Holding her breath in anticipation, Danae watched in awe as the huge iron behemoth chugged into view, belching clouds of smoke as it slowed down on its approach into the city's denser surroundings. It was so overwhelming in its proportions that she had to strain her head to look up and take it all in. And it was so close! "Oh, look at it! It's so big and dirty and beautiful."

Seeing her like this, Sion saw her as the lonely child she had been, angry and hurt, refused even the simple delight of dreams to ease her sterile existence. Anger and sadness warred in him at the sight of her childish glee. So much of her life had been stolen from her. His jaw clenched as he swore to himself that if it was the last thing he ever did, this woman would know everything that life had to offer. From tasting her first dish of ice cream to the joy of living it all over again through the eyes of their own children and then their children. She would experience it all. That would be his gift to her. And when he had given her the world, then maybe—just maybe—she would then give him her complete trust.

With a sigh, he propped himself up against the corner opposite her and waited for what was to come next. Of course, she would blame him. With a grin, he sat back and waited, the kerchief, which had fallen to the floor in all the excitement, held at the ready.

First, he heard the inevitable cough. Then came the slight intrusion of a smoky stench, which she batted at as she chattered away, "Look at all the things it's pulling. What are they called? Why there must be over ten, I vow! No, I think there's—"

It was then that the coughing started in earnest. Her shoulders heaved, and he quickly reached out to assist her, pulling her back into the coach. He winced as she struck her head on the top of the window frame, and when she collapsed onto the opposite seat, her hat askew, she was followed closely by a cloud of a sooty, noxious smoke that billowed in with her and seemed to cling like a heavy haze about her.

Sion caught her hand and pressed the linen into it, and again her face disappeared into it. Reaching over her, he snapped the window shut, which only succeeded in trapping them in the close, smoky air.

"Is it always this terrible?" she asked with distaste.

He shrugged. "Depends where you are. As I said, we are very close to Paddington Station right now, so the noise and air is worse. The Mayfair district is much better. The more crowded the district, the more nauseous the surroundings; and, of course, the poorer the section, the more populated. You'll get used to it," he assured her.

Wiping the soot from her cheeks, she murmured, preoccupied with the problem at hand, "I rather doubt I shall be here long enough to worry about it." She winced as she looked at the dirty smudges on the pristine cloth, then applied it to her forehead.

Sion's eyes narrowed as he studied her profile. *Don't wager your jewels on that, Danny, my love.* "I find it hard to believe you have never been to town, never seen a train. How is that possible?" Sion mused as he watched her again gaping out the window. It was obvious that something else had just caught her attention.

"Did Camden appear to you a man who would be concerned about the interests of anyone, let alone a detested daughter's?" Danae inquired casually, without any bitterness.

"True, but he wasn't always in residence. What about when he was gone?"

"I was never allowed off the property. I told you that."

"You were forcefully contained?" It never ceased to amaze him what an inhuman monster Camden was.

Danae shrugged as she wiped the soot from her cheeks. "I wasn't about to get anyone into trouble, so I never tried to fight them. In their own way the people of the Abbey were kind to me.

Camden was not someone a servant was going to defy for fear of being turned out without reference. Camden never forgot when he was crossed, and his reach was endless. How could I blame the unfortunate people caught in his web? We were all his victims."

Sion was amazed at her matter-of-fact attitude. If that had been his life, he didn't think he could be so blasé about it. "Don't you want restitution for what he did to you?"

Danae gaped at him. "Heavens, no! I want nothing to do with Camden. Now that I feel confident he doesn't know me, I want to stay as far as I possibly can away from the man. Revenge is a silly waste of time. After all, it doesn't change anything—won't change him—so what is the point of it? I never could understand the concept."

She looked out the window again and gasped in wonder as the carriage was traveling alongside an expanse of green. The sight of the manicured land, in itself, did not amaze her, for she had been raised amid such huge stretches of monotonous beauty. It just seemed so strange to see it in the middle of this maze of buildings and streets, with a pall of dirty sky looming over it.

However, it was not the gently curving paths intersecting the grounds, or the towering monuments, or the sparkling display of water shooting toward the heavens from the mouths of dolphins. It was the pedestrians, arrayed in elegant, expensive fashions, flaunting the vibrant colors of graceful butterflies that caught her curiosity. She envied the delicate ladies, meandering idly about on the arms of dashing gentlemen, who appeared so attentive to their every word. She smiled at the gay cries of the numerous children racing about

their frazzled nannies. Then her mouth fell open
as she caught sight of the most delicate little dog
she had ever seen, prancing gracefully beside the
flowing skirts of its beautiful owner. Again scoot-
ing over to the window, she fumbled with the latch
until it dropped down. The rush of cool air was a
comforting respite.

"What is that?" she wanted to know, pointing at
the fragile creature. She had never owned a dog before—or any pet. Now she could have whatever she
wanted, and she wanted one of those, or maybe
even two.

Sion's gaze followed her rudely pointing finger
before he gently pulled her hand back in. "Being
an Italian *contessa*, you should know that particular
breed of dog. It is an Italian greyhound, known for
being the lapdog of noble ladies. It was bred especially for sitting on their laps to relieve them of
fleas, I believe."

Poking her head slightly out, she watched the little tan-colored hound for as long as she could. A
flea catcher? Ridiculous—the pretty little thing was
as smooth as an alabaster carving. Frowning, she
shook her head. "What a terrible use for such a darling dog. Where can I get one?"

Sion smiled, enjoying the sight of her enthusiasm. "I'll see what I can do." Hearing a racket on
the other side of the coach, he saw her turn her attention quickly to the opposite window. Her knees
brushed his as she scooted over just in time to
watch an omnibus rattle by, people hanging off its
sides. She laughed at the absurd sight. He found
himself chuckling with her, seeing the comical side
of the ordinary activities. "Don't strain your neck;
you will have plenty of time to explore the city as
soon as we are settled."

Beginning to feel immature and gauche under his indulgent smile, Danae sat back in the seat, and adjusting her twisted skirts, she glanced at him with an uncertain frown. Noticing Sion's indifference to everything about them, she felt a sharp and unexpected anger at him. It was so unfair on her part, but she couldn't help it. He had seen and done so much, while her entire life was spent behind the walls of the Abbey and the world blithely passed her by. It made her feel ignorant. He must think her such a pitiful creature.

Feeling an unusual wave of self-pity, Danae again looked out the window, her earlier enthusiasm dimmed.

"May I?" Sion entreated softly. He drew the linen out of her lax fingers and gallantly wiped away the last smudge of dirt. The texture of her skin was amazing. Never had he seen such perfection, creamy-soft and delicately tinted. Leaning forward a bit more, he kissed the tip of her nose. He felt the slight inhalation of her breath fan his neck. Slowly he lowered his lips. Hers were open, waiting for him. . . .

"Berkley Square, my lord!" a voice shouted from above.

Danae's eyes jerked open as she instinctively pulled away from him, embarrassment heating her cheeks. Then she looked at him and froze.

The tenderness in his gaze was gone and in its place was an emptiness that worried her. Without a word, he pushed himself back against the squabs and stared out the window, leaning with the sway of the coach as it turned onto another street. He looked to be carved out of stone, his jaw clenched tight, his languid slouch anything but relaxed. She could literally feel his disquiet; it seeped across to her like a frozen mist, smothering her.

All during their plans and travel to London, Danae had studiously avoided the subject of what awaited them at the end of this trip. She had always believed that if you did not talk about a problem, it simply did not exist. But his wife's horrible death did exist, and now after long, painful years of a self-imposed hell, he was returning to the scene of the madness. She was frightened—for him, but mostly for herself. She was frightened of losing him. Did she have what he needed to hold him safe from the memories waiting to devour him?

Taking a deep breath, she plunged into this subject she hadn't wanted to touch. "What are you feeling right now?"

"What should I feel?" he queried softly, his hooded eyes suddenly watching her.

Danae clenched her fidgeting fingers together. "Fear?"

He smiled slightly, coldly. "Precisely."

Swallowing nervously, Danae leaned forward, her hand reaching out to clench about his knee. "Sion, maybe we should stay elsewhere. Maybe stepping back into old memories isn't the best thing for you right now. After all, you still couldn't even deal with . . ." Her words trailed off into a stiff silence.

Feeling like a fool for letting her emotions get the better of her, she sat back and looked blindly out the window. She was surprised to see none of the bustling crowds that were an integral part of the road that had brought them to this historic city. Instead, there was a genteel serenity to the pristine square they were entering; an air of wealth and elegance hung about the beautiful homes lining the clean cobbled street. Nevertheless, even as she admired Berkley Square, her every sense was still attuned to Sion.

"I couldn't even face her portrait, so how am I capable of walking into that house? That is what you wanted to say, isn't it?" His voice was toneless, his gaze hard when she peeked up at him.

Feeling guilty, for he had it exactly right, she looked down at her hands. "And if it is?" Tipping up her chin, she bravely met his eyes, then lowered them again; his gaze was just too stark right now to face. "Please, let's go somewhere else."

Sion, noticing how pale she looked, thought it over for a moment and then sadly shook his head. "I have to do this, Danae." *God, I don't want to do this,* he agonized for a brief moment. "Though I think it best I send you to a hotel for the time being."

Fear flashed in her amber eyes. "No!" she almost shouted. "We stay together. I will not allow you to leave me behind. You need me." She bit off the rest, not able to let him know how much she needed him.

Sion breathed deeply in relief, yet guilty and terribly torn between the two. Not liking himself very much at that moment, he smiled into her fiercely determined glare. Not knowing what to say, how to explain his thankfulness, he simply said softly, "Thank you."

She offered him a wobbly smile. "You're welcome."

The carriage rocked as it rounded another bend, and by the look on his face, she knew that they had reached their destination—Dereham Court. It was with a strange sense of reluctance that she turned to view the magnificent town house, which was set back from the square, giving it a feeling of isolation.

It was larger than most of the stately homes along the square. His ancestors had spared no expense on the building of this imposing edifice. As Danae stared at the front door, her suddenly clammy hands clenched about her reticule. This was the moment that counted. Her new identity would be made or exposed the moment she stepped out of this carriage. There was no cannier breed than servants. A shiver of frigid unease ran along her arms as the door opened and a small contingent of retainers trooped out and fell to their tasks.

The carriage door was flung wide, the steps dropped down, and it seemed to yawn before her, mocking her. She froze, pressing tighter into the opposite corner.

Sion cast her a searching glance before he stepped out onto the cobbled walk and briefly looked about him. Damn! He'd been hoping to enter unobserved, but unfortunately, the staff were lined up in front of the steps that led to the front door. Irritated, he waved the footman away and turned to help Danae down.

He reached inside for her hand, and she resisted. She just stared back at him with a wide, fearful gaze.

"Danae," he urged her, his hand closing about hers with painful pressure. He cursed again when she twisted it out of his grasp. For a tense moment she stared at him as if she didn't know him. "Danae, don't fall apart on me. We have a bloody audience."

She blinked, then glanced over his shoulder at the unwelcome sight. On unsteady legs she stepped down and stepped close to his side. "Sion," she whispered, keeping her face turned from the curious stares. She couldn't remember a single dratted word of Italian! For heavens' sake, what was wrong with her? "I can't do this right now."

Empathizing with her, he nonetheless said sternly, "It's not as if we have a choice, Danae."

He thought he heard her murmur, "The hell I don't." Then she went limp.

Shocked, Sion caught her up in his arms. There was an eruption of babbling voices around him, several of the footmen rushing in trying to help him. With one explosive curse from him, they fell back and he hurried into the house, his long strides taking him to the library. Gently he set her down on the leather sofa facing the fire.

The first thing he did was open the liquor cabinet and splash a bit of brandy into a glass. Kneeling beside her, he lifted her head, and forcing the rim between her lips, he ruthlessly poured it down her throat.

He fell back startled as she shot bolt upright, spitting the expensive liquor out with a screech. Blankly he looked down at his now stained clothes. "Feeling better, are we?" he asked dryly.

Aware that the servants were hovering anxiously in the door, Danae was only able to glare at him through watering eyes. Lord, her throat burned! She looked about, desperate for a glass of soothing water. "Water," she croaked.

Sion didn't even have a chance to rise when a stately figure of a man rushed over to the cabinet and poured a glass. With a murmured, "Madam," he extended it with a low bow.

However, Sion took it and held it to her lips. "Thank you, Seadon. That will be all for now." They both watched as the door was shut behind the butler. Relieved, Sion sat back on his haunches and reproached her with a shake of his head, "You know, you could have warned me. I was terrified, thinking you had truly fainted."

"So this is how you show your concern, by poisoning me?" she accused, stroking her throat and sipping her water. "What is that vile stuff?"

He glanced with a rueful grimace at his ruined suit. "That was *very* expensive Napoleon Brandy, smuggled at the cost of life and limb and stored, with the utmost care, in the cellars for over fifty years. My father would only drink the best." Not being able to stop himself, he licked stray droplets from his hand. Thank God, those precious bottles had not been at the country seat. He would have consumed them all, not even aware of what he was pouring down his throat. What a waste that would have been. He inhaled the fumes deeply as if it were nectar from the gods.

"Don't even think it!" Danae warned in a low voice. "Besides, how could you actually like that wretched brew? It's a wonder your insides are not rotted away."

With a sigh, Sion had to agree: it was a wonder, indeed. He glanced about the library, noticing that everything was pretty much as he had last seen it. The centuries-old paneling was gleaming and smelling of beeswax and lemon oil, the rare Persian rug he was kneeling upon was as spotless as the day it had been acquired, and the gold-embossed bookbindings of his great-grandfather's vast collection winked at him in the light streaming in through the immaculate windows. At least here, the staff had taken their jobs to heart and had kept his property in excellent order. No doubt, a great deal of the credit was due to his long-time factor and close friend, Jonas Glendower.

Closing his eyes, Sion rubbed his brow, wincing as he remembered the last time he had seen Jonas. He had been in his typical drunken state, angrily lashing out at anyone who tried to help him. Jonas's kindness had earned him a fist in his face before he had been summarily kicked out the front door. He could still hear the echo of the obscenities he had shouted after Jonas to mind his own bloody business.

Though Jonas had respected his wishes concerning Dereham Hall, thankfully it had not stopped him from poking his nose into his other affairs. For the first time this year, Sion felt a lightness of hope concerning his friend. Maybe not all was lost yet. God, he hoped so. He owed Jonas more than he could ever hope to repay. He had been the only person who had stood at his back during the trial. If it hadn't been for him . . . He should have written Jonas months ago, but the thought of his letter being returned unopened had held his hand suspended over many a blank page. It had seemed too cowardly to offer his apology in such an impersonal way. Jonas had earned the right to be able to spit in his face when he begged his forgiveness. Sion knew it was only what he deserved.

The enticing smell of the brandy was cramping his belly. His brow felt warm and damp from perspiration even as a shiver trembled over his body. Feeling his head begin to throb, Sion wearily rubbed his eyes, wanting nothing so much as to call his coach back and escape to the safety of the country. Away from the condemnation of Tory and Jonas. He even wanted to leave Danae behind. In his state of mind right now, he was certain it was only a matter of time before he failed her also. Just the thought of losing Danae made him yearn for the blessed oblivion of the bottle.

Not liking the look of distress tightening his lips, Danae, with the ageless instinct of Eve, reached out and led him back to her, away from the demons already trying to reclaim him. Determined to keep him safe, she knew she would do *anything* to accomplish this.

Sion flinched as he felt warm fingers brush his cheek. Stunned, he glanced up, and his breath caught in his chest. Danae's lips were a hairbreadth away, her eyes offering all the safety and forgetfulness he could ever want. He had to physically restrain himself from reaching out with both hands and grabbing all he could get from her.

When their gazes met, Danae knew that he was hers again. His eyes now blazed with an emotion she was becoming all too familiar with, and for the first time, she reveled in this strange power she seemed to hold over him. Her heartbeat seemed to slow, becoming a heavy, driving pulse beneath her aching breasts. Looking at his lips so close to her own, she wanted to be the aggressor this time, staking her claim on him. Not even aware of the seductive action, she slowly moistened her lips with the tip of her tongue. His eyes flared with feral intensity as he waited for her next move.

Smiling into the burning ebony of his eyes, Danae cupped his cheeks and urged him closer. Her lips blended with his, and after a brief moment of hesitation she slid her tongue into the warm cavern of his mouth.

Groaning, Sion felt his world scatter into a thousand fragments as her tongue stroked his, mating with his. Then she was slowly pulling away, leaving him starved for more. With their gazes locked, her long fingers traced the lines of dissipation and fatigue on his face. With a sigh of pleasure, he let her soothe his pain away. In the wake of each caressing touch, his skin felt rejuvenated.

Looking at the vulnerability in his expression, Danae felt startled, feeling as if she had just given him a piece of her soul and was now exposed to him. Almost callously she had to remind herself that no matter how much she liked and needed him, he was just a man—and in the end they were all the same. She pulled herself away from the beckoning desire simmering in his eyes.

Sion shifted back onto his heels as Danae rose to her feet. His blood surged at a furious pace through his trembling body as his eyes came level with her stomach. With a gentle sway of her hips, she stepped around him and out of his view. Sion bit down savagely on a moan as his swimming senses breathed in her essence.

Hearing the door sweep inward, Sion stiffened in frustration. Damn her wicked eyes, but he was getting tired of these teasing little games. Pretty soon her fledgling wings were going to beat him to death, and he knew he had no defense against her.

Was he an utter fool, jumping from the embers of his doomed marriage into the raging inferno that was Danae?

Then he heard her voice in the hall, and she seemed to be back in form, the lyrical Italian tripping off her tongue without hesitation. He listened to the melody of her voice a long moment and smiled.

Hell or not, he wanted her and she would be his.

Twelve

Early the next morning Danae made her way downstairs, surprised to find that she was looking forward to breakfast. Actually, she was ravenous. Twisting and turning all night was quite taxing on the body, she was beginning to learn.

Reaching the foot of the stairs, she paused, then heard the rattle of silver beyond the closed door to her right. Cautiously she opened the door, and found the room as pleasing to the eye as the heavenly aroma of food was to her palate. And centered in the early morning rays of the sun was Sion, basking lazily like some satiated beast waiting contentedly until the urge to hunt stirred him again. He appeared to be deeply engrossed in the morning paper as he lingered over coffee. Waiting for her? she wondered with a touch of uncertainty, not sure what to say after last night's confrontation. When a footman stepped forward to close the door behind her, she was forced to move farther into the room.

Sion glanced up and politely rose to his feet to assist her into her chair. His smile was courteous, his gaze cool. "Good morning, my dear."

She took her place and responded warily, *"Ciao, caro."*

She wanted to ask how he had slept, if he had

had any nightmares, but did not dare in front of
the footman. Did mistresses sleep in their lovers'
bed or depart directly after the deed? She was not
sure and she certainly could not ask Sion in front
of the servants.

As she picked up her napkin, Danae noticed a
morning daily, freshly pressed and folded, resting
beside her setting. It was curious to see one provided for her, as such a courtesy had never been
extended to her before. Always she had read whatever dailies and weeklies she could get her hands
on, without her father's knowledge, before they
had been discarded, usually crumpled and stained
with refuse.

Picking up the paper, she glanced sideways at
Sion to see him again immersed in *The Times*. As
she opened her mouth to speak, Danae paused,
brought up short by the silent footman as he
leaned over her to pour tea. Realizing she had been
about to speak out of her role, she silently admonished herself. A slip like that could be devastating.
Again she glanced at Sion, and indicating the
paper, she thanked him in Italian.

He glanced up. "*The Morning Post* will tell you
what is going on in town and about the *ton*. It is better than the busiest gossipmonger on the street. I
thought you might find it useful. I have ordered
you a subscription." Straightening in his chair, he
threw the paper down and gave her his undivided
attention. "What were your plans for the day?" he
asked casually.

She had not a clue. She only knew she wanted
to do and see everything. "I 'ave not give it much
thought. I would like to do some . . . 'ow you say,
see sight?"

Sion's lips twitched. "Sightseeing." Resting his

elbows on the table, he buried his lips in his hands. The footman was trying his best not to stare at the foreign lady but was not succeeding very admirably. By nightfall, Sion knew that most of London, below stairs, would know of his guest. By morning next, the *ton* should be humming with avid curiosity. He hoped Danae was up to this task she had set for herself.

"Might I suggest a modiste as your first stop? If you wish, I could give you directions to a couple of reliable couturiers."

"*Si, prego.*" She glanced at him over the cup. "Shall my style be vulgar or merely flamboyant?"

"You couldn't be vulgar if you tried."

Danae felt a warm glow lighten her heart. She had to admit she would rather enjoy cutting a dashing figure and turning a few heads. She was planning on spending an atrocious amount of money; after all, she had quite a few years to make up for. Her sense of freedom made her light-headed and eager to get on with her life. She turned quickly to Sion before the footman came back.

"Sion," she spoke in a low voice, "I have some jewels I need to sell for capital till the estate is settled. Can you do this for me or direct me where to go?"

With an immediate shake of his head, Sion said forcefully, "Nonsense. The modistes I will direct you to know of me. Just have them bill me."

Danae sat back. "No."

Sion frowned at her. She sounded suddenly angry. "There is no need to hock your jewels."

"No."

Staring at the obstinate woman, he tried another tack. "You can pay me back when everything is settled." He noticed a slight easing in her proud posture. His eyes began to twinkle as he added teasingly, "After all, one day you will want to give them to our daughters."

Her spine snapped taut. The door snicked open, cutting Danae off before she even had a chance at rebuttal, and the footman entered with a fresh service of tea.

Sion rose and came to stand over her. She flinched when his warm hand cupped her chin and drew her head back till she was staring into his mocking smile.

"Most likely you will not see me till dinner," he murmured.

Just loud enough for him to hear, she snapped peevishly, "One must be thankful for small miracles."

"Till later, my love." Then his mouth was covering hers. Heat shot through her as his teeth nipped her stubbornly sealed lips. Even with her mind swimming, she realized he would not stop till she surrendered. Almost frantically she relaxed her lips and again jumped as his tongue swept in, then was gone. "Tit for tat, Danny," he whispered, the words tickling her ear as he straightened again.

Her narrowed eyes focused on his back as he strolled to the door. Unconsciously she reached up to rub her earlobe as if she could wipe the words away. Her lips were still tingling, so she licked them and tasted coffee.

Noticing the footman unobtrusively studying the wainscoting, she turned back to *The Morning Post*, her smile a secret behind that raised paper.

The St. James Workhouse in Soho was the same as it had been for the past sixty years, no matter how many acts of Parliament were enacted to change its conditions. Though Parliament had its

heart in the right place, very few members cared
enough to do any more than was required of
them—meaning, they sat in the comfortable hal-
lowed halls and debated passionately on the
atrocities being committed against the down-
trodden citizens of England. As long as these
bastions of human rights passed the beneficent
acts to relieve their suffering, they didn't really
care how they were enforced. They had done their
duty well, and now it was the concern of the people to carry through with their good work. And
so the greedy still continued to prey on their
weaker fellows with little fear of retribution. Thus,
the workhouses, in the worst sense, still abounded
in the hell known as London.

And it was in this workhouse off Poland Street in
Soho that the Earl of Camden came for the third
and final time.

No emotion other than boredom flickered in
Camden's shadowed eyes as he followed the beadle
down a dingy corridor. Twisting his mouth in disgust, he pressed a snowy handkerchief to his nose,
thankful this would be his last visit to this putrid
hellhole.

"It be good t' see yer lor'ship agin," whined the
irritating little pisspot. Camden's gaze slithered
over the man's filthy back as he silently suffered the
fool. But not for much longer. In fact, he had already arranged for the fool's fatal accident. The
fewer tongues speaking his business, the better.

"How long ago did she die?" he inquired, almost gagging as they passed a particularly noxious
doorway.

"The boy's mum?" The beadle shrugged, unaware of the eyes glaring balefully at him. "Been a
bit ago. Year, I'm thinkin'."

Camden nodded. "Good." His gaze shifted about as the corridor opened upon a murky great room. The tall walls, whitewashed decades ago, supported a ceiling of an inferior glass so filthy that no light filtered through. The cavernous hall's dimness was barely illuminated by the few gaslights scattered along the soot-stained walls, and the vast space was packed tight with hundreds of emaciated and dull-eyed human refuse, toiling blindly in the stifling atmosphere.

The stench of unwashed bodies and urine permeated even the heavily scented linen Camden had pressed over his nose and mouth. With a repulsed glare at the offending creatures, he quickly followed the beadle to a far corner where a number of children were jammed into a small area, young shoulders hunched bleakly as their little fingers stitched endless seams on countless piles of gloves. Camden's irritated gaze fell upon one boy of indeterminate age sitting close to the front row. His empty eye socket was a grim testimony to his failure to pay attention to the job at hand. Doubtless, he had been idly dreaming when he had failed to dodge the needle of the child next to him. However, even despite that gruesome lesson, the boy's face was scarred hideously from his hairline to his jaw. The stupidity of these people never failed to amaze him, Camden thought, uncaring, hoping that Halsingham's brat was unmarked.

The beadle beamed proudly at the pile of white kid. "Got an order jus' last month from the Duchess o' Kent for 'er get-to at Chris'mus. 'Undred an' fifty pair. Gor, jus' 'bout shit me knickers . . ." He paused as he caught sight of the earl's withering appraisal. Clearing his throat, he swung about and bellowed, "Timmy Parker!"

There was a shifting of bodies and a scuffling of feet as a lone figure, gaunt and frail, stepped carefully between bony knees and bent backs. When the child stood before them, hollow-eyed, he stared without interest at the imposing figure looming above him.

"Aye, sir," the boy whispered hoarsely, not used to talking.

Camden took note of the emaciated condition of the child: bruised and battered, all hope having been beaten out of him years ago. Camden gave a silent sigh of irritation. It was clear that the money paid over the years to ensure the boy's health had done little more than line the pockets of the greedy bastard hovering behind him. He didn't mind the money so much as being played for a fool. Just as well that the man would not see another day.

Again he critically studied the child. It was going to be a good many weeks before this pathetic creature could be shown. Nevertheless, he would serve very well; the resemblance to his father was startling, even beneath all the filth and sharply protruding bones. Thank God, Halsingham's seed was so potent. This was one bastard he would have a hard time disclaiming as his.

Camden motioned the beadle away and waited till the man had moved to oversee the men pounding hemp before he addressed the boy.

"How long have you been here, boy?"

The child shrugged. "Always, sir."

"Do you know who I am?"

Uninterested, he shook his head.

"I am your grandfather."

Darkly smudged lids lifted as the child's gaze slowly climbed the vast distance to the stranger's impassive face. Not having the strength to hold his

head up too long, he again wearily looked down.
"Got no one. Mum's gone."

"She was not your mother. That woman had kidnapped you when you were in swaddling," Camden
lied brutally. "I have just recently tracked you down.
I'm here to take you home."

"Me mum?" Fear and confusion warred in the
child's haggard features.

Eager to get out of this pesthole, the earl
snapped impatiently, "She was not your mother.
Come, boy. We will go home and I will explain
everything." Camden turned on his heel, pausing
long enough to thrust a wad of bills into the beadle's outstretched hand.

The child looked behind him and stared at the
huddled mass of abused, thin bodies, slumped over
the endless white piles of kid, bony hands wielding
the menacing needles with mindless speed. None
had the energy even to care what happened to one
of their own.

"Come along, boy!"

Conditioned to obey, Timmy turned and followed the cold stranger out of the only shelter he
had ever known. He was not the least bit curious
as to where he was being led. It couldn't be any
worse than where he had been.

The beadle turned away with an uninterested
shrug as he watched the nobleman exit the hall
with the slight boy trailing submissively behind. He
seldom cared where he sold the little buggers off.
There was always another to replace the vacant seat
soon enough.

Thirteen

"My God, Sion!"

The look of stunned surprise on Jonas's face was almost comical, but laughter was the furthest thing from Sion's mind as he stood poised uncertainly on the threshold, hat in hand. Damn, but he had not felt this uncomfortable since his salad days. His smile was hesitant. "Hello, Jon. Am I welcome?"

Jonas Glendower surged to his feet and came about his cluttered desk in his usual haphazard way, hand extended. Sion felt himself relaxing as he took his friend's hand, then laughed as Jonas continued to pump it enthusiastically. At last, Jonas stepped back and, adjusting his spectacles, squinted through the thick lenses as he took in Sion's immaculate person. Even the distortion of the lenses could not hide the joy and affection Sion saw in those familiar blue eyes.

Again shaking his head, Jonas snatched up Sion's hat and carelessly pitched the expensive beaver onto his cluttered desk as he grabbed Sion's arm, "Come, come, have a seat. I want to know everything!"

Sion smiled, taking in the familiar mess. As he stepped carefully around piles of books and files, Jonas navigated them with inattentive ease, having traversed this same maze for years. It still baffled Sion how this man, who could manage extensive estates, keep meticulous records, and account for every pound down to the last farthing, could live in such utter chaos.

With a muttered, "Blast!" Jonas snatched up an untidy sheaf of papers from a decrepit wing-backed chair set before a sooty fireplace. Glancing about, he finally just tossed them over the chair's back. Sion chuckled as he watched the sheets float to the floor every which way, one even settling onto the burning embers before it snapped into a small flame. He felt himself pushed into the dusty leather and then watched as Jonas manhandled its mate closer, again shoving haphazardly stacked files out of the way. Eagerly he sat on the chair's edge, hands clasped between his knees, and smiled at Sion.

"So, how have you been? You appear in splendid mettle. Just down from Wiltshire? Are you at Dereham Court?" Finally, Jonas paused, squinting through his thick lenses.

Same old Jonas, Sion thought with relief. Years ago he had spent many an evening, lounging in this same old battered relic, bamming Jonas on his dull lifestyle. The two of them had met at Cambridge as youths and had been oarsmen on the same team. Jonas had been a sizar, the only one of their team not of the aristocracy. And the shy, lanky teen had paid dearly for that deficit, easy prey to the snobbish brutality of the other team members. But Sion had liked him from the moment they met, and they had been steadfast allies since. It was at Cambridge that Sion had learned to fight dirty in order to protect his friend, whereas to this day Jonas couldn't throw a credible right to save his life. Sion smiled wistfully as he remembered Jonas as he was then and indeed was to this very day—a shy, unassuming man whose keen mind set him apart from the crowd. For close to twenty years, Jonas had been walking in his shadow, always there in the background. To this day he still didn't know what he would have done without Jonas's support during those hellish days after Tory's death. And it humbled him yet again to see Jonas welcome him so open-heartedly after the unconscionable way he had treated him that last time, two years ago, at Dereham Hall, when he had so callously tossed his worried friend out, telling him to go to his own hell and leave him to his.

"I am quite well, Jon. Yes, I am down from Wiltshire. You will be very pleased to know that Dereham has improved since the last time you saw it, and I would be much honored to have you factor it for me once again."

Jonas clapped his hands together and rubbed them almost greedily, except that there wasn't a greedy bone in his lanky body. "Capital! Dashed, if you don't look top-notch, Sion. Lord, the last time we had met . . ." Jonas stumbled into an awkward silence. Clearing his throat, he nervously adjusted his spectacles and glanced at his relaxed companion, his cheeks sporting a ruddy shade of embarrassment.

Sion felt his own sense of acute embarrassment. "I must apologize for that unpardonable scene—"

"Pish-tosh! No such thing! My fault for intruding and trying to run your affairs. After all, such a dashed sad time and all. I still think of Lady Victoria, don't you know." Again he paused, the look in his eyes sad. "It was a bad time for us all. No one can blame you for . . ." His cheeks burned even brighter as Jonas looked down at his hands.

Wanting to put his friend at ease, Sion spoke quietly, "Jonas, I haven't had a drop to drink in months. That's behind me now. Not only did I want to see you as soon as I got to town, to apologize, but I wanted to thank you for all your caring and support. The Court looks fabulous, and I know that was due largely to you. I may have lost myself for a while, but I never forgot you." Jonas shook his head, clearing his throat. Not giving him a chance to speak, Sion forged ahead, "I have come back, Jon. And I am not alone."

Sion paused, staring intently at this man he trusted above all others. "What I am about to share with you must be held in strictest confidence. I am entrusting you with a very precious life."

Always sensitive to Sion's needs, Jonas's somewhat flighty facade slipped away as he carefully observed Sion's every mannerism, every expression, and he listened to the telling of a rebirth of life and hopes. As the shadows lengthened on the wall, Jonas learned of a young woman who would risk all, even challenge centuries of biased laws and censure to attain her one desire: a simple chance at happiness.

Jonas was awestruck. She was like no one he had ever met before, and he had seen many beautiful women before. But it was something he could not quite put his finger on. Here was a girl who had been brought up in obscurity. Lord, Sion had said she had never even seen a train! However, the lady who sat before him now was anything but reclusive. The alleged *contessa* was exquisite. Petite and graceful, with her long silky hair hanging casually down her back to her tiny waist. Her complexion had an exotic cast to it, like a creamy coffee, and doubtless sweet to the taste. Jonas sighed when he looked into those long-lashed almond-shaped eyes of hers. And the color! Set against the delicate patina of sun-kissed cheeks, they were startling gold. Well, maybe not quite gold, but somewhere in between delicious whiskey gold and a golden brown, with the barest hint of green? But it was the way she would look sideways at him that set his heart aflutter. Seemingly shy, yet bold as Delilah herself. It made even his usually ascetic thoughts whirl dizzily. When her luscious lips turned up slightly at him, he grinned back with idiotic fervor.

Danae was seated beside Sion, smiling politely at Jonas as she listened to Sion give a brief history of their friendship. Jonas's attention snapped back to the conversation when he watched her face pale and her polite smile slowly disappear.

"You did what?" In her shock, Danae's quaint Italian accent was forgotten and her furious whisper grated across the sudden silence. Jonas watched Sion's lips flatten in a grimace of annoyance as he girded himself for the battle to come. Sion had warned him that she was a force to reckon with.

Sion glanced over at his friend, noticing his avid attention to the scene about to erupt about his ears. He had to admit that his friend's appearance did not come off as that of someone of impeccable character. His cravat had been carelessly tied, there were numerous ink stains about the cuffs of his wrinkled jacket, and his trousers had seen better days. With a sigh, he squared his shoulders and faced a furious Danae.

"We are going to need help, Danae, in order to claim the inheritance. Papers need to be filed with the courts, and Jonas is the only one I would trust with this delicate situation."

"Do you realize it is my life you are entrusting to this"—Danae shot an angered glance Jonas's way—"this . . ." She broke off again, trying to gather her scattered wits. Narrowing her eyes, she glared directly at the man in question, taking in every detail of his shabby appearance. "What is it you do, Mr. Glendower?"

"I am a solicitor, among other things, madam."

"Are you good at what you do?" Again she took in his well-used attire, a rather telling hint to her of a lack of steady patrons.

Jonas's lips twitched. "I do an excellent job at whatever I choose: I just don't particularly care how I look as I do it. Many brilliant minds have this affliction. Have you seen Mr. Edison lately?"

Choosing not to be humored, Danae's glance sliced to Sion, who was struggling valiantly to keep a straight face. "I thought you detested solicitors."

Sion shrugged, a lopsided smile curling his lips. "Jon is not your typical shyster. I grant you that most are backstabbing, cutthroat, materialistic . . ."

"Please don't feel you must help me, Sion. I can sink my own ship, if needed." Jonas's dry voice cut in.

Danae threw her hands in the air. "Oh, well, that makes it *ever* so much better. As you are not the *typical* shyster, Mr. Glendower, just what kind are you?"

Jonas glanced at Sion only to see a bland smile and cocked brow directed his way. Knowing he was on his own, he bravely turned to face the magnificent virago. His myopic eyes smiled warmly at her. "Quite a harmless one." When he saw her lush lips compress ominously, he hastened to add, "Levity aside, I assure you, my lady, that your secret is safe with me. Not only is Dereham my best friend, but he saved my life once and I owe him dashed more than I could ever repay. I know how important you are to him, and therefore, you are now as equally important to me. I swear before God, I mean you no harm."

Danae shifted a speculative gaze at the now expressionless face of the marquis. His voice was low as he addressed her. "We have to be prepared for a fight if Camden or Halsingham—more likely both—contest the will. Jon is in the position to assist us with this, and he will be better able to plan for any problem if he is knowledgeable of your situation."

Danae listened closely while Sion spoke, but all the while she studied Jonas as he sat across from her, returning her perusal calmly. When Sion finished, she addressed Jonas cautiously, "You realize what I am attempting to do is completely illegal. Are you willing to break with your ethics to assist in this duplicity?"

A man of impeccable morals, Jonas paused for the longest moment before answering carefully, "I am fully aware of your story, my lady, and I truly feel for your circumstances. However, if I did not feel that years of injustice had been perpetrated against you, even as a favor to my close friend I would not undertake to go against the laws I believe in. I am not saying they are all right, but they do govern us and give us our backbone. Sion has never lied to me, and I don't believe he would begin now; nor does he give his trust and friendship easily. He believes in you, which says much to your credit in my eyes. I also have had unfortunate contact with Lord Camden, and what little knowledge I have of this man's character has also swayed me to champion you. I am at your service, my lady, and more than willing to assist you in any way I can."

Sion looked over at Danae and noticed how intently she studied Jonas. The two sat opposite each other, each quite openly assessing the other. Jonas not only had to pass muster with Danae, but she also had to pass Jonas's strict codes of character. He watched as they slowly smiled at each other. Closing his eyes, he gave a relieved sigh.

When Danae rose to her feet, both men came politely to theirs. Stepping forward, Danae held out her hand to Jonas. Without hesitation, he also stepped toward her and clasped her fingers warmly.

"You now hold my life in your hands, Mr. Glendower," she murmured, looking at him sideways out of those magnificent eyes of hers.

Jonas felt himself blushing. "And they shall hold you safe. Please, I would be honored if you would call me Jonas or Jon, as Sion does."

Danae searched his eyes through the distortion of the lenses. What she saw there eased her doubts considerably. "Thank you, Jonas." She turned to Sion with a sigh. "Well, I have to admit, you have not been wrong so far."

"Nor will I ever, where you are concerned, my love."

Her eyes narrowed again, even as a blush stole across her cheeks. "You don't have to pretend in front of Jonas."

Sion smiled slowly, a devilish twinkle in his eyes. "Who says I am pretending?"

Danae paused for a second before she stepped close to Sion. Her own smile played seductively about her lips, and reaching up, she drew her finger along his jaw. After a long moment of staring deeply into his mesmerized eyes, she allowed the teasing finger to rest upon his lips. *"Lei è un cafone che stuzzica e può andare al diavolo per tutti curo."*

Sion blinked as she turned away and glided to the door, pausing before Jonas to wish him a good day. Her accent was impeccable once again. When the door had clicked shut behind her, both men turned to each other. Sion was speculative, Jonas plainly smitten.

"Lovely lady. Quite rare, indeed!" Jonas gushed as he looked toward the door again.

Sion's eyes followed his. "I wonder what she said to me."

Distracted, Jonas answered casually, "She told you to go to the devil, my friend. Yes, indeed, a lady of wit, wisdom, and loveliness. Dashed if you aren't blessed, you lucky bastard."

Sion shot him a look of disgust before turning away.

Fourteen

"My God, are you mad?" Halsingham watched in fascinated horror as Camden's thin white fingers stroked the blond curls lovingly.

Eyes devoid of any human emotion shifted up to meet his, and Halsingham shivered as he stepped back.

"What was the amount of your debts again?" the sibilant whisper floated across to him.

"Don't threaten me, Camden." Halsingham's throat almost choked on the brave words. "The duns know of my wife's death and are content to wait till the estate is settled."

A lethal smile spread across Camden's bloodless lips. "But do they yet know your beloved wife left you not a farthing?" Camden drew a finger down the child's delicate cheek.

Halsingham shifted his gaze away. Out of nervous habit, he fiddled with the cuff of his expensively tailored coat. "My solicitor assured me it won't stand in court."

"Your solicitor is apparently as big an ass as you." The whispery voice hardened. "I am all you have, my dear. And if you don't want to once again find yourself a guest of that same hellhole I fished you out of before, you had better heed me."

Even as anger boiled over his wise intentions to remain calm, Halsingham knew how cravenly helpless he was. But the powerless anger eased him somewhat as he faced his father-in-law. Repulsed, he stared at the five-year-old child standing docilely under Camden's cold fondling. "This whole scheme is preposterous. It won't work, I tell you!"

That empty stare again impaled him. "Oh, but it will. You cheated me once, but never again."

Desperate, Halsingham began to pace the room. Lord, the man was becoming more insane, if that was possible. He rued the day he had let the bastard buy him out of Sidwell. At least the rats nibbling at his flesh there he had been able to fight. This madman was devouring his soul, and he didn't know how to stop it.

"But what is the point? This . . . this"—he waved toward the boy—"is not of your blood. Why would you want to claim the brat as your heir? To what purpose?"

Camden's hand tightened imperceptibly about the child's thin neck. "I want a grandson. You cheated me out of one; Katherine, the ungrateful bitch, cheated me. So I will provide my own. The blood of Camden will not die."

"It is dead." The cruel words fell heavy in the tense air.

Camden slowly raised his face, and what Halsingham saw there froze his body in terror. Those typically dead eyes glittered with a feral light that burned into his brain.

"You will claim this child as your son. You will do it convincingly, or you will not simply find yourself back in Sidwell, but at the bottom of a pauper's grave."

Halsingham swallowed and again glanced at the child. Camden had chosen well. The boy was beautiful: gleaming golden curls, eyes bluer than the clearest spring day, features aristocratically fine. He could very well pass for his son.

His jaw clenched as he realized how well he had been cornered. *Damn Katherine.* What did he ever do to the bitch that she should have betrayed him in such a calculated manner? Again he met Camden's eyes; the gates to an abyss of utter madness.

With a weary sigh, Halsingham turned away. He was so tired of it all. How in hell did one fight madness? For the first time he was beginning to regret his profligate younger years that had led him to this dead end in his life. "Very well. But"—he again hardened his voice as he strode to the door—"I will not have the brat in my home."

Camden watched with satisfaction as the door slammed shut after the fool. Smiling, he stroked the silken curls, thanking God that the conceited ass was such an imbecile.

Then the smile froze as he remembered Halsingham's words. *It is dead.* But the Camden blood was not dead, not while he still lived. His fingers tightened on the boy's curls. No, this boy was not of his blood. Not yet.

But, soon this beautiful child's body would mingle with, and then grow to manhood sustained by the noble blood of Camden.

The child looked up, timid and yet so eager to trust.

"Are you thirsty?" Camden inquired gently.

With a hesitant smile, the boy nodded.

"Well, Edward, let us see what we can find." With a final pat on a downy cheek, the earl walked over to the liquor caddy. He poured a tumbler

full of cool water, then calmly picked up an old
Saracen dagger he had placed there earlier, just
for this purpose. Taking note of the child's stance
in front of the chessboard across the safe distance
of the room, Camden made a slight cut on his
forefinger.

As the drops of blood sank into the crystal water,
he swirled the tumbler till the water pinkened,
then turned a transparent red. After a moment
of thought, he pinched down on the cut. He
would strengthen the other doses as the boy became used to the taste. Then he squeezed a slice
of lemon into the mixture and added a touch of
sugar.

As Camden took the glass to the child, his hand
trembled slightly. The familiar numbness again
shivered over his arm and up into his neck. "Here
you go, my child. I believe you shall like this. It is
called lemonade." When the child had obediently
grasped the glass, Camden snatched his hand back
and jammed it into his coat pocket. The tumbler
looked oversized in the minute fingers.

"Now, drink up, Edward; then we will find you
something to eat."

As the boy obediently emptied the glass, the
earl smiled, satisfaction gleaming in his chilling
eyes. There was scarcely a flicker of emotion on
the earl's pale face as the searing pain ripped
through his neck, sending throbbing shards of
agony pounding in his temples. The endless torture was so much a part of him, just as mundane
as breathing in and breathing out, that he now
knew how to control his reaction to the attacks.
The hand resting in his pocket clenched and relaxed in tandem as he strove to regain the
circulation in his arm. The recurring numbness

was becoming more and more of a nuisance. He did not have time for such weaknesses now. There was still so much to be done.

He took the glass extended to him so politely. Such impeccable manners. Surprising, considering where he had found the child. Nevertheless, blood would tell.

Soon this beautiful child would be of his own blood.

The next Earl of Camden.

Halsingham strode onto Mayfair, barely acknowledging the greetings thrown his way.

Damn, damn, damn. Shit! Would he never be free of the whoreson? Camden had seemed such a godsend all those years ago when he was languishing in Sidwell, all his so-called friends and lovers conspicuously absent. When the earl had come to him with his proposition, he hadn't even thought twice about it. He would have married Medusa herself to get out of that rat-infested hellhole. The terms were explained in great detail, and he had signed the carefully drawn contract. Truthfully, he had had every intention of abiding by the terms. Until he had seen her the day of the wedding, that is. Then there had been no way in hell or beyond that he would have bedded the sow. Hell, for what purpose, as he certainly wouldn't have been able to get hard for the creature? Fortunately for him, it had been quite easy duping the earl, considering how much Katherine had disliked her father and seemed just as eager as him to forgo the trials of the marriage bed. Thank God! He had been very happy to go his way and he hadn't given a damn what his wife had done. To be honest, he couldn't even remember exchanging two words with Katherine beyond the night of their marriage when they had agreed to their pact. Now she was dead. And with her death, she had tied his hands in a royal way.

Feeling a twinge of remorse, Halsingham paused in the mad rush of Mayfair's daily traffic, surprised that he felt such a strange emotion. He had to admit he had not done well by the old girl. He could have at least treated her with a modicum of respect. She had been the Viscountess Halsingham, after all. With a sigh, he shrugged and turned to move on, only to pull up short at the sight before him.

Well, well, well. Pasting his most charming smile on tense lips, he moved toward the elegant creature paused before the window of a milliner.

"Good afternoon, madam."

Danae jumped and spun about, stifling an oath. *"Signore,* you startle me!"

Halsingham bowed gracefully, and taking her gloved hand, he brushed his lips slowly over the warm kid. "My apologies, madam. Do you remember me? Reidlen Carey, Viscount Halsingham? It is good to see you again. Have you been in town long?"

My, he can be charming when it suits his purposes, Danae thought cynically as she smiled with false warmth up into his handsome face. *"Si, signore,* I remember you. Poor Katarina's husband. No, I been in London only short time. I am out seeing sights."

Halsingham looked ironically toward the milliner's. "Yes, indeed. London has many fascinating sights. You must allow me to escort you. The city can be very confusing to anyone unacquainted with its madness."

The countess looked perplexed. "What is this 'madness'?"

Staring into her golden eyes, he waved a negligent hand about. "Madness. London. They are synonymous with each other. You will understand soon enough when you try to cross a street. That is where I can come in handy. I will simply throw my body in front of all traffic for you." Danae blinked as Halsingham blinded her with the full force of his beautiful smile.

She had to glance away and found herself becoming increasingly frustrated by the minute. The dratted cad was making it very difficult to dislike him. Why could he have not wasted a bit of that charm on Katherine? *Because he is a heartless, conceited bastard, that is why,* she reminded herself sternly. Straightening her shoulders, Danae stared the appealing worm down. *"Grazie mille, il mio signore,* but no. I am to meet Lord Dereham. He will show me London."

Halsingham's smile became strained. "My apologies, madam, if I came across too bold."

Danae waved a hand with Latin goodwill. "No, no, *signore.* I would be, um, pleased to, how you say, accept you to show me London on other day, *si?"*

With a slight smile, Halsingham relaxed and bowed again. *"Si,* madam. I would be honored. Maybe you would permit me to call on you?"

Danae paused, wondering if there could be any benefits to this. Receiving a slight nudge behind her, she spoke up. *"Si,* signore, I think this would be fine. I am staying at Dereham House. *Numero uno,* Eight Berkeley Square." Her accent faltered charmingly on the address.

Halsingham frowned. "You are staying with Dereham?"

Danae laughed. *"Ma, certamente!* I stay always with Dereham. I am his; he is mine."

The sinfully blue eyes narrowed. "I see." After a moment, he gathered his thoughts. "Well, then, I hope to see you soon, madam." Then with another graceful, if now a bit curt, bow, he was gone.

"Now, just what sort o' mischief ye tending tae brew, lass?" came Mrs. Turlow's gruff voice behind her.

Danae smiled as she watched Halsingham's impeccable broad shoulders disappear around a corner. "Oh, not much, Mrs. T. Just planning to add a little spice to what is already on the fire."

Mrs. Turlow, loyal down to her bunions, huffed as she pulled Danae along. "And I dinna like what I'm smelling. What would his lordship say if he ken ye were a speaking tae that mongrel?"

"I would appreciate it, Mrs. T., if you did not mention this meeting to his lordship."

The old dame stopped so abruptly, Danae careened into her. When she spun about, she glared suspiciously at the irritated girl poking at her bonnet, which now tilted awkwardly over one ear. "Why, if I may be askin'?"

Danae glared in return. "Because I wish it," she stated succinctly.

Obviously put out with the answer, Mrs. Turlow turned and continued to march down Mayfair with Danae in hot pursuit. Danae grimaced, knowing the spectacle they were probably making, and finally, desperate, she reached out the handle of her parasol and snagged the other woman's arm.

"Mrs. Turlow, as my companion it is your position to follow where I lead, not vice versa. You are making a spectacle of us, and I do not wish to draw any more attention than absolutely necessary." Danae panted, again jerking at her askew bonnet. She wished she could just yank the dratted thing off. It itched and pinched and the ribbons under her neck were strangling her. It was utterly ridiculous to have to wear the contraption *and* carry a parasol. At least the parasol was good for something. She almost smiled as Mrs. Turlow, with as much dignity as possible, unhooked her arm and shawl.

"It be wrong tae keep things from his lordship."

Danae rubbed her temple. Why did she always get headaches around this woman? She sighed. "Mrs. T., I am asking you not to tell his lordship of this meeting simply because he has enough on his mind at present. I don't wish him to worry about Halsingham bothering me. Please?"

Mrs. Turlow pondered the ethics of this as she squinted down the street.

Biting her lip in vexation, Danae wheedled, "If we can come to an understanding on this, we could finish our shopping. I noticed you had your eye on a lovely shawl back there."

Mrs. Turlow's stubborn gaze slid sideways to study the young woman. After a long moment, she nodded, albeit reluctantly. "Verra well, I'll keep me tongue, but I dinna like it."

Danae patted her shoulder, relieved to have that behind her. "Good. Then let us go back to Johnson's. I believe that is where we saw the shawl," she prattled hurriedly, hoping to deter any further discussion about his lordship. "I think it is going to look divine on you."

Mrs. Turlow followed along obediently, muttering about it not being right to bribe an honest old widow. After all, she had her pride, she did, and she was only playing along as she didn't want his lordship to worry.

Danae closed her eyes, the pounding in her temples deafening.

The next afternoon Danae strolled into the library humming a jaunty ditty, smiling, for she dared not give voice to the risqué words. Lord, how she loved London! The hustle and bustle, the sheer exuberance with which life was lived. The costermongers hawking their wares, the hackneys and growlers vying for passengers. The shops, the museums, the parks. Even the Punch and Judy show she had come across today had held a peculiar charm despite the violence. How she had laughed as she watched the enthralled faces of the children scattered upon the lawn before the crude stage. It was all so earthy and gaudy. She had even grown accustomed to the smell, though she would never be able to claim any liking for it.

She pulled up short as she caught sight of a pair of well-muscled legs sprawled out before the fire. Forgetting the book she had come to return, Danae sauntered across the room and sank gracefully into the matching wing chair. Her smile froze as she took in a pair of stormy eyes telling a different story from the polite smile curling his lips.

"Apparently, you forgot to inform me of something yesterday." Sion's words were smoothly snide. The vulnerability of the night before was gone as thoroughly as the remnants of dawn's elusive mist.

Danae sighed, unconsciously riffling the pages of the book. Drat that woman! And the old biddy had accepted the shawl, too!

"Be sure you deduct the cost of a shawl from Mrs. Turlow's wages," she informed him, deciding it was best just to be done with it. There was no change of expression on his face, but for the inquiring lift of a brow. "It was purchased for her in the form of a bribe. Obviously, it didn't work." Her lips tightened with irritation. Glancing down, she missed the smile that quivered momentarily on his lips and was quickly suppressed.

"Maybe that will teach you to whom Mrs. Turlow is ultimately loyal," he replied softly, still nursing his anger.

"Fiddle!" she scoffed. "Your bribe was obviously more lucrative. I had better become more acquainted with her needs."

Watching her peeved expression, Sion finally gave up and laughed. Taking pity on her, he gave her a tidbit to mull over: "Silk."

She was clearly thrown. "Silk?"

He nodded, grinning. "I broke down her resistance by offering her a pair of silk unmentionables."

Danae stared at him, blinking. "How would you know she had a weakness for silk unmentionables?"

Chuckling, he waggled his eyebrows with a humorous leer. "Now, how do you suppose I know?"

Danae shot to her feet. "That's disgusting!" Throwing the book at him, she stormed for the door.

Howling with laughter, Sion beat her there, and blocking her escape, he grabbed hold of her waist. It took a minute of tussling with the infuriated woman before he realized how good she felt in his arms. Leaning against the closed door, he pulled her closer, amazed how his hands spanned her corseted frame, his fingertips touching. His laughter died abruptly. Giving her a slight shake, he finally snagged her furious glare.

"Don't be ridiculous, my love. Mrs. Turlow is safe

from my lecherous endeavors." He paused as his thumbs rubbed erotically over her midriff, the sensitive tips barely skimming the undersides of her heaving breasts. She gasped and froze, her shocked gaze meeting his heated eyes.

"Why didn't you tell me Halsingham had accosted you on the street yesterday?"

She swallowed, her words coming out on a breathy sigh, "He didn't accost me."

His fingers tightened. "Did you encourage his advances?"

Angered, Danae tried to pull away from the iron grasp. "Now who's being ridiculous?"

Sion studied her face for a moment, torn with jealousy as he remembered Halsingham's golden beauty. A woman would have to be either blind or of another persuasion not to be tempted by him. He had to constantly remind himself that Danae had every reason in the world to hate the viscount. But on the other side of the coin, the woman who had reason to hate Halsingham was dead, and Danae was very much alive, exotically beautiful and a target for the full force of the bastard's calculated charm. "I just don't want you to be alone with him."

Danae stared at him amazed. "I wasn't alone with him! I was in the middle of Mayfair with Mrs. T. breathing down my neck, the Judas!"

He shook her gently. "Danny, you know what I mean."

The look in his eyes took her breath away. "You're jealous," she breathed in wonderment.

"Damn right," he growled as he pulled her into his arms. He inhaled the scent of lemons and drew a shaky breath as she leaned against him; then he groaned when she threw her arms about his neck.

If he weren't already acquainted with her naïveté, he would swear she was deliberately provoking him as her hips pressed feverishly against his now painful erection. Even though the layers of cloth absorbed it, his mind reveled in the heat he knew would be emanating from the moist juncture of her thighs. God, he probably would never be able to smell a lemon again and not become immediately aroused.

His teeth nipped at her neck, and then his tongue soothed the sting as he breathed in the scent of her. "Oh, God, Danny, how I need you."

Danae shivered as she felt his tongue tickle along her neck and then encircle the lobe of her ear. Her fingers entwined in the silky hair at his nape as she pressed the burning hunger between her legs even tighter against him. It felt so strange, this elongated, hard flesh she knew to be his manhood. Never in her wildest imaginings had she thought it would feel this good. Pictures certainly did not do justice to the erotic feel of him, nor to the feelings that were tripping wildly through her dazed body.

She gave a shuddering sigh as his hands roamed over her tensed buttocks under the cumbersome bustle. "Sion, you are confusing me and . . ."

"And?" he breathed moistly into her ear.

"I want you too," she groaned as she felt his fingers, somehow miraculously, under her skirts, skimming the thin silk covering her buttocks. "My goodness," she whispered into his neck as the teasing fingers insinuated themselves beneath the slit in her drawers. He stroked the rounded flesh; then, delving along the cleft, his fingers searched lower yet, drawn by the feverish dew between her legs. She stiffened as they plunged into her moist heat, impaling her. Having no time to even ponder the thought of fear or impropriety, her body arched as she opened herself even more to his thrusting fingers. His breath was harsh in her ear, his other hand pressed rigidly against her back.

Sion's fingers plunged again into the wet heaven, and he thought he was going to die on the spot. His other arm supporting her straining body, there was nothing more consuming at that moment than to have her come apart in his arms. His hips flexed as he rubbed himself almost brutally against her. "Danny," he rasped, "give me your mouth."

There was no hesitation as she turned her face up to him, dragging his head down to meet her. When his tongue plunged into her mouth and mated with hers, she shuddered, and, pressing into his frantic fingers, her body began to convulse mindlessly. He swallowed her scream as her hips jerked spasmodically against his, her silky dew drenching his fingers, and his heart pounded with deafening force as his own body shattered into a million pieces.

Exhausted, he caressed her tongue a final time before he dropped his head back and gasped for air. Her skirts fell back into place when he removed his hand and holding her trembling, limp body against him, he breathed in her essence, starved for the scent.

"My . . . my goodness." Her muscles quivered like jelly.

"Goodness, indeed," Sion murmured as he leaned his forehead against hers. "And it will only get better."

This could become entirely too addictive, she warned herself as she pushed out of his arms. And he was all too sure of himself. "I need to go to my room. Now, please." She heard an edge of hysteria in her voice, which Sion didn't seem to miss either.

Sion quickly stepped aside to open the door and felt his spent semen slither down his inner thigh. With a grimace, he looked down on his soiled trousers.

"Oh, my." Danae's voice was breathless, and looking up, Sion was glad to see irrepressible humor twinkling in her eyes.

He shrugged with a self-deprecating grin. "Oops."

"I wager this is one of those rare circumstances when you wished you had skirts, hmm?" Then she was gone, calling for Mrs. T. as she flitted through the door. When the old lady answered, Sion stopped short, his grin fading for the little witch was telling Mrs. T. that his lordship had spilled something on himself and needed help.

Taking a deep breath, Sion sprinted for the stairs, pausing by Danae's side to whisper in her ear of retribution to come. He gave her impudent bustle a pat before he took the stairs two at a time.

"I'll be waiting, my lord," he heard her voice float after him, and he grinned thinking he couldn't wait, either.

Fifteen

Sion walked into White's not knowing what to expect. When he left London all those years ago, it seemed everyone had turned their backs on him. Now he was curious to see if those same backs were still turned to him.

Thinking he might as well just dive in, he wandered into the card room to look for a game of whist. What he encountered were familiar faces turning to stare at him in anything from amazement to huge smiles of welcome.

Sion blinked as several old cronies actually left their seats to approach him, hands extended. His own face probably reflected his surprise, but he didn't neglect one outstretched hand, nor fail to return any of the greetings tossed at him. After several minutes of this openhearted welcome, he began to doubt his own recollections of the events that took place upon his departure from London. With a wry twist of his lips, he could just hear Danae berate him on his abysmal ability to blow unfortunate circumstances out of all proportion. He winced when he guessed at the tongue-lashing he would suffer tonight under her caustic criticism. Maybe he would lie and tell her they had tossed

him out of every club on St. James and that his arse
was as numb as a penguin's tail.

Sion's words of greeting to an old friend of his
grandmother's were cut short when a very familiar
face that he would dearly have loved to keep in the
past was thrust before his. He stepped back slightly
as the sour fumes of port struck his senses. With an
obvious show of distaste, Sion drew his handkerchief from his breast pocket and waved it pointedly
before his face. "Evening, Saegar. Just as inebriated
as ever, I see."

Silence, as thick as the soot hanging over London, settled over the small group of men. After a
few muttered comments and much shifting about
uneasily, they finally melted into the background
until Sion was left confronting the belligerent lord
on his own. Sion's lips twisted wryly. How typical.

"You're back." The absurd comment was made
through gritted teeth.

Sion laughed, "Damned astute, Saegar. Your level
of intelligence always did stagger me."

A rough finger jabbed Sion painfully in the
chest, causing a murmur of low-voiced comments
among the spectators. "You should be five feet
under feeding the maggots, you bastard."

Sion's eyes narrowed as he brushed the offending hand away. "You are drunk, Saegar—nothing
out of the ordinary, to be assured. However, that
pitiful advantage won't deter me in the least from
laying you out flat if you so much as lay a hair on
me again. Your obsessive attitude will not be tolerated by me ever again. My wife is no longer here to
protect you." Gasps surrounded him, but Sion
barely heard them, his attention was fixed so avidly
upon the man weaving slightly in front of him.

Saegar flushed a dull red, and the hate radiating from his bloodshot eyes gave Sion cause to doubt the man's sanity. Sion could barely hear the words whispered through white lips, spittle forming in the corners, "You didn't deserve her, you filthy prick. She was mine!"

Sion's hand shot out before he had the good sense to think twice. Digging his fingers in the baron's rumpled cravat, he hauled him up on his toes, not even noticing the fetid fumes fanning his face. "If I even sense her presence in your putrid little mind again, I'll throttle you to within an inch of your life and leave you licking the gutter." Disgusted with himself as much as with the worm dangling in his hand, Sion unclenched his fingers and watched Saegar stumble back.

The baron tugged his twisted cravat into its previous untamed folds, all the while glaring belligerently at Sion. As he struggled to master his drunken rage, he cast an irate glance over the silent men watching the fiasco. Finding no sympathy there, he shouldered them rudely aside and grabbing up his greatcoat from an attentive footman, he left the club.

Realizing the scene he had precipitated, Sion grimaced inwardly, damning his temper. Now everyone was likely to look upon him as the lunatic he was trying to disprove. This whole situation could not have come at a worse time, right at the moment of his reemergence into Society. Forcing a smile to stiff lips, he wiped his hand on the linen still in his hand and calmly moved farther into the room. The men fell back like the parting of the Red Sea and watched speechless as the marquis moved to take up a position at one of the whist tables.

Glancing over his shoulder, he inquired of a footman, "Five thousand pounds' worth of counters, please," Then turning to the gaping faces seated at the table, he stated affably, "Well, gentlemen, I am a bit rusty, but I believe I can give you a bit of a go at it."

Several of the men again extended their delight in seeing him back. Never very good at dissimulating, Sion spent several uncomfortable minutes planting the fictitious story of his trip abroad, and when he was done, he hurriedly, and with a forced nonchalance, shifted the men's interest onto the reason they were all there: an evening spent at whist. As one, they all turned their attention on the gentleman holding the deck, and he immediately shuffled and dealt.

Even though Sion sat back, casually making all the right plays and chatting amicably with the other players as they finally relaxed, his mind was a seething cauldron of twisted emotions. For too many years Saegar had been a thorn in his side. He remembered the *ton's* surprise when Tory had accepted Sion's suit instead of her lifelong sweetheart, Baron Saegar—and the baron had been devastated. Even since, Saegar had made it a point of twisted honor that he was alive to do nothing but make Sion's life a living hell. Whenever Sion had questioned his wife on their relationship, Tory had never hesitated to tell him of her love for Royce Saegar. She said she couldn't love him any more dearly if he were her own brother. Saegar's love, though, had never been even close to the same familial emotions. His had bordered on the obsessive.

That final night had been only one of hundreds of arguments that he had shared with Tory over her childhood sweetheart. If he hadn't been such a jealous fool, Tory would be alive today. Now Tory was gone and it was clearly apparent that Saegar was still a thorn in his side.

"You mustn't mind Saegar. He can be a real rotter at times, but he's harmless enough," a young man by the name of Yardley commented, noticing Sion's preoccupied frown.

Sion glanced at him, smiling faintly as he threw down a card. He was thankful that someone had finally brought the man up. "What has he been doing lately?"

Yardley shrugged, frowning at his hand, "Brooding, mostly. Damned if he ain't gettin' more bloody mental with each passing day. Never did get over losing Lady Victoria, oow!" He jumped as someone's foot trod his instep, "Eh, watch your ruddy foot, Peckham! I ain't sayin' anything more than what everyone does. After all, Dereham should know what's going down, eh what, Dereham?" His irritated gaze swung over to Sion.

Sion was carefully studying his hand. "In what way do you mean, 'mental'?" he asked casually after a moment.

Colonel Handford spoke up then, "Have to say as I agree with Yardley. The baron is gettin' out of hand, if you ask me. Just last month, a sweet little actress almost had him taken up, he was givin' her such a hard time. Terrified of him, I heard."

Yardley nodded, remembering the tale. "Ruddy right. She looks a dashed sight like Lady Victoria. Saw her in *Macbeth*. Resemblance was dashed eerie."

Sion's hand paused slightly as he tossed down a card. "Anyone recall her name?"

Both men shrugged and shook their heads. "Not

a bit," Yardley said, trumping Sion's card, "but last I heard she was at the Coburg."

After another twenty minutes of social conversation, Sion excused himself, leaving the other players in accord with the newly arrived marquis, especially since he had just dropped a considerable amount on the green baize table.

Intending to visit the Coburg, Sion stepped quickly into the street, to hail a hackney, when he spotted Saegar down the street. Curious why the man was still lurking about after having quit the club hours before, he told the driver to head for Pall Mall. As expected, Saegar hurriedly hailed a growler, and then Sion watched, surprised, as the vehicle veered off down another street. He thought for sure that the man would follow him.

Rapping sharply on the roof, he instructed the driver to turn about and follow the cab heading down Rider St. Even though there was still a bit of traffic on the streets, the driver had no difficulty keeping the other carriage in sight.

"He's stoppin, m'lord. You's want me t' stop, er what?"

Sion saw that the growler had pulled up outside the gates of the St. James burial grounds. "Go on past and pull up around the next corner."

"Righto."

When the carriage came to a halt, Sion leaped out and, telling the driver to wait, backtracked swiftly to the gates. After a slight, hesitant pause, he headed off down the path curving to the right. He knew where the baron was heading. His footsteps echoed in the cloying vapor swirling about his legs, the moon casting luciferous shadows about the centuries-old gravestones, and old memories surged painfully to life. The last time he had trod these grounds he had been following Tory's coffin. He had planned on visiting Tory's resting place while the sun was shining, not in this sinister mist where the night's moisture resembled blood. He was gritting his teeth so hard they began to ache as he followed the path to the family crypt. Rounding a bend, his steps slowed to a stop as he spotted the feeble glow of candlelight through the crypt's grilled gate. Silently he slipped into the yawning mouth and carefully navigated the shallow steps.

As he figured, the baron was there, paying homage to his wife. In fact, the bastard was lying atop her sepulcher, muttering to himself.

"Get the hell out of here," Sion's soft voice cracked through the fetid air.

With a gasp, Royce Saegar rolled to his side, and stumbling to his feet, he leaned heavily against the cold granite. Sion moved farther into the room, his gaze pinning the man helplessly before his rage. "You have no right to be here."

Saegar laughed drunkenly. "No right? Where the hell have you been all these years? You left her alone. Someone had to take care of her and you weren't here. But, I have been. She needs me."

"If it weren't for your mad obsession and your interference in our lives, Tory would still be alive."

Sion was shocked to see the younger man's swollen eyes begin to redden and tears form. "You think I killed her? Are you mad? I worshipped her from the moment I met her. She was always mine. It was just too late when she realized the terrible mistake she had made. Everyone knows you couldn't deal with her affections for me." He shook his head sadly as he gave the infuriated man a wide berth and backed up toward the gate. "You delude yourself if you think Victoria rejected me. You

found out she was carrying my baby, didn't you?
She was going to leave you and you found out,
didn't you? I will have my vengeance, Dereham.
Where justice failed, I will prevail." Then he was
gone, only a hint of sour port to tell of his presence
in the stifling air.

Sion stood staring at the rusted gate standing
ajar, the mist swirling eerily beyond the candlelight.
There wasn't a thought in his mind. It had ceased
to work.

He felt nothing but a deep, dark void.

Danae stirred, easing out of sleep, drowsily aware
that something was not right. Disturbed, she sat up
and squinted over at the mantel. She could barely
distinguish the hands on the clock: twenty past
three. Rubbing her eyes, she shoved the covers
back and swung her legs over the side. Almost unconsciously, she trod barefoot over to the fireplace
and stirred the glowing embers.

Again something niggled at her.

Confused, she looked around, wondering what
had disturbed her. Going to the door, she cracked
it opened and listened. She was just about to close
it again when something caught her attention. Her
eyes sharpened and she pulled the door open farther. She wasn't mistaken, for again she heard the
faint tinkling of crystal. Not even bothering with
her dressing gown or slippers, she moved hurriedly
down the stairs and crept silently into the hall. The
door to Sion's study stood ajar, firelight flickering
about its edges.

Just as she feared, Sion was there with glass in
hand, staring morosely into the fitful flames struggling to keep alive.

Not wanting to startle him, she spoke quietly as she moved closer, "Sion, what are you doing up so late?"

He didn't even acknowledge her as he swallowed the contents of the tumbler in his hand. Turning about, he strode over to the liquor caddy and re-filled the glass. Swiftly Danae moved to his side and gently she placed her hand over the glass as he was raising it.

"Please, Sion, don't." The glass paused in midair. He didn't lower it but merely waited patiently for her to remove her hand. With a sigh she pried it out of his hand and tossed it onto the marble hearth. The tumbler shattered, and brandy bled onto the carpet amid the sparkling shards. When he reached for another glass, she calmly picked it up and sent it after its mate. When Sion finally turned his gaze to meet hers, she gasped. She could swear at that moment he hated her.

"Go back to bed, Danae. I don't want you here."

"I beg to differ with you; I think you need me now more than you ever have."

"There's only one thing I want from you right now, and if you don't leave, I'll take it." His cold glare backed up the threat most impressively.

Unflinching, she stared back. "Then take it."

Sion clenched his hands and was shocked to re-alize that he wanted to hurt her. She was all his pain combined, standing calmly before him, and he wanted desperately to exorcise it. He wanted to crush her, before she had a chance to crush him just as Tory had. Frightened, he backed up, need-ing to get away from her. Sweat beaded his forehead and shivered along his feverish body. His torn emotions screamed for another drink, and Danae stood in his way.

"Please," he begged hoarsely. "Get out of here, Danny. I'll hurt you. Please, I don't want to hurt you."

She slowly followed. "I'm already hurting. When you hurt, I hurt, Sion. Something happened tonight. Tell me; share with me. What happened?"

His eyes misted over, and his throat choked painfully on the sob he swallowed. Looking down, he closed his eyes, blocking out the sight of Danae standing before him, offering him succor. Finally, he whispered hoarsely, "She betrayed me, Danny."

Danae brow furrowed. "Who?"

"Tory."

Danae shook her head unhesitatingly. "Impossible."

"The child she was carrying was not mine."

She was suddenly furious. "Where did you hear such rubbish? How could you even listen to it?"

Sion's haunted gaze trapped her. "From her lover."

"And you believed some man who probably wanted nothing more than to hurt you? Did Tory ever once give you cause to doubt her?"

He immediately shook his head, the look in his eyes telling her to stop tormenting him.

"Sion, how could you accuse her of something that she gave you no cause to blame her for? She died from a horrible accident. She wasn't to blame; you weren't to blame. It just happened. Why are you even listening to this man?"

Sion scrubbed his eyes with a shaking hand. He didn't know what to believe; all he could remember were the times she had defended the scum, always making allowances for him. Was there something deeper there that he had refused to see?

Trying another tack, Danae ventured slowly. "You know this man better than I, but it sounds to me as if he is a soul in torment and has been since the day you married Tory. Considering what has happened, you will probably never be able to forgive him, but also, considering the pain you yourself had fallen into, can't you at least try to understand? You, thankfully, had the strength to save yourself, but this man"—she shook her head sadly—"he sounds like he is very much alone."

"And he doesn't have you," Sion added quietly, his smile sending a warm shiver over her. "But you are right. I have mistaken so much in my life, it seems. This entire evening has been one surprise after the other. It seems I have a habit of turning melodramatic, doesn't it?"

Danae simply smiled at him. She moved toward him, and her gasp of pain had him stepping quickly to her side as she tottered on one foot. Lifting her into his arms, he stepped over to the wing chair and set her gently into it.

Her laugh was a bit shaky as she raised the hem of her gown and stared down at her bare foot. "How silly. This must be God's way to tell me to mind my own business."

Sion lifted her foot and gently plucked the shard of glass from her tender instep. Placing her bloody foot on a footstool, he went to douse his handkerchief with brandy, then came back to kneel before her. The firelight flickered over her exposed leg, and even as he carefully soothed the saturated cloth over the shallow cut, the fingers of his other hand unconsciously traced over her silky flesh.

His eyes searched her flushed profile. "Danny?"

Swallowing, her gaze shifted from watching his hand as it moved under her gown, erotically stroking the back of her knee. She met his intently questioning eyes. He was silently asking her what she wanted.

It was suddenly crystal clear to her what she wanted.

Her lips parted as she licked them nervously, her quickened breath then fanning them dry. She felt his fingers slide up her inner thigh, and grasping the arms of the chair, she spread her legs farther apart to accommodate his searching fingers.

That one trusting movement told him all he needed to know.

Sion dropped the linen and pushed the stool out of his way as he shifted to kneel between her thighs. His eyes skimmed over her heaving breasts, her distended nipples visible under the thin silk, down to her downy curls clearly defined by the shadowed darkness between her thighs. Then his right hand came up under her gown and skimmed along her other sleek limb. His gaze flickered up to hers, and he felt a thrill at the look in those heavily lidded amber eyes.

"Lift your gown, Danny," he commanded, his voice low and strained.

She almost had to pry her clenched fingers from the armrests, but she quickly complied. With excruciating slowness, the hem of her gown crept higher. His fingers flexed about her knees, drawing them farther apart as they were exposed to the flickering light. His heart pounded in his ears, and biting his lips, his eyes found hers again. "More, Danny. Higher."

The hem inched up farther, then paused teasingly just as he caught a glimpse of the dark delta between her spread thighs. His hand clenched almost painfully about her knees, then slid beneath, raising them higher and wider.

"More." His whisper was strangled as he leaned

forward and hooked her knees over his shoulder, sliding her buttocks to the edge of the chair.

Danae thought she would faint when his fingers teasingly slid up her inner thighs and brushed ever so softly over the damp curls. Her fingers jerked, and the hem came to settle about her hips, baring her to his avid gaze. His breath fanned her tender skin as his tormenting fingers insinuated themselves into the delicate folds. She felt him tugging, then erotically twisting the curls between his damp fingers.

Her hips bucked, and helplessly she grabbed hold of his hands. "Sion, please!"

The next thing she knew his hands had swept under her, grasping and squeezing her buttocks as he lifted her higher. Dazed, she watched as his head dipped forward and his tongue thrust into her. She screamed and clutched his hair, not knowing whether she was pushing him away or pulling him closer. "Oh, God, Sion! Stop!" Yet, when as he raised his head, she tried to push him down again and cried, "No, don't stop! Please."

Her dew shimmered about his lips as he smiled wickedly. "Talk to me, Danny. Tell me how you want me. Tell me in Italian." When she simply stared at him, he began to withdraw. Almost desperately, she began to beseech him, her husky voice tripping erotically over the Italian phrases.

Sion shivered as he looked at her moist womanhood, open and so vulnerable to him. Never had anything looked so beautiful; the delicate tissues swollen and aching for the stroke of his tongue. He felt her fingers curl about his ears, urging him down. Closing his eyes, he sought her, reveling in her taste, drowning in the sensuous smell of her. His hands clenched about her firm little buttocks, and with a groan he lifted her higher as he tried to get deeper into her. Her voice whispered over him, lulling him, goading him unbearably, and as his tongue speared into her again her thighs clenched about his head, and helplessly she began to shudder under his thrusting tongue. He felt her pulse and contract in his mouth, and her essence drenched his tongue. It was then he lost his mind.

Surging to his feet, he caught her up in his arms, and the next thing he was aware of was her under him on the divan. Her gown was in shreds about her body, and as he struggled with his trousers, she was pulling frantically at his shirt. Finally, blessedly, he was between her thighs, her full breasts cushioning his chest, their sweat and scent mingling. He tried to go slowly, knowing he would hurt her, but Danae was having none of it. Her nails dug into his shoulders as she pulled him down. Silently begging her forgiveness, he surged fully into her tight sheath, breaking her hymen and sinking deep into her silky passage.

The pleasure was so intense, it was as if he had never experienced the act of loving before, and he was sure it could never get better than this. At least, his scattered wits had thought so until her legs came up higher, causing the sleek muscles of her vagina to clench even more tightly about him. Losing all control, his body arched wildly back as he plunged even deeper into her, his face clenched into a rictus of pleasure-pain as he erupted, emptying his seed deeply into her womb. At that very moment he thought his heart had exploded and heaven had showered its stars down upon him.

Danae's pain was nothing compared to the ecstatic feeling of love and power that swept over her as she watched Sion's magnificent body arch and strain between her imprisoning thighs. The firelight glistened off burnished muscles, and his face, clenched with the fury of his release, was the most beautiful thing she had ever seen. To have this powerful animal shaking and helpless to anything but the drive of his manhood thrusting deep into the core of her, made her feel omnipotent. It even superseded the pleasure he had given her earlier, if that was possible.

With a groan, Sion collapsed onto her damp body, and holding her close, he rolled carefully over the edge of the divan and dropped them gently onto the carpeted floor. He held her limp body atop his, waiting for his heart to slow. With a lazy smile, he nestled her hips between his spread thighs, with him still resting snugly in her warm body. When she stirred slightly, his arms subdued any thought other than remaining exactly as she was. He didn't even give a damn if she was uncomfortable; selfishly he refused to let her go.

Arching her back, she crossed her arms on his chest and gazed down at his now relaxed expression. Gently she wiped away a bead of sweat on his cheek, curious as her fingers rasped against the dark growth shadowing his usually smooth skin. She smiled when he raised heavy lids and contentedly watched her.

"You are a constant source of amazement to me," she observed matter-of-factly.

"And by that enigmatic comment I hope it means I pleased you?" He cocked an amused eye at her when she gave him an adamant nod. "I aim to please, madam."

"What can I say but that I am fearful I shall never be able to keep up?" She couldn't stop the yawn that almost cracked her jaw. Covering her mouth, she blushed at the picture she must make, yawning in his face while she straddled his thighs, his now flaccid cock still deeply embedded in her. She shifted above him and grimaced in pain when her torn tissues rubbed against his own flesh.

Sion's smile slipped as he recalled how callously he had just initiated her. He knew she hadn't experienced any pleasure, and he was filled with remorse to realize that at that one tumultuous moment he hadn't cared. God, what an uncaring ass he was.

Raising a lethargic arm, he tenderly swept a silken skein of hair over her shoulder. "Did I hurt you? Are you all right?" His hand moved to soothe her back, stroking the long curve of her spine. When she wriggled her hips and her inner muscles milked his burgeoning desire, his hands clenched about her sleek little bottom, trying to hold her still. The groan that slipped out caused Danae to smile down on him with renewed interest. Lovingly she massaged the impressive bulge of muscles in his chest and arms, the firelight burnishing his skin to an unbelievably sensuous texture she couldn't help but stroke.

Danae drew her knees up until they were hugging his narrow hips, and pushing herself erect, she ground her pelvis almost harshly into his loins. His head arched back, his fingers digging none too gently into the silky skin of her hips. Raising her a bit, he thrust his hips up before he eagerly pulled her back down on his now straining erection. He clenched his teeth as she shifted farther back, forcing the tip of his shaft farther into her until it touched her womb. His slitted gaze reveled in the sight of her arched back, drowned in the sensuous feel of her hair draping his loins and legs, and he reached for her beautiful breasts thrusting forward.

When his warm hands cupped and squeezed her aching breasts, Danae surged forward with a cry, filling his hands to overflowing with her heated flesh.

Again a moan was wrenched from him, and reaching up, his fingers tangled in her hair as he cupped her moist neck and pulled her down. His tongue surged into her mouth as she tightened about his pulsing flesh.

It was the feeling of warmth that finally stirred Danae from her deep sleep. As her eyes slowly opened, her first impression was of a delicious sense of contentment as intense as it was unfamiliar. Her mind became giddy as she breathed deep of the essence of this unique man curled protectively about her. Drowsing, she nestled her head against the forearm pillowing her head, loving each and every irritating rasp of the wiry hairs tickling her nose.

Her gaze lazily drifted about the unfamiliar room, and seeing the faint light foretelling the dawn to come, she frowned. This was not her room or her bed and she now felt distinctly uncomfortable. She suddenly had the urge to snuggle up in the familiarity of her own bed. Biting her lip, she furtively inched each limb closer to the edge of the bed. After slow, endless minutes of patiently trying to slither out from under Sion, she glanced out the window and realized that at this rate it would be high noon before she saw her bed.

"Stop wriggling about and go back to sleep," Sion

groused as he pulled her firmly back into his arms, his warm hips cradling her bum.

Not having to worry about waking him now, Danae scooted quickly out of the warm cocoon of limbs and covers. Again she was yanked back, and when she looked over her shoulder to protest she encountered a very disgruntled and deliciously rumpled male.

"What the hell's the matter with you?" he demanded through a huge yawn.

"I want to go to my bed, Sion." she explained as she tugged tresses of her hair out from beneath him. Deliberately he rolled more fully onto the tangled curls.

"Don't be ridiculous. This is your bed now."

Not even knowing why she was irritated, she just knew she needed the privacy of her own room. "Sion, if you don't get the hell off my hair, I'll cut it." When he still did not budge, she leaned forward and reached for a paring knife poised on the edge of a bowl of fruit on the bedside table.

With a shout of outrage, Sion sprang from the bed and stood glaring down at her, hands resting on lean hips. Danae stifled a sigh of awe. What a sight to wake up to in the morning.

"Are you always this much of a bitch in the morning?"

She pondered this as she looked about for something to cover her. She did not have the faintest idea what being a bitch meant. "I don't know. Can a woman be a bitch? Isn't that a female dog? Are you now saying I am a dog?"

"It is certainly obvious that you do not like mornings," he said dryly as he sat down on the bed again.

Danae snapped about to glare at him and then gave him a reluctant smile when she spotted the smile in his eyes. "Well, then, all the more reason for me to go to my own bed."

With an irritated sigh, Sion raked his fingers through his rumpled mane and finally gave in. "Fine, I'm still so tired I'll do just about anything to shut you up." Squinting at the clock, he shuddered as he stood and rounded the bed. "God, it's only five in the morning."

Then, buck naked, he swept her up and tossed her over his shoulder. The next thing she knew, a blast of cold air struck her equally nude body as she was bounced on his shoulder while he navigated the hall in semidarkness. Through the blood roaring in her ears, she heard the opening and slamming of a door; then she was flying through the air. Even as she landed in the middle of her bed, Sion bundled her beneath the covers, and joining her, he pulled her none too gently into his arms. Before she could gather her wits enough to be enraged by the pompous way he had just manhandled her, he was snoring gently in her ear.

With an irritated sigh, she cuddled herself even more tightly against the warm length of him. As sleep finally tugged at her heavy lids, she smiled deviously and curled her frigid toes into his instep. She was quite satisfied when his body jerked and he grunted his sleepy protest, "Bitch."

Her body shivered with contentment as his warm feet immediately began to soothe hers.

She could get used to this.

As long as they used her bed.

Sixteen

Danae's mouth dropped open, and snapping her eyes forward, she stared into space, too dazed to even react. Then a rush of unmitigated rage surged through her as she turned on an impervious Mrs. Turlow.

"Did you see that?" she demanded.

Engrossed in studying the passing chaos, Mrs. Turlow turned surprised eyes on her mistress. The girl's face was flushed a furious red, and her amber gaze was literally sizzling. "What?"

Danae jerked about on the carriage seat and jabbed a finger behind her. "There!"

Mrs. Turlow's gaze followed the direction of the trembling digit. Other than the usual stream of pedestrians and vehicles, she didn't see anything out of the ordinary. "I dinna see a thing."

Danae's irate gaze swept the street. Hurriedly she spun about again, and leaning forward, she rapped the driver on his shoulder with her parasol. "Turn about, my good man." Even as upset as she was, she remembered her accent.

Shaking off the irritating jabbing, the driver looked over his shoulder. "Eh, what? 'Ow am I suppose t' turn in this crush?"

"An' 'ow should I know this? This is why the

marchese 'ire you. To go where I want to go. Now I want for you to go back this way!"

Mrs. Turlow sat back and watched the squabble, already knowing the outcome. The lassie always seemed to get what she wanted, one way or another.

"Ye tol' me t' go this way!" the driver continued to grouse as he looked about at the crowded thoroughfare.

Knowing she would lose her prey if the man didn't hurry, Danae gave up rapping his shoulder and started on his head, standing to get better purchase. "*Lei uomo stupido! Now* I wish you to go *that* way!"

As Mrs. Turlow became aware of the looks cast their way, she realized she now had no choice but to intervene. His lordship would be in a royal pet if his lady's name was bandied about. Leaning forward, she grabbed a handful of bustle and yanked the girl down. "What be wrong wi' ye? Sit down and behave!"

Pulled off balance, Danae plopped down onto the seat, but not before she got another whack at the impossible man. "Turn around!"

Swearing loud enough to be heard across town, the frazzled driver yanked on the reins. Slowly the cabriolet jockeyed about and began to turn about, but not without causing a traffic jam of sizable proportions. A good half-dozen drivers cursed as they struggled with their spooked horses, which began to buck their braces in the ensuing chaos. A costermonger hysterically berated his donkey when the stubborn ass collapsed with weary belligerence in front of an oncoming omnibus. The furious conductor ignored the braying laughter of the ass as he yelled obscenities at the helpless owner.

In addition to all this mayhem, pedestrians were

hurling scorching epithets at the unfortunate cabby's head as the mud from last night's storm splattered about with indiscriminate equality. Then, as if the harassed jarvey didn't have enough to contend with, trying to turn his skittish horse around before the milling mass of Londoners banded together and hung him from the nearest lamppost, the madwoman behind him lost what little patience the older woman had demanded of her. With an unladylike curse, she surged to her feet and smacked him squarely on the noodle—then once again, just to be sure his attention was not in question.

"What is taking you so long, eh? I could 'ave crawled there by now!" she shouted at him above the ruckus she had perpetrated.

Spinning about in his seat, he glared at her in a most unprofessional manner. No amount of fare was worth sharing his carriage with this she-devil. Throwing down the reins, he jumped to his feet and yelled back, "An' so who's stoppin' you?"

Seeing the flush of rage on both of the combatants, Mrs. Turlow wrapped one hand securely into the cords and tassels of Danae's fashionable bustle and again dragged her down. However, this time she did not make the mistake of letting go. "Will ye hush, the both of ye!" She yanked again on the handy bustle as Danae tried to leap to her feet again. Still the girl and cabby glared malevolently at each other. Blood could be shed if she didn't do something fast, Mrs. Turlow thought with a tremor of amusement. She had to admit, even a simple drive in the park turned into an adventure when Danae was around. Turning her attention on the furious jarvey, she shouted at him, "Ye best get this rattletrap moving, else I'll be a-tellin' the authorities that fleatrap of a horse has anthrax. Then we will be seein' how braw ye can be, shouting at a lady this way!"

The poor cabby stared openmouthed at the older woman before he spun about and grabbed hold of the reins. Even a hint of the dreaded disease could cause mass hysteria among the thousands of cabbies across London. Mrs. Turlow was pleased to see that her threat gave a new meaning to the word *fast*.

Soon the carriage was heading down Regent Street, in the right direction, and all the while Danae's gaze cast about frantically. "Drat, we took too long. I'm sure he is gone by now." Suddenly she latched on to Mrs. Turlow's arm. "There! Now do you see?" Triumphant, she pointed at a couple strolling leisurely along the street.

Mrs. Turlow squinted with dutiful care at the pair and then looked back at Danae. "So, it be his lordship. What of it?"

"He's with another woman!"

"So?"

"So!" Danae was amazed that the woman was so obtuse. "That lecherous swine goes right from my bed to walking down the street with another woman!" Her glare told Mrs. Turlow just what she thought of her shoddy loyalties. Again she turned and watched the marquis and his lady friend. Her eyes narrowed and her nails curled into the leather squabs, scoring the aged smoothness.

"He's just walking with her; he ain't humpin' her," Mrs. Turlow pointed out reasonably.

Danae paused in her hysterics, confused. "Humpin' her?"

"Ye ken what I be meaning: diddling."

"Diddling?" Danae stared at her friend as if she

was completely mad; then, as the woman opened her mouth to qualify herself again, Danae thrust her hands over her ears. "Stop! I do not want to know!" Parasol in hand, she turned and whacked the driver again. "Stop here!"

Without uttering all the choice phrases he would love to pour over her head, the cabby jerked his carriage to a standstill in the middle of the busy thoroughfare. Valiantly he ignored the commotion behind him as another traffic tangle occurred. He even had the sense to ignore the jolt to his carriage as some man's skittish horse sidestepped into the rear. With a vengeance, the beleaguered jarvey began tallying up what he was going to charge the witch when the livid rider rode on by, flinging curses at his head. He glanced sideways just in time to see the vulgar sign being flipped at him, and righteously he doubled the outrageous fare. Glumly he thought it still wasn't enough.

Meanwhile, Danae had jumped from the carriage, telling Mrs. Turlow to stay put. Giving her bodice a tug, she strolled with unhurried steps and an abundance of dignity up behind the meandering couple. She stretched out her hand to tap Sion's shoulder, but when she saw his dark head dip and watched as his lips brushed suggestively close to the slut's ear, her tap turned into a shove that sent Sion stumbling forward.

Stunned, he whipped about, ready for a confrontation, then was pleasantly surprised by the sight of his delicious lady. He smiled with warmth until he looked into her eyes, and his smile froze. His gaze traveled down to the parasol clenched like a club in Danae's dainty hand.

Carefully he spoke, "My dear, what a pleasant surprise. Out for a stroll?"

Danae raised a brow, then smiled with brittle politeness. Pointedly she studied the golden angel on his arm.

With unobtrusive little tugs, Sion tried to detach his arm from the woman's possessive grasp.

"*Cara*, do not be rude. Please introduce me to this . . . um . . . woman."

"But of course. My dear, this is Mrs. Winters. Mrs. Winters, allow me to introduce the *Contessa di Sala.*"

Danae's eyes narrowed. There was something about the woman that niggled at the back of her mind. She had seen her before, which was odd considering the brevity of acquaintances in her past. What was she to Sion, and why was she clinging to him like a possessive leech? Hiding her fear and anger, she shifted her attention back to Sion.

With man's age-old intelligence, Sion knew he would be sleeping alone tonight unless he did some impressive explaining. His jealous mate's feathers were ruffled, and she was making no bones of the fact that this intruder was poaching on territory already claimed and staked. Sion smiled smugly. Now he knew she loved him.

"Good afternoon, my lady." Mrs. Winters dipped a curtsy while clinging tenaciously to Sion's arm. Again he tried to subtly extricate himself.

"Mrs. Winters is an actress at the Coburg." He noticed Danae's posture stiffen slightly as she intently studied the woman. Finally, he was able to twist his arm out of the grasping fingers, and before she could latch onto him again, he moved over to Danae's side.

Then it hit her where she had seen that face before. The pain that washed over her almost brought her to her knees. As Sion reached her side, her gaze swung to him and her condemnation struck him full force. She clenched her hands about her parasol. If she hadn't, she was afraid she would hit him. "She looks like . . ."

"Like an angel, yes, doesn't she?" he intervened quickly, knowing the resemblance to Tory had been noted. *Damn that portrait!* His smile was strained as he reached for Danae's hand. However, she refused to let go of the parasol, so he gave up, not wanting to create a scene. This was not going well at all. He looked into Danae's eyes and was jolted by the pain he saw radiating from the damp amber depths. "Danae," he whispered, "it's not what you are thinking."

"You must have looked far and wide for her."

Sion grabbed her arm as she turned away. His breath fanned her temple as he quietly assured her, "You have to trust me; this is not what it seems. I'll explain everything later."

Pride kept her tears back. *Why am I surprised? All men are the same—selfish, untrustworthy, greedy bastards!* "Don't bother; I'm sure you have much to catch up on with your pseudo-wife." Shaking him off, she marched toward the carriage.

With a curse, his hurried steps gave chase in as unobtrusive a manner as was possible, forgetting the woman behind him. "Danae, don't be . . ."

She whirled to face him, some of the stiffness cracking away. "*Do not* call me ridiculous."

Hurriedly he explained as he tried to keep his voice down. "Remember I told you of Royce Saegar? Well, a couple of nights ago at White's, I heard of this actress that he was pursuing with overzealous insistence because of her likeness to Tory. They even hinted at violence. I simply wanted to ask her a few questions. That is all."

Danae did not look as if she believed a word of it. "Why did you not tell me of this sooner?"

Sion sighed. "To say the least, I've had other things on my mind. Namely, you. And trying to figure out how to get you back into my bed."

Danae's brow furrowed. "I am in your bed."

"No, we are in *your* bed. And damned uncomfortable, if you care about my opinion."

Looking at Mrs. Winters over Sion's shoulder, she snapped, "It is not uncomfortable."

"Well, not for your dainty frame, of course. But I wonder what you would say if you had to sleep in a bed with your feet stuck out over the edge. How in hell am I supposed to keep your feet warm when mine are dripping icicles?"

Danae watched the woman shift about impatiently. The two glared at each other. "This is not the time to debate the issue." She nodded toward the actress. "Your fantasy is getting away." After turning to glare a final time at Sion, she spun about and strode toward the carriage.

Sion kept step with her. "My what?"

"Mrs. Winters."

He grabbed her arm and jerked her to a stop. "Danny, I swear to God that there are more times than not that I would love to throttle you. She is not *my* Mrs. Winters!"

Danae sniffed at him.

"Lord, you are a stubborn woman. I don't know why I put up with you."

Danae wrenched her arm out of his grasp and almost ran the last few steps to the carriage.

Sion had to bite down on a few choice curses when he cast a harassed look back at Mrs. Winters. As Danae said, the actress was walking stiffly in the opposite direction. He still wasn't through with her yet, but . . . His head turned to watch his infuriating lover. As she started to climb into the carriage, he could swear he saw her hitch her bustle at him.

That did it! He was more than willing to pick up the gauntlet. Squaring his shoulders, he set out after her.

Mrs. Turlow had observed the scene from the safety of the cab, and as Danae approached she shifted to the side to make room. She didn't know what to make of Danae's expression, but her eyes were suspiciously bright. The old woman suspected it was more from the threat of tears than the anger staining her cheeks.

Danae was climbing up into the carriage when she saw Mrs. Turlow's eyes glance over her shoulder, then snap wide.

"Oh-oh," she barely heard the woman mutter under her breath.

Feeling herself being yanked back, reaction set in, and with an inborn sense of self-preservation, her fingers clamped over the side of the cab. Glaring over her shoulder at Sion, she hissed, "Let go of my bustle!"

"Not until you come to what little sense you have. You are acting like a spoiled chit!"

Danae shot back with haughty scorn, "Sion, you are making a scene."

"Hell, I'll show you a scene in a minute—me walking down Mayfair with you over my shoulder, with this impudent bustle worshipping heaven!" Another tug brought her off the carriage step and close to his side. "Now, I will expect an apology for this insult to my honor."

Instead, she trod vengefully on his foot.

He hopped onto his other foot, "Ow! Damn it, that's my best pair of boots you have just vandalized!"

"Well, you are ruining my bustle!"

"You'll have more than a collapsed bustle if you don't behave." He jerked again, and she stumbled about like a dog on a leash.

"All right," she hissed. "You . . . you . . . bully!"

"Well, now I'm wounded," he scoffed sarcastically.

"Buffone!" she spat back.

He paused, his eyes narrowed in outrage. "Did you just call me a buffoon?"

She gave him a stiff, angry smile. *"Si, Signore Buffone."* She added a few other choice Italian phrases, gesturing widely for emphasis.

Stunned, his eyes followed the expansive motions. His mouth snapped shut on his own defense as he caught sight of a couple veering deliberately toward them. Lord, what a spectacle they must be presenting to the masses of Mayfair! With his shoulder, he imperceptibly nudged Danae.

Catching her breath, she looked over her shoulder, following Sion's gaze, and smiled lamely at the couple as they strolled by. *"Buon giorno."*

They nodded politely as they passed by, yet continued to stare at them with impolite curiosity. Embarrassed, she glanced back at Sion.

His cool eyes condemned her. "Now are you satisfied?"

Her brow quirked as she regarded him. "I suppose this is all my fault? I don't see my hand up your bustle."

Sion gave her a reluctant smile, which grew into a chuckle. She felt a slight tug, then watched as his brow furrowed into a frown. Leaning down, he peered into the mass of material at her hip.

"What is it?" she asked as she felt another, more impatient tug.

He glanced up at her, alarm evident in his gaze. "I'm stuck."

She chuckled. "Do stop playing and let me go."

Looking furtively around them, Sion's other hand delved awkwardly into the numerous cords and ruching. She could feel a tug-of-war going on behind her. Panic seized her when she realized that Sion was not jesting with her. "Do you mean to tell me you are truly stuck?"

"Yes," he muttered, irritated. "I am well and—I am emphasizing—*truly*, stuck. It is my stud, I think."

"Well, pup, it is about time you showed yourself again," came a strident voice behind them.

In unison they turned, standing side by side, their hips touching as they tried to hide the fact that his hand was buried in her bustle. As a united force, they faced the impressive matron planted squarely before them, an ancient walking stick clasped with militant verve in one gnarled hand.

Sion forced a stiff smile and bowed, "Good afternoon, Grandmother."

Danae shot Sion a surprised glance before turning back again.

The Dowager Marchioness of Dereham, Lady Vivian Sinclair, stood glaring at her long-absent grandson, her relief in his obvious good health buried deep under her resentment—a resentment that had been festering for three long years. In silent ire, her arthritic fingers clenched about the golden lion's head of her walking stick as her watery eyes studied the couple before her. She had heard about this woman and was not pleased that her grandson was already embroiled in yet another scandal, and before the *ton* was even socially aware of his presence.

Angry as she was, she had to admit they made a

striking picture. Standing beside Sion, one would think that the woman's average height would be overwhelmed by his towering build, but strangely she appeared to fit him with perfect harmony, so regally did she hold her slender form. She dressed with an almost insolent style but managed to carry it off with aplomb. Her complexion was dusky silk, proclaiming her foreign origins, and her eyes, a unique golden hue with a exotic slant, made it almost impossible to look away. The old dame was a bit surprised to see the woman returning her scrutiny with a polite boldness she found admirable, if a bit forward.

Yes indeed, her handsome grandson had a high-stepper on his arm to flaunt, but if she had anything to say about it, he would flaunt her from a house on Half Moon Street, not in the family town house. Already she had heard the rumblings about him and his lover cohabitating.

Quite shocking.

"Well," her voice grated commandingly, "is this the woman I've heard your name bandied with? Speak up."

Sion hesitated for a long moment, debating whether to ignore her altogether, but finally a reluctant sense of social civility, more than familial duty, forced him to disregard the slur against Danae and acknowledge the old dowager.

"Madam, I would like you to meet the *Contessa di Sala, Signora* Danae Suriano. My dear," he went on, turning slightly toward Danae, "this is my grandmother, the Dowager Marchioness of Dereham."

With as much grace as she could manage, considering Sion's hand was wedged in her bustle, Danae dipped a slight curtsy, not too deep; after all, the old crone had just insulted her. Never again would she humbly endure cuts from people she could hardly care less about, and this woman came across as a person who could fit squarely into this category. By the stiff tension radiating from Sion, it was obvious he didn't think too highly of the matriarch of the Dereham clan.

"How have you been, madam?" Sion asked politely, not really giving a damn. Or so he told himself as he stood there just wishing she would leave.

"As if you give a damn how I have been doing," came the bitter rejoinder, almost reading his mind. "Not once in three years have you bothered to correspond to let me know how you were or to ask of my failing health."

Sion looked skeptically at the feisty, wizened lady. Indeed, she looked older but in no way frailer than when he last saw her. "I didn't think you would care to hear from a man who had murdered his wife, madam." He felt the slight jolt that shook Danae's body.

The faded eyes, fastened intently on Sion's face, widened in shock before her papery lids shuttered her feelings. Danae noticed that the hand holding the cane shook and the old woman seemed to wilt, what little starch supporting the frail frame melting away. The dowager's companion, standing at a respectful distance, stepped forward but was abruptly waved away.

When his grandmother again raised her gaze, Danae was shocked to see the hurt radiating from the black eyes that looked so much like Sion's. This woman loved her grandson, but Sion believed she had betrayed him. Danae felt a burning need to learn the truth, for she knew Sion's pride enough to know he would not bend. Tomorrow she would call on the dowager marchioness.

Lady Dereham stared at her grandson, at a loss what to say. He believed she had turned her back on him all those years ago. Now she understood the silence, but why was that the mystery? What had she done to him? Said to him? She couldn't remember. Lud, she was getting old. Her last pride and joy stood but a few feet away, hardly wanting to even acknowledge her. Her attention shifted briefly to the woman standing so close to his side. The amber eyes were studying her intently, seeing more than her stubborn grandson cared to.

A silent message passed between the two women. Once more the marchioness glanced at her grandson; then wearily, without another word, she turned to accept the arm of her companion and ambled off into the crowd.

Danae looked at Sion and her heart wrenched as she spied the moist sheen in his ebony eyes, his gaze fixed bleakly on his grandmother's stooped form.

"You love her but are trying to hurt her. Why?"

Shaking his head slightly, he bent to untangle his stud. "Please, Danae, let it be."

"Of course, if you wish." As if she had any intention of letting it be.

As they turned toward the carriage again, already her mind was working on a plan for seeing the marchioness.

Seventeen

Danae had decided to stay at home today, having overtaxed herself the past week with seeing the sights of London and being prodded by the professional finesse of modistes, milliners, and bootmakers. Besides, Sion had exhausted her last night. She smiled with dreamy contentment, remembering his glistening physique bent over her, demanding endlessly and giving torturous delights all night long and into the subtle light of dawn. He had been very exuberant in thanking her for returning to *his* bed.

She chuckled as she again pictured Sion standing on the bed, straddling her with sketch pad in hand, stating how he had to capture the moment for posterity. The sketch never did get finished, Sion having thrown the pad aside when her mouth had found his deliciously straining manhood. Her cheeks flushed with tingling warmth as she remembered the taste of him; he had tasted of the essence of them. Her smile faded when she again visualized all that masculine beauty and power quivering for the mere touch of her finger or stroke of her tongue. How beautiful he made her feel, how cherished. But, for how long? Until her beauty began to fade, till extra flesh padded her sleek frame, till countless years stole her youth?

On these morbid thoughts, the library door swung wide, and the butler, Seadon, stepped in.

"A visitor, madam: the Viscount Halsingham to see you. Shall I say you are at home?"

Danae thought for a moment before she nodded, "*Si*, Seadon, and tell the *signore* of our visitor, *per favore. Grazie.*"

"Very good, madam. I will show him into the parlor."

Danae watched the closing door with mixed emotions. She wondered what Halsingham wanted, and yet she got a rather precarious thrill at tweaking his nose, so to speak. Standing, she tossed aside the book on her lap and, smoothing her skirts, headed for the parlor hoping Sion wouldn't be too long. Last she had seen of him, he had been sprawled across his bed, snoring gently. So much for his complaint of cold feet, considering he hadn't even bothered to cover himself when he had finally fallen into an exhausted stupor. When she had rolled him off her he hadn't even stirred an eyelash.

Entering the parlor, Danae spied the viscount standing before the bay window, the brilliant morning light surrounding his lithe form. As he turned at the sound of the door's opening, his smile was no less blinding than the light glinting in his golden hair. His fingers were pleasantly warm and soothing as he took her offered hand. Bending low, he brought her hand to his lips, turning it over at the last second and placing his lips upon her wrist.

Danae, shocked at the heat of those lips upon her sensitive skin, inadvertently snatched her hand back, forcing a smile upon stiff lips. *"Buon giorno, Signore* Halsingham. How are you this morning?"

Halsingham smiled with seductive ease as he followed her to a pair of chairs. *"Molto allora, grazie. E lei?"*

Danae spun about to stare openmouthed at him. *Oh, dear! This could be a problem. "Parla Italiano?"*

He shrugged, grinning boyishly. *"Si, ma molte piccolo."*

Gathering her thoughts, Danae sat on the edge of her chair, hoping that for once he was telling the truth. Her own Italian was just adequate. "Where did you learn *Italiano, signore?"*

He sat across from her. "Years ago my father had me assigned as an attaché to an ambassador to Italy. It was only a short stint, not much more than eight months. Just enough to pick up a few words."

Danae hurriedly glanced down when she realized she was staring. "I never knew," she murmured, amazed at how little she knew of this man who had been her husband for three years.

He quirked an eyebrow. "How could you have known?"

"Well, I . . . I . . ." she cast about frantically after that little faux pas. "I never recall *Katerina* tell me of this," she finished lamely.

"I don't believe she knew." He straightened the cuff of his jacket.

When the door opened again, she looked toward it eagerly but was disappointed to see Mrs. Turlow enter with a tea tray. Setting the tray down before Danae, Mrs. Turlow moved across the room to settle into the window seat. There she studied the viscount with suspicious regard, her frown ferocious on her pugnacious features.

Halsingham turned from watching the door

guardian and asked in a whisper, "Did I do something wrong?"

Danae hid her smile as she leaned over the tea tray. "*Si*, you are in room alone with me. *Signora* Turlow is my chap . . . chap . . . how you say?"

"Chaperone," he supplied dryly.

"*Si*, chaperone. Why have you come, *signore*?"

"Well, I . . ." Again he glanced over at Mrs. Turlow, stiffening slightly when he caught her still glaring at him. Danae suppressed her smile when he shifted his confused gaze onto her. "Well, I wondered if you would do me the honor of accompanying me for a ride in the park tomorrow morning."

Observing his tenseness as she handed over the teacup and saucer, Danae doubted that this cordial invitation had been his initial reason for coming. He wanted something but was reluctant to speak in front of Mrs. Turlow. Extremely curious, she was about to send the well-meaning snoop on her way when the door swung inward again and Sion strode in. He paused to take in the scene before he took a seat on the divan beside her, giving Halsingham the barest of civil greetings. Out of the corner of her eye she noticed the viscount's ire at Sion's entrance.

"So, Halsingham, what brings you here?" Sion asked bluntly, his gaze coolly accessing the younger man.

Halsingham looked at Sion over the rim of his cup as he took a sip. After a moment he replied with equal coolness, "I came to ask the *contessa* to come out with me tomorrow morning. You have no problem with this, do you, Dereham?"

"More than you can know." Sion's silky voice established his opposition to the viscount's intentions quite nicely, Danae thought. Flattered, she switched her gaze to Halsingham and watched as the two men stared each other down. It was rather like watching two rams bashing their fool heads together.

Feeling a little devil prod her, she spoke up brightly, "I think I would enjoy to ride with the *signore*."

"No, she wouldn't." Sion's eyes hadn't moved from the viscount.

"Yes, she would." Leaning over, Halsingham placed his saucer on the table with a decided rattle.

"Why don't you just get to the point of why you are here, Halsingham."

Danae's glittering eyes teased Sion. "He is here to see me, *cara.*" Then she turned to Halsingham. *"Si,* I will come with you *domani.*"

Halsingham dragged his gaze from Sion and smiled stiffly at her. Rising to his feet, he bent over her hand, rudely ignoring the earl. *"Excellente, signora. Allora gli diro ciao fino a domani."*

"A cosa tempo incontreremo?" she asked, deliberately prolonging the intimate *tête-à-tête*. In her peripheral vision she noticed Sion's jaw clench, the muscle in his cheek twitching as he vainly tried to control his rage.

With a smug smile flung at the livid earl, Halsingham again pressed his lips to her wrist. "I will call for you at eleven, *signora.*"

"Molto bene. Ciao."

When the door had closed behind the man, Danae fussed with the tray, trying to make herself look occupied. "Please leave, Mrs. Turlow," she heard Sion's voice command with cold precision.

Mrs. Turlow immediately got up and headed for the door. "Aye, ye better beat some sense into the wee wittle." She stubbornly avoided Danae's outraged glare as she slammed the door behind her.

Sion lounged back, studying his perverse lover, then asked while trying to rein in his escalating temper, "Are you deliberately trying to provoke me this morning?"

Danae merely folded a napkin, avoiding his censorious gaze. She didn't like feeling like a reprimanded child.

Crossing his fingers over his stomach, Sion tipped his head back and stared at the neutral territory of the ceiling. "Much earlier than I wished, I was rudely jolted out of a deep slumber, which, if I recall by your ecstatic cries and moans throughout the *long* night, I had definitely earned." He cast a lazy glance at her profile and relished the blush his words brought to her cheeks. "Being informed of the unwanted presence of a certain viscount and advised, *by you,* of the desirability for my presence 'posthaste,' I hurried gallantly to your side. There I was subjected to you and that toad delighting each other in a noxious *tête-à-tête* while your humble servant was all but ignored. Then, as if this were not insult enough, I was also forced to sit by like a docile ass while you flagrantly defied me."

Danae gazed at him in stunned admiration. "That was quite impressive, my lord. You have eloquently explained your ire, and I most humbly agree. My apologies for disturbing your sleep, and yes, you did earn it as I most happily recall, but"—she looked at him with innocent bewilderment—"I am not aware that I have to obtain your permission to enjoy the company of anyone I choose to associate with."

Sion's eyes narrowed to dangerous slits.

Danae shrugged in sham apology. "You, of course, may always discuss your misgivings with me, but you have not the right to order me." She smiled at him, all winsome scorn. "I do not believe a lover has to obey; that is a wife's lot in life." She looked him straight in the eye. "And I am not your wife."

"How true, and with this attitude I don't see any change of that in the near future."

"I am not expecting one."

Tired and irritated with the senseless banter, Sion shot to his feet and stood glowering down on her. "Listen and listen well, Danae. I don't trust Camden and I don't trust Halsingham. Getting into a carriage with the man is, to say the least, a damn foolish chance to take. However, only being your *lover* and having no say as to what happens to you, you do as you bloody well see fit." And with this parting shot he strode from the room, anger dogging his hurried heels.

Well, Danae thought as she sat back, *that certainly puts me in my place.* She felt more than a little irritated that Sion would let her go with Halsingham so easily. It was obvious that he didn't care enough about her to put up much of a fight.

Refusing to admit to her contrary emotions—independence versus the need of depending on the safety of Sion's arms—she had the most absurd urge to burst into a bout of self-pitying tears.

Did Sion care, or was she only fooling herself?

The next morning, heavy-eyed and depressed, Danae patted her chignon a final time, noticing the approach of the eleventh hour in the mirror. With a sigh, she rose from her dressing table, not sure she was curious enough anymore to care what Halsingham had to say to her.

Passing a disgruntled gaze over her rumpled bed, she snatched up her reticule and headed for the door. It was quite daunting to realize how dependent she had become on a pair of warm and comforting arms to hold her through the night before she could find blissful sleep. Sion had avoided her last night at dinner, having retired to one of his odious clubs, not bothering to return until the dawn hours. In a huff she had gone to her own solitary bed, intending to give him the cold shoulder when he finally deigned to make an appearance. The only problem was, he hadn't even bothered to give her the satisfaction of snubbing him. He had never come.

Well, so be it!

Giving her bodice a militant tug, she reached for the handle of the door, intending to fling it open but gasped as she painfully wrenched her shoulder instead. With a confused frown, she again twisted the latch and tugged to no effect. Slipping her reticule onto her wrist, she grasped the latch with both hands and rattled it angrily.

Nothing.

Stepping back, she placed her hands on her hips and glared at the door. Was the dratted thing stuck? Hitching up her skirts, she levered a delicately shod foot against the frame, and again grasping the latch in both hands, she strained backward, but to no purpose for the door held fast.

"Well, for heaven's sake," she muttered as she smoothed her skirts back into place. Leaning forward, she placed her ear to the door, and hearing muted voices in the hall beyond, she pounded on the thick mahogany, *"Mi scusi,* whoever is out there. Could you help me, *per favore?* The door is stuck."

She jumped back, startled, as a very familiar, very smug voice drawled just on the other side of the portal, "No it is not, my love. It is locked and it will stay that way until Halsingham is on his way."

Not believing her ears, Danae stared, stunned, at the door. Then the heat of anger surged into her face as it hit her what he had done. *The dratted man had locked her in!* Leaping on the door, both fists pounding, she shouted, "You low-down, contemptible bastard, open this door this minute!"

Sion smiled as he leaned a shoulder on the door, feeling the vibration of the pounding. "I think not, my love." As her shouts became more profane and the pounding increased, he winced. The woman certainly had a temper. With amused concern he admonished her though the door, "Careful of your hands." Abruptly the pounding ceased.

He cocked an ear against the wood, curious as to what she would do next. When all was quiet, he assumed she had given up, no doubt succumbing to a feminine bout of tears, and pushed away from the door. With a chuckle, he headed down the stairs, thinking how it wasn't so difficult getting the upper hand with Danae once he recognized her perverseness for what it was; an enchanting, vulnerable way of seeking attention.

As he entered his study, he informed Seadon that the *contessa* was not at home to the Viscount Halsingham when he called. It wasn't but five minutes later when a piercing scream shattered the sedate atmosphere. Sion was out of his study and sprinting up the stairs before Seadon could even rise above his astonished confusion. A second later the shout of "Fire!" galvanized a panic among the household.

Sion bounded onto the landing just as he saw smoke billowing out from under Danae's door. Terror constricted his chest as he ran down the hall, fumbling in his pocket for the key.

"Danny," he shouted, his hand trembling so violently he was barely able to get the key inserted into the lock. Throwing open the door, he surged through the pall of smoke, his watering eyes searching desperately for her when a shove from behind propelled him farther into the room. Confused, he spun about and heard the slamming of a door and what sounded suspiciously like the grating of a key in its lock. Jerking his handkerchief from his pocket, Sion scrubbed his burning eyes and then looked about the room.

Her empty room.

In the next moment he found the fire, or the source of the smoke. Not believing his eyes, Sion stood, soot-stained and slack-jawed, staring at the strategically placed pile of dampened and charred towels piled with careful precision into a yellow porcelain chamber pot. The billow of black smoke emanating from the mess was noxious indeed, and he guessed she must have drenched the towels with a toilette water.

Coughing and cursing, he grabbed up a beautiful fur-lined cape and took perverse pleasure in dropping it over the smoking pot, then turned his attention to the door. Even before his hand reached for the latch, he knew it would be locked.

"Danae," he bellowed, "you open this damned door right this bloody minute or your ass is mine and tonight I'll paint it red!" Furious, he kicked aside the chamber pot and leaned against the panel. "Danae, I swear to God . . ."

"Your lordship . . ." The rest of the sentence came across a muffled garble.

He pressed closer against the smoke-stained wood. "Seadon, is that you?"

The voice came through clearer now. "Yes, my lord. I can't seem to find the key."

"Where's the *contessa?*"

The muffled reply was definitely hesitant. "I believe she left with the viscount, my lord."

Pushing away from the door, he glared at it, the whole side of his face, the palms of his hands, and the front of his immaculate jacket smudged black from the soot on the wood. "That *willful little bitch!* When I get my hands on her . . ." He couldn't even finish the thought as his mind stumbled for a hideous enough retribution. Throwing back his head, he roared out to the hapless Seadon, "Get someone up here to open this friggin' door! I don't care if you have to take an axe to it!"

Breathing heavily, he heard the vague sounds of scurrying footsteps, then silence. Bloodshot eyes glared balefully at the covered chamber pot.

The Hellhound of Dereham was back.

Four hours later, Danae stared at the imposing front entrance with a fear she hadn't felt since leaving Camden Abbey. With dragging feet she climbed the stairs, and not bothering to knock, she inched the door open and poked her head inside. When the door was jerked inward, she stumbled forward with a muffled yelp and found herself being scrutinized down the length of Seadon's haughty nose.

Raising her chin and hoping she came across a

bit more composed than she felt, Danae nodded to
the distinctly condemning butler. "*Ciao*, Seadon.
Is . . . is the *signore* in?"

"Not to you, madam," he replied in stately disdain.

Danae nodded, smiling lamely, realizing she was
in deep, deep water. "*Signora* Turlow?"

"Not to you, madam."

Trying for a little levity to ease the tension, she
jested, "Are you in, Seadon?"

When he opened his mouth to reply, she fore-
stalled him by lifting her hand, "*Sì*, I know—not
to me."

He bowed, ever so slightly. "Very good, madam."
Then, without another word he shut the door,
turned his back, and left her standing in the middle of the hall.

At a loss as to what to do now, Danae contemplated her options and didn't like any of them.
Drawing off her gloves, she moved into the salon
and collapsed onto the divan before the fire. Resting her pounding head in her hand, she stared
desultorily into the fitful flames, wondering why
she was always trying to provoke him so. The problem was, she *liked* their altercations. She liked
watching his eyes flash at her; she liked the banter. She loved his undivided attention. She always
felt so alive when she was with him, but when they
were spitting at each other and testing each
other's mettle, she felt more than just alive—she
felt invigorated. She could almost say she enjoyed
it as much as when she was making love with him.
Almost. She sighed and shifted restlessly as she
realized she would doubtless be spending another
long night in her lonely bed.

And in a room reeking of smoke, no less. Lord,

when would she learn to temper her impulsiveness?

She closed her eyes, not even noticing as the tears slipped beneath the lashes feathering her pale cheeks. *God, please don't let Sion hate me.*

Suddenly, an urge she hadn't felt in months swept over her like a tidal wave. Almost against her will, she rose to her feet and walked into the hall and down the corridor till she came to the door of a room she had previously avoided. She pushed the broad door in and it swung wide, whispering on oiled hinges. She stepped into the darkened room and took a deep breath, her eyes closing as the familiar scent of highly waxed wood assailed her senses.

When she moved forward, she walked as if in a trance. A moment later she found herself seated on a hard bench, her back ramrod straight. Blindly she lifted the cherry-wood cover and felt the cold ivory beneath her fingers. She paused, then slowly stroked the tip of one finger along a key, and the reverberating hum called to the lost soul in her. She didn't even hear the haunting melody as it drifted with somber grace through the quiet halls; instead she felt it soothe her anguish and fear. This long-lost friend of hers was back.

On silent feet, Sion entered the music room and sat unobtrusively in a corner, his gaze fixated on her proud back. The music was incredibly poignant, almost funereal in its pathos, and he hated it. It spoke too eloquently of the pain within. His head still pounded from the rage he had suffered through, and it was all he could do not to hurt her as she had him. His hands curled into fists upon his tensed thighs, his body stretched almost to the breaking point. But he persevered, sitting in an almost violent silence, staring at his infuriating lover, hating her and loving her even more. Fear swamped him as he listened to her suffering through the music. Had he lost her? Would she run again as she had fled from Camden? And superimposed on this thought was the fact he knew he could never let her go. Never.

The haunting strains died into the silence. Danae let her hands drop away from the keys, and she looked down at them as they lay like deadened weights in her lap. "I didn't go with him," she whispered into the room, her heart reaching across the vastness to the man sitting in the shadowy corner. When he said nothing, she swallowed painfully. "I went to visit your grandmother."

Still he said nothing.

His condemning silence strangled her. She was finding it difficult to breathe as she stood and slowly turned toward him. Keeping her gaze on her clenched fingers, she tried to speak, but her throat convulsed on the words. Coughing slightly, she forced herself to speak. "I'm sorry, Sion . . . I . . . it was . . ."

Tears stung her eyes. *Please, don't send me away.* But his silence screamed at her. Buffeted by her emotions, Danae went over the edge into familiar numbness. The fear slipped away, the pain slipped away. The void that enveloped her was an escape she had hoped she would never have to suffer again. It was as if Katherine was coming to life again.

Glancing up, she looked at him for the first time. She saw his vague silhouette sprawled in a chair in a darkened corner. Pride stiffened her shoulders.

She couldn't, wouldn't beg. So she had mistaken the depth of his interest in her. She would survive.

"I'll pack tonight and be out of here in the morning, if that is acceptable." The words grated painfully in her throat.

In the tomblike silence she could feel his gaze raking her. She flinched when he suddenly rose to his feet and, with predatory grace, sauntered toward her, his steps echoing around her. Her heart accelerated as he drew nearer, then plummeted when he moved on by, not even deigning to look at her. Her eyes were staring sightlessly at the space where he had almost brushed against her, her starved senses breathing in his scent. Behind her she heard the door snick softly shut. Defeated, she closed her eyes.

Powerful hands grabbed her shoulders, wrenching a startled scream from her. She was spun about and found herself staring wide-eyed into a face of Sion she had never seen. The rage etching into his features held her spellbound in fear of this stranger. His fingers dug cruelly into her shoulders, and suddenly she couldn't take it. The thought of Sion, her lover, hating her was a nightmare twisted into a reality that she had never thought to experience.

Her world shattered, and she collapsed—simply collapsed into his arms. The harsh hands on her shoulders tried to hold her away, and they bit into her flesh with a pain that jolted her. "Sion," she sobbed, frightened by this stranger looming so menacingly over her. "Please, you're hurting me."

"Am I?" his voice rasped out of the darkness. "Am I hurting you, Danae? How does it feel?" When she just sobbed harder, he let go her shoulders and took hold of her wrists, "Tell me. I want to know what kind of pain a treacherous, callous bitch can feel."

When the force of her sobs began to rack her slender body, Sion stepped back so he could look down at her. Cursing his damned temper, he watched as she crumbled to the floor and curled into herself, hugging her knees to her heaving chest. With a shuddering sigh, he squatted down beside her and reached out to touch her flushed cheek.

"Christ, Danny, all I wanted to do was protect you. I don't believe you can have any idea what hell I went through knowing you were alone in his company." So deep was his turmoil that it took him a moment to realize she was speaking.

"I'm sorry. I was wrong. I'm always wrong; I know that. I'm sorry. I'll go. I'll leave, I promise. I'm sorry."

Scrubbing his face with shaking hands, he turned his face to the ceiling, his breathing a harsh background to her garbled litany. After tense moments in the dark room with only her tears, the cold floor, and his helplessness surrounding them, he finally stood. Gently he helped her to her feet, lifted her into his arms, and walked out of the room.

In his room, he placed her in the center of his bed and stood by grimly as he watched her slender body again curl away from him. His eyes never left her as he stripped off his clothes, then climbing in beside her, he pulled her against his body, steeling himself for a fight.

But, with heartwrenching sincerity, at the touch of his hands she turned and blindly reached for him, her heated, damp face pressed into his neck.

Her arms snaked about his neck, almost strangling him. "I'm sorry," she whispered again.

With an anguished moan that became a reluctant chuckle, he buried his face into her sweet hair. "No, you're not; that's why I love you so much, you little witch."

Her body shuddered, then burrowed even closer into his. "Good."

He smiled. "I'm sure you think so." His fingers made short work of the laces at the back of her bodice. In moments she was lying naked in his arms. "Now go to sleep. I'm exhausted."

"I hope you had as terrible a night's sleep as I had last night." When he merely nodded, she murmured groggily, "Splendid," then thankfully drifted off into healing sleep.

As Sion listened to her slumberous breath, he stroked her feverish brow, pondering his contrary lady. Again he wondered at the pain in her past and the formidable and vulnerable woman it had created. She was the epitome of the word *contradiction,* and he had his doubts whether she would allow him to grow to a respectable old age with her. Lord knew he had lost a few of those years today.

After a while, his arms began to loosen as his body drifted free into blessed oblivion. But, niggling just on the peripheral edge of consciousness, he vaguely recalled something she had said earlier. It prodded insistently, giving no peace. Then his eyes snapped open, and it took all his willpower not to shake her awake.

She had gone to see his grandmother.

Leaning on his elbow, he glared at her blissfully slumbering countenance, and resented her for costing him yet another peaceful night's sleep. What had his grandmother told her?

When Danae shifted and snuggled closer, he again glared at her. Reaching down, he tucked the covers closer about her. "You shouldn't have done that, Danny," he whispered in her ear.

She muttered some unintelligent little sounds, and her frigid toes brushed against his. Unconsciously his feet warmed hers, thinking it was strange how the rest of her body was like a little furnace. *Even her damn toes are contrary.*

On a positive note, at least she hadn't gone riding with Halsingham.

Lying back down, he stared up at the ceiling, wondering where Halsingham's sudden interest in Danae was going.

Eighteen

Vivian Sinclair, Dowager Marchioness of Dereham frowned as she tried to keep sight of the spare frame of the Earl of Camden in the milling crowd along Regent Street. Even though it was strange to see the reclusive man out in public, she would never have given it another thought. But now that Danae had apprised her of the whole sordid situation, and making a few conclusions of her own based on what she had not been told, she found herself wallowing in vulgar curiosity. Wondering who the beautiful child at his side was, she dogged the earl's steps, using her cane to advantage when someone was hapless enough to step in her way. Her attention was constantly drawn to the golden curls and angelic profile of the boy trotting obediently at Camden's side. Never had she seen such a beautiful child. As her prey turned into the tailoring shop of Fitch Brothers, she paused, undecided what to do.

"Crandall, I believe I will buy my grandson some fine cambric handkerchiefs. What do you say?" Not really giving a damn what her companion had to say, she squinted through the glass window, and not seeing Camden, she stepped through the door, the bell above announcing her arrival.

With irritating promptness, a salesman stepped forward, blocking her view of the back of the store. "Madam, welcome! How may I help you today?"

Scowling, she shoved him aside with her walking stick, and upon spotting Camden seated in a chair flanking a set of floor-length mirrors, she relaxed. It was apparent the child was being fitted for some suits, for he was standing with stoic disinterest on a platform before the wall of mirrors as he was being measured. When the irritating little man again politely prodded her about her wishes, she snapped, "Handkerchiefs."

He bowed, "Very good, madam. If you will come this way, I will show you. . . ." he paused and looked around when he noticed that he was talking to himself. With a sigh, he retraced his steps, then followed the direction of the old woman's attention. She was staring quite rudely at the Earl of Camden and his grandson. "Is there a problem, madam?"

Using the dangerous-looking cane, she motioned toward the mirrors. "Who is that?"

"That is the Earl of Camden."

"I know that! Who the deuce do you think I am? I'm talking of the child."

Not having the faintest idea who she was but only knowing she was now sounding like someone of importance, he answered a bit more deferentially, "That is the earl's grandson, the Viscount Searling."

Shocked, she jerked about and stared at the clerk. "His grandson?" Her gaze swiveled back to the diminutive figure multiplied in the numerous mirrors. What was going on here? The girl had told her everything. Quite a leap of faith— quite admirable, and quite stupid in many ways.

But she didn't mention anything about a child. Did Sion know?

Her eyes shifted again, and she found herself studying the earl, whose whole attention was riveted intently on the beautiful child. For that matter, did Danae know she had a son? Something was not quite right. When the obsequious little man began to talk again, she gave him her full attention for the first time since entering the shop.

Loving to gossip and finding an opportunity, he leaned forward and whispered in confidential undertones, "It seems that his grandson had been kidnapped years ago and only now just found. The viscount's mother had been so depressed by his disappearance that she had fallen into deep decline and simply languished away. I heard she died tragically last summer. So sad to think she never saw her child again, dying of grief before the joyous event of his homecoming. Beautiful child, isn't he?"

Quirking a dubious eye at the subject of the dismal little tale, she couldn't picture the Danae who had boldly appeared on her doorstep a week ago languishing away over anything, let alone a fictitious son.

In a hurry to be gone, she swung about, and in a rustle of stiff bombazine, her wide bustle threatening the neatness of the narrow aisle, she sailed toward the door. Pushing the clerk out of the way as only a pompous noblewoman with years of experience could, she belatedly felt she owed the man something for his trouble, and paused in midflight. A small commission was in order. After all, she had just received a wealth of information.

"I'll take a couple dozen of your very best handkerchiefs, monogrammed with the initials SS. Send them to my address." She pressed a gilded card into his hand. "Thank you, my good man. Now, out of my way." And before he could even blink, he heard the tinkling of the bell over the door before it was slammed shut.

"Stand aside, my good man; I'll announce myself. Crandall, I would like some of my usual brew right away." There was an ominous crash when the Dowager Marchioness's strident voice reprimanded, "Out of my way, out of my way! Crandall! Get him!"

Marking her place on the same page of the same chapter of the same book she had been trying to read all week, Danae hurried to the doors. Flinging them wide, she almost laughed aloud when confronted by the buxom Crandall tackling a disheveled Seadon, who, with dedicated verve, was trying to intercept the marchioness.

"Seadon, it is all right, *si*." Then she did laugh when abject relief flooded the features of the indignant servant.

"Very good, my lady," he intoned as he jerked his arm from Crandall's now lax grip. "This person would not introduce herself," he defended himself as he returned the old woman's glare.

The insulted lady stepped forward with menacing intent, "You half-wit . . . who the deuce are you, anyway? Where is Grayson?"

"Dead," Seadon intoned archly.

The marchioness looked around at Danae, shocked. "When did that happen? He was younger than me!" She sounded almost indignant that the poor man should have died before her.

Shrugging, Danae stepped between them and

gently took Sion's grandmother's arm. "Seadon, this is the Do-wa-ger *Marchiona, Signora* Dereham." She deliberately made a botch of the title and didn't fail to notice the marchioness's sharp-eyed perusal of her, no doubt not believing a syllable of the faulty accent. And here she thought she was doing so well.

Seadon's hectic flush drained, and then an interesting shade of green washed his stunned features. "Oh, my! Oh . . . *forgive me,* my lady, I . . . oh, my!"

The marchioness turned to glare down her beak of a nose at him. "I don't like you. Go away."

"At once, my lady." Then, spinning about, he almost ran from the hall.

Danae looked at Crandall, still standing mute along the wall. "You see to some, um, refreshment, *si?*"

With a slight nod, the woman followed along in Seadon's wake.

Curious as to the marchioness's visit, Danae ushered her into the library and helped her into one of the massive wing chairs by the fire. As she saw to her comfort, she was a bit concerned over what Sion's reaction would be to his grandmother's presence in his home.

Just as she was settling herself across from her, the old dame came to the reason of the visit with brutal dispatch.

"That is the most execrable accent I have ever heard. Do you really fool people with it? It is also obvious that you didn't tell me everything. Your son, for instance."

Danae just stared at the woman.

"Well?"

"Of course I don't have a son. What makes you

ask?" Now that they were alone Danae didn't
bother with her accent.

"I have my reasons." Even as that unblinking
gaze drilled her, it was also obvious to Danae that
the woman wasn't as in control of the situation as
she would like to think. Her frail kid-gloved hands
were trembling and restless upon the top of her
cane.

"Katherine died a virgin, if that is what you want
to know."

The marchioness ceased her restless fidgeting as
the words sank in. An infinitesimal thrill shot along
her spine as her eyes dipped, involuntary of better
manners, to scan Danae's flat stomach. "And now?"

Danae hid her shock well as she smiled with polite distance. "That is my business, my lady."

"Will it be my business when I am a great-grandmother?"

Danae didn't blink an eye. "Perhaps."

Vivian harrumphed. "You are a cool one. Let
us see how this catches you." Leaning forward,
she announced slowly, wanting to make sure every
word was attended to, "You are the proud mama
of a beautiful, bouncing boy. I'd guess five years
old."

As expected, Danae's cool shell slipped more
than a notch; it disintegrated. She stared at Vivian
openmouthed. "What?"

The old woman nodded, smug in the thought
she had finally found the woman beneath the cara-
pace. "Just so. My reaction exactly."

"What nonsense are you speaking of?"

"I saw Camden on Regent Street and followed
him. Walking at his side was the most beautiful
child I have ever seen—other than Sion, of
course." Even with her mind awash in confusion,

Danae gave a slight smile at the woman's obvious pride and loyalty. "When they entered a haberdashery, I, of course, followed along in. According to the gossipy clerk's rendition, Camden is claiming the child as his long-lost heir, just now rescued after all these long years. A victim of a kidnapping, I believe he said. And you"—she motioned with her cane—"you wasted away from your grief and had tragically died before the miraculous rescue. All very touching. All very melodramatic. All a pile of rubbish."

Danae sat still, stunned into a mindless void. After a few moments, she mused, "I don't believe it. Camden can't be serious." Standing, she paced away and then back, aimless in her direction. "He must be mad to think he can pull this off. Why, even the age of the child is blatantly wrong. I don't think Halsingham was subtle about his marriage into the Camden family at the time we were married; he was too ecstatic at having a fortune finally at his fingertips. There are going to be enough people counting backward. I simply can't believe it. Lord, he must be more obsessed than I thought."

"Delusions of grandeur had never been a problem with Camden. He has always been such an odd duck, if you ask me. I made a point of staying away from him—gave me the shivers, that one did. And that second wife he married. Now, that would be enough to send any man over the edge."

"What is going on in here?" Sion's deep voice intruded, the chilliness in his words reflected in the stark mask he presented to his grandmother.

Danae spun about and hurried over to him as the marchioness devoured the sight of her grandson.

"What is she doing here?" he asked of Danae even though he glared across the dimming room at the old woman.

"Sion, please," she warned in an undertone as she took hold of his arm. "Behave." With a tug, she was able to drag him into the room. "Lady Dereham was kind enough to inform me of Camden's recent machinations. And quite startling they are, too."

The two Derehams hardly paid attention to her ramblings as they studied each other like two wary animals afraid for their lives.

"You are not welcome here, madam. I am sorry if this disturbs you, but your presence here greatly disturbs me." Steeling himself against the sheen of tears in the faded black eyes, he continued, "I ask that you leave."

Danae's nails dug into the sleeve of his jacket. Leaning over, she whispered furiously into his ear, "Sion, you can be such a bastard at times. At this moment I'm seriously doubting my intelligence in trusting such a coldhearted ass. Have you ever thought that you might have been wrong, that there might have been a reason for what happened three years ago?" Stepping away, she glared at him. "I suggest you think about it. You may never have this chance again." Taking a deep breath, she glanced over at his grandmother, who suddenly looked a decade more wizened. Suppressing the urge to go over and comfort her, she turned away toward the door, but not before throwing a lethal glare at her obtuse lover. "I will see to the tea."

At this moment he didn't know whom he was angrier with, and his emotions were too tangled to care. When he turned to follow Danae out, he was brought up short by his grandmother's wavering voice.

"I did not desert you at the trials."

"That is strange, since I don't remember you sitting at my back. I don't remember you responding to my pleas for your support. I don't remember you being anywhere around when I needed you." He was so bitter that the memories of all the years of stark loneliness threatened to consume what civility he had left.

"I don't know what happened, Sion. Apparently there had been a force that neither of us knew about conspiring to keep us apart. I didn't realize until I saw you last week, for the first time in all these years, that you somehow thought I believed you guilty." Her voice grew impassioned as she stood, her legs trembling so much that she had to lean heavily on her cane. But her gaze was steady and direct when she finally made eye contact with him. "If you want me to go, I will. But before I do, know this. Never did I think you guilty of harming your sweet Tory. *Never! Never! Never!*" She pounded the floor with each vow.

Sion's eyes misted over as he stared at this woman who had been such a loving force in his life. The belief of her abandonment had devastated him, and on top of the deaths of his family, it had almost crushed him into inebriated death. Swallowing hard, he asked in a gravelly voice, "Where were you? Why wouldn't you see me?"

She stepped forward, raising her arms, let them fall limp at her sides. "Sion, I thought you knew."

"Knew what?"

"With the shock of Tory's death and your being imprisoned, I . . ." Her words faded away. Looking up at him with tears streaming down her face, she shook her head sadly, whispering, "I am so sorry, Siony, I thought you knew. I thought you had turned against *me*. And then all those years I wrote to you at Dereham Hall and you never answered." She sighed as she sat back down, so terribly tired and old. "I finally just gave up, and then my pride stepped in and I, too, felt anger against you. Siony, I couldn't get to you. I had had a stroke. For close onto a year after Tory's death I was partially paralyzed."

Sion's heart stopped beating. "No," he whispered, refusing to believe. "They would have told me. Jonas would have told me."

She just stared at him, the tears shimmering on her brittle cheeks. "I don't know what happened. Siony, I love you. If I could have been there for you, I would have."

With trembling hands he raked his hair back, still refusing to understand how such a miserable thing could have happened. "God, all these years I thought you believed me guilty. I thought you had deserted me." He turned to her, watching her shake her head, her shoulders stooped and heaving with the quiet sobs. "I didn't know you were ill, Nana; if I had I would have come to you as soon as I was able."

Again she shook her head as a sob burst forth, racking her slight body. Blindly she held out her hand, and in seconds he was beside her, rocking her gently in his arms even as he clutched her, with an almost frantic strength, against his heart.

"Do you realize how long it has been since you called me Siony? I think that's what did me in," he teased fondly, blinking away his own tears.

She gave a watery chuckle as she pushed away, and cupping her hands about that stubborn jaw, she looked deep into his beautiful ebony eyes. The infamous Dereham eyes. "We Derehams do like our little pet names. It is our only weakness."

Danae peeked in, and with a sigh of contentment she quietly shut the door, leaving the two of them to make up for lost time.

"It be a happy day?" Mrs. Turlow's gruff voice queried with her usual tenderhearted prying.

Danae turned with a wide smile and sniffled as she mopped at her brimming eyes. "Oh, Mrs. Turlow, the happiest."

Mrs. Turlow's eyes flicked over to the closed doors. "And about time, too. Day at a time all his lordship's past is layin' tae rest. Soon he will be yours alone, and then we can start on the babies."

"Babies?" Danae stared after her waddling form.

"Aye, the babies."

"That is all I need—more babies. I've got one now that I didn't even know I had yesterday."

Mrs. Turlow stopped dead and spun around. "Ye have a wee bairn?"

Danae shrugged, "So I've been informed. A strappin' bonny lad o' five."

Mrs. Turlow just stood blinking at her, finally at a loss for words.

Danae was staring out into the sunset, the murky sky splashed red and orange through London's infamous smoke, when she felt two arms surround and hold her close. With a contented sigh, she dropped her head back on a wide shoulder and lost herself in the sense of security he always exuded. This was as close to heaven as she had come all day.

"An ass, am I?" He nipped her ear in playful retaliation.

"*Si*, but I am in *amare* with your *assa*," she teased as she reached around his slim hips and pinched a hard buttock, then curled her fingers about the back of this thighs.

"Have I told you how much I love you?" He nuzzled the curls at her nape.

Her eyes opened slowly, and as she stepped out of his arms, her whole body tensed. Turning around, she studied him with somber eyes. "Don't mistake gratitude for love, Sion. A mere thank-you would be sufficient."

He frowned in confusion, not a little hurt. Steeling his emotions, he crossed his arms over a suddenly constricted chest. "I know the difference, Danny, and I know what I feel. Are you trying to tell me, as politely as possible, that you don't love me?" His gaze was raking her features, hoping to get a clue as to what she was really telling him. Then, before she could answer, he hurried on: "Because it doesn't matter whether you do or not. It won't change how I feel."

"Why do you love me, Sion?"

He shrugged, fearful of where all this was leading to. Did she want to leave him?

"You are fascinated with my beauty? I please you in bed? I am a novel experience, a virgin with no inhibitions? But you see, that is all it is to you, right now, right here: a diversion until you decide to get on with the rest of your life."

Sion relaxed, almost smiling when he now realized what the emotional yoke about her shoulders was. It was all her old insecurities coming back to taunt her. That was something he could understand, even if he did have a few doubts as how to dispel them.

"Yes, of course, I love those things. Good Lord, Danny, I'm a man. But, that is just the sugar that sweetens the cake. Above and beyond that, I love you for what you are."

There was a cynical twist to her lips as she moved away from him. "For years I watched Halsingham fall in and out of love like a bouncing ball. Loving obsessively, declaring lifetime fidelity, claiming that never had he felt such a depth of love for the current lady gracing his bed. And it was always delivered with such passion, such sincerity, that even as a bystander, knowing Halsingham for the swine he was, I believed him. And then the next time I saw him, he was spouting the same drivel into the ears of his latest conquest."

Cocking her head to the side, she studied the broad length of him. He was so beautiful. He could have anything and anyone he wanted without even having to go out of his way. "In the throes of passion a man will say anything that makes the taking just that much easier. It is his way of claiming his mate for the moment and sucking her dry of every response she has to offer, because a woman with an emotional investment will give that much more generously, thereby making the conquest sweeter and more soothing to the male ego."

Sion stared at her, shocked. "My God, you are cynical." He shook his head, trying to make some sense of this whole crazy conversation. "Is that what you think of me? Is this drivel what you believe when you kiss me, when you make tender love with me?"

"What women feel and commit to is completely different," she replied evasively.

"That is not what I asked," he snapped. He had an urge to do violence. Burning with restless energy, he began to pace the room. "So, because you had the misfortune to be married to an unprincipled, selfish, lying bastard, I am condemned as such simply because I am of the same gender?" He spun around and glared at her. "Is this correct?"

She smiled grimly, "Let's not forget Camden. Another paragon of manhood."

With a curse, Sion plowed fingers through his disheveled hair, almost pulling it out at the roots. "God! What have I ever done to you to deserve this?" In two long strides he was looming over her, his menacing heat warming her clammy skin. "Have I hurt you? Lied to you? Abandoned you after I had my wicked way with you? Denied you sex when you begged me for it? Not been there when you needed me? What in hell have I done?"

She couldn't refute his angry words. He had been all that was good and decent to her. It was what would happen later. Having no defense, she simply stared back.

"Do you realize what you are doing to me, Danae?" he grimly demanded. "You are angry with the world because you feel it turned its back on you when you were, in your words, fat and ugly. But the truth is, you never gave it a chance. You *allowed* Halsingham and Camden to mold you into the bitter and distrustful woman you are today. You say no one could love you the way you were? Well, look what you are doing to me. You cannot allow yourself to love me because I am a man. Who is being the bigot now, Danae?"

Tears shimmered in her eyes. "You don't understand," she whispered.

"Oh, I understand too well. You are already accusing me of betraying you, because in your twisted little mind that is what all men will eventually do. I am not *every* man, Danae; I am *me.*" He leaned down, almost touching his nose to her as he intoned with sarcasm, "But, don't you worry, my love, I am used to being accused of something I haven't done."

She pushed him away. "And will you love me if I become what I was? Could you love that bedraggled, *fat* and *ugly* thing you found?" She was crying now. "Could you, Sion?"

He shook his head sadly. "No matter what I say, you won't believe me." With a sigh, he walked over to the bed and sprawled wearily onto it. "What do you want of me, Danae? Help me out here."

He watched as she approached him, her own weariness shadowing her eyes. Without a word she lay down beside him, curling with unconscious trust into his side, her breath fanning his neck.

"Don't tell me you love me. I'll be your lover, your friend, and whatever else you need. But what I need is to know that you will not mislead me into dreaming of something that could never be. I am only human. I will grow old; the beauty you love so much will fade and you will move on. I can take just about anything but having to look back and remembering the words of love on your lips."

Sion stared at the ceiling, frustration and anger seething behind his cool demeanor. At this moment he almost hated her. Would his life never be simple again? Just when everything was starting to fall into place she had to rip out his heart again. His fingers flexed with his need to throttle some sense

into her obtuse mind. Lover and friend, indeed!
He could get that anywhere.

Stifling a vile oath, he surged to his feet and
strode to the door.

Startled, Danae tumbled into the middle of the
bed and then sat up, calling to him just as he
reached the door. "Sion, where are you going?"

"Out! I can't breathe in here." He was stepping
through the door when the full power of his anger
erupted. Turning back, he slammed the door with
such force the windows rattled, and came back into
the middle of the room, not trusting himself to get
any closer to her.

"I am not one of your fucking effigies! I am not
Halsingham! I am not Camden! I am not some
shallow ass who can't function unless I have some
empty-headed work of art draped over my arm or
sprawled across my bed. I am not, nor have I ever
been, led about by my prick." Working himself
into a frenzy, he started pacing the confines of
the room.

Danae watched the restless pacing with cautious
attention. She flinched when he came to a stop at
the foot of the bed, glaring down on her, his ebony
eyes glowing feverishly.

"I know what I want from life, and I am damn
well able to muddle through well enough without a woman. Sex does not control me. For
chrissakes, the last woman I made love with was
my wife. Yes, I love making love with you! Yes, I
love to be seen with you on my arm! Yes, I love
your spunk and intelligence. No, I don't give a
bloody damn about your beauty. Beautiful women
can be found on any street corner for the right
price. Of course you will grow old. Of course you
will put on weight; I am hoping for lots of babies.

But"—his hand shot out, and grabbing her ankle he pulled her unresisting body closer to him— "you will never lose your luster. That is what is in your heart, in your soul. What shines from your beautiful eyes every time you look at me. And *that* is what I see when I tell you I love you."

Reaching out, he cupped her pale face in warm palms, pulling her gently to her knees and flush with his chest. His softened gaze probed deep into her amber-colored soul. Brushing his thumbs across her tear-stained cheeks, he whispered, "That never grows old, or gains weight, or has doubts of its right to love and be loved in return. Can you understand this?"

Her smile was tentative, her heart bursting with hope. "I'll try," was all she could manage.

He returned her smile, relief easing his anger. "Well, I can't ask for more than that. At least for now." Bending down, he dropped a tender kiss on her brow, then released her and turned away.

Seeing he was headed for the door again, Danae popped out of the bed to follow him, but he stopped her at the door. Confused, she looked up at him. "Don't you want me to come to your room?"

With a teasing finger he tapped her nose. "You stay here and get some sleep."

"You don't want me?"

"Of course I want you, my ridiculous love. But I think you need to be convinced that I can love you just as much out of bed as in it."

She almost laughed, "But that is silly."

"That may be, but I have decided to woo you."

"Woo me?" she repeated, not understanding a word of what he was saying. All she knew was that she didn't want to sleep alone.

"Trust me." Then he shut the door in her face.

She stood staring at the closed portal, and already she felt dreadfully lonely. At a loss of what to do now, she turned about and stared at her empty bed all the way across the vast empty room. Her lips pursed into a stubborn line. She didn't want to be wooed; she wanted Sion. Stiffening her spine, she yanked the door open and plowed into the broad chest of her man.

He grinned down at her. "What took you so long?" Then, bending low, he tossed her over his shoulder and headed toward his room.

With a smile she watched the muscles flex in his sleek buttocks. Almost to his room, she remembered something. "By the way, did I tell you that I am a mother?"

Her own legs struck the wall just as he walked into it like a drunken lord. While he cursed and grabbed his knee, she was just thankful he hadn't dropped her.

Nineteen

The young nanny's voice dwindled off into silence as she looked across the schoolroom to her young charge perched on the window seat, who gazed with unblinking absorption out onto the bustling London streets. Biting her lip in frustration, she slowly closed the book on her lap, worrying whether she was ever going to reach him.

Weeks had passed since the Earl of Camden had hired her on to take charge of his heir, Edward Arthur Marlowe, Viscount Searling, and in those weeks not one word had she heard pass this solemn little boy's lips. It was unnatural. It was frightening, just as frightening as the earl himself. If she hadn't felt an immediate empathy for the little lord, she would have hied herself out of the oppressive house after the first night. But, once Lord Edward had turned those haunted blue eyes upon her, she knew she could never desert him. And that was saying a bit about her convoluted feelings for him, because the earl scared her silly. The way he could appear with the shift of the breeze through a room was enough to make her secretly cross herself and wish for one of those ridiculous talismans that her batty old aunt was always trying to force on her. For if anyone had an evil eye, it was the Earl of Camden.

She shivered as she thought of those cold, colorless eyes watching his heir with obsessive care—watching her, evaluating her every move as she went about her daily tasks of caring for her charge. It amazed her how little it affected Lord Edward, but she had learned over the weeks that nothing seemed to touch him or the ethereal cocoon he wrapped himself in. Sadly, he never spoke to her, never turned to her for solace or help. It was as if he didn't trust her, as if, because she had been hired by the earl, she was now his creature. And every day her heart wept for this lonely little boy, picturing him as this fragile shell that tumbled about with the ebb and flow of the unholy atmosphere that surged through this house.

Sweet Lord, how she wished she could reach him; if he would just say one little word to her, she would feel she was accomplishing something.

Out of habit now, she glanced over her shoulder, relieved to see that his lordship was nowhere around and the door was still safely shut. Feeling a roiling sense of dread to be gone, even if only for a short time, she looked at the watch pinned to her shirtwaist and was thankful to see that it was time for their afternoon walk in the park.

"Shall we go to the park, Lord Edward?" She was always careful to address him as such. The one time she had forgotten, the earl had swept down on her, like a banshee out of hell, ranting like a bedlamite—so unlike his usual bloodless demeanor—almost striking her for not giving his heir his appropriate address. She had been scared witless when she had looked into the madness festering in this monster. For days she had cowered in her room, berating herself for her cowardice in not attending the poor child, but too terrified that she might have to face the earl again to step outside her door. Each of those days she had given the excuse of illness for not attending her duties, and each of those days she had prayed he would dismiss her and give her the excuse she needed to leave. But there had been no dismissal forthcoming. She wished she had the courage to just pack her bags and leave, but she couldn't in good conscience leave little Edward behind. Who knew what the next woman the earl hired would be like. She might be cold, or abusive, or uncaring. No, she couldn't leave Lord Edward alone and unprotected. Her own kind heart kept her a prisoner here.

When it seemed her charge hadn't heard her, she again gently suggested the walk. Immediately, he rose to his spotlessly shod feet and walked to the door—just like an obedient lap dog ordered to go out. Like a little dog that had had all its natural spunk whipped out of it.

She blinked back her tears as she followed him. Why was it that without even uttering a word he could make her feel so inadequate?

When they had reached the foyer and she was putting on her cloak, she paused abruptly, feeling the hairs on the back of her neck prickle. With her usual sense of dread, she looked over her shoulder and found herself pinned under the earl's reptilian perusal. Without even knowing it, she stepped closer to her charge. She swallowed her fear when she noticed the tic spasming along the left side of his face. It was quite obvious to her that he was in the middle of one of his attacks and, therefore, was at his most unpredictable.

"Off to the park, Miss York?" came his sibilant whisper, his unblinking gaze sliding from her to rest with his usual morbid fixation on his grandson. Lord Edward was lucky in that he didn't have to look at the man but stood before the earl with his head down, studying the floor.

Wetting dry lips, she dipped a slight curtsy, "Yes, my lord." Then, grabbing up Lord Edward's coat from the coatrack, she quickly bundled the boy up, her hands shaking so much, she bungled a task that she could have done effortlessly in her sleep.

"And how is my grandson today?" This was addressed to the top of Edward's head. Silence strained the hall.

Elizabeth, her heart pounding, stepped between them, and taking hold of her charge's cold, limp hand, she steered him toward the door. Eager to get out, she spoke for the boy. "Lord Edward is feeling a bit under the weather, my lord. A brisk walk in the park should be the ticket, I daresay." The last was almost shouted over her shoulder as they stepped out into the blessed sunshine.

Fumbling behind her for the door latch to close it, her wrist was enveloped in a cold mass. Yelping, she spun around, and her eyes widened in terror as she came nose to nose with the earl, those colorless orbs drilling into her brain with merciless intent. With frantic effort she tried to jerk free, but his seemingly frail hand held her with ease.

His sickly-sweet breath fanned her cheek, and quickly she averted her face as he spoke with that eery whisper of his, "I want him home in one hour, my dear Miss York." Then he released her and she stumbled backward almost teetering on the edge of the stoop as he stood there smiling at her.

In the next second she was on the street, pulling the quiet boy after her, almost running for what she felt was her life.

The park was breathtaking; the brilliant shades of green, golds, and reds melding together overhead to create a bower of spectacular beauty. Late-blooming flowers presented a splash of color over the lush carpet crackling under her feet as she strolled down the same path for the ninth time.

Danae's steps slowed to a stop, and with Mrs. Turlow they laughed at the antics of a couple of geese squabbling over a chunk of bread a little girl had tossed to them. Still smiling, Danae turned to again scan the perimeter of the small man-made pond.

"Well, it seems they are not coming today."

"Terry dinna ever be wrong. He said they come everyday at two o' the clock."

Danae cocked a brow at her companion. "I still find it strangely coincidental that your half-brother's stepson from his third wife is working as a footman in Camden's household."

Mrs. Turlow adjusted her shawl—Danae remembered that shawl—and shrugged. "London be a small world, an' the servant class be tight. They dinna mind helpin' each other out. 'Sides, the earl dinna earn the loyalty o' his staff, and if it dinna be Terry it would have been another." She cast Danae a cheeky grin and winked. "I knew the under-butler from way back when I knew me way about a bed."

Deciding not to touch on that any further, Danae spotted a bench not too far off and, with a sigh, eased herself down and wiggled her toes. Her feet ached, and she had the compelling need to strip her half-boots off and rub her toes. She smiled as dreamy thoughts of Sion flashed through her mind.

When Mrs. Turlow plopped down beside her, she was jolted to the present. Feeling her cheeks flush with color, she occupied herself with scanning the park again, becoming more and more discouraged.

It had taken Mrs. Turlow only a few days, and by the end of last week she had the entire schedule of Camden's household down to the last odd detail. And even though she had never been in the Camden town house, she now knew where every room was—every hall, every closet. Her curiosity had ridden her to the point where she had finally decided to hie herself off and beard Camden in his own lair. But both Sion and Jonas had been adamant against this honest approach even when Nana had backed her up, offering to accompany her.

"There they be," Mrs. Turlow's gruff voice announced in an undertone.

Swinging about, Danae draped her arm along the back of the bench and stared as a young woman, presumably the governess, and a boy of about five were settling themselves onto a bench farther down the path. Nana had been right: he was the most beautiful child she had ever seen. And the spitting image of Halsingham. *Well, how convenient for Camden.* He had simply gone out and found one of his son-in-law's by-blows. Pity he couldn't have found one of the right age. *Wily old bastard.*

Standing up, she twitched her skirts into place and took a leisurely stroll along the path toward her subject, all the while trying not to appear too vulgar in her staring. As she came closer, she was taken aback at the utter lack of emotion on the child's face, pale and lifeless as a funeral mask carved of cold alabaster. It was eerie, especially with the backdrop of the dozens of children about the grounds frolicking, laughing, and shouting, giving their governesses a run for their wages. Now that the two were settled onto the bench, they merely sat and ignored each other. The girl watched the other children with a hungry expression while the boy fidgeted with the model boat on his lap with little interest. Danae's heart went out to him as memories of her own painful childhood came rushing over her.

She had not planned on speaking with the child; she had simply wanted to see him for herself, but now wild horses couldn't have dragged her away. Not even her sensible Sion.

When she came abreast of the silent couple, she deliberately caught her heel in the hem of her train and, with a cry, stumbled to her knees. Mrs. Turlow and the governess both leaped to her aid, but the boy just looked on with chilling disinterest.

Dragging her attention away from him, she turned her smile upon the girl. "Oh, *mi scusi*, how—hm, clumsy, *si, clumsy* is the word?" She peered into the plain little face.

The governess had been bent over brushing the grass from Danae's skirts when her curiosity overrode her shyness and she looked up. She gazed with awe at the stunning face smiling down at her. "You are, Italian, madam?" She then blushed at her forwardness.

"*Si, Italiana.* I am Danae Suriano." Danae held out her hand. "And you?"

The girl stared at the outstretched hand, stunned. Never had a woman ever offered her her hand. Especially one of the gentry. Not sure what she should do, she hesitantly extended her own and gave a belated curtsy. "I am Elizabeth York, madam."

Danae took her hand and gave it a small squeeze before she turned and introduced her companion, Mrs. Turlow. The two fellow conspirators' eyes held for just a moment, before the old darling picked up on the plan. After throwing a distracted hello at the governess, Mrs. Turlow plopped Danae down on the bench next to the boy. Then, with a few grunts and groans she managed to settle herself at Danae's feet and, pulling out needle and thread, commenced to repair the torn ruffle.

With an apologetic smile to Miss York, who still stood trying to take in the last few minutes, Danae turned her attention on the boy even as she addressed her comment to the girl, "This is your son? So *bello!*"

"Oh, no, he is my charge. This is Edward Arthur Marlowe, Viscount Searling."

She smiled at him. *"Ciao, Edwardo."* He just continued to stare at her. "That is so lovely a boat." He glanced at the shiny new model sailboat then again turned his serious eyes on her. Her smile cracked a little. "You have sailed it, *si?"* No answer.

"I am sorry, madam, but he doesn't speak. I have been with him for weeks and I haven't heard him utter a single word. He just won't respond to me." It was obvious that the detachment of her charge saddened her.

Danae studied his stoic little face and somehow knew he could talk—he just didn't want to.

Waiting for Mrs. Turlow to tie off the thread, she

took the boat out of his lax hold. She flicked a glance at Miss York. "May I, *prego?*" Not waiting for permission, she tugged him to his feet and pulled him along after her as if he was a reluctant puppy on a leash. As expected, he put up no resistance.

She took him to the edge of the pond and, kneeling down, placed the boat in the water and gave it a push. Edward stood silent, watching it glide through the water lilies.

Dropping her accent and keeping her eyes turned toward the boat, she asked, "Edward isn't really your name, is it? Would you like to tell me what it is?" In her peripheral vision she saw him shift his gaze to her, his little body tensed with indecision. Trusting was not something this child would ever do easily. The minutes stretched out in silence as Danae forced herself to keep her eyes on the meandering boat. Several times she felt his little body shift about restlessly.

"Timothy Parker," came his hesitant voice.

Relieved, she smiled at him. "Timothy Parker," she repeated softly. "I like it so much better than Edward Arthur. It suits you." Standing, she held out her hand. "Come, let us go get your boat."

After a moment in which she held her breath, she felt his cold little fingers slip into hers and curl into her palm. Together they walked along the pond's edge. There was so much she wanted to ask him she was at a loss as where to begin.

"I would like to meet your mother. She must be very beautiful to have such a handsome son."

"Dead."

She glanced down at the top of his golden head. "I'm so very sorry, Timothy. I lost my mother when I was about your age. I know how hard it is." They walked in silence for a bit.

"I hear that you were taken from your mother. Kidnapped? How lucky for you that your grandfather was able to find you."

"No."

"No?" *No, what?* She had better ask questions more concisely, what with his dearth of responses.

"He says my mum wasn't my mum. But we was always together at the house."

"The house?"

"Workhouse."

She stopped and turned toward him. "Camden found you in a workhouse?"

He nodded.

"Where was your father?"

He shrugged. "Didn't have one."

That bastard, she seethed, *condemning this—his child—to a workhouse!*

Kneeling beside him, she suppressed the urge to wrap her arms about the slight body. Instead she reached out and straightened his immaculate little tie. "I would like to be your friend, Timothy. I think you are special and I want to be your special friend. In fact, I want you to call me Danny. There is only one other person who calls me that and he is very, very special to me, too. You will meet him one day soon." She brushed aside a golden curl and cupped his cheek. "If I come tomorrow, will you have a picnic with me?"

For the first time she saw a spark of . . . something in his beautiful blue eyes. She hoped it was joy but would settle on mere interest at this time.

Finally, he nodded.

"Wonderful! Now, shall we get your boat?"

The light left his eyes like a flame blown out, and again the lusterless blue revealed nothing. Now she understood Sion's words. He was right: the luster was everything. She followed Timothy's gaze, and together they looked at the expensive toy tangled in the lilies, listing on its side.

"I don't want it." She was surprised when he reached for her hands. Hand in hand they strolled slowly back, neither of them in a hurry to return him to the reality of his life.

Elizabeth watched, hurt and confused, as the lady brought back her charge. She had actually seen him *talking* with the stranger. So why wouldn't he talk with her? What was wrong with her?

"What is the matter, lass?" the lady's motherly companion asked gently.

Swallowing her tears, she averted her face as she shook her head. Steadily the lady in her elegant walking ensemble strolled closer, Lord Edward's fingers clasped securely in her gloved hand. Never had he extended his hand to her, she thought with jealous resentment.

"Ye must trust us; we mean ye no harm. Do ye love the wee laddie?"

"Yes," Elizabeth whispered. "But he doesn't seem to care for me."

"It just takes time, lass."

Elizabeth turned to glare at the obtuse woman. "It obviously didn't take time for him to open up to the lady. And why should I trust you? I don't know either of you, and if you don't mind my bluntness, you forced your attentions on us."

Mrs. Turlow huffed up a bit, always willing and waiting to take on an opponent. "I can be a wee bit blunt meself, lassie. That lady over there is the kindest heart ye'll ever meet. She's taken a fondness for the laddie, and she would die afore she ever hurt him."

"Enough, *Signora* Turlow," Danae's gentle rebuke cut in, startling the two women. With an apologetic smile, she turned to the obviously irate nanny. "You must forgive my companion; she is, um, 'ow you say, devoted."

In the face of such sincerity, Elizabeth felt herself blushing at her rudeness. The lady had only been kind to an obviously lonely little boy. Under the circumstances, she would have done the same. Swallowing her anger, she looked at Edward and saw a light in his eyes that she had never seen before as he gazed up into the beautiful face of the mysterious lady. Again the hurt dug into her heart as she wished he would, just once, look at her that way. But even through her jealousy, she was happy that at last someone had been able to reach through his shell and touch him. Maybe it was the lady's foreignness that had caught his interest.

"You 'ave a delightful charge, *Signorina* York. He says you come every *domani, si?*"

Elizabeth stared at her, dumbfounded.

"She means ye come here every day?" Mrs. Turlow interpreted irritably as she shot her lady a peeved look. She did not like where this was leading. His lordship would like it even less.

Getting more confused by the minute, Elizabeth nodded. "Oh, yes, we come every day at two."

Danae clapped her hands in delight. *"Excellente! Domani* I bring, um, basket with picnic, *si?"*

Biting her lip, Elizabeth glanced down at Edward and was shocked at seeing the pleading in his eyes as he stared at her. How could she deny him anything? Most reluctantly she nodded. However was she going to get Lord Camden's permission?

As if reading her mind, Lady Danae stepped closer to her and advised in an undertone, "It best, I think, to keep this our little secret, *si?*"

Elizabeth's eyes narrowed, all her suspicions coming to the fore again.

Seeing her reaction, the lady's brows rose in surprise, even as the beautifully accented voice hardened a bit as she continued, "So, you wish to tell of *domani* to Camden? Brave girl. And how will you tell this *bello ragazzo* that he can not have his picnic?"

Not liking the feeling of being coerced, Elizabeth's gaze swiveled to Edward again. She noticed the strain on his suddenly pale face, his hands clenched white-knuckled at his sides. But, other than those little signs, there was, as usual, no expression to be read on his stoic little face. If she was going to win his trust and prove to him she was not his grandfather's spy, it had to start here. In order to earn his trust, she was being forced to trust this strange woman.

Again she gave a reluctant nod. Then, having enough of this queer interlude, she held out her hand to her charge. "Come." Unfortunately, the demand came out too curt. Taking a deep breath, she bit her lip as she counted to ten, slow and even. Then in a calmer voice she said, "It is getting late, Lord Edward. Lord Camden will be wondering where we are." Lord, that made her sound exactly what she was trying to prove she wasn't: Camden's creature.

He just stood there looking at her for a long, pregnant minute before he tilted his head back and looked up into the exotic face of the *contessa*. Smiling, she gave him a slight nod. Immediately, he went to stand beside her, and after another brief pause, he took her extended hand. But, he did not grip her hand as she had seen him doing to *hers*. If she had let go, it would have fallen limp at his side.

Mumbling a hasty farewell, Elizabeth pulled him down the path, just wanting to put a goodly distance between them and the strange duo. Her emotions were so mixed at that moment, she didn't know whether she wanted to cry, scream, or go back there and kick that beautiful woman in her expensive bustle. As they rounded a bend in the path and out of the sight of the two women, she paused and knelt down in front of him.

"Are you all right?" she felt compelled to ask, even though the question sounded ridiculous under the circumstances.

As she expected, he simply stared at her.

The frustration ate at her. "Edward, you can trust me; don't you know that by now?"

His eyes shifted down.

"What is it going to take to get you to trust me?"

He looked up, and his blue eyes spoke volumes to her, only she couldn't decipher them. Brushing a lock of hair off his forehead, she blinked back her tears. "I promise you, I will not tell your grandfather of the lady. You will have your picnic tomorrow. And if you ever need to see her, I will try my best to get her for you. That is the best I can do until you tell me what else you need, all right?"

A glimmer lightened his eyes as he stared solemnly at her, and when his hand tightened about hers, her tears almost spilled.

Sighing, she shook her head, confounded at the whole turn of events this afternoon. "Does she mean that much to you?"

But he only looked down again, hiding his true

feelings for this stranger from her. Slowly she rose to her feet. Without another word she guided him back to the town house. Her thoughts were whirling at an alarming rate. There was definitely a mystery here, and she intended to get to the bottom of it before Edward was hurt.

Twenty

Though Sion was making an admirable attempt at keeping his mind on his tenant's accounts, when Jonas was announced he was relieved for the interruption, for his mind kept replaying all his problems to the point he had a headache that was about to split his skull open.

"Thank God! Where the hell have you been?" Sion demanded as he threw down his pen.

Jonas came to stand before Sion's desk. He was weary and more than a little disheartened; not in the best of moods to put up with Sion's irritability. "What is wrong?"

"Everything. Where have you been this past week?"

Taking a deep breath, Jonas set his case down on the edge of the desk and adjusted his spectacles. "I am sorry I left in such a hurry with no word. I wasn't thinking. My brother passed on last Sunday."

Sion belatedly took in Jonas's haggard appearance. Guilt flushed his face, and if it had been physically possible he would have kicked himself. "Lord, Jonas, I'm sorry."

"Don't. He has been ill for years. His death was a blessing."

"I didn't know he was ill."

There was a subtle note of accusation in Sion's words, and Jonas found he didn't like the tone in his voice. "Well now, you haven't been around the last few years, if you will remember."

"What else did you fail to tell me over the years, Jonas?"

Jonas just stared at him. "Devil a bit, what the hell is wrong with you, Sion? I've never seen you like this. And to be honest, I'm not in the mood to put up with it."

"During the trials why did you keep my grand-mother's illness from me?" He didn't blink an eye as he watched Jonas's reaction. And what flashed across his features was utter confusion.

"Lady Dereham is ill?"

"No, Jonas, not now, during the trials."

Jonas was having a hard time following this. He was tired and actually quite annoyed at the moment, and now Sion was talking a lot of rubbish. "Was she ill?"

"It seems, at the beginning of the trials, she'd had a stroke."

"Good Lord! How could we not have known?"

A wave of relief washed over Sion as the look on Jonas's face revealed nothing but pure and honest shock. Coming about the desk, he pushed Jonas into a chair, then went to get him a drink. "Well, now I know that you didn't keep it from me."

Jonas's startled gaze clashed with Sion's as he reached for the snifter. Anger chilled the usually friendly eyes, and it seemed that the thick lenses just magnified the anger tenfold. "By God, that goes too far, Sion. Are you accusing me of . . . of . . ." He wasn't quite sure what he was being accused of.

Propping a hip on the corner of the desk, Sion

held out his hand as if to stop the anger. "Jonas, please, I'm floundering here. I just find it incomprehensible how such a thing could have happened—and especially *why*. I thought perhaps you might have done so out of a misguided effort to protect me."

Jonas slammed his glass on the desk. "Well, that has got to be the most asinine thing I have ever heard! Hell, when you thought Lady Dereham had turned against you, you almost went insane. Do you honestly think I would have kept something so monumental as her stroke from you in order to ease your bleedin' mind?" He was almost screeching the last words.

Sion flinched, and feeling ridiculously sheepish, he nodded, "Well, yes, it crossed my mind." He looked at Jonas and saw him staring off into space. "I'm sorry . . ."

"If you tell me you're sorry one more time, I'll punch you in the nose. Don't talk to me right now. I'm damned angry."

Sion hid his smile as he moved back around the desk and sat down. Jonas had to have stepped over the edge of mere anger to be cursing like that. Typically, he would have bitten his tongue off before giving voice to such language. With a sigh, Sion leaned back and waited while his friend cooled down. He had to admit, it hadn't been the best of weeks for either of them, and tempers were bound to flare.

"Well, it is obviously Saegar." Jonas rubbed his tired eyes under the heavy spectacles. "Have you questioned Lady Dereham's staff?"

"Nana has. She says they claim that they thought the doctor had taken care of informing me."

"What about that strange companion of hers?"

"Crandall came into Nana's employ during her recuperation. In fact, she had been recommended by the doctor."

"So who is her doctor?" Jonas leaned forward to retrieve his glass.

"A Doctor Harold Benton. He was apparently Nana's doctor for years. And no, I have not spoken with him. Can't even find him. It seems he had retired not long after my trial, so Nana says, and no one seems to know where he is."

Jonas leaned his head back on the soft leather and stretched his feet out. The brandy was doing what it did best: relaxing him. "Wonderful. I'll look into it." He closed his eyes and took another sip.

Sion slipped a crumpled letter out of his breast pocket. "And as if we don't have enough problems, look at this." He tossed the letter across the desk.

Leaning over, Jonas grabbed the note and quickly scanned it. Another curse was spat out, and he shot to his feet.

He really did look ridiculous, Sion thought, with his red hair sticking out in every direction, his eyes bloodshot and spitting fire behind the lopsided lenses that distorted one eye while the other glared at him over the rim. Sion bit his lip to keep from laughing. "Sit down before you spill your drink."

Ignoring the command, Jonas glared at him. "When the bloody hell did you receive this?"

Sion stood, and rounding the desk, he took back the offensive note. "Yesterday. Danae almost saw it." He winced. "Thank God she didn't. I can just imagine how she would take a death threat." It was just pure chance that he had intercepted the note before Seadon had it delivered to her

room. After a stern lecture to Seadon about how
all correspondence would go through him first,
Sion then sat down and did nothing all morning
but digest this latest danger. So who was it? Halsingham? Camden? Saegar? Of course, the coward
hadn't bothered to sign it. Which, the more he
thought about it meant it couldn't be Camden.
Camden was too pompous to have a fear of
reprisal when it came to meting out his vengeance.
With a sigh of tired frustration, he could see none
other than Saegar for this latest menace. The man
probably sensed how important Danae was to him
and was going to strike out at him by taking from
him that which he held most dear.

"I've already contacted an Inspector Brock from
Scotland Yard. Danae doesn't know it, nor do I
want her to, but she is being followed now wherever
she goes."

"Well, is there anything else you would like to
add to the pile, Sion? Every time I see you lately
it just seems to grow and grow and grow. . . ."
Slowly, vertebra by vertebra, Jonas melted back
into his chair, but he didn't look appeased in the
least. If anything, his lips pursed to a degree such
that Sion didn't think he would ever be able to
pry them open again. A lemon couldn't have done
a better job.

"Well, there is this other minor thing. Danae's a
mother."

Jonas shot to his feet. "When did this happen?
Dash it, Sion, I was only gone a week!"

The next day, as Danae approached the same
bench, her heart was lightened when Timothy
came to his feet; it was quite obvious he had been

waiting for her. She handed him the basket and as Mrs. Turlow commandeered Miss York, keeping her busy and out of the way, she walked with Timothy over to an ancient oak. Pulling a linen cloth from the basket, she snapped it open and spread it out under the lush canopy of foliage. Then began the arduous task of settling herself upon the ground with a corset digging into her ribs and the blasted bustle making it difficult to find the seat nature had given her. Finally, she just shifted the blasted thing to her hip and plopped down. She had to suppress a chuckle when she pictured herself seated demurely under an idyllic tree with a hump on her hip.

Timothy sat beside her only when told to, and gazing at her with his usual serious regard, he finally asked, "Why do you wear it? What does it do other than make the back of you look big?"

Did this poor child never see anything as humorous? Danae pondered as she set out their lunch. "Well, it's fashion's way of trying to improve on what the good Lord gave us."

"Do you want a big behind?"

Danae smiled down at him. "You don't like my big behind?"

Timothy shrugged as he eyed the cookies. So there was a touch of the child in that stoic little heart, after all. She had discovered a weakness for cookies. "I've been thinking of getting rid of it. It always seems to be getting in the way. And it's too convenient a handle." She muttered this last to herself as she reached for a cool carafe.

"I like picnics, don't you?"

There was no response.

"Have you ever been on a picnic, Timothy?"

He shook his head.

She poured a glass of lemonade. "Well, to tell the truth, neither have I. So this is a first for both of us." Leaning forward, she handed him the glass. She was startled when he jerked back, staring at the glass with what she assumed to be loathing.

"Don't you like lemonade?"

His response was immediate: an emphatic shake of his head.

When she raised the glass to her lips, she was bothered by the way he was watching her with almost unnatural intent. "Is something wrong, Timothy?"

"Don't you color it?"

"Color it?" She didn't have the faintest idea what he was talking about.

"He always makes it. I don't like it, but I have to drink it."

"He? Your grandfather, you mean? He makes you lemonade?" She was stunned. She couldn't picture Camden doing anything even remotely domestic. Making lemonade? And coloring it?

With a hesitant finger, he touched the glass in her hand. "Do you like it?" His voice was skeptical.

"I love lemonade. I didn't make this; my friend did, Mrs. Turlow, and she makes a great lemonade. Puts lots of sugar in it to make it disgustingly sweet. It's pure heaven. Would you like to try it?" Again she extended the glass.

After a momentary inner debate, he reached for it and took a cautious sip. She actually felt honored that he was trusting her, for she knew this serious child would never give it lightly. But, when his eyes jumped to meet hers, she could hardly believe her eyes. Like the sun coming from behind dark, storm-swollen clouds to shed its healing warmth, he smiled at her. Her breath caught at the beautiful phenomenon.

"It tastes much better without the red."

She frowned in confusion. "Camden flavors it with red? What is the red?"

Drinking deeply of the sweet lemonade, he managed to hold out one hand, his little index finger extended.

She stared at it for a moment, expecting him to do something else. "I don't understand, Timothy."

"He cuts his finger and the lemonade turns red."

Danae could feel her face turn white even as her body shivered. Her stomach twisted, and grabbing a napkin, she pressed it to her lips, swallowing convulsively. "Blood? He puts blood in . . . in . . ." Her whispered words faltered into horrified silence.

He nodded, then finished the glass. "I like this much better."

It took sheer willpower not to be ill. Danae turned her face away and blinked back her tears. What perversity was going on in that man's mind now? Where did Timothy fit into all this madness? *Why?*

She didn't realize she had spoken aloud until Timothy answered her. "He says we will be one."

"Timothy . . ." She reached over and took the empty glass from him. "Does Camden . . ." Lord, she didn't know what she wanted to ask first. It was all spinning about her like some horrible nightmare. "Has Camden ever hurt you?"

Timothy stared up at her with his big blue eyes. Slowly he nodded.

Her heart stopped beating. She unclenched her hands and rubbed her sweaty palms on the pristine white skirt. God, she didn't want to hear this! For a panicked second, she thought of grabbing her skirts and running. Her own father was doing this! Her own flesh and blood! *Oh, please, Sion, where are you? I need you!* She forced herself to look into those beautiful eyes, eyes now trusting her with everything. "Does he hit you, Timothy?"

The denial was immediate.

Her eyes closed with her shaky sigh. *Thank God for small miracles!*

"Does he yell at you?"

Again he shook his head.

Now she was confused. "How does he hurt you?" *Other than force you to drink his blood,* she sarcastically reprimanded herself.

"He says me mum wasn't me mum. He says she was a bad woman who took me. He locks me in a closet." He looked down, almost embarrassed as he told her. "I don't like the dark."

Long-buried memories of a dark, cold place crowded in on Danae. She didn't like the dark, either. "Who does he say your mother is?" She asked this even though she already knew the answer.

"Katherine."

"Timothy . . ." She leaned over and took his cold hands in hers. "I'm going to tell you a secret. Can you keep a secret? This must be just between you and me."

He was solemn as he nodded.

"I knew Katherine. She was my friend and she was not your mother. Camden is lying. Your mother was a good woman and she loved you very much. You must always remember that."

He had been staring down at their clasped hands when he looked up at her. The vulnerability in his eyes was devastating to her raw emotions. "Who is my father?"

She paused for a moment. The words almost

stuck in her throat as she answered him with the honesty he was trusting her with. "I am sorry to say that your father is the Viscount Halsingham."

"He doesn't like me."

Danae bit the inside of her lip as tears sheened her eyes. She cleared her throat. "Yes, I know, darling. But you have me now. I like you so very much." Squeezing his hands, she released him and gave him a cookie. God, what a mess!

"Do you have a little boy?"

She shook her head.

"Maybe one day I can be yours?"

Leaning over, she cupped her hands about his face, and speaking without thinking first, her emotions on the run, she swore, "One day you will be my son. This I promise you."

He nodded, not doubting her for a moment.

The enormity of what she had just done hit her with the full force of a battering ram. What if she couldn't do it? What if she couldn't get him away from Camden? Then something flashed like a heavenly spark. She had one ace up her sleeve, and Halsingham was it.

She looked down on the child munching his cookie. "Now remember, you mustn't mention any of this to anyone. Especially not Camden." The last thing she wanted was Camden to get a whiff of any of this and take it out on Timothy.

Plopping the last bite into his mouth, he crossed his heart.

Sion was sprawled before the fire, watching his love pace back and forth. "I knew this was going to happen when you saw the child. I just knew it."

She spun around. "What are you saying? That I

should just ignore him? You forget I lived with that
monster. I know what he is capable of. I would also
have to be a monster to just walk away as if nothing
was wrong. And I am not like him!"

Sion watched her out of heavy-lidded eyes. "I
never said you were, love. But we have so many
complications right now . . ."

She didn't give him a chance to finish, she was so
livid. "Complications? What complications?"

He smiled slightly. "Your whole life is a compli-
cation, Katherine." He deliberately reminded her
who she really was. It was starting to become too
dangerous for her not to.

She loomed over him, murder in her eyes. *"Don't
you *ever* call me that! She is dead!"

Reaching up, he snagged her waist and pulled
her struggling body onto his lap. Wrapping his
arms about her, he held her secure and when she
suddenly broke into tears he simply held her. "Oh,
Sion, I *promised* that little boy that he would be
mine, that I would protect him. What if I can't do
it?" she sobbed into his neck. "He is so little, so
defenseless, and he trusts me. What am I going
to do?"

He honestly didn't know either, but he knew one
thing: he was going to be a father much sooner
than he thought.

He stroked her damp, flushed cheek and
rubbed his own against her tumbled hair. Never
would he let this woman down, no matter what
she wanted, what it took. Blindly, he stared into
the fire, pondering long and deep. "Do you want
me to kill him?"

Her sobbing ceased and she grew still. She didn't
answer him for the longest time; then she sniffled
reluctantly, "No, I suppose not. Not that I wouldn't

mind seeing that . . . that bastard six feet underground, but the last thing I want is something to happen to you."

His arms tightened about her as he promised, "My dearest love, somehow, someway, we will get Timothy. This I swear to you."

She started fidgeting with one of the studs in his shirt when she looked up with strained hesitance. His jaw tensed as he knew he wasn't going to like what was coming. "You know, I was thinking we could blackmail Halsingham."

His eyes narrowed on her, and she hurried on. "I mean that maybe he could get Timothy away from Camden, even if it's into his own household, until we could figure a way to get Timothy permanently. At least he would be away from Camden." She looked at him, hopeful.

She was amazed when he sat still and actually contemplated her suggestion instead of ranting at the stupidity of her plan.

"There might be something to what you say," he conceded carefully, not wanting to commit himself. "But it's going to have to be handled very delicately or else the whole thing could become exposed."

She nodded in immediate agreement.

"In other words"—he cocked a threatening eye down on her—"you stay the hell out of it. This is going to require tact and diplomacy, something you know nothing of."

Trying to appear humble was becoming more of a strain by the second. Biting her tongue, she rewarded him with her sweetest smile and thought that the day Sion used tact and diplomacy to win the day was the day she would kiss his feet.

* * *

Timothy watched, his eyes expressionless, as the long white fingers drummed with patient monotony on the immaculate knee. He knew the man was angry with him. And when the pain was on him, he knew where the anger would lead to. In fact, Timothy knew this man very well. Like a prey learning the weakness of its predator in order to survive, he watched Camden and he learned.

"I understand you had another visit from the lady in the park today."

Timothy looked Camden straight in the eye and said nothing.

"Who is she?"

Timothy didn't blink.

"What did you talk about?"

They stared at each other in silence.

Camden stood up, shards of agony shooting through his eyes, making him almost nauseous. Pinpricks of pain shivered along the arm that moments ago had been numb and lifeless, and settled with a torturous pounding in his temples. Wanting nothing more than to grab his head and howl in misery, he turned away from the boy and, reaching into his coat pocket, withdrew the little brown bottle that he now carried around with him with frantic obsession. With an unsteady hand he unstopped it, and raising it to numb lips, he took a long swallow of the bitter drug. His pained eyes slid closed as he waited for the laudanum to seep into his tortured body and give him blessed surcease. After a while he was breathing easier, his body relaxed and his mind floating free of all his earthly suffering. Carefully he slipped the precious bottle back into his pocket; then he turned around to smile with cold intent upon this disobedient creation of his.

"Very well, Edward, if we must we will play this little

game of yours through to its usual conclusion. I will hope that after your nap you will wish to discuss it." And walking over to the far wall, he touched a lever hidden in the ornate moulding. On silent hinges a hidden door swung wide, exposing a gaping chasm in the beautiful paneling. "In you go, Edward."

Timothy stared into the black void and shivered. No matter how many hours he spent in that cramped, airless hole, he could not distance himself from the feelings of terror that would grip his trembling body. The fear of hearing the rats scrabbling in the walls only got worse as he imagined them growing in size and coming out of the darkness to eat him. Just like at the workhouse, when he had been locked in with the corpses and forced to watch and listen to the hundreds of them devouring the flesh, crawling in and around the draped, shadowed forms. Only here he had no place to run and nothing to fight them off with. Every time he lay huddled in a tight ball in that darkness, he knew there would be a next time, and then another and another until one day the rats got him, crawling all over him just like on those corpses.

Then he remembered Danny and her promise. It wouldn't be much longer, she had told him. She would take him away from all this and love him. Trusting someone for the first time since his mother had died, Timothy walked into the stifling void and didn't even cry when the prison was sealed tight and the familiar fetidness engulfed him. Huddling up, there was only one thought on his mind as he turned a deaf ear to the screaming in the walls: when Danny would come for him.

Twenty-one

Sion was up and out at a very unfashionable hour, but if he didn't leave he would have done something drastic, like truss Danae up and stick the largest handkerchief he could find down her throat. Love could only go so far, and then there was justifiable homicide. All last night while he tried to make love to her, then while he tried to sleep, then while he dressed, and then over his breakfast, she had coached him on exactly what he should say to Halsingham. She was so intent on getting her point across, she hadn't realized that he had stopped listening to her the first time she had gone over it.

Knowing that Inspector Brock was usually in his office at an early hour, he headed over to Scotland Yard. When Sion was seated, and over a cup of coffee, the inspector gave him a report on Danae's movements and, more importantly, Saegar's. Sion was angered and scared witless to learn that the man wasn't doing much lately but following Danae about. Despite Danae's belief that he should try to understand the baron's pain, this was something he could not ignore.

However, Brock told him not to worry. He was having Saegar tailed twenty-four hours a day, and as soon as the man slipped up in the least little way, he would have him taken into custody.

Just the thought of Saegar watching Danae froze Sion's blood. He mentally made a note to start wearing a pistol and also to buy a small one for Danae's reticule.

Concluding with business at the Yard, Sion hailed a hackney and gave Halsingham's direction. The sooner he got this over with, the sooner he had a chance to restore some peace and quiet in his home. He smiled when he pictured Danae right where he had left her, pacing the front hall. By now she was glaring at the door, sending scathing looks at Seadon whenever he came to stare at her or offer her a chair in his usual weary way. Sion hoped she was fretting, wondering what in hell was keeping him. It was like poetic justice for the misery she had put him through last night.

Changing his mind, he tapped the roof of the cab to get the driver's attention, then directed him to circle the park a couple of times. Then, with a sigh he settled back and closed his eyes with every intention of taking a little snooze. It would do her some good to learn the blessing of patience, for she had surely strained his lately. After all, he wasn't some bloody puppet dancing on the ends of her strings. Well, not much, anyway.

After four leisurely turns around Hyde Park, Sion swung his walking stick between lazy fingers as he approached the door to Halsingham's flat. Eleven in the morning was still a very impolite hour to call. He didn't give it another thought as he pounded on the polished wood. After several long minutes, the door was opened by the viscount himself. It was quite apparent that he had interrupted the man's sleep, by the look of his heavy-lidded, bloodshot eyes and a robe thrown over a sadly rumpled evening rig. *Perfect.* It suited him just fine to have the bastard off balance. And he had every intention to keep him that way.

Striding past the dazed man, Sion headed over to the banked fire and stirred the coals to life. "Good morning, Halsingham. We have to talk."

"Dereham?" The viscount looked out onto the landing before closing the door, then squinted across the room, his confusion obvious on his unshaven face.

After the flames caught, Sion turned back, rubbing his hands together, just beginning to realize how much he was going to enjoy this. With a forced smile, he asked with uncharitable disinterest, "Am I interrupting something?"

Halsingham retied his robe with several abrupt jerks as he went to stand over the intruder now lounging in his favorite chair. "As a matter of fact, you are—my sleep. What the deuce do you want?"

"Your son."

Expecting anything but this, Halsingham froze. After a long, pregnant pause, he managed in a rusty voice, "What son?"

Chin resting on his fist, Sion studied Halsingham's flawless features, hating him more with each minute that passed. "What is your problem, Halsingham? Are you being evasive because you forgot you have a son, or are you trying to decide which one of the several dozen littering England I am referring to?" he asked with lazy sarcasm.

The viscount drew himself up and glared down at Sion. "I think it would be wise for you to leave."

"Why?"

"Because, if you don't, I just might toss you out the window."

Sion looked about and then pointed. "That window?"

"If you prefer."

"What I would prefer is to lighten many a lady's battered heart by putting an end to your worthless life. But I have been told that is not an option, so I must suffer you, pathetic scab that you are. However, since I find you growing tedious, I will get to the point." Leaning forward, he pierced Halsingham's gaze with his own. "Within the next forty-eight hours you will gain custody of your son, the boy being claimed by Camden as his grandson and heir. After this has been achieved, I will step in and relieve you of the onerous task of caring for him."

Halsingham was amazed at the man's audacity. "Why the bloody hell should I?"

Sion's gaze slowly panned about the room and took stock of the expensive paneling, the rare Persian carpets, the priceless artifacts interspersed about the large room. "You live very well, but you are also just one step ahead of your debtors. I notice you have no servants about. Can't afford them this month, Halsingham? It is well known that you live on the sole largesse of Camden. I wonder what the earl would do if it became known throughout the *ton* that the child he was trying to pass off as the legitimate child of Viscount and the late Lady Halsingham was an impossibility."

Halsingham's slim frame tensed as if preparing to take a facer right in the middle of his pretty nose. "I don't follow you."

Sion *tsk*ed in disgust, shaking his head. "Halsingham, Halsingham, of course you do. Even I don't believe you to be that stupid."

Halsingham could feel his body flush with heat

as the blood pulsed through his veins at an alarming rate. He turned away from his nemesis and closed his eyes. He could feel his whole world tilting crazily about him. Not knowing what else to do, he played dumb. Opening his eyes, he was shocked to stare into Dereham's reflected image standing directly behind him. That bastard had been watching his every reaction in the mirror. With a forced laugh he shrugged. "Well, I suppose I must be that stupid, for I haven't the faintest idea what the hell you are threatening me with."

Sion moved away. "You surely do disappoint me, Halsingham. I had been hoping for a worthier opponent. I am speaking of a woman, your late wife to be exact, who lies in her grave as pure as the day she was born. Last I heard, it was still impossible for a virgin to give birth to a child, no matter how far medical science has progressed."

Not only was his world tilting, it was shattering about his feet. Not bothering to hide his loathing any longer, he spun about and confronted the marquis. "You can't prove a damn thing."

"If the signed affidavit from a respected physician is not sufficient, I'm sure an exhumation of her body would put to rest any doubts Camden might harbor."

Making a concerted effort not to stumble, Halsingham walked over to a window and stood staring out at nothing. Why was this happening to him? What had he ever done that was so wrong? Ever since Katherine's death it seemed as if God himself was out to thwart him. He was even beginning to think that his late wife was scheming with the Almighty, seeking reprisal for his so-called neglect, intent on pulling him down. But how in hell did this cocky weasel figure into it? What could he possibly want with one of his by-blows?

With a sigh he turned to face the marquis. "Why are you doing this to me? What more could you possibly want, considering your lover is getting a sizable inheritance that by right should come to me?"

After having been subjected to this slur against Danae, Sion forced himself to keep to the issue at hand, even though he wanted nothing more than to toss the little pisspot out the same window he had been threatened with. Unclenching his hands, he meticulously smoothed the fine kid over his fingers. "I don't give a shit about you. What I do care about is an innocent child in the clutches of that madman. Good God, man, are you that much of a bastard that you don't give a friggin' fart about the seed you planted in some hapless woman's body. Camden found this child of yours in the most disreputable workhouse in England, slaving fourteen hours a day in conditions a rat would have shied of. Have you absolutely no decency?"

"It wasn't my fault that the boy's mother was a lightskirt. I didn't force her, and I shouldn't have to concern myself with her mistakes."

Sion just looked at this man standing before him and was astonished to realize that he truly was unaware of any moral obligation on his part. No wonder Danae thought so poorly of men; look at the standards that had been dealt her. The rawest set he had ever seen. Even though he still hated it, he now had a grudging respect for her obsessive caution. And this joke of a man standing before him was, in large part, to blame for all his headaches.

Walking toward the door, he just wanted to get

out and breathe some clean air—even London's filth was preferable. The refuse behind him was beginning to make him ill.

"I've changed my mind," he announced abruptly. "You have twenty-four hours to get that boy away from Camden. If he is not here by this time tomorrow, all hell is going to break loose; you have my oath on that. And when Camden and I get done with you, not to mention one Italian virago, you will think the inside of a coffin sheer heaven."

Halsingham stood there by the window, staring at the door as it shuddered with the force of Dereham's exit. Then, with a vile curse, he yanked at his rumpled cravat as he headed for the dressing room.

What the bloody hell was he supposed to do now? Having Dereham eliminated was a good possibility. He wouldn't even be averse to Camden's sudden demise. However, that was too risky as he would be in dun city as soon as the coffin hit the ground.

Then he stopped dead in his tracks. "Shit!" he grated out as he struck his forehead with the heel of his palm. "What an asinine idiot I am!" The key to the entire Camden dynasty was actually his by law, and when push came to shove, there wouldn't be a hell of a lot that old bloodsucker could do. Camden could hardly start all over again by latching onto another brat. By the time he was done with the earl, he wouldn't have any choice but to spread the wealth around a bit more. And Dereham could go piss up a tree. He would deal with him in his own good time.

* * *

"Are you truly that stupid that you would sit there and threaten me?" Camden asked in that brittle-cold voice of his.

Halsingham took a deep breath and counted to ten. He was getting real tired of everyone calling him stupid. "All I am saying is that it is going to look a bit peculiar if I have nothing to do with my own son. After all, appearances are especially important in this case."

"The sycophants of our acquaintance hardly give a damn about their own progeny, let alone some-one else's. You had best come up with a better excuse than that." Camden studied the fuming man sitting across his desk for a long moment. "If this is your pathetic attempt to gain control of the Camden fortune, you can forget it. The child is im-portant to me, but bank my words; I would kill him first before I would let you get your mercenary hands on my money." Like hell he would, but this stupid sot didn't know it. "It would be very con-ducive to your continued good health if you simply content yourself with the generous allowance I al-ready give you. Don't get too greedy, Halsingham. You are walking the edge of a blade as it is. I think you are too vain to realize just how much I truly do detest you."

Standing up, the earl walked over to the bellpull and gave it a lazy tug; then he turned again and drilled his son-in-law with pitiless eyes. "You inter-fere in my plans, you approach my grandson in any way, and I promise you, you will never know from what direction you were hit. Now get out." He nod-ded toward the burly footman who had quietly appeared in the open doorway.

Halsingham looked from the servant back to the man he hated more than anything or anyone in his life. And he was getting sick and tired of his life constantly being threatened. What kind of man was he that he simply sat there taking this abuse? He was almost tempted to let Dereham follow through with his threats, and watch Camden's unholy plans collapse about him, ending the long and illustrious history of the fucking Camden dynasty. But he was not the fool everyone claimed him to be. Spineless, perhaps, but not stupid. He was still alive, wasn't he?

He was entering the hall when he heard a noise above him, and turning slightly, he spied his son at the top of the stairs, staring down at him. The boy's serious blue eyes registered nothing as he watched his father, and Halsingham was torn between the insane desires of either snatching him up and running or bounding up the stairs and throttling the life out of that diminutive problem. But, again he assured himself, he wasn't stupid.

With a jerk, he spun about, and as he melded with the congestion on the thoroughfare, he wondered what the hell he was going to do now. If he complied with either man's threats, he was a dead man, and he now had less than twenty hours to make a decision.

Cursing Katherine with every foul epithet he could think of, he headed toward the heart of London's infamous stews.

As soon as he rounded the curve in the path, he spotted Danny sitting on a bench and with a grin he sprinted ahead of Miss York. With a glad exclamation, Danae flung wide her arms; then, as he cannonballed into her, they tumbled back against the backrest, her laughter joyous. After a moment of just holding him, she realized with a chuckle that if she didn't loosen the stranglehold he had on her neck she was going to faint. But, as she gently tried to pry loose his arms, she felt tremors racking his little body. The smile melted from her face as concern took over.

Looking at an equally concerned Mrs. Turlow, she asked, "Timothy, love, what is it? Are you hurt?"

Burrowing his head farther into her neck, he shook it.

Tightening her own hold, she shifted him about, then drew him onto her lap. Murmuring soothing nonsense, she rocked him gently, then started as a shadow fell across them. Looking up she saw Miss York standing over them, obviously distraught and close to tears herself. Without a word, her eyes questioned the young governess.

Miss York watched her young charge being held lovingly in the *contessa's* arms; then, casting her gaze about nervously, she explained in an undertone, "It was his lordship. He somehow found out about Edward's visits with you. When he questioned him yesterday, the young master, of course, clammed up as usual and wouldn't admit to a thing. He put him in the closet and left him there all night."

Danae's breath caught, and kissing Timothy's ear, she murmured softly, "I'm so sorry, Timothy. It was all my fault."

Almost frantically he shook his head.

"When I went to get him early the next morning, I thought he was dead, so cold and still was he," Miss York's quivering voice continued. "And there *he* sat, just sitting in front of the closet, staring at me with those reptilian eyes of his. Didn't say a word as I carried the young master away. Just watched." Wringing her hands, she sat down beside them. "Oh, ma'am, he scares me, he does. I don't know what to do. I want to protect the young master, but I'm so afraid." The girl's tear-swollen eyes gazed on the tousled head resting on Danae's breast. Misery drenched the pretty brown eyes she raised to Danae. "Oh, Lord, ma'am, I just don't know how to protect him."

Leaning over, Danae grasped one of the girl's cold hands and squeezed tightly. "It's not your fault, Elizabeth. You are doing your best and no one knows that better than Timothy."

His head bobbed in confirmation.

Miss York's sniffles cut off abruptly, and suspiciously she glared at Danae. "Who are you? Where's your accent?" she demanded with a little hiccup. "And why did you call him Timothy? I knew something strange was going on here." Her own distress gone, Elizabeth stood her ground and glared at this mysterious woman who was turning all their lives upside down and now even endangering her little charge.

Just realizing her terrible blunder, Danae cast a frantic gaze over the girl's head to Mrs. Turlow.

Immediately the old woman came about the bench and grabbed hold of the girl's elbow. Ignoring the girl's indignant cries, she then, without a by-your-leave, tugged the struggling lady along after her as she headed down one of the paths.

Confident that Mrs. Turlow would handle that problem, Danae turned her attention to Timothy, only to notice his serious gaze following after the duo.

He turned with a frown to her. "Are you in trouble now?"

Touched that after all he had suffered the past

night, he could worry over her, she gave him a teary smile as she brushed aside a few burnished curls from his flushed face. "Don't you worry about me. What about you?"

Dropping his face, he shrugged.

She tugged at his rumpled tie while swallowing her tears. "Oh, Timothy, I don't know what to say. I promised to take care of you and yet, right now, I can't."

His wounded gaze jumped to hers, and reluctantly he slid from her lap. Taking his hands in hers, she tugged him close again. "Do you remember when I spoke of Sion?" When he nodded, she continued, "He went to see your father this morning."

"I saw him."

"Who? Sion?"

He shook his head. "Hal . . . sing . . . ham." He stumbled over the name.

"Your father."

Adamantly he shook his head. He steadily returned her stare, needing her to understand. "No. Halsingham."

And she understood only too well. Neither did she ever refer to the man who sired her with the honored title of "Father." "How did he look?"

"Who?"

"Your fath—Halsingham." She knew her impatience was getting the best of her, but that rat Sion had never come back to clue her in on what was happening. God's teeth, just what wasn't she going to do to him when she got her hands on him tonight?

"Mad." Timothy answered with a succinct nod.

"Oh, dear." She sat back, dejected. It apparently hadn't worked. Damn, but he had always been such a spineless fool. Now whatever were they going to do?

"Good afternoon."

They both jumped as that sibilant whisper floated over them. As if they were joined at the hip, they turned to stare up at the Earl of Camden. And, as Miss York so aptly described, those reptilian eyes were zeroed in on Danae, pinning her with eerie accuracy.

"Buon giorno," she finally managed.

"I see you have made the acquaintance of my grandson." Ignoring Timothy, the earl looked about with negligent unconcern. "And his governess is nowhere to be seen. Ah, such a pity, and she has been such a pliable little thing. But, it seems I'll have to get rid of her. Can't have her shirking her duties and endangering the life of the heir to Camden."

Danae knew that defending Miss York would be useless, so she didn't even bother. Again those cold, colorless eyes came to rest on her.

"Do you realize that since the first time I saw you I've had the uncanny feeling that I know you. And my instincts are never wrong."

Danae raised equally expressionless eyes to clash with his. "Well, as we have never had prior acquaintance, *signore,* I would say they are failing you now."

Camden's eyes narrowed ever so slightly as he studied her. Again, as many times in the past, she felt like some specimen squirming under his regard, a pin stuck through her middle.

"No," he reiterated slowly, "they are never wrong. I'll have to ponder this some more." Then he smiled.

And chills raced along her body. It took every

bit of strength she could muster not to shudder
visibly.

Snapping his fingers, like calling a dog to heel,
he commanded, "Come, Edward, we must be leaving."

Resisting the urge to snatch him back, she had to
sit there as she watched Timothy leave her and
docilely go to that monster's side.

Then, as Camden was turning away, he paused.
"Oh, by the way, tell that girl not to bother coming
back. Her services are no longer required. I simply
cannot tolerate disloyalty." And again he smiled
that mirthless smile of his. "But, somehow I think
you already know this."

Danae watched the two of them as they moved
down the path. Silently she prayed for Timothy to
look back. But, as they slowly began to disappear
around the bend, she felt tears well in her eyes. He
was giving up on her.

Then, at the last possible moment, his diminutive
figure paused and he looked over his shoulder before continuing on. Danae closed her eyes as her
breath left her in a shaky sigh. She literally had to
pry her fingers from the bench, they were clamped
so tightly about the edge of the wood.

Just keep faith with me, Timothy. I will get you out, she
swore, her gaze pinned to the last spot she had seen
him. Even if she had to kill that bastard herself, she
would see him free.

"This is all your fault!" Elizabeth's tearful voice
accused from behind.

Turning around, she faced the distraught young
woman, knowing she had no defense; she was at
fault. Taking a deep breath, she linked her arm
about the girl's waist but was shaken off.

"No! I've got to go after Lord Edward. Heaven

knows what the beast will do to him, and it's all your fault!" With that, Elizabeth spun around to follow the earl and her charge, but Danae's voice caught her up short.

"The earl has dismissed you. I think it would be best if you just stayed away. Better for you and better for Timothy."

Shocked, Elizabeth dropped onto the bench and stared off into space. "What am I going to do? All I own is in that house. What's going to happen to Edward?"

Danae sat beside the stunned woman and stared off into space with her. Neither noticed when Mrs. Turlow arrived, huffing, for she had bustled to follow the girl after the determined nanny had given her the slip several paths away. Looking around, she asked, "Where's the wee laddie?"

Immediately, Elizabeth broke into tears, covering her face as she quietly sobbed.

Danae reached into her reticule and drew out a fine linen kerchief. Leaning over, she tried to soothe the girl the best she could. "I suppose I should tell you the whole story. You've proved your love of Timothy enough, and your present unemployed status is now my fault, as you say. But, I warn you, if you try to expose me, ultimately you are only going to hurt Timothy. And I'm not saying this to protect myself but to protect him."

So, as Elizabeth's sobs slowed and the stooped, shaking shoulders straightened into rapt attention, Danae told her the entire story from beginning to the tangled mess they were now enmeshed in. When she was finished, Danae raised her reluctant gaze and met the incredulous stare of a pair of wet, reddened eyes.

"I don't believe it. I've never heard such an absurd story in my life!"

"It be true, every blessed word." Mrs. Turlow supplied in a surly voice.

Elizabeth, openmouthed, stared from woman to woman, sitting on either side of her, not knowing what to do. Should she run? Go to the police and report these two lunatics? Would they hurt her?

Seeing the girl's inner turmoil and disbelief, Danae sighed in frustration at her own stupidity in trusting this young woman. "Well, there is not much more I can say except this: as I stated before, think twice before you do anything concerning me, for ultimately you could be endangering Timothy's life." Standing, she made to move away from the bench. Almost desperately the girl's hand shot out and grabbed hold of Danae's skirt.

"No! Don't go. I do want to help. I love that little boy and I'll do just about anything to help him—even assist you in this ridiculous plan, if need be."

Danae and Mrs. Turlow exchanged a relieved glance, then Danae linked her arm with Miss York's. "Thank you. Now, first thing first. Let's get you home and settled and we will think where we go from here."

"What are you going to tell his lordship?" Mrs. Turlow wanted to know as she fell in behind them.

Shooting the old woman a warning frown, Danae told her, "We shall tell him nothing right now. He thinks I am irresponsible as it is, so why reinforce his belief until it is absolutely necessary." Glancing sideways at Mrs. T., Danae noticed the stubborn purse of her lips and sighed. "Promise me you won't tell him."

This was starting to be all too familiar and frequent, Mrs. T. thought sourly as she returned Danae's pleading gaze. Reluctantly she nodded, knowing no good would come of it.

After all, it wasn't as if Miss York was a stray puppy they could hide in a closet.

Sighing and muttering dire predictions, she trudged after the pair.

"Just how stupid do you think I am?" Halsingham asked in disgust, eyeing the behemoth across from him.

The bilker simply sat there cleaning his filthy nails with the tip of his cuttle, eyeing him.

"But I can get the job done for half that," Halsingham argued as he swatted at the smoke drifting about his face.

"Takes it or leaves it, guv. Makes no never-mind t' me." The man shrugged as he took a swill of his pint.

Halsingham scrubbed his face in frustrated irritation. *God, would this day never end?* With a sigh, he looked about at the dregs of society swilling down their rag water, belching, farting, and blowing foul-smelling smoke into the already fetid air.

Just wanting to get out of this pesthole, he threw up his hands as he spat out, "Fine, anything, just get it done and get it done right, or else you will never know what hit you."

The ape simply smiled, showing a row of rotten, tobacco-stained teeth and black gums. "Now, that's right funny, guv. So, tells me, who's goin' t' do the 'ittin'? You?"

Was he the only one in this world who took threats seriously, Halsingham wondered as he threw half the blunt down on the table. "When the job is completed you will get the rest."

"Righto." A huge paw came out to swipe the gleaming coins away.

Then, as he left the dive, he heard the behemoth laughing behind him.

Twenty-two

Danae slammed into the house and glared at Seadon, who stood in front of her with his hand still extended to open the door.

"Where is he?" she demanded as she strode toward the library.

"His lordship is resting in the library, madam," Seadon intoned in his weary way as he made sure she had slammed the door securely.

Her skirts rustling angrily about her, she made a beeline to Sion's lounging figure. "Where have you been?"

Sion paused in the midst of sipping his tea and took note of her too-bright eyes. He knew when Danae was on the verge of tears, and he felt a storm coming on. "I've been here waiting for you, love," he answered calmly.

Collapsing into the chair opposite him, she stared into the fire, dejected. "Oh, Sion, it didn't work." Then she looked at him sharply. "You did go to Halsingham this morning?"

"Yes, just as planned. So, what didn't work?" He poured her a cup but she waved it away.

"I saw Timothy in the park. He said he saw Halsingham at Camden Hall and that he looked mad.

Obviously, Camden didn't bite. God, how I hate that bastard!" she spat out, impassioned.

"Halsingham?"

"No. Yes! Him, too, but I was referring to Camden. Do you know he put the poor child in a closet all night simply because he wouldn't answer a few questions."

Sion's body stiffened imperceptibly before he leaned forward to replace his cup. "I gave Halsingham until eleven tomorrow to get Timothy away from Camden. Don't lose all hope quite yet."

"I was too optimistic, putting any faith in that spineless fool. Of course, he won't buck Camden." Restless, she jumped to her feet again. Sion hardly noticed, he was so used to her pacing now.

"He is not going to have much choice in the matter if he doesn't want Camden to learn the truth about the marriage," Sion argued reasonably.

"You don't know Halsingham like I do. Right now he is feeling like a rat trapped on a burning ship, and none of his options are going to be to his liking. So he will get desperate, and Halsingham's too stupid to get desperate. He'll likely come up with some brainless scheme that will get someone killed, and unfortunately, it won't be him."

Sion stifled a smile. Getting weary just by watching his lady pace herself into a frenzy, he got up and, coming up behind her, captured her in his arms. "Relax. One way or another we will get Timothy. We will just have to exercise a little patience and see what tomorrow brings. Besides, we have a ball to attend tonight, and I have a surprise that should arrive"—he glanced at the clock—"at any moment."

She spun out of his arms and confronted him, caught off guard. "What ball?"

"Nana's, of course."

"What do you mean, 'of course'? I know nothing of it."

He looked a little sheepish. "You mean I didn't tell you?"

If she was upset before, she was furious now. "No, you didn't tell me! Sion, how could you do this? On top of everything that is happening, now you throw this at me! Well, I won't go. I don't even have a ball gown."

"You will. That is your surprise. The seamstress should be here momentarily." Reaching out, he soothed her arms, trying to pull her closer. But, Danae was not Mrs. Turlow and couldn't be bribed so easily. With an unladylike oath, she jerked away and headed for the door.

"I don't care if you bought me a dozen gowns; I'm not going. Please extend my apologies to Nana."

Getting equally angry, he strode after her, shouting, "You most certainly will go. We are the guests of honor. You will not disappoint her, Danny."

Danae did an about-face, intending to do some shouting of her own, when she spotted the interested Seadon polishing the handle on his beloved door. Putting a hand to his chest, she pushed Sion backward into the library and slammed the door. Then, nose to nose, she argued in an undertone. "You listen to me, Sion Sinclair. I have no intention of going to Nana's ball no matter how much I love her. I will not be some freak, displayed and gawked at."

Taken aback, Sion just stared at her; then, with an exclamation of disgust, he threw his arms into the air. "What nonsense are you rattling on about? Why would you be considered a freak? And how could you believe I would subject you to something like that?"

"I am an unmarried woman cohabiting with a man who is my lover. How did you think your precious Society would receive me? With open arms? One of our plans when we came here was to live as quietly as possible, away from snobbish interest. We have too much to do to start a scandal of major proportions."

"Danny, because you are a widow and a foreigner into the bargain, you will be considered a woman of the world and above such strict conventions. You have already been a mystery and on the curious minds of the *ton* since the day we arrived. If nothing else, you are going to garner an eccentric notoriety and the secret envy of every woman because of your freedom to do whatever the hell you want." When he saw she wasn't convinced, he added, "Do you really think Nana would do anything to harm you. She loves you."

Danae looked sideways at him, and he knew he had her. "Besides, just wait until you see my gift. I designed it especially for you."

She relented a little more. "I don't want to be laughed at and shunned, Sion." Fear and uncertainty tinged her words.

Taking her into his arms, he promised, "At the first snigger, we will be out of there. How is that?"

Finally giving in, she wrapped her arms about his neck, and dropping her head on his shoulder, she nodded. He nuzzled the curls at her temple and breathed deeply of her lemon scent. "I've missed you, Danny. I need you." And turning her face to his, he kissed her deeply, not really meaning to take it any further. But, when she strained against him, thrusting her tongue into his mouth with equal fervor, he shoved her against the door with a rattle, and before either of them knew it, her skirts were up about her thighs.

Suddenly, Danae wrenched her mouth away from his and panted, "What was that?"

"What?" he mumbled, dazed to everything but her luscious breasts in his hands.

"That!" she snapped as she pushed him away, twitching her skirts back into order.

Sion, angry, frustrated, and ready to commit murder, spun about and glared at the door when he heard the timid knock. Within a heartbeat he threw the portal wide and yelled, "What the hell is it?"

Seadon blinked a few times, then announced calmly, "Mrs. Auriville, my lord."

Feeling like an utter ass, Sion smiled lamely at the beautiful woman standing behind Seadon, trying to hide her amusement. "Julita, how are you?"

Julita bit her lip before she said slowly, "A bit more rested than you, *cherie.*" And her gaze flickered down for a brief second.

Sion's smile was brittle as he reached behind him and pulled Danae to his side. "My dear, you remember Julita Auriville? She has come to fit your gown."

Danae's face was a rosy shade of embarrassment as she fidgeted with a few stray curls falling down upon her shoulders. *"Buona sera, Signora* Auriville."

"My timing always was execrable. Please call me, Julita. Shall I come back later?" she offered graciously. After years of fitting men's mistresses, wives, and even the occasional catamite, nothing bothered her. On the contrary, it was good to see Dereham back and so obviously in love again. And his lady was stunning. She had thoroughly enjoyed dressing her. But, this gown was the *pièce de résistance*. Tomorrow she would be turning patrons from her door, unable to keep up with the orders she was going to receive.

Being a typical female, Danae's attention latched onto the large box held carefully in the modiste's assistant's arms. "No, no, now is fine, *si*." She slipped past Sion, and escorted the ladies to her rooms. After the modiste had entered, followed by her assistant, Danae turned to close the door only to find it blocked by a pair of broad shoulders. "What do you want?" she asked with a preoccupied frown.

"I want to watch."

He sounded so much like a sulky little boy that she couldn't resist smiling at him. "Does baby want his treat?" she teased in a singsong undertone.

Suddenly, he was all roguish man as his sizzling gaze swept the svelte lines of her body. "Yes, he does. And I promise you, I'm always a good boy; I always finish my treat down to the last lick."

Her face flamed bright red, and quickly she looked over her shoulder, relieved to see the two women engrossed in opening the boxes. "Why can't you play fair?" she groused as she pushed the door closed behind him with a rattle.

Grabbing her chin, he leaned over and gave her a slow, gut-wrenching kiss, reluctantly releasing her lips when he finally pulled away. "I always play fair with you, Danny," he whispered. "I wouldn't want to do it any other way."

With a dreamy sigh, she turned away and stopped short. "Oh, my!" she breathed in awe.

"You like?" his moist breath whispered in her ear.

"I love." Like a sleepwalker, she walked over to the gown spread out on the bed, and reverently she smoothed her hand down the luxurious emerald green velvet. It was elegant in its simplicity. There was no fussy lace or furbelows, no ponderous draping.

In short order, the women had her out of her day ensemble and lovingly slipped the masterpiece over her head. It fit like a glove, and with few tugs here and there, the rich velvet fell in long, elegant folds with a slight draping effect of chiffon velvet of the identical color sweeping up around her hips. Where there should have been a massive bustle, the delicate material was drawn up into a simple bow, the underside having been lined with gold tissue. The tails swept down into the graceful demitrain, the light shimmering off the gold interspersed about the deep-hued velvet. The whole effect was spectacular. "Oh, *cara mia*," she breathed as she postured in front of the beveled mirror. "It is *splendido!* You design this, *si*?"

Sion's gaze lovingly traced the exquisite lines of Danae's body framed by the lush folds. "*Si*, and you are gorgeous, as always." Then he frowned.

In the mirror she saw his expression, and turning about, she asked, "What is the matter, *cara*?"

He waved a hand, pointing somewhere about her chest. "That. I didn't draw it that way," he accused Julita.

Both women turned back to the mirror and stared, "What?" they asked in unison.

Coming to his feet, Sion came up behind Danae, and reaching over her shoulders, he tugged sharply on her decollete, causing her to stumble. "What are you doing, Sion? That hurt, and you'll ruin it. It looks *bello, si*?" She looked at the modiste in the mirror, now uncertain.

"I agree. What is wrong with it?" Julita slapped

Sion's hands away as he went after the offensive neckline again.

"It shows too much bosom."

Both women gaped at him. "That is modest by any standard," Julita exclaimed, pointing at the velvet bodice gracefully exposing Danae's beautiful shoulders, but only giving a teasing hint of cleavage.

"It shows too much," he reiterated in a steely voice.

Danae's eyes narrowed, and Sion thought she was going to argue, so he was stunned when she suddenly nodded.

"*Si, cara mia.* You are right."

Suspicious, he asked warily, "I am?"

She nodded vigorously. "The dress is unacceptable." Shrugging she said sadly, *"Bien.* I shall have to stay home."

Sion, knowing he had just lost this battle, cast a disgruntled stare at Julita. "I did not design it that way!"

Julita pondered on just exactly what "part" of his pride she appealed to; then, with a shrug she smoothed the velvet where Sion's jealous fingers had mussed the simple lines of the decolletage. "No doubt, by the end of the evening, he will be complaining it is not low enough. Men are such contrary creatures, but we do what we must to humor them."

"Amen," Danae sighed.

The ball was a stunning crush. Everyone who was anyone was there to become reacquainted with the Marquis of Dereham and to view his lady-love. Equal parts of jealousy, admiration, and lust were bestowed on the exotic Italian *contessa,* but above all, Danae's first appearance in Society was a fabulous success. The only thing that marred an otherwise perfect evening was the fanatical regard of both Camden and Halsingham. If Camden was a bit more circumspect about his spying, Halsingham didn't even try to hide his attraction for her. All she had to do was turn about and she was bumping into him.

"You simply must tell me who created that absolutely stunning gown, my dear," the Duchess of Lancaster said, eyeing the creation enviously.

Danae knew she had heard that name before, and the teasing memory was beginning to rankle as they talked of fashion and modistes. Listening with half an ear and smiling, hopefully at the right times, she was like a dog worrying a bone in her attempt to recollect. She had a vague reminiscence of a conversation between Sion and Jonas. Then, she gave a start as something the duchess said jolted her memory.

"Oh, yes, I throw the most simply marvelous weekend hunts. You must come. And bring Dereham along if you wish, though you would not be lacking in companionship, I'm sure."

Ignoring the subtle slur, Danae commented carefully, "*Si*, I have 'eard of your parties. In fact, I believe it was *Barone* Saegar who 'ad spoke of them."

"Oh, *that* man." The woman's onerous voice dripped with disgust. "He is simply not allowed at any party of mine anymore."

Danae's heart accelerated. "You 'ave trouble with him? He seems a *gentile signore.*"

"That sot?" Lady Lancaster scoffed. "I remember one year he got cup-shot to the point of idiocy. Had to have him thrown off my property. Thank God, all my guests hadn't arrived at the time. You know, that scandal he caused with Lord Dereham had been so blown out of proportion. But politics, don't you know. It was a shame what that man had to put up with. Delightful man, Dereham. You are a lucky woman. I must admit that if you were not here I would throw my cap at him. I vow, I would throw my body at him if I thought he would catch me." The lady heaved a great sigh; then, with a slight shrug of regret, she turned and sailed into the crowd.

Danae stared in openmouthed wonder after this luminary of London Society.

When someone touched her shoulder, she almost jumped out of her beautiful gown. "Oh, Sion!" Then she nodded toward the impressive figure of Lady Lancaster. "Did you know that your hostess is carrying a tendre for you?"

Sion grinned. "Don't be too jealous. Cathy is in love with every man she meets. She has insatiable appetites, so I have heard."

Danae shrugged. "I don't know about that, but don't you see? She is supposed to be the reigning leader of the *ton*. If she is so well disposed toward you, so must the rest of them be. Now, doesn't this make you feel just a bit foolish, worrying all those years over your lost reputation? It seems no one ever did believe Saegar but a few ambitious or political characters that have long since lost any interest in you."

Sion glanced about him with a jaded eye. "You weren't there, Danny. It may have been of fleeting interest to the great majority of the herd, but the sheep that mattered the most to me believed it at the time. It is not something I will forget or forgive easily."

Wrapping her arm about his, she told him softly,

"You are wrong about one thing: the ones *most* important to you never stopped believing in you. Don't you ever forget that."

His hard gaze softening, he leaned down, and his lips touched her cheek in the merest wisp of a kiss. "I love you, you know, and I can't wait to get you alone."

Her body heated and tingled, and glancing sideways at him, she whispered back, "There must be someplace where we can find a moment of privacy in this mausoleum of a home."

Their playfulness came to an abrupt end when their eyes met and the same wonderful current coursing through her body passed into Sion's, fusing their thoughts in delicious need. In the next moment, they were leaving the stifling crowd and set out in search of a bit of privacy. One long corridor to the left, Sion pushed open a door, and after a quick glance in, he pulled her into the room with him. The door was slammed shut and the latch secured, and Danae was in his arms before either could do any more than groan with the growing demands of their impatient bodies.

"Sion," she gasped as his teeth gently nipped her throat, "Sion, make love to me. Right now, right here. I want you naked in my arms."

Having no intention of arguing with this demand, Sion swung her up into his arms and carried her over to the divan.

Halsingham's eyes narrowed in rage as he watched Sion undress her. Casting a furtive look about, he stepped into the shrubbery to get closer, thankful the moon was hidden behind the clouds as he watched the impassioned couple inside. His fingers clenched about the window's frame as he watched Danae step out of that provocative gown that had teased him all evening. His breath caught with strangling suffocation as the perfection of her body was revealed in the flickering gaslight. With reverent care, Dereham unlaced her corset, his lips worshipping the skin revealed with the loosening of each lace.

Halsingham ran a shaky hand over his own tingling lips, then uttered a vile curse as she came to stand almost directly in front of him, nude except for a pair of sheer silk stockings gracing long, supple legs. It was as if she was taunting him, teasing him. He watched, helpless, as Dereham threw off his own clothes, ripping the studs from his shirt; then Halsingham grew almost frenzied when the bastard stepped in front of her, blocking his view of her body. When Dereham knelt in front of her, Halsingham's starved gaze ranged obsessively over Danae's exposed silhouette. She shifted slightly to watch her lover's hand stroke up and around her body, opening to those questing hands with low moans that bedeviled Halsingham's taunted nerves. The voyeur was struck with the force of her beauty as his gaze greedily fed upon her heavy breasts thrusting high, the dark nipples distended and swollen, aching for the touch of his tongue, the long, supple curve of her waist sweeping into the graceful hips and rounded buttocks. And those sinful legs. He could almost feel them clamped about his waist as he thrust into her.

Dereham sat back on his haunches and just admired the play of the light burnishing the sensuous sight before him. Slowly he extended a hand to stroke the tender skin of her inner thighs, and with a groan, Danae threw her head back and again licked her swollen, glistening lips. Halsingham wasn't even aware of the trickle of sweat that rolled down his temple as he watched that hand, so dark against the delicate creaminess of her skin, stroke closer to that dark shadow that constantly drew his avid gaze. His jaw clenched painfully as Dereham dipped his fingers deep into those silky, wet curls, then withdrew them, the flickering light glistening on her essence now coating the long fingers that splayed possessively over her. Breathing deeply, Halsingham had to clench his middle, and controlling the wild urge to hurl himself through the window, he leaned his feverish forehead against the cool glass.

He cursed the marquis in the vilest terms possible as he watched the bastard lean forward again and drag his tongue slowly along the taut lines of her belly, his hands reaching behind her to cup her buttocks and pull her even closer to that ravenous mouth. When his tongue dipped into her naval, she groaned, and convulsively her fingers gripped his hair as if to urge him on. Dereham then looked up and spoke to her, directing her, and like the bitch in heat she was, she complied immediately. Releasing her hold on him she leaned against the back of the divan, and supporting herself, she raised one long, supple leg and draped her thigh over his shoulder. Again the dark head dipped forward, but not before the frantic eyes of the voyeur caught a glimpse of those pink, pearlescent tissues hidden in her moist delta.

Panting with erratic gasps, Halsingham's hand went to his erection and grasped it painfully as impotent rage consumed him. That should be him in there. That should be his tongue now delving deeply into that glistening thatch of down. Those should be his lips gleaming with her essence, his ears drinking in the sounds of her cries as she spasmed down into his arms, helpless to any and everything he wanted to do to her.

Furious at the injustice of it all, he pumped his erection as his feral eyes watched Dereham cover her sprawled body, his buttocks pumping tensely between those splayed thighs. He could picture his own cock pumping in and out of that warm delta as her hands came up to grip and claw at his own back. And just as he heard Dereham's roar, his own ejaculation saturated the wool of his trousers.

Still breathing heavily, he looked with narrowed, enraged eyes down upon the embracing lovers, promising retribution for this vile episode. She belonged to him. On silent feet he turned and headed for his carriage.

Soon her luscious body would be in his bed and his alone.

Danae lay curled in Sion's warm arms, staring up at the flickering light, her voluminous petticoat covering them.

"Did you do this with Tory?" She didn't know what compelled her, but she had to know.

"What?" he sighed as he shifted her about and then nuzzled the curls falling about her shoulders. The way they both looked, a little sneaking out the back was is order.

"This." Danae persisted, the wave of her hand encompassing the room and them.

Sion chuckled and nipped her ear. "Good Lord, no."

"Why not?"

He thought for a moment, then shrugged. "I don't know. I guess I never thought of Tory in this way: spontaneous, ravenous."

Danae sat up and glowered down at him. "Meaning she was a lady and I'm not?"

He pulled her back down. "Meaning, I loved her in a different way." He kissed her temple. "It seems strange, but now after having known you, loving you, I realize that what I felt for Tory was more . . ." He searched for the right word.

"Duty?" she supplied dryly.

"No!" Coming up on an elbow, he stared off into a dark corner. "No, never that. I loved her because she saw the best in me and was willing to look past the worst. You didn't know me then, Danny. I wasn't very endearing. I was wild, rough, and more times than not, completely undependable except when it suited me."

"I don't think I would have liked you then."

He turned to her, almost eagerly. "You see, that is what I mean. No one did, but Tory saw deep down and knew what I needed. She brought stability into my life. Except for Nana, I really had no other influence, and she spoiled me rotten." Tears glimmered in his eyes as he looked deep into hers. "Tory brought out the best in me, Danny, and she will always be a very special part of my life. But I never loved her like I love you. What we have is wild, passionate—a rejuvenation of life."

When she turned away, he caught her chin and forced her to face him again. "What is it?"

"I don't want to be the subject of a wild, passionate love. Passion dies. *I* want stability and security and a comfortable love that will survive no matter what."

He smiled tenderly at her. "You have that."

"And when you get bored with me?"

The muscles in his jaw clenched as he tried to contain his impatience. "Our passion will never die, Danae."

She sat up with a jerk. "That's trite!"

"God, here we go again!" he spat out as he reached for his trousers and yanked them on. "I am getting so sick and tired of this, Danae. I am not going to continually beat my head against that wall you call a heart."

Sion strode about gathering up his clothes, throwing them on as he punctuated his words while thrusting his arms into shirt, vest, and jacket. "I am not afraid to commit myself to this relationship. I will not be unfaithful to you! I will not betray you! And I will never leave you! *Now* it is *your* turn. You either accept this love and all the pitfalls and peaks that come with it, or *you* "—he jammed a finger at her—"walk away."

Finished dressing, he loomed over her. "There are no other options here, Danae. But whatever you decide, I'll always be here for you if you ever need me." Not bearing to see her sprawled on the floor at his feet, her body gleaming in the light, an almost luminescent glow about her, he turned away. He suddenly realized he was scared to death because he wasn't sure what her decision would be. He had just made the biggest gamble of his life.

He paused at the door, steeling himself. "I will wait for you in the carriage around back at the delivery entrance. If you don't come, I'll know your decision. I know Nana would love to have you stay here with her, and I'll send your things around in the morning. But"—his ebony gaze clashed with hers as he commanded harshly—"don't bother coming unless you are willing to risk just as much as I. You are going to have to trust your stubborn heart to me someday, Danny, and if we are to spend the rest of our lives together, that someday starts tonight!" Then he left the room, closing the door quietly behind him.

He waited a minute outside the door, listening. Then, when he heard nothing, his heart plummeted, and straightening his shoulders, he headed for the servants' stairs.

"Sion."

He stopped sharp, his heart beating like thundering drums. Schooling his expression into an impassive mask, he turned slowly and waited. There she stood in the doorway, her petticoat draped modestly about her. Thank God, they were down in the far reaches of the mansion. Her own expression was composed, calm, revealing as little as his. Finally, he asked, "What?"

"If I recall, earlier today you were raving on about my decollete, and now here I stand, bare-arsed, and you don't say a word."

His stern posture didn't ease. He saw no humor in the situation. "I'm through playing games, Danae."

"I agree."

He knew what she was doing, and it wasn't good enough. In a hard voice he demanded, "Say the words, Danae."

She looked down at her toes peeking out from beneath the lacy hem. She couldn't count all the lonely years she had dreamed of speaking those precious words to someone. And when she did, she knew there would be no going back. She was entrusting her very soul to this man. It was all a matter of trust. It was everything. "I love you."

"I didn't hear you."

Suddenly, she was angry—with herself for giving in, with him for forcing her—but she was so frightened she was horn-mad. She threw down the petticoat, along with years of suspicions, qualms, and above all, loneliness. Taking a deep breath, she threw her head back and shouted, "I love you, you dratted beast!"

Before she was even able to finish she felt herself being swept up in his arms and born backward in the room.

"It's about time!" he growled as his mouth came to claim his hard-won bounty.

Twenty-three

A dispirited mood hung heavy over the couple seated before the crackling fire, as both of them stared into the flickering flames. Mesmerized by the hypnotic dance, their dismal thoughts ran along parallel lines and yet were eons apart.

With a sigh, Danae shook her head. "I knew he wouldn't do it."

Sion's eyes narrowed as he watched a log disintegrate in a puff of glowing embers. "It is obvious I didn't make myself clear enough," his grim voice intoned.

He had been furious that Halsingham hadn't been at home when he had arrived at eleven sharp. Not in the best of humors to begin with, he had been forced to waste precious hours pacing the bastard's salon while an uneasy valet looked on. When he had slammed out of the building at one o'clock, he was almost thankful Halsingham hadn't shown his pretty face, for he was afraid he would have shot it off and landed himself before the Queen's Bench again.

Danae glanced sideways at his hard profile. "What are we going to do?" Knowing he was not in the best of moods—*volatile* would even be more apt to describe his glowering temper—she wasn't sure she wanted to know.

"*We* are not going to do anything. Don't worry, I'll handle it." The tone of his voice was warning her that this issue was not open for discussion.

Danae closed her eyes, fearing her concern had been well founded. The last thing she wanted was for him to "handle it." In his current mood, the word "bloodshed" sprang uncomfortably to mind. If she wasn't careful, Sion could very well end up in prison for trying to help her.

"Mr. Glendower, my lord," Seadon announced, startling them.

As Jonas strode into the room, Danae smiled with relief, knowing that he would divert Sion's attention from Halsingham. She only hoped he wasn't bringing more bad news. She wasn't sure how much more they could take.

Sion shot to his feet, his hand held out. "Jonas, thank God! What news?"

Jonas walked over to the liquor caddy and poured himself a glass of water, and returning to the fire, he sat opposite Sion and Danae. "Well, I met with the doctor. As Brock had said, the man is quite ill. Consumption. Most of the time he was coughing so bad I could scarcely understand a word he said."

"Jon, get to the point," Sion snapped out, irritated.

With a deep, fortifying breath he plunged on. "Yes, he was the attending doctor at the time of the marchioness's stroke, and yes, he did keep the information from you. He said he had no choice in the matter; he was being blackmailed."

Without hesitation Sion supplied dryly, "By Saegar, of course."

Jonas just shrugged.

"The bloody little worm," Sion bit out. "Will I ever be rid of him?"

Seadon strode in, an envelope on a silver salver. "This just arrived, my lord."

Danae watched as he ripped off the seal and quickly perused the letter. "Bloody hell!" he swore harshly. He glanced over at Danae, and she saw fear in his eyes. "It's Nana. On her way to the country she collapsed. They barely got her home."

Danae stood and hurried to his side. Without asking, she snatched the letter from him. "Is she all right?" she demanded, even as she scanned the missive herself.

Dragging shaking fingers through his hair, he glanced as if in a daze. "We will have to leave immediately." Then cursing long and viciously, he strode from the room, calling for Seadon as he climbed the stairs.

Helplessly, Danae looked over at Jonas. "My God, Jonas, what else can possibly go wrong?"

Early the next morning, after an evening of arguing back and forth, Sion gave up on Danae and reluctantly agreed to leave her in London. As she watched Sion's carriage disappear around a corner, she wondered if she was doing the right thing. She cared deeply for Nana, and was just as worried as Sion. But she also had Timothy to worry over, and she knew that Nana would understand her need to be close to him.

Sion had promised he would be back no later than tomorrow. It already seemed like an eternity yawning before her, but knowing what she had to do in those two days, it was not nearly enough time.

Even as Sion's strict admonition to her to remain in
the house till he returned echoed in her mind, she
was already making plans to disregard it. She had
no choice. She had to beard Halsingham in his lair,
and it was best done while Sion was far away from
London.

Sighing, she turned away from staring down the
street where she had last seen his carriage, and entered the already lonely town house.

Waving over a hovering footman, she handed
him an addressed envelope and told him she
wanted it delivered as soon as possible and would
wait for an answer.

"And now what are ye planning to do?" Mrs. Turlow demanded to know from behind her.

Knowing she would need her friend's help as
usual, she replied stiffly, expecting a fight, "I have
sent a note to Halsingham asking him to meet me
in the park."

"Are ye daft?!"

Danae turned to glare at her. "More than likely,
but I have to do this, Mrs. T. You can either help me
by accompanying me, or else you can stay here and
fret. You have no other option."

"I would have one right enough if his lordship
were here," Mrs. Turlow threatened, giving a last-
ditch effort in a cause she knew she had already
lost.

"But, he isn't here, is he?" Danae turned away to
climb the stairs to her room.

Mrs. Turlow sniffed, then ambled off toward the
kitchen. "Let me know when we are tae go. I dinna
like it, but I'll be there."

Not quite an hour later, the answer came back: *I
will be honored to attend you in the park at 11:00. Your
most humble servant, H.*

"Humble, my arse," Danae mumbled as she tossed it into the fire.

"Are you sure this is such a good idea?" Elizabeth fretted for the fourth time in almost as many minutes.

Danae sighed, trying to hide her irritation. "Yes, Elizabeth, I believe it is. It is obvious Halsingham wants me. I have to use that."

"That is the silliest idea I have ever heard."

"Do you have a better one? Every day that passes and we do nothing is one more day Timothy is held hostage to Camden's madness. Our options are narrowing day by day."

"What reason are you going to give him for wanting Timothy?" None of this made any sense to her, but Elizabeth knew she would do anything needed, just like Danae, in order to get Timothy away from the earl.

Danae gave a weary sigh as she shook her head and lied, "I don't know. I haven't figured that out yet." Again she worried whether she was noble enough to sacrifice herself to save Timothy.

Elizabeth sliced a shocked glance at the mantel clock. "Well, you had better think of something soon, it's already ten-thirty."

Spinning around, Danae stared in dismay at the clock. "Gracious, where has the time gone?" Bustling over to Sion's desk, she jerked on her gloves and then picked up her hat and parasol and practically flew into the hall, shouting for Mrs. Turlow.

Danae had every intention of speaking honestly with Halsingham that very afternoon. It was the only way, for all their sakes. Sion would be better off without her, the child would be out of Camden's clutches; and even if Danae had to disappear and Katherine rise from the dead, she would never allow herself to be a victim ever again. She was stronger now. She would be able to survive, just as long as Sion was safe from this debacle she had created.

Then she saw Halsingham striding down a path toward her, and the park tilted about her. This man was her husband. She was about to hand her life back into his hands. She stared blindly at him as he moved rapidly toward her, his smile radiating warmth and pleasure at the sight of her.

"I was pleased to get your message this morning, my lady. I'm only disappointed it took you so long to send it."

Danae felt her cold hand enclosed in his, and the open air suddenly narrowed down to a tight, confining vaccuum about her. She couldn't breathe; she felt faint. Seeing Halsingham's slight frown as he studied her closely, she forced a smile to numb lips and pulled her hand out of his detested grip. Thankful that Mrs. Turlow was so close, Danae turned to direct their steps down a path, Halsingham matching his long strides to her smaller steps.

At that very moment she knew she couldn't do it. How could she ever allow this man back into her life again? She just couldn't. Desperately she began to think of alternate solutions to Timothy's plight. This was becoming a horrid habit—these endless lies and deceits. And with each one, she was only digging herself deeper into the mire.

"I 'ave been much busy since coming 'ere. I feel so bad I 'ave not seen you since your so kind invite to show me London. Now I 'ave the time."

"I have no doubt Dereham has kept you very busy," Halsingham interjected dryly, remembering just how busy the bastard had kept her the other night. His memory was still all too vivid. Even at that moment, he was prick-proud just thinking of the gaslight shimmering over her damp flesh. Wordlessly he cast a surreptitious glance down her figure, recalling every luscious inch of her.

"Oh, *si*, but he is gone today."

He perked up at that. "Gone?"

"Just for the day," Mrs. Turlow's gruff voice assured him from behind.

Halsingham shot her a look of loathing. Mrs. Turlow stuck out her chin and returned it.

Deciding not to waste any more time and fearing this might turn into a donnybrook, Danae felt it expedient to get to the point.

"I 'ave met your oh-so-*bello* son."

He immediately became on guard. "Yes, so I understand. In fact, Dereham visited me the other day about him. But I suspect you know this."

Danae looked at him in all innocence. "But, no, *signore!* I know nothing of this." Halsingham narrowed his gaze on her. "I must admit, though, I find it most, 'ow you say, strange, that Camden is claiming a grandson from Katerina, when we both know this to be *impossibile,* 'Ow can this be, *signore?*"

Silently Halsingham cursed that idiot Camden as he thought furiously of a plausible explanation. "The boy is actually from another daughter of Camden's—"

"*Signore,* do not mistake me for a fool." Danae's voice became a bit more clipped as she interrupted this brainless attempt.

Halsingham stopped and turned to look at her full on. "All right, what do you want, *contessa?*"

"I want the *ragazzo.*"

"Why?"

Why, indeed? How about the truth for a change? Danae thought quickly. "Because I 'ave no liking of *Katerina's padre.* He treated her bad; he must treat that beautiful boy bad. *Katerina* would want me to help the *ragazzo povero.*"

He did not look impressed. "You do this because Katherine meant so much to you?" he asked in derision.

Danae stared straight into those sinful blue eyes so like Timothy's. "*Si*, she meant that much to me."

"And what do I get for my troubles? Camden is not the easiest person to deal with, as I am sure you are well aware."

Danae had been expecting this. When she had embarked on this improbable scheme, she felt confident she could handle Halsingham when it came to this. *I can do this,* she assured herself. Girding herself, she looked up coolly. "And what would the *signore* request of me?"

"What Dereham got the other night," he told her with brutal dispatch.

Danae was confused. "I don't know what you mean," she said slowly, confused.

He leaned closer, his lips almost brushing her ear. "Must I spell it out? I . . . want . . . what . . . Dereham . . . got . . . at . . . the . . . ball," he spoke with insulting specificity.

"You saw?" she gasped, fear and revulsion gripping her after the initial shock.

"*Si.*" He kissed the sensitive spot behind her ear. "Every stunning inch of you."

Repulsed, she quickly stepped back from him,

curbing the urge to scrub at her ear. He had watched them? How could he have? Thinking of Halsingham spying on her with Sion made her physically sick. Breathing deeply, she swallowed down the bile that threatened to rise.

When he stepped closer again, Mrs. Turlow growled low and stepped between them, a menacing mask covering her usually benign features. "Dinna think to take another step, me fine bucko!"

Danae spoke over her, "You are disgusting!" Then, with that stunned exclamation thrown at him, she spun about and marched down the path away from him. Not caring where she was going she fled from him, with Mrs. Turlow hard on her heels. Then she heard him call out at her.

"I take it this means you no longer want the *bel ragazzo?*"

She stopped short, and Mrs. Turlow plowed into her. Taking a few deep breaths, she turned toward him again. There he stood, in the middle of the path, supremely arrogant and utterly spineless. She saw him as a canker on the arse of posterity, and how she wished she had a long, dirty lancet!

"Watch what ye do, lassie," Mrs. Turlow warned her in an undertone.

Too upset to speak, Danae simply nodded, then walked back to where he postured, too conceited for his own good. With a hard-won nonchalance she was far from feeling, she ambled over to him till they were almost standing toe to toe. There she stared him down in disgust. "Do you realize I could ruin you, *signore?* One word from me and *Katerina's padre* would not see you long in this world, *si?*"

Halsingham's arrogant facade cracked slightly as he tried to stare her down. "You do that and you ruin his plans for the boy. The boy would then become an embarrassement—and expendable. I believe you are only too well aware of what Camden is capable of when challenged."

He had her there, blast his eyes!

In silence they measured each other, both at a stalemate for the moment. When he next spoke, it was like hitting her broadside with his entire arsenal.

"Marry me."

Danae just blinked at him. She opened her mouth to speak, then realized she didn't know what to say. Out of habit now, she looked to Mrs. Turlow, to see the widow's eyes blazing across the narrow space at her. No help there, for she didn't like what Mrs. Turlow was communicating to her. Again she looked at Halsingham's smug face and hated him all over again.

"But why would you want this? I am another man's mistress, a fallen woman by your *societa's* standards."

He shrugged. "It's rather simple. I want you in my bed and Katherine's money back in my pocket."

If Timothy's life was not hanging in the balance at that moment, she would have laughed in his face. But she couldn't afford that luxury. She saw only one advantage to this bizarre turn—it gave her the perfect excuse to get Timothy into her hands. That she had no intention of actually marrying the bastard didn't pang her ethics in the least; after all, they had been buried long ago with Jassy.

"*Si*, I will marry you, but I 'ave a *condizione* of my own." It was hard to ignore Mrs. Turlow's gasp of outrage behind her.

Halsingham bowed, baiting her. "At your service, my love."

"The *ragazzo* must be put into my care before the vows are spoken."

His gaze narrowed on her face, not trusting her. "I may not be able to do that."

Danae shrugged with an insouciant smile. "Then I do not marry you and *Katerina's* money remains mine."

He hesitated for long minutes, Danae's breath held for the interminable length of time, when he finally drawled, "Very well." Then, stepping closer, he grabbed her into hurtful arms. "Shall we seal our pact with a kiss?" and as his mouth came down on hers, he bent her over backward with the intent to throw her off balance. She almost gagged when he forced his tongue into her mouth.

Revulsion froze her for an eternal moment before she finally wrested herself free with the help of an enraged and spitting Mrs. Turlow.

"*Signore,* are you mad? *Pazzo?*" She drew her hand over her lips and scrubbed, furious. Swallowing her nausea, she looked furtively about, then froze, stunned into immobility. There at the edge of the path was Sion, eyeing her coldly, his gaze unblinking.

Following her shocked gaze, Halsingham turned and saw the marquis. He smiled with broad malice as he latched on to Danae's arm and dragged her over to where her lover stood rooted.

"Dereham, old man, how fortuitous to see you here. Danae said you were gone for the day."

"I was." Sion's stiff lips hardly moved as he continued to glare at her.

"Well, since you're here, congratulate me. Your lady has agreed to marry me."

Sion's eyes sliced toward Halsingham before they returned to blaze down on her again. "Is this true?"

She had to bite her tongue, so much did she want to shout her denial, but with Halsingham right there, she could do nothing but nod in dumb resignation. She would explain it later. He would understand.

"Is this true, Danae?" he demanded of her again, rage and disbelief choking his voice.

"Yes," she whispered in misery, hating to hurt him even for this short time till she could get him alone.

He ignored Halsingham as a myriad of conflicting emotions played across his strained features. He waited, silent, compelling—waited for her to say something, anything that would make sense of what was happening. When she remained quiet, only her turbulent golden eyes trying to make him understand, he clipped out a forced, "Congratulations."

The word flayed her as he turned his back on her and strode off down the path without another word.

"I say, he is a poor loser, isn't he," Halsingham laughed.

Wrenching her arm out of his hold, she called out, "Sion!" and tried to follow him, but Halsingham grabbed on to her again, laughing all the while.

"Let go!" she hissed as she struggled to get free. Having enough, and not thinking quite clearly of the consequences, she brought her sharp heel down with an impressive crunch on his tender instep and leaped free of his clutching hands.

"I will not be manhandled, *signore!*" she lashed out at him; then, spinning about, she took out after

Sion, her steps almost running down the long path to the entrance where he had disappeared.

Behind her, Mrs. Turlow huffed along, mumbling all the way about her stupidity.

"Shut up, Mrs. T.!"

"Ye sure as not muckled it bad. His lordship willna forgive ye for this," she predicted sourly.

"I know, I know. But, what else could I do? Of course I'm not going to marry that snake. I just said I would to gain time."

"He willna care why."

Sweat broke out between her shoulder blades. Could Mrs. Turlow be right? Would he not listen to her reason, try to understand? Reaching the park's gates, she looked about, frantic, praying for a sight of Sion.

"Saints preserve us, here he comes."

Spinning about, she saw Halsingham bearing down on them, not too far off down the path. Not thinking of the danger of her action, she grabbed hold of Mrs. Turlow's arm and stepped off the pavement into the dusty street, right in the path of a swiftly approaching growler. Wrenching back on his horse's reins and standing on his brake, the cabby was able to come to a sliding stop directly in front of the two white-faced women.

Ignoring the vitriolic cockney obscenities being thrown at her head, Danae hustled Mrs. T. into the blessedly empty cab, and as she climbed in after her she glanced over her shoulder. Halsingham was now through the gate, and she could see the whites of his eyes. With a yelp, she tumbled the rest of the way into the cab, not even caring what she exposed in her graceless haste.

"Berkeley Square, and hurry!" she shouted at the growler. When the carriage didn't move, she stood up and whacked the hapless cabby across the head with her reticule. "Now!"

Immediately, the whip cracked and the horse surged forward with a lurch, tumbling Danae back onto the worn squabs. Out the window she saw Halsingham's furious face flash by, then felt safe enough to collapse back, exhausted. The rushing air felt cool on her cheeks, and she was surprised to find tears blurring her eyes. When had she started to cry?

As the cabby took them through the congested streets of London, she prayed Sion would be there waiting for her, demanding an explanation of her. And as the minutes dragged on, punctuated by Mrs. Turlow's fatalistic predictions, Danae began to believe she might be right this time.

Twenty-four

Danae heard Sion's muted voice as she approached their rooms with leaden steps. As he instructed his valet, Majors, she didn't know whether his composed voice was soothing or irritating, a sign of calm or stormy weather ahead. She paused outside the double portals with her ear to the door, eavesdropping, afraid to go in, when she heard Sion ask Majors to fetch another valise out of the attic.

Heart thudding, she threw back the doors and stood looking at the disarray about her in stunned dismay. Forced to notice the valet when he murmured some indefinable words to her, she realized he wanted out. Good, the sooner the better, she thought with ungracious preoccupation, and quickly she stepped aside to let him by. As soon as he was out in the hall, she slammed the doors shut, blind to everything but Sion's tall form stooping over the bed as he stuffed a pile of clothing into a battered valise.

Startled, he glanced up; then, seeing her, his face became an emotionless mask as he went back to what he was doing. "I came back for you. I was so bloody worried I couldn't just leave you behind. Damn asinine of me, wasn't it?"

"Why are you taking so much?" she demanded as she crossed the room to stand beside him. Unhurriedly he stepped away and moved to the other side of the bed. Tears stung her eyes.

"Are you planning a trip beyond what you intended?" she tried to ask in as casual a tone as she could manage with the fear choking her.

"Yes," he replied curtly.

"Where to?"

"Dereham."

"How long will you be gone?" She turned slightly away from him so he couldn't see her distress.

"Does it matter?" He closed his valise with a snap.

"Of course it matters, Sion."

Frigid black eyes came up to clash with hers, his disgust and disbelief plain to see. Without a word, he turned away to open a few drawers in his dresser, pulling out toiletry articles. She also turned away, going to the window to stare blindly out while tears streamed down her pale cheeks. He was leaving her. Strange how much it hurt, even though she had been expecting it sooner or later. She just hadn't thought it would be this soon.

The silence stretched thinly between them when his enraged voice startled her. "Is that boy so important to you that you would sell yourself, or is it Halsingham you want?"

She spun around, dashing the tears from her face with trembling fingers. "God, no! How can you even think that?"

"Maybe seeing you in Halsingham's arms, as soon as I am conveniently out of the way; maybe hearing from your own lips that you had agreed to marry him gave me an idea!" he sneered as he threw a carefully folded shirt into another valise.

"Christ, what a bloody fool I've been! Here you are, a beautiful deceiver, going behind my back the minute it is turned, to rendezvous with Halsingham!" As his ranting words came to an end, he was standing in front of her, shouting, "Why, Danae? Why do you constantly fight me, go behind me, never put your trust in me? What in the hell can that spineless jackass get you that I can't?"

The pain in his eyes devastated her far more than his anger could ever intimidate her. So, like the coward she was, she dealt with the anger by becoming incensed herself. "I . . . Sion, I don't intentionally go behind your back; it's just that I know what a problem I have been in your life. Timothy is *my* fight! I am not completely helpless, no matter how little faith you have in me. I asked to speak with Halsingham to find out his frame of mind—what he was doing, if anything. When he asked me to marry him, I was so flustered I just said yes to gain time and hopefully get Timothy from Camden. That is all! I have no—and never will have any—intention of marrying the fool."

"Tell me, if it gained you more time, would you have jumped into bed with him?" His cold gaze raked her.

Pulling back her hand, she slapped him, and he didn't even give her the satisfaction of a flinch. Breathing unevenly, holding back a new onslaught of tears, she stood tall before his unblinking perusal. Finally, he shook his head sadly, and turning away from her he resumed his packing.

"I don't know you anymore, Danae," he said in a weary voice. "I doubt I ever did. I guess I've wanted so desperately to believe in a fairy tale of my own making that I failed to realize that maybe my princess is no more than a figment of my starved imagination. You have no substance, Danae. You awoke in my home telling a lie, you entered London Society enacting another lie, and every time I turn around you are covering up even more lies." He looked over his shoulder at her, tears reddening his own eyes. "So tell me, Danae, what about you is real?"

"My love for you," she whispered, the tears she had been fighting streaming down her cheeks again.

He smiled sadly as he lifted the two valises. "I just don't believe you anymore." He stood across the room from her, an abyss of swirling doubts and suppliance between them, and just looked at her, as if truly seeing her for the first time. There seemed to be a world of regret in those beautiful Dereham eyes. She was almost thankful when the sad scrutiny was over and he headed for the door.

She sniffed, pressing a hand to her pounding forehead, her head stuffy and yet so empty of all thoughts but one. "So this is good-bye?" She realized, as though through a long tunnel, that she was about to faint, her body starting to float away from her conscious self, looking down upon two strangers who had once upon a time loved each other so extravagantly, so . . . selflessly.

He paused in the portal, head down as if pondering her question. "I don't know," he finally said on a tired sigh. "I'll let you know."

She felt the room tilting as giddy relief rushed through her, robbing her of breath. "I'll be waiting," she managed to get out as she clung tenaciously to consciousness.

He made no comment; he didn't turn around, just walked away wondering if she was lying to him yet again.

He never knew that as he climbed into his carriage Danae lay crumpled on their bedroom floor, scarcely breathing, her face pale as death.

"I'm all right, I tell you! Leave me be!" Danae cried out in testy anger as Mrs. Turlow stuck another spoonful of broth under her nose. Closing her mouth mutinously, she glared at the frowning widow, then mumbled unintelligibly through her clenched lips.

Jonas's smile twitched as he bent over and, with a solicitous hand, drew Mrs. Turlow gently but firmly to her feet and away from the beleaguered patient.

"I believe she has had enough, Mrs. Turlow."

But Mrs. Turlow ignored him as she replaced the bowl on the tray with a clatter, returning Danae's glare. "Ye are a beastly wee gilp, that's what ye are, and I'm that ashamed of ye." Then, throwing her apron over her face, she broke into tears and fled the room.

Danae's glare turned into a comical mask of stunned surprise as she turned to Jonas and Elizabeth who were both staring at the door. "Did I hear her *crying*? Tell me she wasn't crying."

Jonas and Elizabeth looked at each other, then turned uneasily toward Danae. Both nodded.

"Well, this is just wonderful! First I chase Sion away, and now I've reduced my dragon to tears." Her own voice thickened with self-righteous tears as she plucked at the blankets. "What did I do that was so wrong? I never intended to hurt anyone; I just wanted to make everyone safe. Was I wrong?" Her teary eyes looked up, beseeching them, as two fat tears rolled down her flushed cheeks. "Well, was I?"

Again they both nodded.

The tears stopped abruptly. Holding their collective breath, they eyed her warily, since for the past few hours her aberrant moods were swinging about as wildly as a drunken monkey in a tree full of fermenting fruit. Before they could blink twice, she was glaring again, the full brunt of her anger now directed on them. "So, what do you know, anyway? None of you can appreciate the lengths I go to on behalf of all of you. How I struggle day in and day out. Fine, I refuse to try again. Now, leave me!"

Relieved, they began to back out, but before they made it halfway across the room, she shot out of bed and ran through the dressing room into the washroom. Not knowing what to do, Elizabeth and Jonas bumped into each other as Elizabeth tried to follow Danae and Jonas leaped for the door, shouting for Mrs. Turlow.

A few short minutes later she came sniffling into the room, and Jonas, beside himself with anxiety, hustled her toward the washroom, babbling a gaggle of nonsense she didn't bother to listen to. Then they stopped abruptly as the sounds of retching emanated from behind the closed door.

Jonas was surprised to see a wide smile crease the worried lines on Mrs. Turlow's face. "And dinna I know it! Our lassie is having a bairn. At last!"

Jonas swayed on his feet. "A bairn," he parroted weakly. "You mean as in 'baby'?"

"Aye," the enraptured widow breathed, clasping her hands together as if in prayer. "His lordship's own bonnie bairn. I just felt it in me bones as she hasna flowered in months."

Hearing a thud behind her, Mrs. Turlow looked down in surprise to find Jonas sprawled at her feet. *Tsk*ing in disgust, she stepped over him and barged into the washroom, chasing Elizabeth out, then cooing over her lamb, all past sins forgiven and forgotten.

Holding a towel to her perspiring face, Danae asked faintly, "What is a 'gilp'?"

"An ungrateful lassie," Mrs. Turlow supplied as she stroked back tendrils of hair clinging to Danae's damp cheeks.

The expectant mother shot her a hurt glance, "I'm not an 'ungrateful lassie,'" she argued in a teary voice.

"Nay, ye're a pregnant lassie."

Danae stared in horror over the towel at her smugly smiling friend. Then her face screwed up and she started wailing. "And Sion doesn't even like me anymore!" she sobbed.

Mrs. Turlow enfolded her in an embrace of maternal understanding as she rocked the emotionally stressed girl in her arms, telling her everything was going to be just fine—how, she wasn't sure, but just knowing it would.

"When?" she sniffled.

"Now, how should I be knowin' the when? The two of ye were going at it like a couple o' wee bunnies. About seven months is my guess."

Danae flushed to the tips of her freezing toes, even as she gave a reluctant chuckle. "No, I mean how long have you known?"

"Och, a month or more. Dinna ye notice ye dinna flower last month an' more?"

With all that had been happening, she hadn't even given it any thought. Sion's baby was growing in her.

Just then an agitated Elizabeth stuck her head in. "Mrs. Turlow, Mr. Glendower has fainted! I can't revive him; what should I do?"

"Throw a bucket o' water over him."

Unsure of such a drastic solution, Elizabeth just stared at her; then, when Mrs. Turlow shooed her away again, she closed the door quietly behind her. Biting her lip, she stood looking down at the lanky body spread-eagled on the floor; then, with a sigh she looked about the room, her gaze alighting on a crystal vase stuffed with yellow daffodils. Hurrying over, she carefully took out the flowers, set them aside, then carried the heavy vase over to the oblivious man. Holding her breath, she tossed the contents full on him and jumped back when he surged to his feet with a satisfyingly healthy roar.

She beamed at his dripping, stunned face. "There, now. Isn't that ever so much better?"

Staring at her guileless face, he subdued his confusion and initial anger, then looked down the sodden length of himself, as he dripped with monotonous plops onto Sion's prized Kurdistan rug. Deeply mortified, he removed his glasses with fumbling fingers, then tried, unsuccessfully, to polish them dry. When he felt her soft, warm fingers take them from him, he blinked in myopic embarrassment as he watched her dry them on her own skirt. Satisfied with the clear lenses, she replaced them with gentle care on his nose, and he smiled down at her, besotted. Blushing, she looked down.

"Yes, thank you, I am much better now. How resourceful of you to douse me with water."

Her eyelashes fluttered as she peeked up shyly.

"Actually, I can't take all the credit. It was Mrs. Turlow's idea."

Jonas shot a peeved look at the washroom door. "How kind of her. I must remind myself to thank her later. However, now I fear I must leave you. I have some pressing business to attend to. Thank you again for all your . . . help." Grimacing, he turned, and as quickly as his sodden trousers clinging to his unmentionables would allow, he escaped.

Later that afternoon, much more subdued and reflective, Danae lay stretched out on the library divan, staring blindly into the fire. She smiled slowly when she thought that her child could have been conceived on this very divan.

She thought long and hard on how Sion would take this news. Again and again she pondered the wisdom of telling him right away of his impending fatherhood or waiting to see whether he still wanted to go on with their relationship. If she told him now, she feared he might feel pressured into doing something he no longer wished to do, and never would she hold Sion—or any man, for that matter—in a relationship based solely on embittered obligation. She had had enough of that in her life. On the other hand, if she didn't tell him, he would doubtless accuse her of lying to him again, not trusting him.

She sighed in frustration as she rubbed her forehead. She just didn't know what to do. The only thing she did know for absolute fact was that she was ecstatic knowing Sion's child was growing in her. Again she looked down in wonder at her flat stomach, and with a gentle hand she stroked the tiny being nestled warmly within her. Her and Sion's child. What could be more miraculous than knowing she would soon bring to life a product of their love, a love she thought she would never know in her lifetime? A tear slipped down her cheek as she thought of her beloved Jassy and how happy she would have been to hold her Katherine's child in her arms.

A tap on the door stirred her from her meditations, and as she looked over her shoulder, Jonas walked in, a sheepish smile flushing his boyish features. In his hands was a long, slender box banded with a red ribbon.

"How are you feeling, Danae?" he asked as he came around the divan to sit in the matching chair beside her.

Her smile was wry as she surreptitiously wiped the single tear away. "Calmer, you will be relieved to hear."

His shoulders relaxed with a long exhaled sigh of relief, "Well, that is good to hear."

She cocked her head at him, looking him over. "And you look no worse for your little dilemma this afternoon."

Again he flushed bright red. "Well . . . yes, that is . . . I . . ."

She laughed outright at his embarrassment. "I can't tell you how truly flattered I was to hear that you had actually keeled over for me."

Jonas chuckled, while his embarrassment had him plucking at the satin ribbon.

"For me?" she asked gently.

He blinked in confusion down at the box. "Oh, yes, I forgot. An urchin delivered it just as I was entering the house." Quickly he thrust it into her hands.

She beamed as she yanked the bow loose. "Do you suppose it is from Sion?" she asked in hopeful delight as she peeled back the top.

Inside, on black tissue lay a perfect, single red rose in full bloom. With a murmur of wonder, she lifted it out and held it to her nose, inhaling the delicate scent.

"Good Lord!" She heard Jonas exclaim in horror as he snatched the bloom out of her hand.

Her eyes blinked wide in amazement as he whipped out his kerchief and began to rub her fingers. "Jonas, what on earth are you doing? What is the matter?"

"I don't know," he muttered as he continued to bend over her, scrubbing furiously at her fingers. Confused, she looked down into the box and saw its bottom coated with a shiny substance, then looked down to where the rose lay on the carpet, dark smudges surrounding it.

"What is it?"

"Blood," Jonas hissed as he finished wiping her fingers clean of the sticky, metallic-smelling substance.

"Blood?" she parroted in numb amazement. "Sion sent me a bloody rose?" Then she gave a hysterical little laugh at what sounded like a jest.

Jonas looked up at her, shocked. "Of course not! Of all the ridiculous things to accuse him of!"

"Well, who sent it?" She was completely bewildered by the past few minutes, the laudanum, forced on her by the doctor, still dulling her wits.

"Saegar, of course. He must know Sion is out of town."

"Why would Saegar do something like this to me?"

"Because you are alive and Victoria is dead,"

Jonas mumbled as he picked up the blood-coated rose with his ruined kerchief and stuffed if back into its delicate box. Snatching up the lid and ribbon, he tossed the whole into the fire. Together they sat in silence and watched as it caught fire and burned steadily into a pile of glowing ashes.

"I had better send word to Brock." Then, with a hasty farewell he was gone, calling out to Mrs. Turlow as he slammed the door behind him, leaving Danae again in solitude, now colored with a sinister shade.

Camden cried out as his shoulder struck sharply against the newel post, the room tilting crazily about him, throwing him off balance. Blinded with pain, he reached out for the wall and sagged against it as the relentless torment slithered behind his eyes, slicing into his temples, causing waves of nausea to gag him. His body doubled over as a merciless tidal wave of torturous sensations surged over him then retreated again. After a few moments, the torment subsided to a bearable level, and breathing heavily, he struggled to straighten himself, wincing as he realized his left arm was again numb, paralyzed to any sensation.

Casting a surreptitious glance about the empty hall, he took hold of his limp hand and shoved it into his pocket and out of the way. Then, with a shaking hand, he withdrew his handkerchief and dragged it over his perspiring face and neck. Bit by bit, as he mastered control over his quavering legs, he was finally able to push himself erect from the wall. Turning, he faced the steep ascent of the staircase, his pain-dulled eyes tracing the intimidating rise. Taking a deep breath, he placed one foot on the first riser and, step by painful step, he climbed the mammoth obstacle, all his concentration riveted on his reward to be found at the top.

By the time he reached the first-floor landing, his breath was rasping with sluggish exertion and his perspiring body quivered with debilitating weakness. Again another steep staircase loomed before him, and this time he almost had to drag himself up the risers. As he reached the second floor, he wanted nothing more than to collapse where he stood, but strangely enough, his pain-fogged attention was snagged by the schoolroom door. Limping over to the closed portal, he pushed it inward on silent hinges and, as expected, peered into the dark stillness. He knew where to look for his prey.

And there he sat, his grandson, perched on the window seat, gazing with tenacious faith out onto the bustling streets of London. Every day, he sat there, expecting the mysterious *Contessa di Sala* to come to this house to see him since he was no longer permitted out for his daily walks in the park.

Camden glanced about the room shrouded in gloom and abandoned by life, as he had yet to replace the duplicitous Miss York. And now he had no intention to do so. It was better that the child was totally dependent on him, with no outside influence to interfere in their relationship.

He swallowed painfully, his rasping whisper echoing off the walls and reverberating back into the bleak, stifling air. "So, Edward, what have you been doing with yourself today?"

Timothy glanced over with dark, listless eyes before resuming his tireless vigil out the window, out beyond the gates closing the Camden town house off from the rest of the world. Every day, he hoped she would come, praying she would remember her promise. But she never did. Yet still each day he climbed up onto his uncomfortable perch and scanned the countless faces that passed by, fearful to look away, for in that one distracted second he might miss her.

"She won't come, Edward. You were simply a toy to amuse herself with, and now she is bored with you. She doesn't care about you, Edward. Only I care for you. I found you, didn't I?"

His only change of expression was the tightening of his lips as he continued to scan the streets. Suddenly, his eyes narrowed as his gaze sharpened on a bobbing, stylish hat perched atop a head of reddish brown hair. He held his breath; he leaned forward, his little fingers tightened on the sill as his gaze remained riveted on that hat. Then it passed in front of the grilled ironwork of the gate. He sat straighter, his heart stopped . . . then plummeted. It wasn't her.

He almost jumped as the hateful whisper chuckled over his head. "As I said, she will not come, Edward."

Timothy glared down on the street, again searching every face. He didn't even notice when the door closed again.

Out in the hall, Camden leaned against the closed portal as shards of the excruciating pain again shot up and down his previously numbed arm. His eyes focused with difficulty on the last flight of stairs leading up to the attic, his sanctuary. Stiffly he move toward it. Finally—how, he wasn't sure—he stood panting before the door to the attic. With a shaking hand he pushed it open; then with dragging determination, he made his way through the gloom to a far corner, where a bare and dusty mattress lay on the floor.

His steps echoed hollowly on the splintered wooden planks, announcing his presence, and almost immediately a silent, dark figure slipped from behind an ancient oak screen, a sheet draped over its arm. With smooth, economical movements, the figure snapped the sheet open and draped it over the mattress.

With a relieved grunt, Camden fell prone on the welcome comfort. The Chinaman disappeared again to reappear with a long, thin pipe, about eighteen inches long and made of bamboo. At the closed end, a small iron bowl was screwed into the pipe, where a smoking, sticky pellet of raw opium was pushed into the small hole entering the hollowed bamboo. Greedy for the relief the pipe would give him, Camden snatched it from the Chinaman, then waved him away. After the man disappeared behind the screen, Camden collapsed back on the mattress before he drew long and deep on the blessedly mind-numbing opiate. Soon the racking pain was only a distant irritant as he floated above and beyond it all.

Sharp, black eyes watched out of slitted lids as the lord drifted off into a deep, drug-induced sleep. Silently the Chinaman rose from his cross-legged position on the floor and retrieved his pipe from the slack fingers. With quick, economical motions he cleaned the bowl of the sticky residue, picked up his hollowed lemon of raw opium, and on silent feet left the attic, disappearing down the back stairs until he was summoned again, with more and more frequency as the months went by.

Hours later, Camden stirred to the oppressive quiet, the darkness relieved only by a single can-

dle placed at a safe distance from the mattress.
Dulled eyes blinked wearily up at the cobwebbed
ceiling, the flickering shadows moving eerily
across the exposed A-frame of the roof. Turning
his head, he let his bored attention wander aim-
lessly over what he could see in the limited circle
of light; then it narrowed on a stack of holland-
covered portraits leaning against the opposite
wall. His eyes sharpened as he studied the stacks
of huge canvases, and a niggling sensation teased
along his memory.

With a grunt, he stumbled to his feet, taking up
the candle before he pulled himself erect. Walking over to the stacked canvases, he yanked off
one of the dusty covers, and suddenly he knew
what he was looking for. His colorless eyes panned
each canvas as he flipped them forward, working
faster as his obsession to find it grew. When he
didn't find it in that group, he pushed the lot of
them back against the wall with a clatter and
moved on to the next. The second pile also offered up nothing, and moving on to the third, he
whipped off the sheet. He froze as a pair of
painted golden eyes stared up at him, bringing
back a flood of lost memories, some good, some
bad, but mostly bitter regrets. His thin lips curling into a smug smile, he stepped back and
studied the twenty-year-old portrait. Yes, indeed,
his instincts were never wrong.

There, lounging back amid the May flowers of
Camden Abbey with her three-year-old daughter on
her lap, was his first wife, Lady Beatrice Kersey
Camden—the spitting image of the mysterious
Danae Suriano, *Contessa di Sala.*

Absently Camden stroked his numbing arm as he
contemplated the pretty face of the child. *Well, this*

certainly puts a different perspective on things, and he smiled for the first time in years.

Early the next morning, Timothy was hustled out of bed and downstairs to the earl's study. He was pushed inside and the door was shut soundly behind him.

"Come forward, boy. Here." A pale hand extended from behind the leather expanse of Camden's favorite chair and pointed to a spot directly in front of the fire.

After a slight pause, Timothy went to stand where commanded. Camden was gazing at a point above the mantel and with a wave of his hand he directed Timothy's attention there. When he saw the image of Danae staring down at him, he stiffened, shocked and confused to see her image in this house.

"Do you know who that is, boy?" came the hateful voice.

He shook his head.

"That is your grandmother, and the girl is your mother. Remind you of someone?"

Blanking out everything around him, Timothy again shook his head.

The earl's cold hand shot out and painfully grasped Timothy's chin, forcing him to face him. "That woman in the park lied to you. She is your mother. And she abandoned you, just as she abandoned me and her husband. But, you now have the chance to get her back." Two pairs of expressionless eyes each drilled the other. "Wouldn't you like that? Wouldn't you like her back in this home where she belongs—with you?"

Timothy's heart raced. Danae here, with him. Always. "Yes," he said.

Releasing the boy's chin, Camden sat back, satisfied. This was going to be easier than he thought. Now he just had to deal with that fool Halsingham. Remembering how the fool had panted after her at the ball and chased her outside the park, Camden knew he would find no opposition from that front. Not only would Halsingham get his lovely wife back, but the money would be his. And this time he would make damn sure she was held secure at the Abbey until he was done with her.

Contented, he sat back, having forgotten the presence of the boy, and stared at the portrait of his late wife. Life was good again.

Twenty-five

Halsingham paced the length of the path again for what seemed the tenth time in as many minutes.

"Well, I can't look *too* conspicuous pacing this bloody path *again!*" he castigated himself, irritated, frustrated, and harried with the whole damned morning. He was still waiting for that filthy behemoth he had hired the other night to do the dirty work, and now here he was, waiting in the bloody bushes (skulking in bushes, for God's sake!) for that damn boy that Danae wanted so bloody much, to show up on his daily walk. Why in hell couldn't she just want one of those God-awful ugly pug dogs that were so popular with the ladies? No, she wanted Camden's brat! And with each minute that crept past two on the clock, the more it appeared he wasn't going to show.

"Shit!" he kicked a stone out of his path, then smiled and bowed gracefully to a couple of ladies who sauntered by, glaring down their noses at him.

"Where the hell is the little sod? If she wants the little blighter, by God, she'll get him!" he swore softly as he sliced another glare down the path toward the park's entrance. Then his eyes widened as he saw Danae herself step through Green Park's gate. Alone, and heading directly toward him.

He cursed long and low as he dived into the bushes and into the malodorous embrace of his hired thug. "Where the hell have you been?" he hissed, quickly stepping downwind of the cumbrous giant.

Beady black eyes stared down on him with a cunning intelligence Halsingham was reckless enough to ignore. Slipping his cuttle back into the pocket of his filthy jacket, the hulk pushed away from the tree he had been leaning against and started to come too close for Halsingham's sensitive nose.

"So, where's 'e?" Hulk's deep bass voice rumbled.

Halsingham glanced over his shoulder just in time to see, through the thick foliage, Danae hurrying by. "I don't know where the bloody bugger is! He's supposed to be here by now. Just like Camden to make a hash of my plans!"

"So, where's 'e?"

Halsingham whirled on him. "I don't bloody know where he is! What am I, a damn seer?"

The hulk hawked, spit, and went back to supporting the tree.

Halsingham stared down at the puddle of phlegmy spittle shimmering a scant inch from the toe of his shiny half-boot, then glanced up with revulsion. "Do you try to be disgusting, or does it just come naturally?"

Looking up farther, Halsingham found himself the object of an intent scrutiny from the beady eyes. Damn if the bastard wasn't looking him over as if he were a pile of shit he had just stepped in!

"So, guv, yew wants me t' nab the chip, or yew wants me t' tip yew a muzzler?"

Halsingham stared at him. "What the hell is that supposed to mean?"

"It means I won't haf ter stare at yer bleedin' pretty face fer long."

Halsingham took a deep breath. Another damned threat, and this one didn't even make him blink. He must be getting immune to the bloody things!

"Listen, just take the woman instead," he finally decided in a rush. He might as well get his money's worth out of this fiasco, and without the boy he'd never get Danae any other way.

Hulk glanced around the park grounds. "Which mort do yew want, or don't it matter?"

Halsingham felt like hitting him. "Of course it matters, you imbecile! You take the wrong 'mort' and you won't get another blessed farthing out of me, you understand? That is the one I want." And he pointed through the bushes at Danae.

The hulk parted the bushes and squinted. "Cor' blimey! Yew mean the bushel-bubby?"

"What?"

Hulk's huge paw came up and pantomimed an impressive bust on his own bulky chest.

"Oh, for chrissakes, just get her and keep your filthy hands off her bubbies; they're mine!" Then, not wanting to be anywhere around the ape, he skulked off into a closer set of bushes, where he would get an unobstructed view of the scene to come.

Smirking after the flash cove, the hulk stepped out of the bushes and began to head toward the mort when a johnnie strolled into sight. Cursing, he tugged the brim of his hat down, hunched his shoulders, and turned his back on the johnnie. Then, as inconspicuously as his massive frame would allow, he dived back into the coverage of the park foliage. Holding his breath, he watched the distinctive uniform amble slowly, too slowly, by him, and stifling another curse, he cast his eyes about the meticulous paths, sighing in relief as he spotted the mort again.

There she was, not too far off, pacing back and forth in front of a bench, impatiently checking a small watch pinned to them be-u-ti-ful titties. He felt himself starting to salivate.

Dragging a hand across dry lips, his calloused fingers rasping over stubbled cheeks, he forced his attention to more important things. He cautiously checked both ways before stepping out onto the path again, and with the way clear, he became a bit more cocky. A smirk splitting his face, he strode up to her, again taken aback by her looks. *Blimey, what a bleedin' stunner! No wonders the cove wants 'er.* For a second his greediness whispered tantalizing alternatives into his ear, but, not needing any more trouble in his life, he grimly ignored them.

Her back was to him as he moved in closer, and scanning the area with a final furtive glance, he pounced. And what he found in his arms was not the typical hysterical woman, but a screaming, spitting, kicking virago. Shouting a few curses and threats of his own as she managed to hit vital body parts, he finally managed to clamp a sweaty paw over her open mouth. Twisting and turning, he struggled to drag her into the bushes, getting more desperate by the second. Then she sank a set of sharp, healthy teeth viciously into his palm.

Bellowing in pain, wondering what in the frigging hell he was doing here, he failed to hear the pounding feet, shouts, and the shrill blare of whistles until it was too late. One second he was trying to rid himself of the madwoman in his arms, and the next he found himself yanked around and thrown, face first, onto the path, with his arms wrenched behind him.

"Are ye all right, ma'am?" Brock asked worriedly as he steadied Danae, who was bent over spitting and rubbing a lacy kerchief furiously over her mouth. Not knowing what else to do, he dragged out his flask and held it out to her.

Not caring what it was as long as it was wet, Danae thankfully grabbed it and took a healthy swig. Nothing could be worse than that sweaty, grimy hand and the sour, salty taste of it as she had sunk her teeth into it. She glanced over at the prone figure, and seeing the filth caking his skin and clothes, she shuddered and bolted down another fortifying dose of whatever it was.

"Thank you," she finally managed as she handed the flask back to the kind gentelman.

His eyes widened slightly as he shook it, then turned it upside down. A lone drop slid out of a previously more than half-full container of good Irish whiskey. He shot her a speculative peek from under bushy brows before turning around to address his men.

"Good job, boyos. Let's take 'im in." And when they had hauled the hefty bilker up, he turned and tipped his bowler at Danae. "I am sorry for this, ma'am. It won't happen again."

A hiccup caught her unawares, and with an embarrassed sound, she covered her mouth with her kerchief. Trying for some dignity, she asked, "Do you know who he is?"

Brock extended a cautious hand, not really steadying her as she swayed a bit, but there just in case. He frowned as he thought that maybe he should take her home. "Are ye all right, ma'am?"

With a bright smile, she reassured him. "Oh, I'm fine, just fine," she addressed the bush over his head. "I'll just sit here for a while. I feel a little warm, I think." And after a moment of serious thought, she fanned herself with the kerchief while she squinted up at him. "Aren't you warm?"

"No, ma'am." He wondered if he should tell her that her accent was slipping.

"That's nice. I think I'll sit down."

"That's a good idea, ma'am." And when she turned in the wrong direction, he latched gently on to her elbow and guided her over to the bench. "Why don't I escort you home, ma'am?"

She gave him an adamant shake of her head. "Oh, no, I am waiting for someone." Her brow furrowed in thought.

Stymied with indecision, Brock looked after his men, who had paused a distance away and engaged in a scuffle with the hulking thug. Biting his lip, he looked down at the little lady. "All right, then, but ye sit right here until ye feel better," he admonished as sternly as possible.

She reached over to pat his hand and missed. "You are such a good man, Mr . . . ?"

"Brock, ma'am. Inspector Brock. Thank you, ma'am." Then, with a last vacillating perusal of her flushed face, he followed his men.

Danae watched him hurry down the path, and when it started to tilt and sway she was surprised that he didn't fall down. Shrugging, she looked about, wondering what had just happened. One minute she was waiting for . . . She frowned as she leaned back her head and blinked up into the swaying trees. Who *had* she been waiting for? With an unsteady hand she raised her pin watch and carefully tried to make sense of the four hands.

Halsingham struck the tree, cursing roundly as he watched the behemoth being dragged off by the police. Was nothing ever going to go right for him again? he wondered savagely. Catching his breath, he swung around, and thrashing at the bushes in his way, he glared at the woman who was single-handedly making his life utter hell.

After being turned away four times from her town house by that dragon of hers last night, he had taken himself off, in a frenzied panic, to his favorite brothel with every intention of plowing as much of the merchandise as he was able. But less than an hour later, he had slammed out of the establishment in another rage, too humiliated to see straight. Never had that happened to him before. His performance in bed was legendary, but last night, even with a beautiful whore's mouth working her magic on him, he couldn't perform. She hadn't had the right color of hair, the right body. Her eyes hadn't had that exotic slant with amber gold glittering sensuously from beneath heavy lids. The gaslight hadn't flickered over her curves the way it caressed Danae's. No matter how beautiful the whore, she hadn't been the one he wanted. He wanted *her!* And tonight, if that ape hadn't scuffled it, she would have been writhing beneath him, wrapping those sinfully long legs about him as he plunged into her blessed heat.

Now what the hell was he going to do? He didn't have the boy to bargain with, and he didn't have her. At this rate he never would!

As he ran his hands through hair usually arranged to perfection, his mind sped along any alternate plan he could think of. Then the glimmer of an idea came to him. In fact, it was a bloody fantastic idea. He smiled to himself. Too bad he hadn't thought of it sooner; it would have saved him the quid he had wasted on that pathetic excuse for a thug.

Just as he was stepping forward, a hand came down heavily on his shoulder, jerking him around. Stunned, he found himself staring into the face of the man who had just botched his last plan.

"Good afternoon, sir. Out fer a stroll in the bushes?" Brock asked sarcastically. He couldn't believe it when he had spotted the viscount lurking in the bushes just off the path, making a pathetic attempt to camouflage himself in the shrubbery. Glancing over Halsingham's shoulder, he saw that the man had a nice, unobstructed view of Dereham's lady sitting on her bench.

Halsingham drew himself up and spoke in his haughtiest voice. "Is there some law against that, my good man?"

With a wry twist of the lips, Brock pointed to the back of a sign not far from their feet. Curious, Halsingham took a few steps backward and read *PLEASE STAY ON THE PATH*. Lips pursed and eyes narrowed, Halsingham glared sideways at the tedious little toad. With dignified hauteur he adjusted the cuffs of his immaculate jacket and, looking down his nose, intoned gravely, "I had to take a piss. Should I have done so on the path?"

Brock's lips twitched as he looked around, struggling not to laugh, when he saw something that drove out all thought of humor, and he froze.

Halsingham's gaze couldn't help but follow, and

then both stood there staring, rooted to the spot, as Danae was being hustled down the path by a man in a voluminous cape. Shocked, the viscount wondered vaguely why she wasn't struggling, when he caught the glint of dull metal. The man had a pistol dug into her side.

With a shout, both men dived through the bushes, Halsingham cursing vilely as a branch snapped back into his face.

"Saegar!" Brock bellowed as he took out after them at a dead run, pulling out his pistol as he went. He was vaguely aware of Halsingham's footsteps pounding after him while they narrowed the distance. As they drew closer, he again bellowed at Saegar to stop.

Saegar whipped about, and his bloodshot eyes widened at the sight of the two men charging down the path toward him, baring down on him fast. His hand convulsed about the arm of Dereham's tart, and jerking her closer, he snarled in her face, "I'll be back for you. Tell Dereham." Then he shoved her away with enough force to send her sprawling across the path. As he turned to run he caught sight of several men converging on him from different directions, expecting to trap him. Desperate, he fired into the crowd, then turned and ran for his life, heading for the only place he knew he would be safe.

As Brock came even with Danae's prone body, he flung out his arm toward her and shouted at Halsingham, "Take care of her!" then continued after Saegar, who was fleeing as if the fires of hell were nipping at his heels.

Panting, Halsingham fell to his knees beside Danae. Turning her gently, he drew her into his arms and frowned as he studied her unconscious face.

"Poor baby," he crooned, brushing away bits of gravel embedded in her cheek. Leaning over, he kissed her forehead, then laid his cheek against hers. "Don't worry. I'll take care of you now."

As he climbed to his feet with her safely tucked in his arms, he brushed aside all offers of help from the growing crowd, and heading off down the path that led out of the park, he didn't give another thought to the inspector and his quarry. He had what he wanted.

The sky was just beginning to darken as the hackney pulled up outside his rooms. Flinging open the door, Halsingham jumped down, and as he was turning back to reach in, his attention was caught by a movement off to the side. He frowned as he recognized Camden's coachman, a huge bear of a man, picked more for his stupid blind devotion than for any claim to handling horses.

The man tipped his hat with a thin veneer of respect, his voice expressionless as he delivered his message. "His lordship sends his respects and wishes your presence immediately, my lord. He sent his carriage for your convenience."

Convenience, my ass, Halsingham thought sourly.

"I can't come just now. I have some pressing business, but assure his lordship I'll be there—"

"Now, my lord." The man's demeanor was inflexible.

Halsingham's jaws flexed as he compressed his rage. His head started to throb unmercifully, and if he had a gun he would not have hesitated to put a bullet through the flunkey's eyes.

"I said—"

"Now, my lord." His dead eyes stared into Halsingham's, and the viscount knew he could either climb into that coach on his own two feet or be thrown in unconscious.

Leaning into the hackney, he drew Danae's limp body into the fading light. "And what do you suppose I do with her?" he asked sarcastically as he cradled her with tender care in his arms.

The henchman looked into her face, and an evil smile lit his piggish eyes, "Why, I'm sure his lordship would be honored to have her as a guest, my lord. In fact"—those chilling eyes shifted to him—"I know he will. Don't keep his lordship waiting, my lord."

"All right, damn your eyes!" Halsingham shot a lethal glare at the man as he stepped forward, intending to take his precious burden. "Back off! I have her."

With a slight bow, the coachman strode ahead to open the carriage door.

Halsingham sat with her on his lap, and dropping his head back, he sighed wearily. Would this bloody day never end? He was tired, he was hungry, and above all he was randy for his lady. He was in no mood to put up with Camden's machinations. And now he was going to be forced to carry Danae into that viper's nest.

Twenty-six

Danae came slowly awake to the feel of her face being tenderly bathed with a warm cloth. Her head pounded, her mouth felt painfully dry, and various parts of her body throbbed. She winced as the cloth touched her cheek.

"Sion?" she murmured, reaching for his hand.

He took it and held it tightly, only the voice that reassured her wasn't his. "Take it easy, my love."

Her eyes shot open and she stared up at several faces staring down at her, some alarmingly familiar, others she had never seen before. Even though her mind was foggy, she still had enough sense to know she was in danger, and realizing her head was resting on Halsingham's lap, she struggled to sit up.

He helped her to sit upright but allowed her no more distance as he put a possessive arm about her and drew her tightly to his side.

Frightened and confused, she tried to push away, but as her struggles were useless, she stopped and took in the situation. Camden sat across from her, legs crossed elegantly, with his chin propped on his hand while he studied her with his usual predatory interest. Timothy stood quietly at his side, not looking at her.

"How are you feeling, Katherine?"

Her heart stopped beating, and almost desperately she looked at the two strangers. "Please, *signores,* where am I?"

One of the men cast a surreptitious glance at Camden before he answered hesitantly, "There is no reason to be alarmed, Lady Halsingham. You are safe at home."

Danae started to tremble, for her worst nightmare was coming true. Gathering what strength she had, she yanked free of Halsingham's imprisoning embrace and jumped to her feet. *"Signore,* what joke is this. I am the *Contessa di Sala,* Danae Suriano, and this is not my home. I demand to be taken out of here at once."

Camden chuckled as he turned his attention to the men. "Do you see what I mean? She is quite insane. The only thing her husband and I can assume is that the accident damaged her mind. She truly believes herself to be this *Contessa"*—he turned an amused gaze upon her again—"what was that outlandish name again, my dear?"

With sheer force of will, Danae fought back. "I don't know what sick game you are playing at, *signore,* but I warn you it will not work." She turned in earnest appeal to the two strangers. "This is some trick, some sad joke. This *Katerina* they speak of is dead. I try to nurse her back to health after carriage accident, but it was no use. When she die she leave her money to me, and this they do not like!" She flung her hand back to indicate the amused Camden and Halsingham, still looming close to her.

"My poor love," Halsingham murmured as he wrapped arms like steel bands about her waist, pulling her tight against his body.

Helpless tears sprang to her eyes as she strove to

throw him off. Desperate, she turned toward the men and begged, "Please, *signores*, please, you will take me out of here."

The other gentleman, who had sat silent, watching the episode with a grim expression, cleared his throat and stood up abruptly, startling the man at his side. "Enough of this. We have heard what you have to say, Camden, but I am not wholly convinced. We will take her into our custody, and an informal hearing before the QC will decide if she is indeed your missing daughter, and then if she is mentally incompetent or not."

Stepping forward, he took hold of Danae's arm in a firm grip and pulled her out of Halsingham's clutches. Camden had also come to his feet, his lips set in a grim line. "How soon can the hearing be arranged? I won't be able to rest well until my daughter is home and safe again."

She stared at him in amazement. When had he ever cared if she was safe?

"I understand your concern. I will try to put a priority check on this. With any luck, it will be heard within the week, two at the outside."

Camden gave a reluctant nod, and his gaze shifted to her. What she saw there sent her tumbling backward to a time when she had eaten, breathed, and slept with a constant companion: fear. She truly believed she would rather die than be delivered into his clutches again. Just before she was pulled from the room, she sought out Timothy and almost wept at the pain radiating from his dark eyes.

Stepping out of the town house, she blinked as the early-morning sun struck her and set her head to pounding again. She was amazed to see it was early morning. What had happened to last night?

Had she been in that house all night? With Halsingham? Starting to panic again, she scanned the street, contemplating her chances of outrunning her escorts when she caught sight of a blessed miracle. Jonas stood across the street, watching her, a stranger at his side—her savior from the park.

Jonas gave her a reassuring nod and then waited until she had been bundled into the carriage. She looked back as they pulled away from the curb, and saw the two men stride off briskly in the opposite direction.

Halsingham watched as the carriage ambled down the street. When it was out of sight, he turned to face his father-in-law. "You said there wouldn't be any problems," he accused, his manner sullen.

He hadn't been surprised to learn that Danae was his wife. In a strange, elemental way he had always known that she belonged to him. But she was going to have to pay for making a cuckold of him, for letting another man touch what was his, for putting him through hell. Weary beyond belief, he flung himself down on the divan where he had so recently held her in his arms, and closed his eyes.

Camden stepped over to the fireplace and gazed up at the portrait, ignoring the pain ripping at his eyes. He wasn't pleased with what had just happened. When he had asked the Home Secretary, the Rt. Hon. Frederick Tennant, to his home regarding a delicate situation, he had been fairly confident of the outcome. And here he stood, yet again having to wait just when everything was so close to falling neatly into place. He wasn't worried, though, for there could be no doubt whatsoever as to the outcome. No matter how hard she fought, she would be returned to him.

He smiled as he pictured the beautiful woman

she had become. She was going to bear him a magnificent heir.

From a distant corner of the room, Timothy watched Camden as he stared up at the portrait. Curling himself into an invisible little ball, he hugged his knees and remembered the fear in Danny's eyes as she had looked at Camden. And it was all his fault for wishing she were here with him. He was weak and bad, and now she wasn't going to like him anymore. Now he would never be her little boy.

Putting his head down onto his knees, he silently wept.

It was well into the evening when Sion arrived at home. He stared up at the brightly lit town house and knew something was wrong. He took the steps two at a time, and just as his hand reached out to open the door, it was flung open. Jonas appeared before him, obviously distraught. Babbling almost incoherently, he dragged Sion into the library filled with people.

Sion's gaze swept the assemblage of people, but she wasn't there. Grabbing hold of Jonas's shoulder, he shook him quiet. "Where is she?" he rasped out.

Jonas ran an unsteady hand through his tangled hair. "That's what I've been trying to tell you! She's gone!"

Sion's blazing eyes swiveled to the only man who he knew would make sense. Brock stepped forward and, keeping his feelings to himself, recounted with cool professionalism, "I made a bloody botch of it, my lord. An attempt had been made to kidnap her ladyship, which we foiled, and had the bloke taken into custody. Then I found Halsingham skulking in the bushes, and I was questioning him when Saegar appeared and made an attempt to take her ladyship. I was alone at the time, as my men had left with the bloke, and I'm afraid I left her ladyship to Halsingham, feeling Saegar was the bigger threat. I chased him down to your late wife's grave, but he killed himself before I could take him into custody." When Brock had finished and the room was silent, Sion stepped over to the liquor caddy and, with deliberate care, poured himself a dollop of brandy. It seemed everyone in the room held their breath as he bolted it to the back of his throat and then stood there staring at the crystal tumbler in his hand.

"So Saegar's dead?"

Jonas and Brock exchanged troubled glances. "Aye, my lord."

It was strange, he should have felt relief, but he was too numb to care one way or the other right now. Danae was out there somewhere, alone and frightened, and he couldn't get to her. And he had always promised to protect her.

"We found her ladyship in Camden's house. But in the morning she had been taken out, by the home secretary no less." Jonas had supplied this.

He turned to address Brock again. "Are you sure she is out of Camden's house?"

"We saw her taken out with our own eyes. We don't exactly know why Tennant is involved in this."

"Camden knows," the dowager marchioness's voice broke in. "And he's going to push this into a public scandal so there can never again be any doubt as to who she is."

Sion spun around. "Nana, what the hell are you doing here?" He moved over to her. "I chased after you all the way to your dower house only to be told you had never been there." Of course, it had been another damn ploy of Saegar's to get him out of the way.

She was sitting in the large armchair before the fire, all but hidden from the room, with her legs wrapped warmly in a blanket. Shaking her head at his stupidity—he was sure—she admonished him, "You have much to answer for, my boy. How could you blindly follow such a missive before first checking it out? Where is your sense lately?"

Sion, Brock, and Jonas all exchanged exasperated looks. Too preoccupied with Danae's danger to take issue with this attack, Sion demanded, "Where is Halsingham now?"

Jonas and Brock shrugged, and they both answered, "Don't know for sure." "At Camden's would be best guess."

Sion was staring at his grandmother. "Nana, how strong are your connections in the Cabinet nowadays?"

She shrugged, "They've been better. All my old beaux are mostly dead." She smiled a little winsomely as she admitted, "Though there is one rather formidable barrister, a QC who is still somewhat smitten with me."

"I think we will have a little better luck getting some questions answered if we have your old flame at our side," Sion speculated as he poured himself a glass of water.

As gently as possible, the marchioness warned, "If Camden has the home secretary on his side, there is not much we are going to be able to do to get her back, Sion."

There was a hardness in his profile as he looked out the window. "I will get her back, Nana. One way or another."

No one liked the sound of that, and they all sat back in their chairs, brooding.

Mrs. Turlow, who had been standing just inside the door, slipped silently out of the room. Wrapping herself in her precious shawl, she stepped out into the fog-enshrouded evening, and with a determined step she headed off down the street, following the gaslit street lamps.

"Goin' somewhere, are ye, Mrs. Turlow?" Inspector Brock asked as he fell into step with her.

"Aye, and it be none o' yer concern," she snapped.

"It is if ye're goin' where I ken ye're goin'."

She stopped abruptly and faced him. "And just where do ye ken I'm going, me boyo?"

"Camden's."

She blinked up at him, taken aback. "Ye're right," and tugging her shawl closer, she trudged on.

"O' course, I'm right."

"So what do ye want?"

"I want to talk with your brother's stepson from his third wife."

Mrs. Turlow's turned to him in amazement. How did he know about her snitch? Then her laughter boomed out into the night. "Ye are a rum one, ye are, Inspector."

"Call me Thaddeus," he coaxed.

She looked sideways at him. He was an appealing bear of man. "Ye may call me Fenella," she offered graciously.

He nodded his head, "I'm well honored, Fenella."

"Just don't let it swell yer britches, laddie."

Twenty-seven

Danae was reading the *London Post* when she heard the grating of the key in the lock. Expecting Halsingham again, she deliberately ignored looking around and continued with her reading. Then she felt a pair of warm lips nuzzle the nape of her neck.

With a cry she sprang to her feet and, swinging around, whacked the paper across his face, the room echoing with the rewarding sound of it slapping against his insolent mouth. Her smile froze when she stared into the stunned face of Sion blinking at her.

"Sion!" she cried, flinging her arms about his neck. "Oh, God, you're here! Are you still mad at me?"

Holding her waist with one arm, he rubbed his cheek, thoroughly confused. "What was that for?" He voiced the question cautiously. She seemed glad to see him, and yet here she was, slapping him again.

Standing on tiptoe, she soothed his reddened skin with her lips. No matter how hard she tried she couldn't stop herself from chuckling, especially when he looked down at her with such a wary eye. "I am sorry, darling, I thought you were someone else."

The muscles beneath her lips clenched as he intoned ominously, "Don't tell me—Halsingham."

"All right, I won't tell you. Oh, Sion, I've missed you so. I had such a day yesterday. Or was it the day before? What day is—" The rest of her words were swallowed by his hot mouth as he shut her up in the only way he cared to. Equally greedy, her lips latched on to his, and for endless minutes they were insensate to all but their respective hungers, tongues stroking with wild fervency and their breathless moans and sighs mingling.

"Oh, God, Danny, I . . ." His words trailed off when his dazed eyes opened and he noticed the strange surroundings. For one shattering moment he had forgotten where they were and what was at stake. When he felt her hand squeezing and massaging his engorged shaft, he thrust her almost violently away from him. He raked shaking fingers through his hair, but when he saw her coming at him again, he held his hands out in front of him, desperate to ward her off. Just looking at her slumped backward over the table, staring at him with feverish eyes, her magnificent breasts heaving, made every part of his body ache. God, even his skin hurt.

It was with formidable effort he controlled his rampant lust and got the blood rushing back into his brain from another, less cooperative part. He closed his eyes to block out the confused hurt in her tawny eyes. "Danny, please, love, don't look at me like that. There is nothing I would rather do than throw myself down on that table and let you have your wicked way with me. But we have work to do and not a lot of time to do it in. Nana and Mr. Abbott will be here directly."

Gathering her dignity about her, she tugged on her bodice and sat down, refusing to look at him again. She knew if she did, she would probably throw all maidenly restraint to the four winds and ravish him. Never had she wanted him so much. She wanted his body, his tenderness, his wildness, and, most especially, his love. Clearing her throat, she touched a lace kerchief to her upper lip and blotted it with a delicate touch. "Who is Mr. Abbott?"

Straightening his tie, he moved over to the window away from her. "He is a very respected barrister, a Queen's Counsel, in fact. The only reason he was available on such short notice is that he is an old flame of Nana's." He sounded distracted as he walked restlessly about the small room.

"How is Nana?"

He gave her a preoccupied hum of an answer that she assumed was good news. Feeling that something was not right, she studied him as he paced about the room. He looked tired and tense. And extremely worried. "I heard about Saegar." Her voice was soft as she tried to get his attention. "He is finally out of your life. You must be pleased." She watched as he continued to pace about. It was obvious he hadn't heard a word she had just said. "Sion?"

Hearing her at last, he threw a preoccupied glance over his shoulder, a frown marring his weary face, "Hm? Did you say something, love?"

She gave him a slight smile and shook her head.

When the lock rattled, he turned eagerly toward the door. The dowager marchioness and an older gentleman, presumably Mr. Abbott, stepped into the room. Both were frowning. Danae quickly stepped to Nana's side. She looked done in. Worried, Danae helped her to the closest chair.

Sion tensed as he stepped forward. "Well?" he snapped, unmindful of his rudeness.

Mr. Abbott exchanged a glance with the dowager before he faced Sion, clasping the lapels of his frockcoat, an age-old habit acquired from close to thirty-five years debating on the QC. "It doesn't look good, my boy." He was ever one for plain speaking.

Sion rubbed his forehead in weary despondency. "When is the hearing?"

"It has been set for tomorrow morning."

"So, give me the best and worst that can happen."

"Very well. I will begin with the easiest to foresee; worst case. She will, in all probability, be charged with calumny and adultery, and found mentally incompetent. You will be charged with complicity and held as the respondent in the issue of adultery."

Danae glanced quickly down at her clenched hands, refusing to look at Sion. She didn't know if she could bear to see what was in his face. She blinked back her tears and swallowed heavily. This was all her fault. Her selfishness had dragged him down to this, and all he had ever done was offer his help and love. And what had she done to repay him but destroy him?

"She must have some recourse?" Sion's voice was strained.

Mr. Abbott shrugged and spread his arms wide. "What recourse could she possibly have when they exhume the body of a twenty-two-year-old woman and uncover the body of a fifty-year-old woman? She has nothing to back up her claim: no birth cer-

tificate, no family bible, no marriage papers, no
family to step forward and claim her, no one to
vouch for her but you and your servants. *You* tell
me where her recourse is. *You* give me something
to defend her with. Best case: there is none."

Sion just stood there, staring down at the floor,
his arms hanging limp at his sides. Danae saw his
defeated posture and she cried inside—not for herself, for she was beyond help, but for this noble
man whose only crime was to love her.

After a moment, he looked up and their gazes
met. A shiver ran down her spine when she saw an
almost fanatical fire burning in the ebony depths of
those beautiful eyes.

"I will get you out, Danny. There has to be a way,
and I will find it. No matter what it takes."

She was almost relieved when the door swung
inward and the matron informed them that visi-
tation time was over. Coming gracefully to her
feet, she walked around the table to stand beside
him and took hold of his hand, her fingers entwined with his cold ones. "I know you will, Sion.
I'm not worried. But, you had better go and get
some sleep. You look dead on your feet. There
will be time enough to talk after you have rested.
And get Nana home; she looks about to collapse
again." Sion cast a guilty look at his grandmother
and frowned even more, if that was possible.

Danae traced her fingers lovingly over the deep
grooves in his taut cheeks. "You look exhausted, my
love," she whispered before stepping away and
going over to his silent grandmother.

Taking her frail hands into her own, she kissed
the old woman on her cheek. "Thank you, Nana,
for all your kindnesses to me, and your support."
Glancing up, she met Mr. Abbott's unnerving stare.

"And you also, Mr. Abbott. I appreciate your plain speaking. It is very refreshing."

Sion had come up behind her and wrapped his arms about her slim body. He pulled her back against his chest and held her almost painfully tight. "I will see you tonight, my love," he whispered gruffly against the nape of her neck.

Trying to hide her eyes by keeping them cast down, she nodded. She was thankful when they were hustled out the door by the burly matron.

After the door was closed she waited a few minutes, then knocked upon it. It was opened with prompt attention, and the matron stuck her head in. "Yes, my lady?"

"Could you please send for Lord Camden and tell him it is important I speak with him as soon as possible?"

The matron bobbed her head. "Of course, my lady. It will be sent immediately."

"Thank you."

When she was alone again she stood at the window staring up at the evening sky, and found contentment in knowing that at least, for a brief, fantastical moment in her life she had lived among the stars.

Camden stood before her with those unnerving eyes of his studying her, a derisive smile curling his thin lips. "You rang, daughter?"

"Don't call me that." She wasn't about to get into a sparring match with him. After all, she was going into this already knowing she had lost.

Camden dipped his head in silent acknowledgment, his empty gaze never leaving her.

"You win, Camden. I will do whatever you want,

but I have to have your word"—she paused, wondering at her folly of asking this dishonorable man for his word—"I want your assurance that Sion Sinclair will be hurt in no way. No accusations made against him, no retribution sought."

"And if I don't," he inquired with silky disinterest.

"Then I will kill myself."

The two combatants' gazes clashed, both cold and mercenary. Neither giving nor taking an inch. But Danae knew she had the advantage here, for she knew too much of his obsessive drive. The need for her body with the precious Camden blood flowing through it was as priceless to him as the Holy Grail was to the idealism of Christendom.

He turned around and walked over to the window and watched as the setting sun glinted off the rooftops and spires of London. "Suppose I cede to your demands and you still give me no heir. After all, you failed before."

"No, I didn't. Halsingham failed." She felt no guilt or hesitation whatsoever of throwing the blame on that vain man.

Camden spun around, for once caught off guard. His gaze pierced the dimming room, sharp and lethal, boring into her with a ruthlessness that tested her newfound strength. "What are you saying?"

"I'm saying that on that day you sent Katherine off to London she was untouched, a virgin, *virgine.*" She was not surprised, knowing she also could take delight in cruelty, especially inflicting it on this person. Her smile, as she watched him walk toward her, was cynical, derisive, and filled with hate.

She hardly saw him lift his arm, but she felt the impact of his clenched fist as it slammed into the side of her face. Blessedly, she felt nothing but numbness as the force of the blow sent her sprawling. Like a vulture he hunched over her, and wrapping one hand into her hair, he dragged her viciously off the floor, glaring down at her with undisguised hatred. At least the facade of gentility had finally been stripped from him, she thought with contempt.

"You bitch! All those fucking years I waited, and you were making a mockery of me?" He shook her like a dog shaking a rat. She winced as she felt her neck crack.

"It wasn't difficult, you pathetic fool," she deliberately goaded him, even as she lay before him, panting with pain.

Bellowing in rage, he drew back his arm again, then caught himself at the last second while she laughed in his face. The blood smearing her lips made a travesty of her smile, and her jaw was already swelling, but she came back giving as good as she got. Suddenly, he knew what she was doing, why she was goading him, and he had almost fallen again into her trap. With a curse, he threw her down and stepped away.

Sitting up, she wiped the blood off her lips and only managed to smear it more. "Go on, Camden; kill me! Do you think I give a damn? Truth be told, I would prefer it. My death would prevent one more mad creature being brought into this sad world."

There was only one other time he had ever been this close to a complete loss of his sanity, and it was with supreme effort that he fought for control. The little bitch knew him too well. He would have to be more careful around her for the present. But there would come a day when he wouldn't need her anymore. His gaze slithered over to her when she started talking again, making her pithy demands.

"I mean what I say, Camden. You harm Lord Dereham in any way and I will take your precious obsession and cram it down your throat." Her hatred was palpable, every bit equal to his own. And as he watched her, he couldn't help but admire her as she stood before him, blood smearing her beautiful face, defiant and spitting. His daughter. The mother of the future Earl of Camden. God, what a man he will be!

"I agree. He is of no importance to me any longer."

But he was of every importance to her, Danae thought as she gingerly touched her jaw. Now he could be no more than a beautiful chapter in a life that was over. Tears filled her eyes as resignation stiffened her back, for she could only pray she would never see him again.

Out of sight, and—hopefully—out of Camden's mind.

Please, my love, just stay away.

Sion strode down the corridor several hours later, wondering where the matron stationed outside Danae's room was. He was anxious to hold her in his arms again, and even this minor delay was wearing thin on his edgy nerves.

He stopped before the door, paced back and forth a few times with surly impatience, then, with a vile curse, reached out and gave the handle a testy rattle. Surprise froze him to the spot when the door swung free and, creaking inward, revealed the interior of a darkened room.

Heart pounding, he stepped into the shaft of

light from the corridor, then fumbled with the gas lamp on the wall beside him. As the gas hissed and the light dispelled the shadowy corners, he scanned the empty space, already feeling her absence.

"Danae?' he called out, even though he knew it was useless.

"She is gone, my lord."

He spun about and found himself facing Mr. Abbott.

"Where is she?"

"She has gone with Lord Camden."

The room tilted crazily, the lack of food and sleep contributing to his sense of confusion and loss. "What do you mean she has gone with Camden? The hearing isn't until tomorrow; isn't that what you said?"

"There is to be no hearing. Knowing she had no choice, she made a bargain with the devil."

Sion's clammy skin began to sweat. "What bargain?"

Abbott stared at the dazed man, trying hard to mask his sympathy. In another time, in another life, this man could have been his grandson. "She would go with him as his undisputed daughter and he would leave you and your grandmother alone."

"And you let her go?" The look in Sion's eyes was enough to give the indomitable barrister pause.

"I had no say in her decision. Besides, as hard as it is to accept, she did the right thing. You could have been ruined, Lord Dereham. She knew this, and she did what she felt was best."

"Best!" he grated out. "Best that she is in the hands of that madman? Best for whom, man? Certainly not best for her, and certainly not best for me. I love her!"

Mr. Abbott toughened his resolve. This was for Vivian. She was weak enough without having to suffer seeing her grandson involved in yet another scandal in the courts. "She is in the hands of her father and her husband, my lord. You were in breach of the laws of this land and before God. She is doing what is right. There was no other choice, except to see her placed publicly into their custodianship and you socially ruined, perhaps to the point of serving time in jail. She had the sense to see this, and she did what was right!"

Sion looked at the pompous fool with hate burning his heart. "God damn you to hell." And not trusting himself to remain in the same room with him, he pushed past the barrister and fled, never having noticed the note, addressed to him, sitting in the middle of the table.

But Mr. Abbott noticed it. With a heavy conscience he picked it up and ripped it in half. He closed his eyes, again telling himself this was for Vivian. He felt so old as he stared down at the pieces in his hand.

"It is for the best," he whispered. Then he turned down the gas and left the room, closing the door quietly behind him.

Danae opened her eyes as the train began to slow in preparation for its stop at the station of Aylesbury. She ignored the men on either side of her and instead concentrated on not being ill all over herself. She couldn't understand it; she was never ill, not that she didn't have enough reason lately, but now it seemed that was all she was. And so very tired.

Pressing a kerchief to her lips, she swallowed heavily and took a deep breath. The sooty air certainly didn't help, so she closed her eyes again. Then they snapped open in horror. *Oh, my God, my baby!* How could she have forgotten! What kind of mother was she? A mother with the infamous Camden blood, it would seem, she thought bitterly. Already she had no care for her precious burden, and she felt like crying again at her own heartlessness. The safety of her child should have been paramount to everything, and here she was, forgetting its very existence.

I'm going to be a terrible mother!

Then the enormity of it struck her, and she blanched. *My God, what am I going to do? I can't let Halsingham touch me now,* she thought frantically. And Camden had such a hatred for Sion, she feared what he would do when he learned of it.

"Are you all right, my dear?" Halsingham asked solicitously as he put an arm around her. He wasn't surprised when she shook him off.

"Don't touch me!" she hissed at him.

He flushed a bright red; then turning his shoulder on her, he stared out the window, his perfect profile still. She couldn't tell if he was hurt or angry, and she couldn't care less. He was nothing but a bloody puppet, with no more sense than the pathetic cur in the street, begging for scraps and thankful when it got them, even if they came with a kick in the ribs.

She slid a sideways glance at Camden and saw him sitting as cold and derisive as usual, the eternal spider weaving his web. Across from her, Timothy watched her with hungry eyes.

For him alone she curbed her anger and offered a comforting smile. He blinked once and then hurriedly looked away. She frowned at this odd attitude.

The train was coming to a stop and she leaned over, intending to take his hand when a curious sight caught her attention. She stared over Timothy's head, and with her heart pounding, and a smile tugging at her lips she watched a disheveled Mrs. Turlow yank a bag off the rack overhead and, without so much as a glance in her direction, step off the train.

Danae's suddenly interested gaze scanned the other passengers for a familiar face, but she was disappointed. What was she thinking? The last thing she wanted was for Sion to follow her. *Or did she?* her more selfish and honest voice prodded.

"Come along, Timothy," she urged softly as she took his hand and drew him along after her. His hand twisted in hers, and for a moment she thought he was going to pull free, but he only turned it so he could cling to hers with desperate need. She glanced down, and the two smiled at each other. Well, if nothing else came out of this whole sordid situation, she would now be able to watch over Timothy. Her heart lightened a bit at this thought.

Stepping off the train, she searched the depot, needing to catch sight of her friend again. She had almost given up when Timothy tugged at her hand, and looking down, she saw his golden head nodding off to the right. There, in the shadows of a baggage cart, Mrs. Turlow stood waiting. When their eyes met, Danae felt a warm, comforting feeling in the pit of her stomach, and she smiled at this woman who was always there when she needed someone—ever since that day so long ago when she had opened her eyes to a strange new life. Mrs. Turlow returned her smile, and then, with a reassuring nod of her gray head, she disappeared around the corner. Danae had to bite her lip hard, so tempted was she to call out to her.

"Come along, my dear," Halsingham directed stiffly, grabbing her other arm at the elbow and ushering her toward a waiting carriage, with Timothy trotting along at her side.

He ignored the stiffening of her body, and when she tried to shake him off, he simply punished her with his grip, pleased to know her skin would show the mark of his possession just as much as her face showed the mark of Camden's. She had embarrassed him for the last time. It was about time she was made aware of the fact that she belonged to him.

"You have it wrong, Halsingham," Camden murmured in his ear. "She belongs to me. I have only given you the loan of her body for a while. And don't forget that, lest you find yourself gasping for the last breath of your pathetic life. I can always find another stud, one even more worthy of her." And with these malicious words, Camden walked on ahead of the little group.

Halsingham stared at that narrow back and wished he had his pistol. He was going to have to kill that cold bastard after all.

Danae stared with disinterest at the dinner tray beside her, debating the merits of starvation. Then her eyes sparked with interest as she thought, with cynical humor, that what she really needed was more food. Much more food. No one knew as well as she just how quickly Halsingham's interest would shrivel as her curves increased. Of course, her baby would take care of that dilemma soon enough.

The snap of pebbles hitting the windowpanes startled her, and flinging back the covers, she ran barefoot to the bay window. Luckily, they hadn't been nailed shut, and flinging one wide, she leaned out. As expected, there stood the sturdy Scottish widow, hands on hips, squinting up at her through the moonlight.

"Mrs. Turlow," she called down in an undertone, "why are you here? You shouldn't have come."

"And who else will take care o' ye, I'd like to be knowin'?" she demanded imperiously. "Especially with ye breedin' and all."

Danae again felt shame. Even Mrs. Turlow remembered, when she, the mother, had forgotten.

"Does Sion know?"

Mrs. Turlow shrugged, "I dinna think so. I dinna tell him."

"Good. He mustn't know. At least not yet." And then she leaned out farther and glared down at the busybody. "And I am not going to bribe you about this, Mrs. Turlow. Lives are at stake here, and if anything happens to his lordship because of him finding out about this baby and rushing in with foolhardy bravado, I will take your da's claymore, the one you are so proud of, and skewer you with it! Do you understand me?"

"Aye." The sullen reply floated up to her. "But, dinna ye forget what happens every time ye tell me not tae tell his lordship."

Danae ignored this bit of wisdom, for it was true—whenever she said not to tell Sion, it always came back to haunt her. But this time it truly couldn't be helped. "I have enough to worry about right now. Where are you staying?"

"I was a hopin' ye could arrange for me to stay here."

Frowning, Danae glanced behind her, uncertain. "I don't think that would be wise just yet. I would prefer them not to know you are here till I know more what is going to happen. For now you'll have to go into the village and stay at the inn there. Tell them that the Marquis of Dereham is expected and you were sent ahead; that way they will put it on credit. Do you understand?" She saw her friend nod.

Hearing a key grating in the lock, she frantically waved Mrs. Turlow away and, latching the window, ran to the bed. She didn't even bother with the steps as she leaped under the covers, barely catching the tray before it upended. Holding her breath, she watched as Camden strolled in. Closing the door, he leaned back against it and stared at her. The look in those eyes had always instilled such fear in her—now she only felt deep hatred.

"You amaze me, you know."

"I don't care. You can't keep me here under lock and key forever. Never again will I let you hold me a prisoner."

Camden tipped his head to the side and just smiled at her. "Do you wish to see Edward again?"

Breathing heavily, Danae just glared back at him.

His eyebrows rising in taunting inquiry, he asked again, softly, "Well, do you?"

Hating him more with each second that passed, she finally spat out, "You know I do."

"Then behave and do what you are told and you will see him again. If you don't do what you are told, then I shall punish . . . Edward."

Danae wanted to tear his throat out.

Camden pushed away from the door and opened it. "Do we understand each other?"

"I understand that you are completely mad. Why would you even want your cursed blood to live again?" she demanded spitefully.

Camden paused. When he spoke again his voice was a sibilant whisper that brushed over her with his madness. "I shall remember what you just said when next I speak with Edward."

The door snapped shut, and the lock grated even as Danae hit the door, her screams and pounding falling on deaf ears.

Sion had reached Victoria Station around midnight only to be told that the next train out to Aylesbury wasn't until nine the next morning. Swearing long and fluently, he took himself back to Berkeley Square, where he picked up his horse, not bothering with a carriage, and pressed the poor beast to within an inch of its last heartbeat.

Twenty-eight

Danae sat in the window nook and watched as dawn's light began to glow on the horizon. She was so tired, but she was afraid to sleep. She wondered where Sion was and prayed that he stayed away. Even if he came, what could he do? She was Halsingham's wife, and as far as the law was concerned, she belonged to him.

Dropping her forehead against her knees, she despaired of ever seeing Sion again. Never would his arms hold her. Never again would his smile soothe her fears or make her laugh. But she had a piece of him under her heart, and she would cherish and protect this precious being to the last inch of her life. She would survive Camden. She had no other choice.

Alert to every whisper and creak around her, Danae's head came up when she heard the faint sounds of a disturbance deep in the center of the house. Getting to her feet, she ran over to the door and pressed her ear against it. After a moment, she slumped against the door with a groan.

She heard Mrs. T.'s strident voice growing stronger the closer she got to the door, the sounds of furniture being tipped over, the crash of a vase hitting the floor. "Let me be, ye bloody half-wit.

Take yer lecherous hands off me person. I wilna leave before I see me lamb!" Then the door shook on its hinges. "M'lamb, are ye in there? Are ye well?"

Steeling herself, Danae stepped away from the door just as it was thrown inward. There, standing in the corridor, forcibly restrained by a burly footman on either side of her, was a panting, furious Mrs. T.

She was still muttering and threatening when her wild eyes settled on Danae, and in a last-ditch attempt to get to her, she kicked one servant in the shin and sank her teeth into the arm of the other. She had almost made it to the door when an arm dropped across the entrance, and Camden's cold, reptilian gaze froze her midstep as several brawny lads could never have done. "Do you know this person, my dear?" he asked of Danae while he held Mrs. Turlow pinned to the floor with that inhuman stare.

Danae's gaze darted between her friend and the madman who held all their lives in his hand. It wasn't as if she could lie, not with Mrs. T. screaming her threats all through the house. Sighing, she admitted with tired resignation, "Yes. She is my companion. She means no harm. Please, don't hurt her." Her fear was palpable and all too obvious to Camden, for he glanced over his shoulder at her, a morbid interest flaring in his eyes.

"Another Achilles heel, is she? How convenient." He turned back to the old woman and studied her for a moment. Finally, he directed in a bored drawl, "Take her below and lock her in the pantry for now. I may have use of her later."

Danae closed her eyes, cursing her stupidity at

letting him see such a weakness, when Mrs. Turlow called to her again.

"Are ye well, lass?" she needed to know, her soft burr heavy with worry as she quickly scanned Danae's person for signs of abuse.

"I'm well, Mrs. T. Please go with them and don't give them any reason to hurt you." These last words were directed to the two young men who had hold of her friend's arms. "She's just an old woman. I am asking you to be gentle with her." One of them nodded to her as they pulled her resisting body down the corridor.

Danae stepped backward into the room as Camden moved forward, shutting the door behind him. "So, have you resigned yourself to your duties in the night?"

Danae didn't say anything, her stubbornness holding her mute.

Camden looked her over, amusement in his pale gaze. "Even though this new backbone of yours is admirable, my dear, in the long run all that will happen is your willfulness shall be meted out in punishment on those dear to you."

"You may be able to get away with keeping me here, but what you are doing to Mrs. Turlow and the boy is criminal. Just because you are a peer of the realm does not give you the omnipotent power to do as you please."

Camden stepped closer to her and drew a cold finger down her cheek. "And who is to know what I do or don't do?"

Danae stepped away from him.

His face looked carved in stone as he walked over to the bed and stood beside it, fingering the silk counterpane. "I have sent for Halsingham. Of course, the sooner he impregnates you, the sooner we can be done with him." His voice was as brittle as the autumn leaves carpeting the ground outside.

"This is barbaric," she whispered, clasping her hands tightly before her, for if she didn't she was afraid she would grab the closest possible weapon and kill him.

His empty gaze found hers. "No, this is the continuation of an old and noble line."

"What will happen to Timothy when I give you your vaunted heir?"

"I will put him back where I found him, of course."

Never had she been so frightened as she was at that moment, knowing she was the product of this man's blood and heart and soul. Would she one day turn into this? Was this what she would pass on to Sion's child?

And into this spiraling fear walked Halsingham, staring at her with an avid, possessive smile.

Halsingham barely spared a glance for his father-in-law as he came to Danae's side and crowded close upon her back. She could feel his warm breath on her neck, and she shivered with loathing. When she slid her gaze to Camden, she wasn't really surprised to see the hate burning in those colorless eyes as he watched Halsingham.

"I will give you fifteen minutes and then I'll be back," Camden reported curtly as he stepped to the door.

She felt the jolt of Halsingham's body behind her. "What the hell are you talking about?" His voice was livid with astonished anger.

Camden sliced his son-in-law a lethal glare. "You have fifteen minutes to plant your seed in her body, and then you will get out! Whether you are finished or not, I will have you dragged off her body."

"How the hell am I suppose to get her pregnant under those demands?" Halsingham asked, incredulous.

"I'm beginning to have my doubts that you are even capable. After all, for over three years you failed to produce any results." Camden's eyes stared unblinking into those of his puppet.

And Halsingham couldn't respond to this accusation, for he was damned if he did, maybe even more so than he was already.

"Very well," he grated out as he swept an arm about her middle, pulling her back against his rigid body.

Camden's lips tightened slightly, the only emotion crossing his expressionless facade, and reiterated in a soft voice, "Fifteen minutes." And then he was gone.

As soon as the door clicked shut, Halsingham ripped the back of her dress open with one vicious movement, and before she even had a chance to struggle, he caught her up in his arms and tossed her on the bed, following her down, his body suffocating her. All the anger he felt toward Camden and was too much the coward to do anything about, exploded onto her. Looking up into his wild eyes, she thought incredulously, *My God, he's going to rape me!*

For a minute she lay there stunned, until he straddled her and, sitting back on his haunches, fumbled with the buttons on his trousers. Then pure, cleansing anger sparked her survival instincts to life. Shoving her hands against his chest, she was lucky to catch him unawares, and as he tumbled backward off her, she was free for one precious second. But it didn't last long. With a shout, he grabbed her shoulders as she tried to twist from the bed, and shoving her back, he again climbed on top of her. Fists flying and teeth snapping, she fought back as if her life depended on it—and the life of her baby.

I can't let him do this; he can't do this. My baby is in this body; I can't let him in, was the litany pounding through her head as she scratched at that beautiful face, feeling a savage delight when she felt his skin tear under her nails.

"You fucking whore," he panted as he succeeded in flipping her over, and holding her down with a knee in her lower back, he shoved her face into the mattress. Now beyond rational thought, he knew only one thing: this woman was his, and he had to lay claim to her right now or she would never learn.

Tearing at her skirts, which were already in shreds, he finally bared her lower body, and the sight of those beautiful legs and her sensuously rounded buttocks exposed to him made his already accelerated heart jump painfully in his heaving chest. Licking dry lips, he stared down at her thrashing body, and the compulsion to conquer her was deafening, overriding any little sense of morals he had ever possessed. He freed his engorged shaft even as his knee was digging between her tightly clenched thighs, forcing them apart. His hands clenched about her hips, and he was just pulling them up in preparation to thrust home when her shouts finally pierced the violent numbness that had claimed his mind.

"What?" he slurred, feeling as if he were struggling into awareness after a long sleep. He watched in a daze as a drop of his sweat fell onto one of those beautiful globes of flesh and rolled with agonizing slowness into the vulnerable cleft.

"You can't do this," she sobbed, almost hysterical. "I'm going to have a baby. You can't do this." And her shoulders shook uncontrollably as she cried, her fists buried in the bedding.

He dropped her as if her flesh was suddenly a live coal in his hands, and slipped off the bed. He stood there staring down at her, when a hate such as he had never felt before filled his mind, suffocating his lungs and dimming everything around them into vague shadows. That bastard's seed was growing in her body. His body.

Flinging back his head, he screamed his fury; then his hand shot out, and grabbing a fistful of her hair, he dragged her tear-ravaged face around to confront him. "It will not be," his hot breath panted in her face. Then, striding to the door, he threw it open, bellowing for Camden to get his ass in there.

And Camden came, walking slowly into the room after a few minutes, his gaze sliding to the bed, taking in his daughter huddled back against the headboard, clutching the tatters of her dress around her, her eyes reddened and wide in her bruised face, watching him with uncertainty. Drawing his pocket watch out, he glanced at it and reported dryly, "My dear boy, you still had four minutes left—"

"The bitch is pregnant with Dereham's brat. I want it ripped out of her. I will not bed her until it is done." Halsingham's demands were couched in a vicious undertone, all the while glaring at the girl shivering on the bed.

Camden turned a speculative look on her. "Are you indeed, my dear?"

Stretched to the limit of her endurance, Danae didn't know what to do or think anymore. She knew she should think this through, for the thought of putting Sion's child into this madman's control froze the very heart of her. She had to think, but as hard as she tried, her muddled mind just spun faster and faster in a terrified vortex. Closing her eyes, she felt her life funneling down into the heart of the whirlpool. "Yes," she whispered.

"Well, well, well," his silky voice mused. "This changes everything, now, doesn't it? Dereham's brat. Though I can't say I like the man, his blood is good."

Halsingham, not liking the way things were progressing, shouted, "I want a bloody leech sent for, right now."

Camden turned to watch the ranting man, and a look of disgust twisted his mouth. "Do you realize that all I have done is put up with your endless demands, and what did you give me in return?"

Halsingham paused in his tantrum, and his skin prickled at the speculative gleam in Camden's eyes. He flicked his wife an uneasy glance; then, in a calmer, more careful tone he persuaded, "You know she can't have this baby."

"Why not?"

He stared at Camden in amazement. "You hate Dereham."

"And I despise you. What is the difference? I'll tell you what the difference is, my boy. The seed in her body in now of a nobler, more ancient lineage than yours would have provided." He tilted his head, studying Halsingham, noticing how he was becoming more agitated by the minute. "I don't need you anymore, Halsingham. And I thank God for that, for you have been nothing but a pain in my side since I first bought you."

And with these softly voiced words, he drew out a small derringer, aimed it at his heart, and fired.

Danae screamed and was leaping off the bed when the door flew open and Sion, followed by Mrs. Turlow, burst into the room.

"Sion," Danae sobbed as she tried to run to him, but Camden latched onto her arm and drew her backward with him.

In a single glance, Sion took in the scene: Halsingham's crumpled body bleeding on the floor, Danae bruised and nearly naked in Camden's arms, and Camden's gun, still smoking, pointed at the middle of his chest.

"Does he know?" Camden whispered in her ear.

Too confused and frightened to even try to dissimulate, she shook her head.

"Good, then maybe I'll let him live."

Sion held his arm out, for Mrs. Turlow was about to move past him. His whole attention was on that immaculately clothed arm wrapped around Danae's middle. Catching her gaze, he asked, "Are you all right?"

Here she was, standing before him: bruised, almost raped, her gown hanging in tatters about her shivering body, practically being held at gunpoint by a madman, and he asked if she was all right? If she weren't so frightened she would have laughed. Instead, she looked directly into his beautiful ebony eyes, and her voice quavering, she unfortunately said the first thing that came to mind, "I want to go home, Sion."

He smiled slightly at her, trying to appear calm when all he wanted was to jump the bastard and crush his throat with his bare hands. "I know, love, and we will. Soon."

"What you are going to do, Dereham, is leave,"

Camden's dry voice cut in. "Even now Halsingham's seed is smearing her lovely thighs. I would like to get her back into bed before she loses any more of it."

Mrs. Turlow's gasp echoed in Sion's mind as a roaring filled his ears. He looked into Danny's bruised eyes and didn't care. Nothing mattered but her, safely back in his arms. "It doesn't matter, Danny. Do you hear? I love you."

Camden's insidious whispers fanned her ear. "If you want him to live, send him away."

Tears filled her eyes as she stared at her love, needing him so much and yet needing to send him away. "I . . . I . . ." Camden's arm tightened painfully about her. "It does matter, Sion. You see, he didn't rape me. I lay with him willingly."

"She's lying," Mrs. Turlow's gruff voice prodded him. "She dinna lay with him, not willingly."

Looking into her eyes, Sion didn't need Mrs. T. to tell him what he already knew. But, if he was going to get her out of this impossible situation with all of them in one piece, he would have to retreat—for now.

Fortunately, he was never given the chance, for all of a sudden, from the courtyard below came a cacophony of sounds: carriages arriving, horses neighing, and commands shouted. He was shocked when he made out Brock's voice in the melee.

Distracted, Camden started to back up into the bay window in order to look down upon the disturbance, when Sion saw his chance and dived at them. The gun exploded, and for a split second, Danae had thought she had been hit. She felt herself caught up in Sion's arms, and together they tumbled to the floor, leaving Camden standing to face the influx of Brock and several London constables, with weapons out.

Danae looked down to see her body covered in blood, and knew it wasn't hers. "Sion," she gasped, turning in his arms as he held her safe.

"I'm all right, Danny. Its just a scratch," he assured her with a grunt, trying to stanch the flow of blood from his shoulder.

The sight of his blood swept away any residual numbness. Relieved that he was alive, she shouted at him, "That was the most stupid, foolhardy stunt I have ever seen. You could have gotten us killed. Why the hell didn't you just wait for them to get here? Now look what you've done—ruined a perfectly good suit."

He smiled up at her. "I love you, too."

They both looked over to see Camden taken hold of by a constable. Brock hurried over to them and knelt down. "It is a good thing the home secretary sent me. He didn't like the earl taking the lady out of his custody without permission." He glanced at Halsingham's body. "Camden do that?" They both just nodded.

Brock grinned. "Seems we got the right to arrest him now."

Danae looked over at the man who sired her and felt nothing but relief. "Is it finally over?" she asked tonelessly.

"You'll never have to see him again," Sion assured her gently.

Danae watched as Camden was pushed out into the corridor. At the last minute, he looked over his shoulder at her. Even at this distance she saw the madness in the cold, hateful stare. This madman was her father. His blood ran in her veins. In her baby's veins.

"Oh, God," she whispered, anguish clenching her gut. Blindly she turned toward Sion, and he pulled her close, even as Mrs. Turlow was trying to wrap his shoulder.

"It's all right, love," he murmured against her ear.

Desperate, she looked over his shoulder into Mrs. T.'s sad gaze.

Twenty-nine

One week later

Danae stared up at the portrait and wondered about this woman who was her mother. She wished she remembered her better, but she could hardly recall anything about her anymore. Perhaps it was because she didn't want to remember the Abbey anymore, and all the wasted years before she had been dropped into Sion's world.

Camden Abbey. She wanted it burned to the ground, but Sion had wisely talked her out of it.

"Love," Sion's low voice broke into her thoughts. Smiling, she turned about and drank in the sight of him. It still seemed the sweetest of miracles to her that Sion was now her husband. Her own love.

Crossing the room, Sion took her into his arms and held her close. He looked up at Danae's mother, seeing so much of Danae in the lovely woman. "I wish I had known her."

Sighing, Danae turned in his arms, and together they studied the portrait. "I don't know. I think it was best that she escaped Camden when she did. Her life would have been hell with him."

Sion, sadly, had nothing to say to this bit of wisdom. Instead he said, "There is someone here to see you."

After a moment, Danae took Sion's arm, and together they joined their guest in the parlor. Danae recognized him immediately and she stiffened. He brought into her home too many bad memories. "Dr. Grieves," she inclined her head coolly. "What brings you here?"

Knowing well how much Lady Dereham disliked him, the doctor bowed and came directly to the point. "My lady, I thought it my duty to inform you in person of the passing of your father."

Sion and Danae were shocked. They looked at each other, and it was Sion who asked him to explain.

"Due to complications from his condition, and the stress of the past week, he had an aneurysm of the brain. For days he was in a coma before passing quietly away."

Danae frowned at him. "What condition?"

The doctor looked at her in surprise. "Why, I thought you knew, my lady. Lord Camden was in the advanced stages of syphilis."

"Good God," Sion swore in amazement, "Well, that certainly accounts for much, doesn't it?"

Completely confused, Danae looked between the men. "I don't understand."

Taking his wife's hand in his, Sion led her to the chaise and sat down with her. "Love, syphilis is a disease that is contracted through . . ." He paused. "It is sexually transferred."

Still confused, she looked at the doctor. "Who gave it to him?"

"The second lady Dereham," Grieves supplied, a tinge of embarrassment staining his cheeks.

Danae was silent for a moment, then said in a musing voice, "The baby was diseased, too, wasn't it?"

The doctor merely nodded.

Sion looked between them. "What baby?"

Danae told him, her voice heavy, "When Camden was told that Janet was to have a baby, my life was actually quite bearable. Unfortunately, she had an early labor, and the baby didn't live above a day. It was all so sad; the baby was terribly undersized, wizened and malformed. His nose was almost flattened against his face, making his breathing difficult. And I remember the doctor so clearly checking his eyes and telling Camden that he was blind. The poor little soul never had a chance. I never saw a rage such as Camden's fury that day; I remember it as if it were just yesterday. After the little body had been bundled up and taken away, Camden turned and looked at me. From that day forward, my life became a living hell."

"What happened to Janet?"

Danae looked at the doctor, for she had always wondered about that herself.

The man looked uncomfortable, but he told them the truth. "Camden refused to let me care for her. He sent me away, practically had me thrown off his property. Worried, I went back the next day and demanded to see her ladyship, but she was already dead. She had bled to death."

Sion said quietly to Danae, "So the child was born syphilitic. I must say I remember Janet Kenley. She was a very promiscuous girl and the *ton* was shocked when Camden married her. The child probably wasn't even Camden's, as ironic as that probably sounds."

"He must have known then he would never be

able to sire a healthy son," Danae mused. "No wonder he never tried to marry again." She looked up sharply at the doctor. "So his madness was generated because of this disease?"

"Oh, yes. Syphilis attacks the nervous system and promotes any variety of madnesses. Unfortunately, Camden was a . . ." The doctor stumbled over his thought and paused. He stared at Danae and noticed her avid attention. He could be nothing but honest with her. "Though Camden had some tendencies toward a sociopath nature, the disease fed upon it."

She only cared about one thing. "So his madness is not hereditary?"

Dr. Grieves looked surprised. "No, absolutely not! If I had known of your fears, my lady, I would have laid them to rest long ago."

Danae turned and threw her arms about Sion's neck. "Sion, I'm healthy! Our child is going to be blessedly healthy!" Then she broke down in tears. Blinking back his own, Sion crushed her close.

They didn't even notice when the doctor slipped from the room.

Out on the street, Grieves stepped up into a waiting carriage.

"So how did it go?" the marchioness demanded before he could even sit.

Which he did heavily, and shaking his head he marveled. "I never knew that she didn't know of Camden's condition. Poor girl, what she must have lived with all these years."

"Did they believe the story?"

"Of how he died? Oh, yes. Why would they not?"

"Good, I don't want Danny to know the truth. She has enough on her plate to deal with." Her father's suicide was something she would never learn of.

"As far as the world is concerned, Camden died at home in his sleep. There should be no scandal."

"Good. Good."

The good doctor leaned back with a sigh. "God, I'm just glad it is finally over. Working with that man these past years has been pure torture."

Nana looked him over cynically. "Well you could have said no to him, y'know."

He looked insulted. "I'll have you know that with what he was paying me, I was able to devote most of my time to research."

"Humph, doubtless," she scoffed.

Dr. Grieves sat back and glared at her.

Looking out the window, Nana smiled and commented, "It is a bright new day, Horace. And I am going to be a great-grandmother. Can you believe it?"

Horace smiled benevolently down on one of his oldest friends, "Not a bit of it, Vivian. You look the same as the day I met you."

She slid him a disgusted glance. "Going blind, are you?"

"Unfortunately, yes," he sighed.

Seven months later

"Is he not perfect, Sion?"

"Perfect," came the rote answer.

Turning over, Danae hit her husband's shoulder. "Wake up, and don't be so grumpy. He is absolutely perfect, no?"

Sion groaned out, "Yes. He is beautiful, gorgeous, exceptional, but at the moment I just want some sleep. Our splendid son will have us up soon enough as it is. Can't we worship him then?"

"Next, a daughter."

"That goes without saying."

"You know I can't get into my clothes." Danae sighed into the dark canopy. "I got so big with Justin. I will lose it, I promise."

Sion sat straight up in bed, turned, and glared down at her. "I swear to God, Danny, if I hear this one more bloody time, I'll move into the next room. I don't give a bloody damn if you go down five pounds or up twenty. I love you. Now, please, can I just go to sleep?" And he collapsed back into his pillows. "God, I just wish you would choose a nurse. Tomorrow Nana is bringing a gaggle of them over for you to look over, and you had better damn well choose one, or I will! Miss York would have been perfect, but, no, you had to act matchmaker and throw her at Jonas."

Taking pity on her exhausted husband, for she had to admit he had been doing nothing but running and caring for her and Justin since the baby's birth a week ago, she softly kissed his shoulder. "Yes, and now they are as happy as we are." With a contented sigh, Danae snuggled down beside him and pressed her cold toes against his warm feet.

Immediately Sion turned about, pulled her against his body, and mumbled, "Finally. Now hush and sleep."

The new mama and papa were just drifting off into blissful sleep when their perfect little son bellowed out into the night, proving that his lungs were just as healthy as could be expected of a new lord of the realm.

"Mama, the baby's crying," Timothy's worried voice floated above the indignant wails.

Groaning, Sion stuffed the pillow over his face.

"I guess that means it's my turn." Smiling, Danae jumped out of bed and took hold of Timothy's hand. "Let's go see what he wants, shall we?"

"I sure hope it's not changing the nappy thing," he told her solemnly.

"Me too," she agreed heartily as they left the room together.